A prolific author of more than one hundred books, **Diana Palmer** got her start as a newspaper reporter. A *New York Times* bestselling author and voted one of the top ten romance writers in America, she has a gift for telling the most sensual tales with charm and humor. Diana lives with her family in Cornelia, Georgia. Visit her website at www.dianapalmer.com.

Books by Diana Palmer

Long, Tall Texans

Fearless
Heartless
Dangerous
Merciless
Courageous
Protector

The Wyoming Men

Wyoming Tough
Wyoming Fierce
Wyoming Bold
Wyoming Strong
Wyoming Rugged
Wyoming Brave

Visit the Author Profile page
at Harlequin.com for more titles.

DIANA PALMER

TEXAS PROUD
&
CIRCLE OF GOLD

HARLEQUIN
SPECIAL
EDITION

HARLEQUIN®
SPECIAL EDITION™

Recycling programs
for this product may
not exist in your area.

ISBN-13: 978-1-335-01599-0

Texas Proud & Circle of Gold

Copyright © 2020 by Harlequin Books S.A.

Texas Proud
Copyright © 2020 by Diana Palmer

Circle of Gold
Copyright © 2000 by Diana Palmer

This edition published by arrangement with Harlequin Books S.A.

For questions and comments about the quality of this book, please contact us at CustomerService@Harlequin.com.

Harlequin Enterprises ULC
22 Adelaide St. West, 40th Floor
Toronto, Ontario M5H 4E3, Canada
www.Harlequin.com

Printed in U.S.A.

CONTENTS

TEXAS PROUD

In loving memory of Glenda Dalton Boling
(1945–2019) of Homer, Georgia.

You were my cousin, my friend,
my favorite bookseller, my hostess
for over twenty years of book signings with
my friend Jan Walker. You left a hole in the world
with your passing, Glenda. And all of us
who loved you will miss you, as long as we live.

Chapter One

Her name was Bernadette Epperson, but everybody she knew in Jacobsville, Texas, called her Bernie. She was Blake Kemp's new paralegal, and she shared the office with Olivia Richards, who was also a paralegal. They had replaced former employees, one who'd married and moved away, the other who'd gone to work in San Antonio for the DA there.

They were an interesting contrast: Olivia, the tall, willowy brunette, and Bernie, the slender blonde with long, thick platinum blond hair. They'd known each other since grammar school and they were friends. It made for a relaxed, happy office atmosphere.

Ordinarily, one paralegal would have been adequate for the Jacobs County district attorney's office. But the DA, Blake Kemp, had hired Olivia to also work as a part-time paralegal. That was because Olivia covered for her friend at the office when Bernie had flares of rheumatoid arthritis. It was one of the more painful forms of arthritis, and when she had attacks it meant walking with a cane and taking more anti-inflammatories, along with the dangerous drugs she took to help keep the disease from worsening. It also meant no social life to speak of. Bernie would have liked having a fellow of her own, but single men knew about her and nobody seemed willing to take on Bernie, along with a progressive disease that could one day make her disabled.

There were new treatments, of course. Some of them involved weekly shots that halted the progression of the disease. But those shots were incredibly expensive, and even with a reduced price offered by kindly charitable foundations, they were still out of her price range. So it was methotrexate and prednisone and folic acid. And trying not to brood about the whole thing.

She was on her way to her room at Mrs. Brown's boardinghouse. It was raining, and the rain was cold. It was October and cool. Not the best time to forget her raincoat, but she'd been in a hurry and late for work, so it was still hanging in her closet at home. Ah, well, she thought philosophically, at least she had a nice thick sweater over her thin blouse. She laughed hysterically to herself. The sweater was a sponge. She felt water rolling down over her flat stomach under her clothes.

She laughed so hard that she didn't see a raised portion of the sidewalk. It caught her toe and she tripped. She fell into the road just as a big black limousine came along. Her cane went flying and she hit the pavement on her belly. She was fortunate enough to catch herself on her forearms, but the impact winded her. Luckily for her, the driver saw her in time to stop from running over her. It was dark and only the streetlights showed, blurry light through the curtains of rain.

A man got out. She saw his shoes. Big feet. Expensive shoes, like some of the visiting district attorneys who showed up to talk to her boss. Slacks that were made of wool. She could tell, because she used wool to knit with.

"You okay?" a deep, velvety voice asked.

"Yes," she panted. "Just…winded."

She rolled over and sat up.

A tall man, built like a wrestler, with broad shoulders and a leonine head, squatted down, staring at her with deep-set brown eyes in an olive complexion. His jet-black hair was threaded with just a little silver, and it was thick and wavy around his head. A lock of it fell onto his forehead as he bent over her. He had high cheekbones and the sort of mouth that was seen in action movies with he-men. He was gorgeous. She couldn't help staring. She couldn't remember ever having a man send her speechless just by looking at her.

"Nice timing," he mused. "Saw the limo coming, did we? And jumped right out in front of it, too."

She was too shaken to think of a comeback, although she should have. She checked her palms. They were a little scraped but not bleeding.

"I tripped."

"Did you really?"

That damned sarcastic, mocking smile made her very angry. "Could you find my cane, please?" she asked.

"Cane?"

She heard his voice change. She hated that note in it. "It went flying when I hit the raised part of the sidewalk. It's over that way." She indicated the sidewalk.

"On the other side, probably. It's red enamel. With dragons on it."

"With dragons. Mmm-hmm."

A car door opened. Another man came around the front of the car. He was older than Bernie but younger than the man squatting down next to her. He was wearing a suit.

"What's that about dragons?" the man asked, faintly amused.

"Her cane. That way, she says." He pointed.

The other man made a sound in his throat.

"Look anyway," the big man told him.

"All right, I'm going." There was a pause while Bernie sat in the road getting wetter by the minute.

"Well, I'll be…!"

The other man came back, holding the cane. He was scowling. "Where the devil did you get something like that?" he asked as he handed it down to her.

"Internet," she said. The pain was getting worse. Much worse. She needed a heavy dose of anti-inflammatories, and a bed and a heating pad.

She swallowed hard. "Please don't…stare when I get up. There's only one way I can do it, and it's embarrassing." She got on all fours and pushed herself up with difficulty, holding on to the cane for support. She lifted her head to the rain and got her breath back. "Thanks for not running over me," she said heavily.

The big man had stood up when she did. He was scowling. "What's the matter with you? Sprain?"

She looked up. It was a long way. "Rheumatoid arthritis."

"Arthritis? At your age?" the man asked, surprised.

She drew herself up angrily. "Rheumatoid," she emphasized. "It's systemic. An autoimmune disease. Only one percent of people in the world have it, although it's the most common autoimmune disease. Now if you don't mind, I have to get home before I drown."

"We'll drive you," the big man offered belatedly.

"Frankly, I'd rather drown, thanks." She turned, very slowly, and managed to get going without too much visible effort. But walking was laborious, and she was gritting her teeth before she'd gotten five steps.

"Oh, hell."

She heard the soft curse before she felt herself suddenly picked up like a sack of potatoes and carried back toward the limousine.

The other man was holding the door open.

"You put me down!" she grumbled, trying to struggle. She winced, because movement hurt.

"When I get you home," he said. "Where's home?"

He put her into the limousine and climbed in beside her. The other man closed the door and got in behind the wheel.

"I'll get the seat wet," she protested.

"It's leather. It will clean. Where's home?"

She drew in a breath. She was in so much pain that she couldn't even protest anymore. "Mrs. Brown's boardinghouse. Two blocks down and to the right. It's a big Victorian house with a white fence around it and a room-to-rent sign," she added.

The driver nodded, started the engine and took off.

The big man was still watching her. She was clutching the cane with a little hand that had gone white from the pressure she was using.

He studied her, his eyes on the thick plait of platinum blond hair down her back. Her clothes were plastered to her. Nice body, a little small-breasted and long legs. She had green eyes. Very pale green. Pretty bow mouth. Wide-spaced eyes under thick black eyelashes. Not beautiful. But attractive.

"Who are you?" he asked belatedly.

"My name is Bernadette," she said.

"Sweet," he mused. "There was a song about Saint Bernadette," he recalled.

She flushed. "My mother loved it. That's why she gave me the name."

"I'm Michael. Michael Fiore, but most people call me Mikey." He watched her face, but there was no recognition. She didn't know the name. Surprising. He'd been a resident of Jacobsville a few years back, when his cousin, Paul Fiore of the San Antonio FBI office, was investigating a case that involved Sari Grayling, who later became Paul's wife. Sari and her sister, Meredith, had been targeted by a hit man, courtesy of a man whose mother was killed by the Graylings' late father. Mikey had made some friends here.

"Nice to meet you," she managed. She grimaced.

"Hurts pretty bad, huh?" he asked, his dark eyes narrowing. He looked up. Santelli was pulling into a parking spot just in front of a Victorian house with a room-to-rent sign. "Is this it?" he asked.

She looked up through the window. She nodded. "Thanks so much…"

"Stay put," he said.

He went out the other door that Santi was holding open for him, around the car and opened her door. He reached in and picked her up, cane and purse and all.

"Come knock on the door for me, Santi," he told his companion.

Bernie tried to protest, but the big man kept walking. He smelled of cigar smoke and expensive cologne, and the feel of his big arms around her made her feel odd. Trembly. Nervous. Very nervous. She had one arm around his broad shoulders to hold on, her hand spread beside his neck. He was warm and comforting. It had been a long time since she'd been held by anyone, and it had never felt like this.

Santi knocked on the door.

Bernie could have told him that he could just walk in, but he wasn't from here, so he didn't know.

Plump Mrs. Brown opened the door, still wearing her apron because she offered supper to her roomers. She stopped dead, with her mouth open, as she saw Bernie being carried by a stranger.

"I fell," Bernie explained. "He was kind enough to stop and bring me home…"

"Oh, dear, should you go see Dr. Coltrain?" she said worriedly.

"I'm fine, really, just a little bruised dignity to speak of," she assured the landlady. "You can put me down," she said to Mikey.

"Where's her room?" Mikey asked politely. He smiled at the older woman, and she flushed and laughed nervously.

"It's right down here. She can't climb the stairs, so she has a room near the front…"

She led the way. He put Bernie down in a chair beside her bed.

"You need a hot bath, dear, and some coffee," Mrs. Brown fussed.

There was a bathroom between Bernie's room and the empty room next door.

"Can you manage?" the big man asked gently.

She nodded. "I'm okay. Really. Thanks."

He shrugged broad shoulders. He frowned. "You shouldn't be walking so far."

"Tell her, tell her," Mrs. Brown fretted. "She walks four blocks to and from work every single day!"

"Dr. Coltrain says exercise is good for me," she retorted.

"Exercise. Not torture," Mrs. Brown muttered.

The big man was thinking. "We'll see you again," he said quietly.

She nodded. "Thanks."

He cocked his head. His eyes narrowed. "First impressions aren't always accurate."

Her eyebrows arched. "Gosh, was that an apology?"

He scowled. "I don't apologize. Ever."

"That didn't hurt, that didn't hurt, that didn't hurt," she mimicked a comedian who'd said that very thing in a movie. She grinned. Probably he didn't have a clue what she was talking about.

He threw back his head and roared. *"Police Academy,"* he said, naming the movie.

Her jaw fell.

"Yeah. That guy was me, at his age," he confessed. "Take a bath. And don't fall in."

She made a face at him.

His dark eyes twinkled. "See you, kid."

He walked out before she could correct the impression.

He stopped at the front door. "That room to let," he asked Mrs. Brown. "Is it still available?"

"Why, yes," she said, flushing again. She laughed.

"You'd be very welcome. We have three ladies living here, but…"

"I'm easy to please," he said. "And I won't be any trouble. I hate hotels."

She smiled. "So do I. My husband was in rodeo. We spent years on the road. I got so sick of room keys…"

He laughed. "That's me. Okay. If you don't mind, I'll have my stuff here later today."

"I don't mind at all."

"How much in advance?" he asked, producing his wallet.

She told him. He handed her several bills.

"I don't rob banks, if that's what you're thinking," he said with a wry smile. "I'm a businessman. I live in New Jersey, and I own a hotel in Vegas. Which is why I hate staying in them."

"Oh! You have business here, then?"

He nodded solemnly. "Business," he agreed. "I'll be around for a while."

"It will be nice to have the room rented," she confessed. "It's been vacant for a long time. My last tenant got married."

"I'll see you later, then." He hesitated, looking back toward the room where he'd left Bernadette. "She'll be okay, you think?"

"Yes. She might look fragile, but Bernie's tough. She's had to be."

"Bernie?" His eyes widened.

She laughed. "That's what we call her. We've known Bernadette all her life."

"Small towns." He smiled. "I grew up in one, myself. Far from here." He pulled out a business card and handed it to her. "The lower number is my cell phone.

If she needs anything tonight, you call me, okay? I can come and drive her to the hospital if she needs to be seen."

Mrs. Brown was surprised at that concern from a stranger. "You have a kind heart."

He shrugged. "Not always. See you."

He went out, motioning for Santi to follow him. They got in the limo and drove off. Mrs. Brown watched it go with real interest. She wondered who the outsider was.

Mikey was all too aware of the driver's irritation. "They told me to keep an eye on you all the time," he told Mikey.

"Yeah, well, I'm not sharing a room with you, no matter what the hell they told you. Besides," he added, settling back into his seat, "Cash Grier's got one of his men shadowing me with a sniper kit."

"It's a small town," Santi began.

"A small town with half the retired mercs in America," Mikey cut in. "And my cousin lives right down the road. Remember him? Senior FBI agent Paul Fiore? Lives in Jacobsville, works out of San Antonio, worth millions?"

"Oh. Him. Right."

"Besides, I know the sniper Grier's got watching me." He chuckled. "He doesn't miss. Ever. And they snagged *The Avengers* to watch when the sniper's asleep."

"The Avengers?" Santi roared. "That's a comic book!"

"Rogers and Barton. They're called the Avengers because Captain America's name in the series is Rogers, and Hawkeye's is Barton. Get it?"

"Yeah."

"I know how bad Mario Cotillo wants me, Santi," Mikey said quietly. "I'm the only thing standing between Tony Garza and a murder-one conviction, because I know Tony didn't do it and I can prove it. Tony's in hiding, too, in an even safer place than me."

"Where?" Santi asked.

Mikey laughed coarsely. "Sure, like I'm going to tell you."

Santi stiffened. "I'm no snitch," he said, offended.

"Anybody can hack a cell phone or the elaborate two-way radio we got in this car, and listen to us when we talk," Mikey said with visible impatience. "Use your brain, okay?"

"I do!"

"Well, you must be keeping it in a safe place when you're not using it," Mikey muttered under his breath, but not so that Santi could hear him. The guy was good muscle and a capable driver. It wouldn't do to upset him too much. Not now, anyway.

Mikey leaned back with a long sigh and thought of the woman he'd met tonight. He was sorry he'd misjudged her, but plenty of women had thrown themselves into his path. He was extremely wealthy. He had money in Swiss banks that the feds couldn't touch. And while he'd been accused of a few crimes, including murder, he'd never even been indicted. His record was pretty clean. Well, for a guy in his profession. He was a crime boss back in Jersey, where Tony Garza was the big boss. Tony owned half the rackets around Newark. But Tony had some major new competition, an outsider who saw himself as the next Capone. He'd targeted Tony at once, planned to take him down on a fake murder charge with the help of a friend who worked in the federal attorney's office. It had backfired. Tony also had friends there. So did Mikey. But Mikey had been with Tony in a bar when the murder had taken place and by chance, Mikey had a photo of himself and Tony with a date stamp on his cell phone. He'd sent copies to Paulie and Cash Grier and a friend down in the Bahamas. Before the feds could jump Tony, who might have been dealt with handily and at once before it even came to trial, Mikey and Tony had both skipped town.

The next obvious play by Cotillo would be to put out contracts on Mikey and Tony. Mikey smiled. He knew most of the heavy hitters in the business. So did Tony. It wouldn't work, but Cotillo didn't know that. Yet. Meanwhile, Mikey and Tony were playing a waiting game. Both had feds on the job protecting them. Mikey wasn't telling Santi that, however. He didn't trust anybody really, except his cousin Paul. The fewer people who knew, the safer he was going to be.

Not that life held such attractions for him these days. He had all the money he'd ever need. He had a fearsome reputation, which gave him plenty of protection back home in New Jersey. But he was alone. He was a lonely man. He'd asked a woman to share his life only once, and she'd laughed. He was good in bed and he bought her pretty things, but she wasn't going to get married to a known gangster. She had her reputation to think of. After all, she was a debutante, from one of the most prominent families in Maryland. Marry a hood? Ha! Fat chance.

It had broken his heart. Even now, years and years after it happened, it was a sore spot. He was more than his reputation. He was fair and honest, and he never hurt anybody without a damned good reason. Mostly, he went after people who hurt people he cared about.

Well, there was also the odd job for Tony when he was younger. But those days were mostly behind him. He could still handle a sniper kit when he needed to. It was just that he didn't have the same need for notoriety that had once ruled his life.

Nobody needed him. Funny, the main reason he'd enjoyed the debutante was that she'd pretended to be helpless and clingy. He'd enjoyed that. Since his grandmother's death, there had been nobody who cared about him except Paul, and nobody who needed him at all. Briefly, he'd helped his cousin protect a young woman from Jacobsville, Merrie Grayling, before she married the Wyoming rancher. But that had been sort of an accessory thing. He'd liked her very much, yet as a sort of adoptive baby sister, nothing romantic. It had been nice, helping Paulie with that little chore, especially since he knew the contract killer who'd been assigned to get Merrie. He had known how to get the hit called off—actually, by getting Merrie, an artist of great talent, to do a portrait of Tony. The contract killer had ended badly, but that happened sometimes. Most sane people didn't go against Tony, who'd told the guy to call off the hit.

But all that had been three years ago. Life moved on. Now here was Mikey, in hiding from a newcomer in Jersey, trying to protect his friend Tony.

He thought again about the young woman who'd fallen in front of the limo. He felt bad that he'd misjudged her. She was pretty. What had she called herself—Bernadette? He smiled. He'd been to France, to the grotto where Saint Bernadette had dug into a mudhole, found a clear spring and seen the apparition she referred to as the Immaculate Conception, and he'd seen Bernadette in her coffin. She looked no older than when she'd died, a century and more ago, a beautiful young woman. He wondered if her namesake even knew who Saint Bernadette was. He wondered why she'd been given that name.

So many questions. Well, he was going to be staying in the same rooming house, so he'd probably get the chance to talk to her, to ask her about her family. She was nice. She didn't like pity, although she had a devastating medical condition, and she had a temper. He smiled, remembering that thick plait of blond hair down her back. He loved long hair. It must be hard to keep, for someone with her limitations.

His little Greek grandmother had been arthritic. He recalled her gnarled hands and the times when she hadn't been able to get out of bed. Mikey had carried her from room to room when she had special company, or outside when she wanted to sit in the sun. He couldn't remember what sort of arthritis she'd had, but it was in the family bible, along with plenty of other family information. He kept the bible in a safe-deposit box back in Jersey, along with precious photographs of people long dead. There had been one of the debutante. But he'd burned that one.

The car was eating up the miles to San Antonio, where Mikey had left his luggage in a hotel under an assumed name. He'd send Santi in to pick it up and pay the bill, just in case, while he waited outside in the parking lot. You couldn't be too careful. He needed to send a text to Paulie, as well, but that could wait until he was back in Jacobsville. He should ask Paulie about hackers and what they could find out, and how. He still wasn't up on modern methods of surveillance.

He leaned back against the seat with a long sigh. Bernadette. He smiled to himself.

Bernadette took a hot bath, and it did help ease some of the discomfort. Mrs. Brown had been kind enough to add a handhold on the side of the tub so that Bernadette would find it easier to get in and out of the tub. She took showers, however, not baths. It was so much quicker to stand up. Besides, the bathroom was used by all the boarders on the ground floor, although there had been just Bernadette for several weeks, and poor Mrs. Brown had enough to do without having to scrub the tub all the time. She did have a daily woman who came in to help with the heavy chores. But Bernadette was fastidious and it bothered her, the idea of baths when at least one of the former boarders had been male and liked lots of musk-smelling bath oil. For women, especially, baths in a less than spotlessly clean tub could lead to infections. Bernie had enough to worry about without those. So, she took showers.

She dressed in her pajama bottoms and one of the soft, thick T-shirts that she wore with it.

There was a tap at the door and Mrs. Brown came in with a cup of tea in a beautiful ceramic cup on its delicate saucer. "Chamomile tea," she said with a smile. "It will help you sleep, sweetheart."

"You're spoiling me," Bernadette complained softly. "You have enough to do without adding me to your burdens."

"You're no burden," Mrs. Brown said gently. "You keep your room spotless, you never mess anything up,

and I have yet to have to pick up after you anywhere."
She sighed. "I wish we could say the same for the two
nice women on the second floor, and don't you dare tell
them I said that!"

Bernadette laughed. "I won't. You know I don't gossip."

"Of course you don't." She put the cup and saucer
on the bedside table. "What a nice man who brought
you home," she added with a speculative glance that
Bernadette missed. "He's renting a room here, too!"

Bernadette caught her breath. "He is?" she stammered, and flushed a little.

Mrs. Brown chuckled. "He is. The one on the other
side of the bathroom, but that won't be a problem. I'll
make sure he knows to knock first when he needs to
use it."

"Okay, then." She sipped tea and smiled with her
eyes closed. "This is so good!"

"I put honey in it, instead of sugar, and just a hint
of cinnamon."

Bernadette looked up at the older woman. "You
know, he thought I'd fallen in front of his car on purpose."

"You fell? You didn't tell me!"

She sipped her tea. "The sidewalk was slippery and
my toe hit a brick that was just a little out of place. I
went flying into the street. Lucky for me that his driver
had good brakes." She frowned. "It was a limousine."

"I noticed," Mrs. Brown said with a wry smile. "He
was wearing a very expensive suit, as well. I think I
recognized him. He looks like Paul Fiore's cousin."

"I heard about that," Bernadette said, "when I was
working as a receptionist for a group of attorneys, be-

fore I got my paralegal certification from night school and Mr. Kemp hired me. I never saw him, but people talked about him. He was helping protect Merrie Grayling, wasn't he?"

"That was the gossip. Goodness, imagine having contract killers stalking two local girls in the same family!" She shook her head. "I had it from the Grayling girls' housekeeper, Mandy Swilling. She said the girls' father had killed a local woman for selling him out to the feds on racketeering charges, and the woman's son put out contracts on both Grayling's daughters, to get even. He thought their father loved them so much that it would really hurt him." She sighed. "Well, the man was dead by then, and the woman's son was charged with conspiracy to commit murder. They say he'll be in prison for a long time, even though he did try to help them find the killers."

"Good enough for him," Bernie said. "Murder is a nasty business."

"That's another thing. They say that Mr. Fiore's cousin Mikey is mixed up with organized crime."

"His cousin?"

"The man who carried you inside the house tonight," Mrs. Brown replied.

Bernie sat with the cup suspended in one hand. "Oh. Him." She laughed. She hadn't really been paying attention.

"Him." She laughed. "But I don't believe it. He's so nice. He was really concerned about you."

"Not when I first fell, he wasn't," Bernie said, wrinkling her nose. "He thought I did it on purpose to get his attention." She hesitated. "Well, you know, he is drop-dead gorgeous. When I first saw him, I could hardly

even get my breath," she confessed. "It was like being
hit in the stomach. I've never seen a real live man who
looked like that. He could be in movies." She flushed.
"Well, he's good-looking, I mean."

"I suppose some women do find excuses to attract
men like that," Mrs. Brown said in his defense.

"I suppose. He changed his mind when he saw the
cane, though." Her face grew sad. "When I was in high
school, there was this really nice boy. I thought he was
going to ask me to the senior prom. I was so excited.
One of my girlfriends said he was talking about me to
someone else, although she didn't hear what he said."
She looked down into the now-empty cup. "Then another friend told me the truth. He said that I wasn't bad
to look at, but he didn't want to take a disabled girl to a
dance." She smiled sadly, aware of Mrs. Brown's angry
expression. "After that, I sort of gave up on dating."

"There must have been nicer boys," she replied.

"Oh, there were. But there were prettier girls who
didn't walk with canes." She put down the cup and saucer. "I didn't need the cane all the time, of course. But
when I had flares, I'd just fall if I made a misstep." She
shook her head. "No man is going to want a woman who
may end up an invalid one day. So I go to work and save
all I can, and hope that by the time I need to give up
and apply for disability, I'll have enough to tide me over
until I can get it." She made a face. "Gosh, wouldn't it
be nice not to have health issues?"

"It would. And I'm sorry that you do. But, Bernie, a
man who loves you won't care if you have them." She
added, "Any more than you'd care if he had them."

Bernie smiled. "You're a nice woman. I'm so lucky
to live here. And thank you for the tea."

"You're very welcome. You get some sleep. Tomorrow's Saturday, so you can sleep in for a change."

"A nice change." She grimaced. "But I don't want you to wait breakfast for me...!"

"I'll put it on a plate in the fridge and you can heat it up in the microwave," said Mrs. Brown. "So stop worrying about things."

Bernie laughed. "Okay. Thanks again."

"You're very welcome." She hesitated at the door. 'What a very good thing that we don't have many young women living here, except you."

"Why?"

"Well, that nice man who brought you in is really good-looking, and we don't want a line forming at his door, now do we?" she teased.

Bernie blushed, but Mrs. Brown had closed the door before she saw it.

Chapter Two

Mikey waited for Santi in a parking spot near the front door of the San Antonio hotel. He hoped it wouldn't take too long. The streets were busy, even at this time of night, and some of the people milling around were wearing gang colors and had multiple tats. He knew about the Los Serpientes gang. Although they were technically based in Houston, they had a presence here in San Antonio. Paulie had told him about them. They looked out for children and old people. Amazing. Kind of like the Yakuza in Japan.

Japan was a great place to visit. Mikey had gone there for several weeks after his tour of duty in the Middle East. He'd needed to wind down and get over some of the things he'd seen and done there. He'd been with a group of military overseas that included two men from here, Rogers and Barton, who'd been protecting the Grayling girls from contract killers. He hadn't served directly with them, but Cag Hart and the local DA, Blake Kemp, had been overseas at the same time. From Afghanistan to Iraq, he'd carried a rifle and served his country. The memories weren't good, but he had others he lived with. He just added the more recent ones to them.

He'd been surprised to find his company commander involved with Merrie Grayling. The Wyoming rancher, Ren Colter, had been the company commander of his sniper unit overseas. In fact, the Grayling girls' protectors, Rogers and Barton, had also been part of his group. What a homecoming that had been. Not a really great one, because Mikey had gotten in trouble scrounging materials for a brothel. But his commanding officer had gotten him out of trouble with Ren, because Mikey had the greatest luck in the world at poker. He never lost. It was one reason he was so rich. Of course, he couldn't get into casinos anymore. He didn't cheat. He didn't have to. But that luck had gotten him barred all over the world, even in Monte Carlo. He chuckled. It was sort of a mark of honor, being barred from those places. So he didn't mind that much. He had all the money he'd ever need until he died an old man, so who cared?

The car trunk opened suddenly. Mikey's hand had gone automatically under his jacket to the .45 he'd put there before Santi went into the hotel. He kept it in a secure compartment under the seat, custom-made. He hadn't needed it in Jacobsville, but this was unknown territory, and it was dangerous not to go heeled. He had a concealed carry permit, but for Jersey, not here. He supposed he'd have to go see the sheriff in Jacobs County and get one for Texas. That would be Hayes

Carson. He knew the sheriff from three years ago. They got on.

Santi opened the door and got in behind the wheel. "All the bags are in the trunk, chief," he told his boss. "We need to stop anywhere else before we head south?"

"Not unless you're hungry."

"I could eat."

"Well, there's a nice restaurant in a better part of town. Let's go looking." He glanced out through the tinted windows at a young man who was giving the limo a real hard look. "I'm not overjoyed with the clientele hereabouts."

"Me, neither."

"So, let's go. We'll drive around and see if we can find someplace Italian. I think Paulie said a new place had just opened recently. Carlo's. Put it in the computer."

Santi fed it into the onboard GPS. "Got it, chief. Only three blocks away."

"Okay! Head out."

They were well into their plates of spaghetti when Mikey noticed a couple of customers in suits giving them a cursory inspection.

"Feds," Mikey said under his breath. "At the second table over. Don't look," he added.

"Know them?"

"Nope," Mikey said.

"FBI, you think?"

Mikey chuckled. "If they were, Paulie would have mentioned that I had a tail here in the city."

"Then who?"

"If I were guessing, US Marshals," he replied. "The

big dark one looks vaguely familiar, but I can't quite place him. He was working with Paulie during the time I spent in Jacobsville three years ago."

"Marshals?" Santi asked, and he shifted restlessly.

"Relax. They aren't planning to toss our butts in jail. There's this thing called due process," Mikey said imperturbably. "We'll have fewer worries down in Jacobs County. Jacobsville is so small that any stranger sticks out. Besides, we've got shadows of our own."

"Good ones?"

"You bet," Mikey replied with a smug grin. "So eat your supper and I'll move into my new temporary home."

"I don't like being down the road in a motel," Santi muttered. "Even with all the other guys watching your back."

"Well, I'm not sharing the room," Mikey said flatly. "It's barely big enough for me and all my stuff, without trying to fit you into it. No room for another bed, anyway."

"I guess you got a point."

"Of course I do. Besides, it's not like I'm going to get hit until they track me down here."

"The limo is going to attract attention," Santi said worriedly.

"Yeah, well, no more attention than the gossip will, but there's not a place in the world I'd be safer. Strangers stick out here. Remember, I told you about Cash Grier's wife being tracked here by a contract killer, and what happened to him?"

Santi chuckled. "Yeah. Grier's wife hit him so hard with an iron skillet that he ran to the cops for protection."

"Exactly. Nobody messes with Tippy Grier. What a

knockout. A movie star, and she's married to the police chief and has two kids. I never thought Grier could settle down in a small town. He didn't seem the sort."

"That's what everybody says." Santi paused. "I feel bad about that poor girl we almost hit," he added, surprisingly, because he wasn't sentimental. "She was nice, and we thought she was trying to play us."

"We come by our suspicious natures honestly," Mikey reminded him. "But, yeah, she was nice. Needs looking after," he said quietly. "Not that she seems the kind of woman who'd let anybody look after her."

"I noticed that."

Mikey glanced at his watch. "We'd better go." He signaled to a waiter for the check.

Bernadette was reading in bed. The pain was pretty bad, a combination of the rain and the fall. She needed something to take her mind off it, so she pulled out her cell phone, on which she kept dozens of books. Many were romance novels. She realized that her condition would keep most men away, and it was nice to daydream about having a kind man sweep her off her feet.

She couldn't stop thinking about the big dark-haired man who'd done that earlier in the evening. He was kin to Paul Fiore, who was married to Sari Grayling. Bernie worked with Sari in the local DA's office. She wondered if she could get away with asking her anything about the man, who'd been very kind to her after mistaking her for some kind of con woman.

She shouldn't be thinking about him. A man that handsome probably had women hanging on to his ankles everywhere he walked. He was apparently rich, as well. There was another woman in her office, the receptionist, Jessie Tennison, a gorgeous brunette in her late twenties, who was crazy about men and openly solicited any rich one who came into the office. Mr. Kemp, the DA, had already called her down about it once. A second offense would cost her the job, he'd added. Her position didn't include sexual harassment of clients.

What a new world it was, Bernie mused, when a woman could be accused of what was often seen as a man's offense. But, then, her coworker was very pretty. She was just ambitious. She had a failed marriage behind her. Gossip was that her ex-husband had been wealthy but had a gambling habit and lost it all on one draw of a card. Nobody knew, because the woman didn't talk about herself. Well, not to the women in the office.

A sudden commotion caught her attention. There was movement in the hall. Some bumping and a familiar deep male voice. Her heart jumped. That was the man who'd brought her home earlier. She knew his voice already. It was hard to miss, with that definite New Jersey accent. She knew about that because of Paul Fiore. He had one just like it.

There was more noise, then a door closing. More footsteps. Voices. The front door opening and closing, and then a car driving away.

Mrs. Brown knocked at Bernie's door and then slipped in, closing it behind her. "Sorry about the noise. Mr. Fiore's just moving in," she added with an affectionate smile.

Bernie tried not to show the delight she felt. "Is he going to stay long? Did he say?"

"Not really," she said. "His driver is staying at a motel down the road." She laughed. "Mr. Fiore said no way was he sharing that room with another man, especially not one as big as his driver."

Bernie laughed softly. "I guess not."

"So you'll need to knock before you go into the bathroom, like I mentioned earlier," Mrs. Brown continued. "Just in case. I told Mr. Fiore again that he'd need to do the same thing, since you're sharing." She looked worried. Bernie was flushed. "I'm so sorry. If I had a room with a bathroom free, I'd—"

"Those are upstairs," Bernie interrupted gently, "and we both know that I have a problem with stairs." She sighed and shook her head. "The rain and the walk and the fall pretty much did me in today. You were right. I should have gotten a cab. It isn't that expensive, and I don't spend much of what I make, except on books." That was true. Her rent included all utilities and even the cable that gave her television access—not that she watched much TV.

"I know that walking is supposed to be good for you," the older woman replied. "But not when you're having a flare." She drew in a breath. "Bernie, if you wrote the company that makes that injectable medicine, they might…"

"I already did," Bernie said softly. "They offered me a discount, but even so, it's almost a thousand dollars a month. There's no way I could afford that, discount or not. Besides," she said philosophically, "it might not work for me. Sometimes it doesn't. It's a gamble."

"I guess so." Mrs. Brown looked sad. "Maybe someday they'll find a cure."

"Maybe they will."

"Well, I'll let you get back to your book," she teased, because she knew about the late-night reading habit.

"Need anything from the kitchen before I turn out the lights?"

"Not a thing. I have my water right here." She indicated two bottles of water that she kept by her bedside.

"You could have some ice in a glass to go with it."

Bernie shook her head. "It would just melt. But thank you, Mrs. Brown. You're so good to me."

The older woman beamed. "I'm happy to have you here. You're the only resident I've ever had who never complained about anything. You'll spoil me."

"That's *my* line," Bernie teased, and she laughed. It made her look pretty.

"Sleep well."

"You, too."

Mrs. Brown went out and closed the door.

Bernie thought about that injectable medicine. Her rheumatologist in San Antonio had told her about it, encouraged her to try to get it. At Bernie's age, it might retard the progress of the disease, a disease that could lead to all sorts of complications, the worst of which was deformity in the hands and feet. Not only that, but RA was systemic. It could cause a lot of issues in other parts of the body, as well.

Chance, Bernie thought, would be a fine thing. She'd have to be very well-to-do in order to afford something so expensive as those shots. Well, meanwhile she had her other meds, and they worked well enough most of the time. It wasn't every day that she fell in a cold rain almost in front of somebody's fancy limousine. She smiled to herself and went back to her book.

Breakfast the next morning would have been interesting, Bernie thought to herself as she ate hers from a tray her kindly landlady had provided. But she couldn't get up. A weather system had moved in, dropping even more rain, and Bernie's poor body was still trying to cope with yesterday's fall. What a good thing it was Saturday. She'd have had a time getting to work.

Just as she finished the last drop of her coffee, there was a perfunctory knock and the man who'd rescued her walked in.

She pulled the sheet up over her breasts. The gown covered her nicely, but she'd never had a man in her bedroom in her life, except for her late father and her doctor. She flushed.

Mikey grinned from ear to ear. He loved that reaction. The women in his life were brassy and easy and unshockable. Here was a violet under a staircase, undiscovered, who blushed because a man saw her in her nightgown.

"Mrs. Brown said you might like a second cup of coffee," he said gently, approaching the bed with a cup and saucer.

"Oh, I, yes, I…thank you." She couldn't even talk normally. She was furious with herself, especially when her hands shook a little as she took the cup and saucer from him. He lifted the empty one from the tray, so she'd have someplace to put the new one.

He cocked his head and looked at her, fascinated. Her long blond hair was in a braid, a little frizzled from being slept on. She was wearing a cotton gown, and he could see the straps with their eyelet trim. It reminded him of his grandmother, who'd never liked artificial fabric.

"You aren't feeling so good today, are you?" he asked. "Need me to run you over to the doctor?"

The flush grew. "Oh. Thank you. No, I'm…well, it's sort of normal. When it rains, it hurts more. And I fell." She bit her lip because he looked so guilty. "It wasn't your fault, or your driver's," she added quickly. "I'm clumsy. My toe hit a brick on the sidewalk that was just a little raised and it caused me to lose my balance. That's why I use the cane on bad days. I'm clumsy even on flat surfaces…"

"My grandmother had arthritis," he said softly. "Her little hands and feet were gnarled like tree roots." He wasn't watching, so he didn't notice the discomfort in Bernie's face—her poor feet weren't very pretty, either. "I used to carry her in and out of the house when she had bad spells. She loved to sit in the sun." His dark eyes were sad. "She weighed barely eighty pounds, but she was like a little pit bull. Even the big guys were afraid of her."

"The big guys?" she asked, lost in his soft eyes.

He shrugged. "In the family," he said.

She frowned. She didn't understand.

"You really are a little violet under a stair," he mused to himself. "The family is what insiders call the mob," he explained. "The big guys are the dons, the men who run things. I'm from New Jersey. Most of my family was involved in organized crime. Well, except Paulie," he added with a chuckle. "He was always the odd guy out."

She smiled. "He's married to Sari Grayling, who works in our office."

He nodded. "Sweet woman. Her sister is one hel— heck of an artist," he said, amending the word he'd meant to use.

"She truly is. They had her do a portrait of our local college president, who was retiring. It looked just like him."

He chuckled. "The one she painted three years ago saved her life. Her father whacked a woman whose son hired contract men to go after Grayling's daughters. Merrie painted the big don from back home, and he called off the hit." He didn't add how Tony Garza had called it off.

"We heard about all that. I wasn't working for the district attorney's office at the time. I was working for a local attorney who moved his practice to San Antonio. But we all knew," she added. "Everybody talked about it. He actually gave her away at her wedding, didn't he?"

He nodded. "Tony's wife died young. He never had kids, never remarried." He grinned. "He tells everybody he's Merrie's dad. Gets a reaction, let me tell you, especially when he mentions that her brother-in-law is a fed."

She sipped coffee, fascinated by him.

It was mutual. He smiled very slowly, his heart doing odd things in his chest. It had been many years since he'd felt such tenderness for anything female, except his grandmother.

"Do you have family?" he asked suddenly.

Her face clouded. "Not anymore," she said softly, without elaborating.

"Me, neither," he replied. "Except for Paulie. We're first cousins."

"Mr. Fiore's nice," she said.

He nodded. He was thinking about Tony, in hiding and waiting for developments that would save him from life in prison. Mikey had the proof that could save him. But he had to stay alive long enough to present it. Here, in Jacobsville, was his best bet. He'd agreed, knowing how many ex-mercs and ex-military lived here.

But as he stared at this sweet, kind young woman,

he thought about the danger he might be putting her in. Even in a foolproof situation, there could be snags. After all, the contract killer who'd been after Merrie actually got onto Ren Colter's property in Wyoming and had her bedroom staked out before she came back to her sister and brother-in-law.

Bernie cocked her head. "Something's worrying you."

He started. "How do you know?"

She drew in a slow breath and averted her eyes. "People think I'm strange."

He moved a step closer to the bed. "How so?"

She shifted restlessly. "I...well, I sort of know things about people." She flushed.

He nodded. "Like Merrie. She has that sort of perception. She painted a picture of me that nailed me to a T, and she'd never even met me."

She looked up. "Oh. Then you're not...intimidated by strange things."

He chuckled. "Nothing intimidates me, kid," he teased.

She smiled.

"So. You think something's worrying me." One brown eye narrowed. "What, exactly?"

She drew in a long breath and stared into his eyes. "Somebody wants to keep you from telling something you know," she said after a minute, and saw the shock hit his face.

"Damn."

"And it worries you that somebody might hurt anybody around you."

"Need to get a crystal ball and a kerchief and set up shop," he teased gently. "You're absolutely on the money. But that's between you and me, okay? The fewer people who know things, the fewer can talk about them."

She nodded. "I don't talk about things I know, as a rule. I work for the DA's office. Gossip isn't encouraged."

He chuckled. "I guess not."

Her coffee was now stone-cold, but she sipped it, for something to do.

He stared at her with conflicting emotions. She was unique, he thought. He'd never met anybody in his life like her.

She stared back. Her heart was almost smothering her with its wild beat. She was grateful that she had the covers pulled up, so he couldn't see her gown fluttering with her heartbeat.

There was another quick knock and Mrs. Brown came in. "Finished, dear?" she asked as she went to pick up the tray. "You can just set that on here, Mr. Fiore," she told Mikey with a smile. "I'll…"

He put it on the tray and then took the tray from her. "You're too delicate to be lifting heavy weights," he said with a grin. "I'll carry it for you."

"Oh, Mr. Fiore," she laughed, and blushed like a girl. "If you need anything, you just call me, Bernie, ok?"

"I will. Thanks. Both of you," she added.

Mrs. Brown smiled. As Mikey went through the door, he turned and winked at her.

That wink kept her heart fluttering all day, and it kept her awake most of the night.

She was able to go to the table for breakfast the next morning, even if she moved with a little difficulty. Her medicines worked slowly, but at least they did work.

She had prednisone to take with the worst attacks, and it helped tremendously.

"You look better today," Mrs. Brown said. "Going to church?"

"Yes," she replied with a smile. "I'm hitching a ride with the Farwalkers."

Mikey frowned. "The Farwalkers? Wait a minute. Farwalker. Carson Farwalker. He's one of the doctors here. I remember."

Bernie laughed. "Yes. He's married to Carlie Blair. Her dad is pastor of the local Methodist church. I don't have a car, so they come by to get me most Sundays for services. Sometimes it's just Carlie and their little boy, Jacob, if Carson's on call."

He didn't mention that he knew that pastor, Jake Blair. He also knew things about the man's past that he wasn't sharing.

"My whole family was Catholic," he said. "Well, not Paulie. But then, he always went his own way."

"The Ruiz family here is Catholic," she said. "He's a Texas Ranger. His wife is a nurse. She works in San Antonio, too, so they commute. They're very nice people."

"I never met Ruiz, but I heard about him. Ranch the size of a small state, they say."

Bernie grinned. "Yes. It is rather large, but they aren't social people, if you get my meaning."

"Goodness, no," Miss Pirkle, one of the tenants said with a smile. "Your cousin and his family are like that, too, Mr. Fiore," she added, her thin face animated as she spoke. "Down-to-earth. Good people."

"Thanks," he said.

"We have a lot of moneyed families in Jacobsville and Comanche Wells," old Mrs. Bartwell interjected with a smile. "Most of them earned their wealth the hard way, especially the Ballengers. They started out with nothing. Now Calhoun is a United States senator and Justin runs their huge feed lot here."

"That's a real rags-to-riches story," Miss Pirkle agreed. "Their sons are nice, too. Imagine, two brothers, three children apiece, and not a girl in the bunch," she added on a laugh.

"I wouldn't mind a little girl," Mikey said, surprising himself. He didn't dare look at Bernie, who'd inspired the comment. He could almost picture her in a little frilly dress at the age of five or six. She would have been a pretty child. He hadn't thought about children in a long time, not since his ex-fiancée had noted that she wasn't marrying some famous criminal. It had broken Mikey's heart. Women were treacherous.

"Children are sweet," Bernie said softly as she finished her bacon and eggs. "The Griers come into our office a lot with their daughter, Tris, and their son, Marcus. I love seeing their children."

"The police chief," Mikey said, nodding. He chuckled. "Not your average small-town cop."

"Not at all," Bernie agreed, tongue-in-cheek.

"That's true," Miss Pirkle said. "He was a Texas Ranger!"

Bernie caught Mikey's eyes and held them. He got the message. Their elderly breakfast companion didn't know about the chief's past. Just as well to keep it quiet.

"Are you from here, too?" Mikey asked Miss Pirkle.

"No. I'm from Houston," she replied, her blue eyes smiling. "I came here with my mother about two years ago, just before I lost her." She took a breath and forced a smile. "I loved the town so much that I decided I'd just stay. I don't really have anybody back in Houston now."

"I'm not from here, either," Mrs. Bartwell said. "I'm a northern transplant. New York State."

"Thought I recognized that accent," Mikey teased.

Mrs. Bartwell chuckled. "I have a great-niece who lives in Chicago with her grandmother. Old money. Very old. They have ancestors who died in the French Revolution."

"My goodness!" Miss Pirkle exclaimed, all ears.

"My sister and I haven't spoken in twenty years," she added. "We had a minor disagreement that led to a terrible fight. My husband died of cancer and we had no children. My great-niece's mother was from Jacobsville. She was a Jacobs, in fact."

"Impressive," Bernie said with a grin. "Was she kin to Big John?"

"Yes, distantly."

"Big John?" Mikey asked curiously.

"Big John Jacobs," Bernie replied, because she knew the history by heart. "He was a sharecropper back in Georgia before the Union Army burned down his farm and killed most of his family, thinking they were slave owners. They weren't. They were poor, like the black family he saved from real slave owners. One of the Union officers was going to have him shot, but the black family got between him and the Army man and made him listen to the truth. They saved his life. He came here just after the Civil War with them. He didn't even have a proper house, so he and their families lived in one big shack together. He hired on some Comanche men and a good many cowboys from Mexico and started ranching with Texas longhorns. He made people uncomfortable because he wasn't a racist in a time when many people were. He married an heiress, convinced her father to build a railroad spur to the ranch, near present Jacobsville, so that he could ship his cattle north. Made a fortune at it."

"What a story," Mikey chuckled.

"And all true," Miss Pirkle said. "There's a statue of Big John on the town square. One of his direct descendants is married to Justin Ballenger, who owns one of the biggest feed lots in Texas."

"All this talk of great men makes me weak in the knees," Mikey teased.

"Do you have illustrious ancestors, Mr. Fiore?" Mrs. Brown asked with a mischievous grin.

"Nah," he said. "If I do, I don't know about it. My grandmother was the only illustrious person I ever knew."

"Was she famous?" Mrs. Bartwell asked.

"Well, she was famous back in Jersey," he mused. "Got mad at a don and chased him around the room with a salami."

There were confused looks.

"Mafia folks," he explained.

"Oh! Like in *The Sopranos*, that used to be on television!" Miss Pirkle said. "I never missed an episode!"

"Sort of like that," he said. "More like Marlon Brando in *The Godfather*," he said, chuckling. "Afterwards, he sent her a big present every Christmas and even came to her funeral. She was fierce."

"Was she Italian?" Mrs. Brown asked.

He laughed. "She was Greek. Everybody else in my whole family was Italian except for her. She was a tiny little thing, but ferocious. I was terrified of her when I was a kid. So was Paulie. Our folks didn't have much time for us," he added, not explaining why, "so she pretty much raised us."

"I never knew either of my grandmothers," Bernie said as she sipped coffee.

Mikey was studying her closely. "Where were your grandparents from?" he asked.

She closed up like a flower. She forced a smile. "I'm not really sure," she lied. "My father and mother were from Jacobsville, though, and we lived here from the time I was old enough to remember things. I have to get ready for church. It was delicious, Mrs. Brown," she added.

"Thank you, dear," Mrs. Brown said, and grimaced a little. She knew about Bernie's past. Not many other local people did. She could almost feel Bernie's anguish. Not Mr. Fiore's fault for bringing it up. He didn't know. "Want a second cup of coffee to take with you while you dress?"

"If I drink two, I can fly around the room and land on the curtain rods," Bernie teased. "I'm hyper enough as it is. But thanks."

She glanced at Mikey, puzzled by the look on his face. She smiled at the others and went back to her room.

Jake Blair was a conundrum, Bernie thought as she walked in line out the front door to shake hands with him after the very nice sermon. He seemed to be very conventional, just like a minister was expected to be. But he drove a red Shelby Cobra Mustang with a souped-up engine, and there were whispers about his past. The same sort of whispers that followed Jacobsville's police chief, Cash Grier, wherever he went.

Bernie gripped her dragon cane tightly and glanced

at the toddler in Dr. Carson Farwalker's arms as he and Carlie walked beside her.

"Imagine you two with a child." Bernie sighed as she went from one face to the other.

Carlie grinned. "Imagine us married!" she corrected with a loving look at her husband, which was returned. "They were taking bets at the police station the day we got married about when he'd do a flit."

"They're having a long wait, don't you think?" Carson chuckled.

"Very long," she agreed. "Imagine, we used to fight each other in World of Warcraft on battlegrounds and we never knew it. Not until my life was in danger and Dad had you watching me."

"I watched you a lot more than he told me to," Carson teased.

She laughed.

They'd moved up to Jake by now and he was giving them an amused grin. "There's my boy!" he said softly, and held his arms out for Jacob, who was named after him."

"Gimpa." The little boy laughed and hugged the tall man.

Jake hugged him close. "If anybody had told me ten years ago that I'd go all mushy over a grandchild, I guess I'd have laughed."

"If anybody had told me ten years ago that I'd be practicing medicine in a small Texas town, I'd have fainted," Carson chuckled.

"I like having family," Jake said, and smiled at his daughter and son-in-law. "I never belonged anyplace in my life until now."

"Me, neither," Bernie said softly.

Jake looked at her kindly, and she knew that he'd heard the rumors. She just smiled. He was her minister, after all. Someday maybe she'd be able to talk about it. Mrs. Brown knew, but she was a clam. Not a lot of other people had any idea about Bernie's background because she'd lived for a few years, with her parents, in Floresville before coming back here with her father just before he died. She didn't like to think about those days. Not at all.

Jake looked behind his family at the few remaining, obviously impatient worshippers and handed his grandson back to Carson. "Ah, well, I'll see you all at the house later. I'm holding up progress," he added, and looked behind Carson at a man who actually flushed.

"Not a problem, Preacher," the man said. "It's just that the line's already forming for lunch at Barbara's Café…"

"Say no more," Jake chuckled. "Actually, I'm heading there myself. I can burn water."

"You can cook," Carlie chided.

"Only when I want to. And I don't want to," he confided with a grin. He kissed her cheek and shook hands with Carson. "I'll see you all for supper. You bringing it?"

"Of course," Carlie replied with a grin. "We know you can't boil water!"

He just laughed.

Bernie walked into the boardinghouse a little tired, but happy from the few hours of socializing with friends.

She wasn't looking where she was going, her mind still on the Farwalkers' little boy, whom she had sat beside in the back seat and cooed at all the way home. She ran right into Mikey and almost fell.

Chapter Three

Mikey just stared at her, smiling faintly as he caught her by both shoulders and spared her a fall. She did look pretty, with her long, platinum blond hair loose around her shoulders, wearing a pink dress in some soft material that displayed her nice figure without making it look indecent. He thought of all the women he'd known who paraded around in dresses cut up to the thigh and slashed to the waist in front. He compared them with Bernie, and found that he greatly preferred her to those glitzy women in his past.

"Thanks," she said, a husky note in her voice as she looked up at him with fascinated pale green eyes. It was a long way. He was husky for his height, and his head was leonine, broad, with a straight nose and chiseled lips and a square chin. He looked like a movie star. She'd never even seen a man so handsome.

"Deep thoughts?" he asked softly.

She caught her breath. "Sorry. I was just thinking how handsome you are." She flushed. "Oh, gosh," she groaned as that slipped out.

"It's okay," he teased. "I'm used to ladies swooning over me. No problem."

That broke the ice and she laughed.

He loved the way she looked when she laughed. Her whole face became radiant. Color bloomed on her cheeks. Her green eyes sparkled. Amazing, that a woman with her disability could laugh at all. But, then, his little grandmother had been the same. She never complained. She just accepted her lot in life and got on with living.

"You never complain, do you?" he asked suddenly.

"Well...not really," she stammered. "There's this saying that the boss has on the wall at work, a quote from Saint Francis of Assisi..."

"'God grant me the serenity to accept the things I cannot change; courage to change the things I can; and wisdom to know the difference,'" he quoted.

She smiled. "You know it."

He shrugged. "My grandmother dragged me to mass every single Sunday until I was old enough to refuse to go. She had a plaque with that quote on it. I learned it by heart."

"It's nice."

"I guess."

He let her go belatedly. "You okay?"

"I'm fine. I wasn't paying attention to where I was going. Sorry I ran into you."

"Feel free to do it whenever you like," he said, and

his dark eyes twinkled. "You fall down, kid, I'll pick you up every time."

She flushed. "Thanks. I'd do the same for you, if I could." She eyed his height. Her head came up to just past his shoulder. He probably weighed twice what she did, and the expensive suit he was wearing didn't disguise the muscular body under it. "I don't imagine I could pick you up, though."

He laughed. "Don't sweat it. I'll see you later."

She nodded.

He went around her and out the door, just as she heard a car pull up at the curb. His driver, no doubt. She wondered where he was going on a Sunday. But, then, that was really not her business.

It was the next morning before Bernie saw Mikey again, at the breakfast table. He was quiet and he looked very somber. He felt somber. Somebody had tracked Tony to the Bahamas and Marcus Carrera had called in some markers to keep him safe. Tony had used one of his throwaway phones to call Mikey—on the number Mikey had sent through a confederate.

Carrera, he recalled, was not a man to mess with. Once a big boss up north, the man had done a complete flip and gone legit. He was worth millions. He'd married a small-town Texas girl some years ago and they had two sons. The wife was actually from Jacobsville, a girl who used to do clothing repairs at the local dry cleaner's. Her father was as rich as Tony. Her mother had pretended to be her sister, but the truth came out when Carrera was threatened and his future wife saved him. Mikey knew Carrera's in-laws, but distantly. At least Tony was safe. But if they'd tracked him down, they probably had a good idea where Mikey was. It wouldn't take much work to discover that Mikey had been down here in Jacobsville three years ago to help out his cousin Paulie. That being said, however, it was still the safest place he could be. He had as much protection as he needed, from both sides of the law.

He looked around at the women at the table. His eyes lingered on Bernadette. He didn't want to put her in the line of fire. This had been a bad idea, getting a room at a boardinghouse. Or had it?

"Deep thoughts, Mr. Fiore?" Mrs. Brown teased. "You're very quiet."

He laughed self-consciously when he felt eyes on him. "Yeah. I was thinking about a friend of mine who's been in some trouble recently."

"We've all been there," Miss Pirkle said warmly. "I guess friends become like family after a time, don't they? We worry about them just as we would about kinfolk."

"And that's a fact," he agreed.

"My best friend drowned in a neighbor's swimming pool, when my family lived briefly in Floresville," Bernie commented.

"Did you see it?" Mikey asked.

She looked down at her plate. Her whole face clenched. "Yes. I didn't get to her in time."

"Listen, kid, sometimes things just happen. Like they're meant to happen. I'm not a religious man, but I believe life has a plan. Every life."

Bernie looked up at him. Her face relaxed a little. She drew in a long breath. "Yes. I think that, too." She smiled.

He smiled back.

The smiles lasted just a second too long to be casual. Mrs. Brown broke the silence by putting her cup noisily in the saucer without glancing at her boarders. It amused her, the streetwise Northerner and the shy Texas girl, finding each other fascinating. Mrs. Brown's husband had died years ago, leaving her with a big house outside town and a fistful of bills she couldn't pay. Opening her home to lodgers had made the difference. With her increased income, she was able to buy this house in town and turn it into a new boardinghouse. The sale of the first house had financed the purchase and remodeling of this one. The new location had been perfect for her boarders who worked in Jacobsville. She found that she had a natural aptitude for dealing with people, and it kept her bills paid and left her comfortably situated financially. But romance had been missing from her life. Now she was watching it unfold, with delight.

Mikey glanced at his wrist, at the very expensive thin gold watch he wore. "I have to run. I'm meeting Paulie up in San Antonio, but I'll be home in time for dinner," he told Mrs. Brown. He got up and leaned toward her. "What are we having?"

"Lasagna," she said with a grin. "And yes, I do know how to make it. Mandy Swilling taught me."

"You angel!" he said, and chuckled. "I'll definitely be back on time. See you all later."

They all called goodbyes. Bernie flushed when he turned at the doorway and glanced back at her with dark, soft eyes and a smile.

She felt good enough to walk the four blocks to work and she hardly needed the cane. Her life had taken a turn. She was happy for the first time in recent memory. Just the thought of Mikey Fiore made her tingle all over and glow inside.

That was noticed by the people she worked with, especially the new girl, Jessie Tennison. Jessie was older than Bernadette's twenty-four years. She had to be at least twenty-seven. She'd been married and was now divorced, with no children. She had a roving eye for rich men. It had already gotten her in trouble with their boss, Mr. Kemp, the district attorney. That hadn't seemed to stop her. She wore very revealing clothing—she'd been called down about that, too—and she wasn't friendly to the women in the office.

Bernie put down her purse, folded her cane and took off her jacket before she sat down.

"I don't see why you work," Jessie said offhandedly, looking down her long nose at Bernie with a cold blue-eyed stare. "I'd just get on government relief and stay home."

"I don't need handouts. I work for my living," Bernie said. She smiled at the tall brunette, but not with any warmth.

Jessie shrugged. "Suit yourself. I'm going over to the courthouse on my break to talk to my friend Billie," she added, slipping into a long coat.

Bernie almost bit her tongue off to keep from mentioning that their breaks were only ten minutes long and it would take Jessie that long just to walk to the courthouse. The district attorney's office had been in the courthouse, but this year they'd moved to a new county building where they had more room. The increased space had delighted the office staff, which had grown considerably. Their new office was closer to Mrs.

Brown's boardinghouse and Barbara's Café, but farther from the courthouse.

She didn't say it, but her coworker Olivia did. "Who's in the courthouse today, Jessie?" she asked with a blank expression. "Some really rich upper-class man who might need a companion…?"

"You…!" Jessie began just as Mr. Kemp's office door opened. She smiled at him, all sweetness. "I'm going to the courthouse on my break to see my friend Billie for just a minute, Mr. Kemp. Is that all right with you?" she added with a cold glance at her coworker.

"If it's absolutely necessary," he replied tersely. He wasn't pleased with his new employee. In fact, he was beginning to think he'd made a big mistake. A glowing recommendation from a San Antonio attorney had gotten Jessie the job, mainly because there were no other applicants. Competent receptionists with several years' experience weren't thick on the ground around Jacobsville.

"It really is," she said, and looked as if it wasn't the whole truth. "I have a friend in the hospital in San Antonio. Billie's been to see him," she added quickly.

"Okay. Try not to take too long." He paused and looked at her for a long time. "You get a ten-minute break. Not an hour."

"Oh, yes, sir." She was all sugary sweetness as she walked out the door in a cloud of cloying perfume.

Bernie's coworker fanned the air with a file folder, making a face.

Not five minutes later, assistant DA Glory Ramirez walked in the door and made a face. "Who's been filming a perfume commercial in here?" she asked.

"Somebody who's mad at me, probably," Sari Fiore,

their second assistant DA, laughed as she came in behind Glory. "Perfume gives me a migraine."

"I'll turn the air conditioner on long enough to suck it out of the building," Mr. Kemp volunteered.

"Ask her to wash it all off. I dare you," Sari said to the boss.

He laughed and went back into his office. The phone rang. Sari picked it up, nodded, spoke into the receiver and pressed a button. It was for Mr. Kemp. She hung up.

"Where's Jessie?" Sari asked curtly. "The phone is her job, not ours."

"There's some rich guy at the courthouse," Olivia told her. "She had a call from her friend Billie, who works as a temporary assistant in the Clerk of Court's office. I guess that was what it was about, although she said she was going to ask about a sick friend."

"She can't do that on the phone?" Sari asked, aghast.

"Well, she can't see the rich guy over the phone," Olivia said demurely and with a wicked smile.

"Jessie's a pill," Glory added. "I wonder how she ever got past the boss to hire on here. She's definitely not like any legal receptionist I've ever known."

"She's big-city, not small-town," Sari said. "She's got an accent like that lawyer from Manhattan who was down here last month."

"I noticed," Glory replied. "How are you feeling, Bernie?"

Bernie flushed and grinned. "I'm doing fine."

"Oh?" Sari teased. "We heard about your new boarder at Mrs. Brown's."

Bernie went scarlet.

"That was mean," Glory told Sari.

"Sorry," Sari said, but she was still grinning. "Isn't

Mikey a doll?" she added. "He could pose for commercials."

"I noticed," Bernie said. "He's very good-looking."

"We heard about the fall. You okay?"

Bernie gasped. "Does he tell you guys everything?"

"Well, not everything. Just when he feels guilty about something." She smiled gently. "He felt really bad that he'd misjudged you. But it's not surprising. He's had women jump in front of his car before."

"My goodness!" Bernie exclaimed, fascinated.

"He is very rich," Glory pointed out. "And some women are less than scrupulous."

"Very true," Bernie said. "But I'm not."

"He noticed," Sari replied, tongue in cheek. "He said you remind him of his grandmother."

Bernie's eyes widened to saucers, and she looked absolutely horrified.

"No!" Sari said quickly. "He didn't mean he thought you were old. He said you had the same kind heart and the same sharp tongue she did. He was tickled when you compared him to that guy in the *Police Academy* movie." Her blue eyes sparkled as she looked at Bernie. "Paul said he really was like that guy, too."

Bernie laughed. "He's a lot of fun around the boardinghouse. He makes our two older ladies very flustered. Mrs. Brown, too."

"He's a dish. But he's not really a ladies' man, despite the appearance," Sari added. "In fact, he doesn't like most women. He had a hard experience some years back. I guess it affected him."

"We've all had hard experiences," Glory remarked. She shook her head. "If anybody had ever told me I'd marry Rodrigo...!"

"If anybody had ever told me that I'd finally marry Paul…" Sari countered, and they both laughed.

Both women had had a hard path to the altar, with some painful experiences along the way. Now they were happy. Glory and Rodrigo had a son, but Paul and Sari hadn't started a family. Despite being filthy rich, they were both career oriented. Paul was FBI at the San Antonio office and Sari was an assistant DA here in Jacobs County. Children were definitely in their future, Sari often said, but not just at the moment.

Bernie would have loved a child. It would have been difficult for her with her physical issues, but that wouldn't deter her if she ever found a man who loved her enough to marry her. She thought briefly of Mikey and her heart fluttered, but she knew she wasn't beautiful or cultured enough to appeal to a man so sophisticated. And if he'd reached his present age, which had to be somewhere in his thirties, unmarried, he was unlikely to be thinking of marrying anybody in the future. What a depressing thought, she realized, and how silly of her to be thinking of it in the first place. He was only here temporarily. He belonged up north.

She sat very still, aware of conversation around her and not hearing it. Mikey belonged up north. But he was in Jacobsville for no apparent reason, and he'd taken a room at a boardinghouse, which meant he was staying for a while. Why?

She knew he was worried about the people around him in the boardinghouse. Had he made somebody really mad, and they were after him? Was he in Jacobsville because he was safe here? She'd heard just a snippet of gossip from Mrs. Brown, that Mr. Fiore was being watched by one of Eb Scott's men. Nobody knew why. But Eb's men were mercenaries, experienced in combat. Bernie hoped that Mikey wasn't being hunted.

What an odd word to think of, she mused as she pulled up the computer program she used in her work. Hunted. She'd guessed that Mikey was worried about somebody else. Her heart jumped. Was it a woman, perhaps? No. Sari said he was sour on women. A man? Somebody from his past with a grudge? He knew a lot about organized crime. Maybe it was somebody he'd come across in his job, because Mrs. Brown said he told her he owned a hotel in Las Vegas. He must, she thought, be very rich indeed if he owned property in that expensive place.

She was well into research on a new case precedent for the boss when Jessie breezed back in, wafting her expense perfume everywhere.

Sari glared at her. "Jessie, I've told you that heavy perfume brings on migraines. I'd hate to have to speak to Mr. Kemp about it."

"Oh, I'm sorry!" Jessie said at once, feigning surprise. "I won't wear so much from now on."

"Thanks." Sari gave her a look she didn't see and went back to work.

"Well, was he there, your rich mark?" Olivia drawled.

Jessie glared at her. "I don't have a rich mark."

"Some wealthy gentleman?" Olivia probed further.

Jessie took off her coat and sat down at her desk. "I don't know. He was riding in a black limousine. He's from New Jersey."

Bernie's heart dropped to her feet. She only knew one rich man in Jacobsville who rode around in a black limousine. It had to be Mikey. Jessie was beautiful and sophisticated, probably the sort of woman Mikey would really go for. Jessie was an oddity in Jacobsville, where most women weren't streetwise. The older woman probably charmed him.

While she was thinking, Jessie's cold eyes stabbed into her face. "He said he's living at Mrs. Brown's boardinghouse. That's where you live, isn't it, Bernadette?"

"Yes," Bernie said shortly.

Jessie laughed, her scrutiny almost insulting. "Well, you won't be any sort of competition, will you? I mean, no sane man is going to want to take on a woman who can't stand up without a cane—"

"That's enough," Mr. Kemp said shortly from his open office door, and he looked even more formidable than usual. "You get one more warning, Jessie, then you're on your way back to San Antonio. You do not disparage coworkers. Ever."

Jessie actually flushed. She hadn't realized the boss could hear her. She'd have to be a lot more careful. There weren't any other jobs available in Jacobsville right now, and she couldn't afford to lose this one.

"I'm very sorry, Mr. Kemp," she began.

"Bernie's the one who's owed an apology."

"Yes, sir." Jessie turned to Bernie. "I'm sorry. That was wrong of me."

"Okay," Bernie said, but she didn't really look at the other woman.

Mr. Kemp hesitated for just a minute before he went back into his office.

"Careless, Jessie," Olivia said in a biting undertone. "Better make sure the boss isn't listening when you start making rude comments about one of us."

Jessie looked as if she might explode. The phone rang and saved her from making her situation any worse.

At lunchtime, Olivia and Bernie went to Barbara's Café to eat. Glory and Sari went home, where Glory had a babysitter and she could visit with her son while she ate. Sari had lunch with Mandy Swilling, the Grayling housekeeper. Jessie was stuck in the office until the others returned, thanks to Mr. Kemp who insisted that somebody had to answer the phone while he was out of the office. Jessie was almost smoking when the other women went out the door.

"Jessie's a pain," Olivia said curtly.

Bernie's pale green eyes sparkled as she dug into her chef's salad. "You really made her mad."

"Well, nobody else says anything," the other woman defended herself. Her voice softened. "Least of all you, Bernie. You're the sweetest woman I've ever known, except for my late grandmother. You could find one kind thing to say about the devil," she teased.

Bernie laughed softly. "I guess so."

"At least Sari finally said something about the heavy perfume. I know it gives her fits. She's prone to migraines from just the stress of her job. Jessie doesn't care what she does or says unless the boss loses his temper." She frowned. "What's she doing down here?" she added with a frown. "I mean, she worked in San Antonio, where salaries are a lot higher. She doesn't know anybody in Jacobsville."

"The boss said she wanted a slower pace," Bernie replied.

"Sure. Like she has any stress. Unless answering the

phone gives you ulcers," Olivia said drily. "Or bending over the desk to show as much cleavage as possible when a wealthy client comes in."

"Oh, shame on you!" Bernie said, laughing.

"I know. I'm bad. But Jessie's worse. She met your fellow boardinghouse occupant, too," Olivia added with a pointed glance at Bernie's flushed face. "She'll be after him soon. Nobody here rides around in a limo except Paul's cousin Mikey. Sari used to, but she mostly just drives now that all the threats to her and her sister are gone."

"He's here for a reason, too," Bernie said.

"A guess, or that intuition that makes most people nervous?" Olivia teased.

Bernie laughed. "Maybe a bit of both."

"Or maybe not." Olivia glanced up and then down again. "Any idea about what he might be doing today?"

Bernie's heart jumped and she felt it flutter. Incredible, that she knew absolutely where he was, without even looking. "He's coming in the door."

She hadn't looked up. She did now, and there he was, in a dark suit with a patterned blue tie, looking around until he spotted Bernie. He grinned as he went to the counter and placed his order, paying for it before he joined Olivia and Bernie at their table.

"Room for one more?" he asked with a grin at both women. "I don't really know anybody else in here, and I'm shy."

"Oh, sure you are," Olivia said with a wry smile. She wiped her mouth. "I have to get back before Jessie turns purple and says we're starving her. You stay and finish your salad, Bernie," she added as she stood up. "You have a half hour before you have to come back."

"Jessie. That the underdressed brunette who works in your office?" he asked.

They nodded.

"Don't tell her I'm here, okay?" he asked Olivia. He shook his head. "I know how deer feel in hunting season."

They both laughed.

"I won't. I promise," Olivia said. She winked at Bernie and went to carry her tray back.

Mikey looked at Bernie slowly, taking in the blond braid and the nice gray suit she was wearing with a pink camisole. "You look pretty," he said softly.

She flushed and laughed self-consciously. "Thanks."

"You're a breath of spring compared to the women I know," he added quietly, watching her. "Brassy, over-bearing women don't do a thing for me these days. I guess I'm jaded."

She smiled shyly. "You're very handsome and you're wealthy. I guess women do chase you. Even movie stars and rich women."

He pursed his lips. "They used to. It's the other stuff that puts them off."

Her thin eyebrows lifted. "The other stuff?" she asked.

He shrugged. "My connections."

She still wasn't getting it. While she tried to, Barbara brought his steak and salad and black coffee, and put it down in front of him.

"I hope it's done right," she told Mikey. "My cook tends to get meat a little overdone. One of our customers actually carried his back into the kitchen and proceeded to show him how to cook it properly."

"Jon Blackhawk," Bernie guessed.

"How did you know?" Barbara asked.

"He's the only gourmet chef I know, and he's Paul's boss at the FBI office in San Antonio. They were both down here recently on a case. And nobody eats anywhere else in Jacobsville except here," she teased.

Barbara chuckled. "Exactly. It didn't come to blows, but it was close. My temporary cook's from New Jersey," she added.

Mikey's ears perked up. He glanced at Barbara.

She made a face. "His people are heavily federal, if you get my meaning. His brother works for the US Marshals Service in San Antonio, and he's a former policeman where he came from. He's retired."

"Oh." Mikey relaxed, just a little.

"I was going to add… Goodness, excuse me," she said, suddenly flustered as she went back to the counter.

Bernie's eyes followed her, and she grinned to herself as she watched a husky man in a police uniform smile at Barbara as she went to wait on him.

"Okay, what's that little smirk all about?" Mikey teased.

"That guy at the counter. That's Fred Baldwin. He worked as a policeman here for a while, then at a local ranch. Now he's back on the police force. He's sweet on Barbara and vice versa."

Mikey glanced in that direction and laughed softly. "I can see what you mean."

"Her son's a lieutenant of detectives with San Antonio PD," Bernie added.

He nodded. "I met him, last time I was here. Nice guy."

"Her daughter-in-law's father is the head of the CIA," she added.

"I heard that, too. Her son's dad is a head of state, down in South America."

"He does have some interesting connections," Bernie agreed.

Mikey finished his steak. "What's there to do around here at night?" he asked.

She pursed her lips. "Well, people go to concerts at the local high school on the weekends sometimes. Other people drive in the Line."

"What the hell...heck's the Line?" he amended.

"A bunch of people drive around in a line. Teenagers, married people, even old people sometimes. They have a leader, and they go all around the county, one after the other, sometimes even up to San Antonio and back."

He shook his head. "The things I miss, living in a city." His dark eyes met hers. "How about movies?"

"Jack Morris and his son just opened a drive-in theater outside town," she said. "He even built a snack bar with restrooms. He says he's bringing back the 1950s all by himself. It's pretty successful, too."

"What's playing right now?"

She named the movie, an action one about commandoes.

He smiled. "You like movies like that?" he asked.

"Well, yes," she confessed.

He chuckled. "I thought you had an adventurous nature. Mrs. Brown told me about those books you read in bed. She said you have some on outfits like the British SAS and the French Foreign Legion."

She blushed. "My goodness!"

"So, how about a movie Friday night?" he asked.

"I'll have Santi rent a smaller car, one that won't get so much attention from the populace."

Her heart skipped a beat and ran wild. "You want to take me out, on a date?"

"Of course I do," he said softly.

She thought she might faint. "But I… I have all sorts of health issues…"

"Bernadette, you have a kind heart," he said quietly, his dark eyes soft on her face. "None of the other stuff matters. Least of all an illness you can't help." He grinned. "I won't ask you to go mountain climbing with me. I promise."

She laughed. "That's a deal, then."

He shook his head. "Why would you think you're untouchable?"

"A local boy told me that when I was in high school. He said he didn't want to get mixed up with a handicapped girl."

"Idiot," he muttered.

She smiled at him. "Thanks."

"How long ago?"

She blinked. "How long ago was it?"

He shifted. "Clumsy way to put it. How old are you?" he added. His dark eyes twinkled. "Past the age of consent?" he probed.

She closed up and looked uncomfortable.

He put a big, warm hand over hers on the table. "I don't proposition women I haven't even dated yet," he said softly. "And you aren't the sort of girl who'd ever get such a proposition from me. Honest."

She caught her breath. He was so unexpected. "I'm twenty-four. Almost twenty-five."

He was shocked and looked it. "You don't look your age, kid."

She beamed. "Thanks."

He laughed and curled his fingers around hers, enjoying the sensations that ran through him. Judging by the flush, she was feeling something similar.

"Careful," she said under her breath as more people came in the front door.

"Careful, why? Somebody with a gun looking our way?" he asked, and not entirely facetiously.

"Gossip."

He scowled. "What?"

"Gossip," she repeated. "If people see you standing close together or holding hands, they start talking about you, especially if you're local and unmarried. You'll get talked about."

"Like I care," he teased.

She felt as if she could float. "Really?"

His teeth were perfect and very white. She noticed, because he didn't seem to smile much. "I don't mind gossip. Do you?"

She hesitated. But, really, nobody here was likely to gossip about her to him, at least. Not many people knew about her parents or, especially, her grandparents. "No," she said after a minute. "I don't mind, either."

"Just as well. I have no plans to stop holding hands with you," he said. "It feels nice."

"It feels very nice," she said.

He had Santi drive her back to her office. He even got out, helped her from the car and walked her to the door.

"That woman in the courthouse said she works here. That right?" he asked.

She made a face and nodded.

"Then I won't come in. Phew," he added. "She could start a perfume shop on what she was wearing."

"She could in there, too," she said.

He laughed. "Well, I'll see you back at Mrs. Brown's later. If it starts raining, you call me and I'll come pick you up."

She looked hesitant.

"Oh. Right." He pulled out his wallet, extracted a business card and handed it to her. "Cell phone. At the bottom. You can call me or you can text me. Texting is better. I hate talking on the damned phone."

She laughed. "So do I."

"Okay, then. See you later, kid."

"See you."

He got back in the car. She went into her office and closed the door behind her.

Jessie was watching. Her face was livid. She'd tried to cadge a ride back to the office in that nice limo and been refused. It made her furious that little miss sunshine there had managed it. And she was late back to work, to boot!

Chapter Four

Bernie didn't have to look to feel Jessie's fury, but she sat down at her desk without even glancing toward the front desk. Apparently Jessie wasn't going to push her luck by attacking Bernie, though. She settled down at her desk and busied herself typing up letters for the boss while she answered the phone.

It wasn't hard to avoid her at quitting time. Jessie was always the first one out the door, just in case the phone rang and somebody had to answer it. She was never on time in the mornings, either, something resented by all her coworkers.

"Phew," Bernie said with heartfelt thanks when Jessie was out of sight. "I thought my number was up when we got back from lunch."

"Jessie won't quit," Olivia said quietly. "She's got that nice rich visitor in her sights and she'll do anything to get his attention. You watch out," she added.

Bernie sighed. "I guess she'll really hit the ceiling when she finds out I'm going to a movie with him."

"Movie?" Sari asked, all ears.

"When?" Glory asked.

She laughed. "Friday night. He's taking me to the drive-in."

"Ooh," Sari mused. "Heavy stuff."

Bernie blushed. "He's so good-looking. Honestly, I feel dowdy compared to Jessie."

"He didn't like Jessie, though, did he?" Olivia reminded her. "He told me not to mention he was having lunch with us when I went back to the office. He wasn't impressed by her. In fact," she added with a chuckle, "he said he knew how deer felt during hunting season."

"Wouldn't that get her goat?" Sari teased. "I wasn't kidding about Mikey," she added to Bernie. "He really isn't a ladies' man."

"He could be in movies," Bernie said.

"Yes, he could," Glory agreed. "I wonder." She glanced at Sari. "Didn't anybody ever try to get him to audition for a movie?"

"In fact, Paul says he was pursued by a Hollywood agent who saw him in Newark. He just smiled and walked away. He's shy, although that never comes across. He puts on a good act," Sari added.

"He's good with people," Bernie told them as they went out and locked the door, Mr. Kemp having gone home from a day in court already. "The ladies at the boardinghouse think he's just awesome."

"And what a lucky thing that Mrs. Brown only had one vacancy," Sari said. "Or Jessie would be over there like a flash."

"I still can't figure what she's doing down here,"

Glory said. "She's a bad fit for our office, and she doesn't mix with anybody in town except her friend Billie at the county clerk's office." She frowned. "In fact, Billie hasn't been here long, either, and she's a city girl from back east somewhere. They're both of them out of step with local people."

"Do they room together?" Bernie asked.

"Yes, at some motel out of town. That's got to be expensive, too, since none of our local hotels serve meals."

"Which one do they stay at?" Glory asked.

"The one where all the movie stars live when they're in town filming," Sari told her. "The one with whirlpool baths and feather pillows and mini bars."

"Ouch," Glory laughed. "That's the most expensive place in town. Jessie doesn't make enough here to afford such luxury."

"Well, she and Billie share," Sari said. "I guess they share meal expenses, too. Jessie would never manage it alone."

"Don't mention your upcoming date in the office," Glory cautioned Bernie.

"I might not need to," Bernie said, waving Olivia goodbye as she drove off in her car. "We were sort of holding hands in Barbara's Café," she confessed.

Sari whistled.

Bernie looked at her curiously.

"And Mikey knows about small towns, too," she mused. "Apparently he doesn't mind people knowing that he likes you."

Bernie flushed. "Really? You think he does?"

"Paul does," Sari said. "And he knows Mikey a lot better than the rest of us do."

"Wow," Bernie said softly.

"There's my ride. My boys," Glory gushed, waving to Rodrigo at the wheel of their car and their little boy in the back seat. "See you tomorrow!"

"Have a good night," Bernie called. Glory waved as she got into the car and fastened her seat belt. Rodrigo waved at the women on his way past.

"There's just one thing," Sari said gently, turning to Bernie when they were alone. "Mikey's down here for a reason, and it's a dangerous one. I can't talk about it. But you should know that there's a risk in going around with him."

"I do know," Bernie replied. "I don't care."

"So it's like that already." Sari smiled. "I'd feel the same way if Paul was like Mikey. You know that Mikey's past isn't spotless?" she added a little worriedly.

"You mean, about his hotel business?"

Sari didn't know what to say. She felt uncomfortable telling tales. Well, better to let sleeping dogs lie. "It was a long time ago," she lied, smiling. "He'll tell you himself when he's ready."

"I don't care about his past," Bernie said softly, and she smiled. "I've never been so happy in my whole life."

"Judging by how much he smiles lately, neither has Mikey," Sari laughed. "Paul said he was the most somber man you've ever seen until lately. They grew up together."

Bernie nodded. "Their grandmother raised them. Mikey loved her."

"Yes, he did. Paul and Mikey had a rough childhood. Their grandmother was all they had. Well, and each other, although neither of them would admit it."

"They seem to get along well, from what Mikey says."

"They do now. It wasn't always that way." She glanced toward the curb. Paul was sitting at the wheel of their Jaguar. He waved. "Well, I'll go home. Can we drop you off?" she added.

Bernie laughed. "I'm doing really good today, and Dr. Coltrain says I need the exercise when I can get it. But thanks."

"No problem. Anytime. See you tomorrow."

Bernie waved them off and walked the four blocks to Mrs. Brown's boardinghouse. She felt as if her feet didn't even touch the sidewalk. Life was sweet.

She got through the rest of the week relatively unscathed by Jessie, although she received a lot of irritated looks when a couple of local people coming into the office mentioned that Bernie had been seen holding hands with Mikey at Barbara's Café. But apparently Jessie still thought Bernie was no competition for her. She did mention, loudly, that she was going to spend more time at Barbara's herself.

"And good luck to her," Sari laughed when Jessie left ahead of them all, as usual, at the end of the day. "Mikey's been in San Antonio for the past two days."

Bernie smiled with obvious relief. She hadn't seen him since their lunch at the café. He'd been out of town apparently. She'd wondered if he was leaving town. She'd hoped he'd say goodbye first, but his absence at the boardinghouse had worried her. Mrs. Brown only said that he had business to take care of, but she hadn't said how long it might take him to conduct it. Bernie figured it was something to do with the hotel he owned. It must take a lot of work to coordinate something so big, and he must have a lot of employees who had to be looked after as well.

"You didn't know," Sari guessed when she noted Bernie's expression.

"Well, no. He just told Mrs. Brown that he had business to take care of. We didn't know where he was."

"He and Paul have something going on together," Sari said, without mentioning what, although she knew. It was top-secret stuff, nothing she could tell even her worried coworker about.

"I hoped he wouldn't leave town without saying goodbye," Bernie replied.

"Are you kidding? He's taking you to a movie, remember?" Sari teased. "How could he leave town?"

Bernie laughed. "I guess he wouldn't, at that." She was beaming. "You know, I've only ever been on a few dates in my life." She hesitated and looked at Sari worriedly. "Mikey's sophisticated, you know? And I'm just a small-town girl with old-fashioned ideas about stuff."

"So was Della Carrera before she married Marcus here in town," she reminded the other woman. "Nobody's more sophisticated than Marcus Carrera."

Bernie smiled. "I guess not." She frowned. "Mr. Carrera was big in the mob, wasn't he?" she added absently.

"He was. He went legitimate, though. He was actually working with the FBI to shut down a crooked crime figure who planned to open a casino near Marcus's."

"I heard something about that." Bernie shook her head. "I don't understand how people ever get involved with organized crime. It seems a shameful way to earn a living."

"That it is," Sari said, but became reserved. Bernie didn't know about Mikey and she didn't feel comfortable blowing his cover. "Well, I'm off. See you tomorrow!"

"Have a good night."

"You, too."

Bernie watched them drive away and started back to Mrs. Brown's. She could hardly contain her excitement about the coming date with Mikey.

Mikey, meanwhile, had been in conference with Paul, Jon Blackhawk and a US Marshal in San Antonio, while the three of them hashed out what they knew and what they didn't know about Cotillo. Mikey had stayed at a safe house with the marshal while they discussed the case and what they were going to do about the threat.

"I don't want the women in my boardinghouse hurt," Mikey said during one long session. "Just being around me could put them in danger."

"They won't be," Paul replied. "You've got more protection than you realize."

"Yeah, well, Merrie Colter had plenty of protection, too, and she ended up in the hospital when that contract man was after her," Mikey pointed out.

"No plan is foolproof," Jon Blackhawk, assistant SAC at the San Antonio FBI office agreed. "But we've got most of our bases covered. And, frankly, no place is going to be perfectly safe. If you leave your boardinghouse, the women who live there could still be in danger if the contract man decides they might know where you were."

Mikey felt sick to his stomach, although nothing showed in that poker face. "I suppose that's true," he said heavily.

"I've never lost a person I was protecting yet," US Marshal McLeod interjected. He was tall and husky like

Mikey, but he had pale gray eyes in a face like stone and a .357 Magnum in a leather holster at his waist.

"You and that damned cannon," Paul muttered. "Why don't you move into the twenty-first century, McLeod, and sport a piece that didn't come out of the eighties?"

"It's a fine gun," McLeod said quietly. "It belonged to my father. He was killed in the line of duty, working for our local sheriff's office back home."

"Sorry," Paul said sheepishly.

McLeod shrugged. "No problem."

"I hope you got earplugs when you have to shoot that thing," Mikey mused.

"I got some, but if I take time to put them in, I'll be wearing them on the other side of the dirt."

Mikey chuckled. "Good point."

"Where's your piece?" Paul asked suspiciously.

"My piece?" Mikey opened his suit coat. "I don't carry a gun, Paulie. You know that."

"I know that you'd better get a Texas permit for that big .45 you keep in your car, before Cash Grier knows you don't have one," Paul said with a smirk.

Mikey sighed. "I was just thinking about that the other day. So. Where's Cotillo?"

There was a round of sighs. "Well, he was in Newark," McLeod said. "I checked with our office there, but he's out of sight now. Nobody knows where he went. We have people checking," he added. "One of our guys has a Confidential Informant who's close to him. We'll find him."

"It's his contract killer we need to find," Paul interrupted. "If he offs Mikey, we have no case, and Tony Garza will go down like a sack of beans for murder one."

"Speaking just for myself, I'd prefer to live a few more years," Mikey mused.

"Especially since you have a hot date tomorrow night, I hear?" Paul said with an unholy grin.

Mikey embarrassed himself by flushing. The tint was noticeable even with his olive complexion.

"Hot date?" Jon asked.

Mikey cleared his throat. "She's a nice girl. Works as a paralegal for the district attorney's office in Jacobsville."

"Bernie," Paul said.

There were curious looks.

"Bernadette," Mikey muttered. "It's short for Bernadette."

"Pretty name," Jon said.

"She's a sweetheart," Paul told them. "Takes a real load off the district attorney, and the other women who work in the office love her, especially my wife." He glanced at Mikey. "Which begs the question, why don't you ever bring her over to the house to eat? You know Mandy wouldn't mind cooking extra."

Mikey shifted his feet. "It's early days yet. I just asked her to a movie."

"A drive-in, at that," Paul mentioned with a grin.

"You've got a drive-in theater in Jacobsville?" Jon exclaimed. "They went out in the fifties, didn't they?"

"In the sixties, mostly, but we've got a local guy who's trying to bring them back. He even built a small café on the premises with restrooms and pizza. So far, he's a raging success."

"My dad talked about going to drive-ins," McLeod mused. "He said it was the only place he could kiss my mother without half-a-dozen people watching. Big family," he added.

"I can't place that accent, McLeod," Paul said. "You sound Southern, but it's not really a Texas accent."

"North Carolina," McLeod said. "My people go back five generations there in the mountains. The first were Highlanders from Argyll in Scotland."

"Mine came from Greece and Italy," Paul said. "Well, mine and Mikey's," he added with a glance at his cousin.

"Mine met the boat yours came over on," Jon said with a straight face. He was part Lakota Sioux.

There was a round of laughter.

"I have some Cherokee blood in my family," McLeod volunteered. "My great-grandmother was Bird Clan. But we're mostly Scots."

"Can you play the pipes?" Jon asked curiously.

McLeod shrugged. "Enough to make the neighbors uncomfortable, anyway."

"I had a set of trap drums," Paul recalled wistfully. "We had some really loud, obnoxious neighbors upstairs when I lived in Newark, long before I moved here." He didn't add that at the time he'd had a wife and child who were killed by operatives of a man he put in prison. "I was terrible at playing, but it sure shut the upstairs neighbor up."

"You bad boy," Mikey teased.

"A man has to have a few weapons," he said drolly.

"Back to Cotillo," McLeod said. "We have someone watching you from our service down in Jacobsville. You don't need to know who, but we're on the job. I offered, but they shut me up immediately."

"They did? Why?" Mikey asked.

"They say my restaurant allowance is abused."

They all looked at him. He was substantial, but streamlined just the same.

A corner of his mouth pulled down. "They say I eat too much. Hey, I'm a big guy. It takes a lot of food. Besides, I hear some of the best food in Texas is at that café in Jacobsville."

"It is," Paul agreed. "Everybody eats there."

"So would I, if they'd let me. The boss said we needed somebody who liked salads and tofu."

Now they all really stared at him.

He glowered back. "She's a vegan," he said with spirit. "She gets upset if anybody mentions a steak."

"Tyranny," Paul teased.

"Anarchy," Mikey seconded.

"She should move back east, where she'll have plenty of company," Jon agreed. "I'm not giving up steaks, and I don't care if the SAC is a vegan or not."

"That's what I told her," McLeod replied. His black eyes sparkled. "Shut her up for ten minutes at least. But that's when she assigned me to him," he indicated Mikey. "She thinks it's a mean assignment." He chuckled. "I didn't try to change her mind."

"Good thing," Jon said. "I know your boss. She has a mean streak."

"She mustered out of the Army as a major," McLeod replied. "Honestly, I think she believes she's still in it."

"They make good agency heads," Jon said.

McLeod nodded. "But I'm still not eating tofu."

They all laughed.

"What about Cotillo?" Mikey asked after a minute.

"Why does that name sound so familiar?" Paul wondered. Then his face cleared. "Of course. It's that town across the border, you know, the one where an unnamed person that we all know offed the drug lord El Ladron and his buddies in a convoy." The unnamed person was

Carson Farwalker, now a doctor in Jacobsville, who'd thrown several hand grenades under El Ladron's limo and was never charged.

"There's a cactus called ocotillo," Jon Blackhawk mused, "but that little town over the border was actually settled by an Italian family back in the late 1800s."

"Interesting," Mikey remarked. He sighed. "But the man is more worrisome than the town right now."

Faces became somber.

"When our CI finds out anything, I'll pass it on," McLeod said. "Meanwhile, he's got somebody watching Carrera down in the Bahamas." He indicated Jon.

Jon nodded. "Our field office has him under surveillance. And Carrera has some protection of his own, for himself and Tony Garza. You know, just because Carrera went straight doesn't mean he doesn't still have some pretty formidable ties to his old comrades. We understand he has two of them staying in the house with Della, his wife, and his two little boys."

"Two of the best," Mikey agreed. "I know them from the old days."

"Mikey," Paul said with real affection, "you never left the 'old days.'"

"Well," Mikey said with a sigh, "we are what we are, right, Paulie?"

"Right."

Bernie didn't really know how to dress for a drive-in movie, so she settled for pull-on navy blue slacks topped with a blue-checked button-up shirt and a long blue vest that came midthigh. She thought about putting her hair up in some complicated hairdo, but she left it long and soft around her shoulders. She'd toyed with having it cut. It was hard for a woman with disabilities to keep it clean and brushed, but she couldn't bear the thought of giving up the length. She had all sorts of pretty ribbons and ties to put her hair up with when she went to work. Even jeweled hairpins for special occasions. Not that there had been many of those, ever.

She glanced in the mirror and smiled at the excited, almost pretty girl in the mirror. She was going on a real date, with a man who made movie stars look ugly, and he liked her. She almost glowed.

There was a hard tap on the door. She got her coat and purse and opened the door. Mikey was wearing slacks and a designer shirt under a nice jacket. His shirt was blue, like hers.

He grinned at her. "Well, we seem to match."

"I noticed," she teased.

He gave her a thorough appraisal and felt his heart jump as he locked eyes with her. She was unique in his experience of women, which was extensive. She was so different from the aggressive, sensual women he'd liked in his youth. His tastes had changed over the years. Right now, Bernie was the sweetest thing in his life. He hoped he wasn't putting her in danger by being close to her.

"You ready to go?" he asked. "We must both be insane. A drive-in movie and it's just a week until Halloween! It's cold, even for south Texas!"

"I love drive-ins," she said softly. "And I don't care if it snows."

He chuckled. "Me, neither, kid." He took her hand in his and felt her catch her breath. He felt just the same. "Come on. I've got something a little less noticeable than the limo to go in."

A little less noticeable, she thought with surprise when she saw what he was driving. It was a luxury convertible, very pretty and probably very fast.

"Oh, my," she said.

"It goes like a bomb," he said, as he helped her inside the late-model Mercedes convertible. It was a deep blue color. The interior was leather, with wood trim on the steering wheel and the dash. She sank into luxury as she fastened her seat belt.

"Oh, my," she said again as he touched a control and her seat heated up and began to massage her back. "This is heavenly!" She closed her eyes and smiled. "Just heavenly!"

He chuckled. "I'm glad you like it. I go first-class, kid. Always have, even when I was young and full of pepper." He didn't like remembering exactly how he'd gone first-class. She made him feel guilty about the things he'd done in his pursuit of wealth. She didn't seem to covet wealth at all.

"I've never ridden in a car that had heated seats," she said excitedly. "And even a massage! It's just amazing!"

He smiled. He hadn't considered how uptown the car was to someone who probably rode around mostly in cabs that barely had heaters and air-conditioning. "Don't you drive?" he asked.

She felt the words all the way to her feet and averted her eyes so that he couldn't see the sadness in them. She couldn't have afforded a car. "I used to," she said softly. "Not anymore."

"You should go back to it," he replied as he pulled the car out into the street and accelerated. "I love to drive."

"This car must go very fast."

"It does. I'd demonstrate," he teased, "but you'd have to come bail me out of jail."

She laughed, the old fear and guilt subsiding. "I would, you know," she said softly. "Even if I had to sell everything I own."

He flushed.

"I mean, I'd find someone who could…" she began, all flustered because of what she'd blurted out. She was horribly embarrassed.

His big hand reached out for her small one and tangled with it. "Stop that," he chided gently. "You shouldn't feel guilty for enjoying somebody's company. Especially not mine." His hand contracted around hers. "I'm used to women who want what I've got," he added coldly.

"What you've got?" His fingers tangling gently with hers had her confused and shaky inside.

"Money, kid," he replied. "I've got enough in foreign banks to see me well into old age, even if I spend myself blind."

"Oh." Her hand stiffened in his.

He glanced at her and chuckled. "Now you think I suspect that you're only going out with me because I'm rich. Not you," he added in a deep, husky tone. "You're not the sort of woman who prefers things to people. I knew that right off. Proud as Lucifer, when you fell in front of the car and I made sarcastic remarks about how you'd fallen." He sighed sadly. "Worst mistake of my life, thinking you were like that. Believe me, I felt about two inches high when Santi found that cane you used."

She bit her lower lip. "I'm clumsy, sometimes," she said. "I fall over nothing when I'm having flares. I wish I was healthy," she added miserably.

"My little grandmother would sit and cry sometimes when the pain got really bad," he recalled quietly. "I'd fill a hot water bottle for her and read her stories in Greek to take her mind off it."

"You can speak Greek?" she asked.

"Greek, Italian, a little Spanish," he replied.

"I learned to read Greek characters," she said. "They're the Coptic alphabet, like Russian."

"Nice," he said, glancing at her with a smile. "Yes, they are. Hard for some people to learn, too."

"I love languages. I really only speak English and Spanish."

"Spanish?"

"Well, we deal with a lot of bilingual people, but some of the older people who come from countries south of ours don't understand English as well as their children. I can translate for them."

"Brainy," he teased.

"Not really. I had to study hard to learn the language, just like I had to study hard to learn to be a paralegal. I went to night school at our local community college," she added.

"I imagine that was hard," he said. "Working and going to school at the same time."

"It was," she confessed. "I wanted to learn the job, but I missed class sometimes. There was a nice woman who was studying it at the same time—Olivia, who works in our office—and she took notes so that I could catch up on what I missed. The professor was very understanding."

"You're a sweet kid," Mikey said softly. "I can imagine that most people bend rules for you."

She laughed. "Thanks." She glanced at him as they

drove a little out of town to the wooded area that housed the new drive-in. "Did you go to school? I mean, after high school?"

"I got a couple of years of college when I was in the Army," he said. "Never graduated. I was too flighty to buckle down and do the work."

"What did you study?"

He chuckled. "Criminal justice. It seemed like a good idea at the time. I mean, considering what I did for a living."

She just stared at him, curious.

He felt his cheeks heat. He glanced at her. She didn't understand. "Didn't Sari talk about me at work?" he said.

"Just that you and her husband are first cousins and that you're close," she replied, and her eyes were innocent.

She wasn't putting on an act. She really didn't know what he'd been, what he still was. He hesitated to tell her. He loved the way she looked at him as if he had some quality that she'd never found in anyone else. She looked at him with affection, with respect. He couldn't remember another woman who'd cared about the man instead of the bank account. It made him humble.

He drew in a breath. "Well, Paulie and I are close," he agreed. His hand tightened around hers. "I meant, didn't you know about the trouble Isabel and Merrie had three years ago, when they were being stalked by a cleaner?"

"Oh, that," she said, nodding. "There was a lot of gossip about it," she added. "I don't remember much of what I heard, just that a man who was big in organized crime back east called off the hit man. She painted him."

She laughed. "They said he walked her down the aisle when she married Paul. I didn't know her then, except I knew the family and that they were well-to-do. I never moved in those circles. I'm just ordinary."

"Honey, ordinary is the last thing you are," he said huskily as he pulled onto the dirt road that led to a drive-in with a huge white screen and a graveled lot with speakers on poles every few feet. "And we're here!"

He paid for their tickets and drove them through to a nice parking spot right in front of the screen. He looked at the ticket. "We've got a ten-minute wait," he said.

"What are we going to see?" she asked. "I didn't pay attention to the marquee."

He chuckled as he cut off the engine and turned to her. "You didn't notice?" he teased, black eyes sparkling as they met her pale ones.

"Not really," she confessed. "I was excited just to be going out with you." She flushed. "There are some very pretty single girls around Jacobsville, including Jessie, who works with us."

His fingers tangled softly with hers, caressing, arousing. "Jessie doesn't do a thing for me," he told her. "She's like the women I used to date back east. Brassy and out for everything they can get from a man."

"I guess so. We're not really like that here," she added. "Money is nice, but I have all I need. I'm not frivolous. My biggest expense is the drugstore. And the doctor," she said sadly.

"It doesn't matter," he said solemnly. "You're not of less value as a woman because you have a disability."

"Most local men thought I was," she replied. "I won't get better unless they come out with a miracle drug," she said. "There are shots I could take, but they're really expensive and there's no guarantee that they'd work. There's also infusion, where they shoot drugs into you with an IV and they last several weeks." She lowered her eyes to the big hand holding hers. It was strong and beautiful, as men's hands went. Long fingered, with perfectly manicured nails.

"I read about those shots," he replied. "Just before my grandmother died, I was researching new drugs that might help her. The pain got so damned bad that they had to give her opiates to cope with it." He made a face. "Then the government steps in and says that everybody's going to get addicted, so now you get an over-the-counter drug for pain even if you've got cancer," he added angrily. "Like that's going to help get illegal narcotics off the street! Hell, you can buy drugs, guns, anything you want in the back alley of any town in America, even small towns."

"You can?" she asked curiously.

"Of course you can. Even in prison."

"Wow."

He chuckled. "Kid, you really aren't worldly."

"I guess not," she said with a good-natured smile. "I don't have much of a social life. Well, I do have Twitter and Facebook, but I don't post very often. Mostly, I read what other people write. My goodness, I must be sheltered, because some of the things people post I wouldn't even tell to my best friend!"

"What sort of things?" he teased.

"I'm not saying," she replied.

He made a face. "That didn't hurt, that didn't hurt, that didn't hurt..." And he laughed, softly and with so much mischief that she burst out laughing, too.

He looked around. "Not so many people just yet.

So." He caught a handful of her long, beautiful platinum hair and tugged her face under his. "Don't panic," he whispered as he bent his head. "This is just a test. I'm practicing mouth-to-mouth resuscitation, in case I ever have to save you…!"

Chapter Five

Bernie held her breath as she watched his firm, chiseled lips hover over hers. She could taste the coffee on his mouth, feel his breath as his face came closer, so that his dark eyes filled the world.

She clutched at his jacket, more overcome with emotion than she could have dreamed even a few weeks ago.

"I love your hair, Bernadette," he whispered as his hand contracted in it and his mouth slowly covered hers for the first time.

She gasped under the soft pressure, but she wasn't trying to get away. He gazed down at her. Her eyes were closed, her eyebrows drawn together. She looked as if she'd die if he didn't kiss her.

Which was exactly how he felt, himself. He settled his mouth over hers, gently because he could sense her attraction and her fear. It was hard to give control to another person. But it was a lesson she would have to learn. He was glad that she was learning it with him.

He guided her arms up around his neck as his lips became slowly more insistent, giving her time to absorb the newness of it, giving her time to let go of her restraint. It melted out of her as he drew her closer across the console, his lips opening now, pressing hers gently apart.

She heard his breath sigh out against her cheek, felt his arms enfolding her, protecting her. She moaned as the feeling became almost overpowering and her arms tightened around his neck.

"That's it, baby," he whispered. "Just like that. Don't hold back. I'll go slow, I promise."

And he did. He didn't force her or do anything to make her uncomfortable. His mouth slid finally against her cheek to rest at her ear. His heart was doing the hula in his chest. He could feel hers doing the same thing.

It was odd, to be chaste with her. Most women in his past would have been tearing his clothes off at this point, but Bernie was gentle and inexperienced. He could feel the need in her because he felt it, as well. It was new to want to protect and cherish someone. He felt as if he could fly.

"You taste like sugar candy," he whispered at her ear.

Her arms tightened and she laughed softly. She didn't know what to say.

His big hand smoothed the length of her hair. "I'm glad you left it down tonight," he murmured. "Just for me?"

"Just for you." Her voice sounded husky. She felt swollen all over. It was a delicious sensation, like going down on a roller coaster.

His face nuzzled hers. "I never expected something like this," he said in a deep, lazy tone. "I was going to stay in this little town for a while and bide my time, maybe find a poker game to get into or something. And here's this beautiful little violet, right in my boarding-house."

"Me?" she stammered.

His hand slid under her hair. "You, Bernadette." His cheek slid against hers and his mouth covered hers again, but harder this time, hungrier.

She couldn't resist him. She didn't have the sophistication to even pretend that she didn't like what he was doing. Her fingers tangled in his thick, cool, wavy hair. She loved what he was doing to her. She couldn't hide it.

And he loved that about her. He loved that she felt the same attraction he did, and that she was innocent, untouched, vulnerable. She needed someone to take care of her. He needed someone to take care of. Since his grandmother's death, there had been nobody in his life to fill that need. Bernie's disability didn't put him off in the slightest. It made him feel protective.

Which made him slow down. He was taking things too far, too fast. He drew back very slowly, his dark eyes intent on her face, her eyes half-closed, her pretty mouth swollen, her body warm and soft in his arms. She radiated tenderness.

"It's been a long time since I felt like this," he whispered at her lips, brushing them with his own. "And even then, it wasn't so sweet."

She smiled against his mouth. "I've never felt anything like this," she confessed softly. "Not with anybody." She grimaced. "Not that there's ever been anybody, except a boy who kissed me at a party when

I was sixteen." She sighed. "That was just before he said he liked me a lot but he didn't want to get involved with a crippled girl."

"You aren't crippled," he said shortly. "You have as brave a spirit as anybody I ever knew. You're strong and capable. You're a woman with a disability, not a disability that's female. If that makes sense."

"You mean, I have a disability but it doesn't define who I am," she translated.

He smiled. "Yeah. It's like that." He searched her pale green eyes. "I don't mind it. I told you about my grandmother, that she had it, too. Somebody who minds it isn't interested in you the right way. He's looking for somebody more…casual."

She knew what he meant. Her fingers went up to his face and traced it while she studied him with fascination. "I never knew anybody like you," she whispered.

"I never knew anybody like you," he replied, and he was serious. "I can't imagine how I missed seeing you when I was here before, three years ago."

"I heard about you back then. I was working for a firm of attorneys. But people just said you were helping your brother-in-law with some case," she added.

That might be a good thing. He wasn't sure how she'd feel if she knew the truth about him, about exactly why and how he'd helped the Grayling girls.

"You don't know much about me," he said after a minute.

"That's okay. You don't know much about me, either," she replied.

He grinned. "Don't tell me. You're a spy and you have a trench coat in your closet back in the boardinghouse."

"Don't you dare tell a soul," she chided. "They'd send people to sack me up and take me away."

"I'd never do that," he said softly, and he smiled. "Not in a million years."

In the back of his mind, he was hearing a song recorded by Meatloaf about doing anything for love. He sang softly, a little off-key.

She caught her breath. "It's one of my favorite songs," she confessed. "Did you see the video?"

"I did. I watch it on YouTube sometimes." He laughed. "It's one of my favorites, too. What other sort of music do you like?"

Just as she started to answer, there was a gentle rap on the window.

Startled, Mikey let go of Bernie and put her gently back into her own seat before he powered down the window.

Cash Grier was standing there with a very knowing smile on his face, in his uniform.

"I have not been speeding in your town, and I never even jaywalked," Mikey began. "Besides that, we are outside the city limits."

Cash chuckled. "That's not why I'm here."

Mikey just waited.

Cash grimaced. "We've had a development," he said. "Nothing major. But Paul wants to talk to you, at the house."

"We just got here," Mikey said, visibly disturbed. "Can't it wait?"

"Sorry. No, it can't. Paul said to bring Bernie with you," he added with a smile in her direction.

"Oh." Mikey brightened. He turned to her. "Okay with you?"

She grinned. "Okay with me."

"We'll catch the movie another time," Mikey promised. He turned back to Cash. "You headed that way, too?"

Cash nodded. "You'll have two other cars following behind you, as well."

"Following us?" Bernie asked, concerned.

Cash and Mikey exchanged a long look. Mikey shook his head, just a jerk, but Cash understood at once that he wasn't to tell Bernie anything. "It's something to do with a case Paul's working on," Cash told Bernie with an easy smile. "No worries."

"Okay," she said, and smiled shyly.

"We'll be right along." Mikey took the speaker off the window and put it on its stand, powering the window up afterward. "Sorry about this," he told Bernie.

"You're related to an FBI agent," she said. "And I don't mind. Really."

He caught her hand in his as he turned onto the road. "You're easy to be with," he said softly. "You don't complain, you don't fuss. Even when you probably should."

She laughed. "I love being with you. Anywhere at all."

"That's how I feel." He curled her fingers into his and drove the rest of the way to Paul's house in silence. He was worried, and couldn't let it show. It must be something big if Paulie wanted to interrupt a date. His cousin wasn't the sort to interfere unless it was warranted. Which led Mikey to worry about exactly what the new development was.

His first thought was that they'd found Tony in some sort of horrible condition. They knew that Cotillo had a contract out on him, and that he could probably figure out that Tony was in the Bahamas since he and Marcus Carrera were close. He hoped Tony was still alive, even though it put Mikey in more danger.

He glanced at Bernadette and felt his heart clench. He was already attached to her. He couldn't bear the thought of letting her get hurt because of him. And she still didn't know anything about him, really, or the danger he was in. He was putting her in danger. If someone came looking for him, they'd go after the weakest link. An hour in any restaurant or bar around, and they'd know that Mikey was dating this cute little paralegal who worked for the DA. Bernadette could be used against him. In fact, so could Mrs. Brown and her other residents. Mikey had a weakness for motherly women, and people knew about it.

"You're worried," she said softly from beside him.

His head turned. His shocked expression said it all.

"You hide things very well," she continued. "You really do have a poker face. But it's inside you. I can feel it."

He let out a long breath and his fingers contracted. "You see deep, just like Paulie's sister-in-law."

"Merrie was always like that, even in school."

"You've lived here a long time, haven't you?"

"Well, off and on, yes. I was born here, but when I was little, my parents moved to Floresville. My dad worked on a cattle ranch there as a foreman." Her face closed up. "Dad and I moved back here when I was about ten years old."

He was reading between the lines. Something had happened in Floresville that still caused her pain after all that time. He wondered what it was. But he wasn't going to ask. Not yet. They had time.

"I lived all my life in Newark," he said.

"Yes, you told me. You said you own a hotel in Las Vegas," she added, fascinated. "It must be a lot of responsibility, taking care of something so big," she added.

He chuckled. "You have no idea. I didn't know what I was getting into. I had some spare cash and I thought it would be fun to own something big and elegant. It's not what it's cracked up to be. The labor problems alone are enough to send me to the nearest bar."

"I guess a lot of people work for you."

They did, but not in the hotel business. He employed a number of men who worked just a little outside the law on various projects for him. He wasn't about to go into that with her. He thought about the life he'd lived, the things he'd done to get rich. It had seemed so important at the time, as if nothing was more important than having things, having expensive things, having money. He'd come out of the armed forces with a lot of contacts and even more ideas, and he'd put them into practice in the years since then. Now, when he thought of Bernadette and what a straight arrow she was, he felt uncomfortable. What would she think of him when she knew what he was, what he'd been, what he'd done? Already, the thought of losing her trust was painful.

"You have to stop worrying about things you can't change," she said, reminding him of a conversation they'd had some time ago about that.

He chuckled. "That's the thing, kid. There's a lot of stuff I *can* change. I just don't know how to go about it without getting thrown in the slammer."

She laughed because she thought it was a joke.

He smiled. It wasn't a joke at all. He had men who

could take on a contract killer with great success, but it would put him in bad stead with the FBI and the US Marshals Service, which was helping protect him. His hands were tied. He couldn't put Paulie on the firing line by acting on his own. Besides, if he helped put Cotillo away, it put him in a great bargaining position with Uncle Sam. He might need a favor one day. It was to his advantage not to use his usual methods of dealing with threats.

"If you get arrested, I can bake a nail file in a cake and come to see you," she said with a wicked little grin.

He sighed. "Honey, they don't have iron bars on the outside of cells anymore. They're all inside and all the doors lock along the way. You'd never get out that way."

She frowned. She'd never been in a real jail, but he seemed to know a lot about them. She reasoned that he'd probably been with his cousin to see somebody in jail on a case or something. It didn't worry her.

He glanced at her and smiled. She really didn't see the bad part of him. It was amazing—that she had such insight but didn't see wickedness in his actions. Probably she didn't look for it. Apparently, her own life had been a sheltered one.

The big house at Graylings was ablaze with lights when Mikey pulled up into the driveway. There were two black sedans and a black SUV. The sedans had government license plates.

"Feds," Mikey said with a sigh as he helped Bernie out of the car.

She glanced at the backs of the cars parked side by side. She smiled. "Government plates. I guess they think people won't know as long as they don't have flashing lights on top," she teased.

He chuckled. "Good one." He caught her hand in his as they walked up to the front door. He drew in a breath. "Listen, kid," he said as they reached it, "there are things going on that I can't tell you about."

"I don't mind," she said, and looked up at him with perfect trust. In fact, she was in so far over her head that she wouldn't have minded if he robbed banks for a living.

He smiled slowly. "You're almost too good to be true," he chuckled. "Don't you have any wicked, terrible things in your past?"

The door opened, but not before he saw the expression that washed across her face, quickly hidden when Sari Fiore opened the door and grinned at them, holding hands.

"Sorry to have to break up your date," she told Bernie, "but we didn't have a choice. You can keep me company while the men talk. Mandy's gone to bed with a headache, so I'm alone. Well, almost alone," she amended when three men walked into the hall.

"Hey, Mikey," Paul Fiore greeted his cousin.

"Hey, Paulie."

"You know McLeod already," he said to Mikey, indicating a big, dark man, "and this is Senior FBI Agent Jarrod Murdock from our San Antonio office."

"I heard about you," Mikey mused as he looked at tall, blond Murdock, an imposing man who never seemed to smile. "Didn't they threaten to dress up like a ninja and throw you in the back of a pickup if you made coffee again…?" he teased.

Murdock made a face. "Not my fault I can't make

good coffee," he scoffed. "I wasn't raised to be a woman."

The two women present gave him a wide-eyed, shocked look.

He cleared his throat. "Well, men aren't built right to make coffee," he amended. "Our hands are too big." He added that last bit tongue in cheek. And he wasn't smiling, but his pale blue eyes were twinkling just the same.

"That's the only comment that saved you from a picket line outside your office," Sari said in a mock threatening tone.

"God forbid!" Murdock said. "They'd fire me for sure."

"Not really," Paul commented. "You're too good a shot. You and Rick Marquez's wife hold the record for the most perfect scores in the city in a single year."

"She missed one shot last month," Murdock replied. He grinned. "Morning sickness. So I hold the record right now."

"She's pregnant?" Sari asked. "Oh, that's so nice! I hope it's a boy this time."

"They already have two girls," Bernie told Mikey with a smile.

"I like little girls," Mikey said. "Little boys, too. Kids are sweet."

"Not all of them," Agent McLeod said coldly with glittering silver eyes.

"Oh, that's right," Paul commented. "That family you were looking after had a kid who stayed in juvie hall most of his life. What was that he painted your car with?"

McLeod eyes narrowed. "Skull and crossbones."

"And you couldn't touch him, because he was in protective custody."

"Oh, I wouldn't say that," McLeod replied. "I had a long talk with his probation officer. He's getting visits at school, at home, at his part-time job…"

"You vicious man," Sari chuckled.

"Maybe the skull and crossbones was more accurate than we know," Murdock commented.

"Watch it," McLeod said, "or I'll buy myself a ninja suit and a pickup truck."

They all burst out laughing.

"Well, come on into the study," Paul said to the men. He glanced at Sari.

"Bernie and I will be in the kitchen, discussing world politics," Sari replied.

Bernie looked up at Mikey with soft, pretty green eyes. "See you later."

He smiled slowly. "You will." He brought her fingers to his mouth and brushed them with it before he followed the men into the study.

Bernie had to be prompted to follow Sari into the kitchen. She was spellbound.

"If anybody had told me that Mikey would fall all over himself for a small-town Texas girl, I'd have fainted," Sari teased. "Honestly, you're all he talks about when he and Paul get together!"

Bernie flushed. "He's all I talk about at the boardinghouse. I've never met anybody like him. He's so… sophisticated and charming and sweet."

"Sweet?" Sari's eyes were popping.

Bernie laughed. "Well, he is."

"I suppose people bring out different qualities in

other people," Sari said philosophically as she made coffee. "I owe Mikey a lot. So does my sister. He helped keep us alive."

"I heard that you were threatened, because of your father," Bernie said quietly. "Not the particulars, of course, just that Mikey helped your husband with the investigation."

"Mikey put us in touch with a gentleman who saved Merrie's life," Sari said, without going into any detail. "She was almost killed."

"I did hear about that. Some crazy man ran into her with a pickup truck, and then died in jail."

Sari nodded. She waited until the coffee perked and poured two cups of it. She put them on the table. She knew from the office that Bernie took hers black, just as Sari did.

Sari sat down across from her. "We lived through hard times," she recalled. "Our father was a madman. There were times when I thought he was going to kill us himself."

Bernie stared into her own coffee. "My grandfather had an unpredictable temper," she said. "You never knew which way he was going to jump. One time he'd laugh at something you said, and the next... Well, Mama and I had to be very careful what we said to him. So did my father."

"Your grandparents lived in Floresville, didn't they?" Sari asked gently.

Bernie's face clenched. She met the other woman's concerned blue eyes. "You know, don't you?" she asked.

Sari nodded. "From a former sheriff who moved here and had dealings with our office. But you know I don't gossip."

Bernie smiled. "Yes, I do." She put both hands around the coffee cup, feeling its warmth. "My grandfather wasn't a bad man. He just had an uncontrollable temper. But he could be dangerous. And he was, one time too many." She grimaced. "We lived out of town on a ranch, but gossip travels among country folk. After it happened, Dad lost his job and wasn't given references, so we came back to Jacobsville. I was only ten. Dad and I were targeted once by one of the victim's relatives."

"I've been through the wars myself, you know. But I don't blame people for what their relatives do," she added firmly.

"Neither do I. But there was some gossip even here. Fortunately, there wasn't so much that Dad couldn't find work. He went to Duke Wright and got a job. He never got like Granddaddy. I used to think if only somebody had forced my grandfather to see a doctor and get on medication. If only we'd realized that he had mental health issues," she said huskily.

"*If.* There's a horrible word. *If only.*"

"Yes." Bernie nodded. She looked up. "You won't tell Mikey? I mean, I'll tell him eventually, but it's early days yet and—"

"Mikey has secrets, too," Sari interrupted. "He won't hold anything against you. He's more worried about what you'll think of him. He's...had some problems in his past."

Bernie cocked her head. "Can you tell me about them?"

"I think he should tell you," Sari replied. "I don't like to carry tales. He's not a bad man," she added firmly. "Everybody has shameful secrets. Some get told, some never do, some we carry inside us forever like festering wounds."

Bernie nodded. "That's like mine. Festering wounds. They blamed all of us, you see, not just my dad. They blamed Mama and me, as well."

"Bernie, you were just a kid. How could anyone have blamed you?"

"They said Mama made him mad in the first place," she explained. She closed her eyes. "I was just ten years old, I didn't have anything to do with it. Neither did Dad. But people died, and I live with the guilt."

"You shouldn't have to," Sari said curtly. "There was no possible way you could have stopped it."

"Losing my grandmother and my mother was the worst of it, especially for Dad," Bernie confessed softly.

She put a hand over Bernie's. "You can't live in the past. I'm having a hard time with that myself. My father killed a woman. He more than likely killed my own mother. I have to live with that, and so does Merrie. We have our own guilt, although I don't know what we could have done to stop it. We were terrified of our father, and he was so rich that nobody around here would go against him. He made threats and people did what he wanted them to." She sighed. "It was like a nightmare, especially when he was arrested. He tried to make me marry a foreign prince so that he'd have money for his defense attorney," she recalled bitterly. "He came at me with the belt and I screamed for help. He died with the belt in his hand. I thought I'd killed him."

"You'd never hurt a fly," Bernie returned gently. "Neither would Merrie. Your father was an evil man. That doesn't mean you'd ever be like him. You couldn't be."

Sari smiled. "Thanks. I mean it. Thanks very much."

"I guess we're all products of our childhoods," she commented. She searched Sari's blue eyes in their frame of red-gold hair. "What was Mikey's like, do you know? He said he grew up in Newark, and his grandmother raised him and your husband."

Sari smiled. "She did. She was Greek, very small and very loving, even though she was strict with them."

"What about their parents?"

"The less said the better," Sari said coolly. "I'm frankly amazed that they both turned out as well as they did."

Bernie sighed. "I know how that feels, except it was my grandfather, not my parents."

Sari nodded. She smiled. "I hope you're prepared for Monday. When Jessie finds out about the hot date, she's going to be a handful. Glory and I will run interference for you. And it isn't as if Mikey even likes her."

Bernie sighed. "That's a good thing. She's really beautiful."

"She is. But as our police chief likes to say, so are some snakes."

They both laughed.

In the office, things were less amusing. One of Cotillo's henchmen had actually managed to get inside Marcus Carrera's Bow Tie Casino in the Bahamas while Tony Garza was in his private study there. Only quick thinking by Carrera's bodyguard, Mr. Smith, who sensed something out of the ordinary, had saved the day. The henchman was arrested and held for trial.

"They found the henchman dead in his cell the next day, of course," Paul told his cousin.

"Of course." Mikey stuck his hands in his pockets.

"It's a good bet that Cotillo knows where I am, as well. I've got no place else to go in the world where I'd have protection like this," he added.

"True enough," McLeod said. His gray eyes narrowed. "Once you testify, we have plans for you."

"They'd better be plans for two people, because I'm not leaving here without Bernadette."

The words came as a pleasant shock to his cousin, who'd only known Mikey to get serious about a woman once in his life, and that had ended badly.

McLeod chuckled. "We can arrange that."

"Okay, then."

"But we're going to have to up the protection," Paul said. "Eb Scott wanted to lend us the Avengers," he added, referring to Rogers and Barton, two of Scott's top men, "but they're on a top-secret mission overseas. He sent us Chet Billings instead. And we've got Agent Murdock here assigned to you as well."

"So long as he doesn't try to make coffee for me, we're square," Mikey said with a glance at the tall FBI agent.

Murdock just laughed.

"What about Carrera?" Mikey asked. "Is his family going to be under threat, as well?"

"He hired on some old friends," Paul said. "Several old friends, from back home."

Mikey knew what he meant, without explanation. "If I were Cotillo, I'd fold my tent and go back to Jersey."

"Not a chance," Paul said quietly. "He thinks he has what it takes to put Tony Garza down and take over his whole operation."

"Sounds to me like a man with a huge narcissistic complex," Murdock murmured.

"Or a man on a raging drug high," McLeod inserted.

"Maybe both," Paul replied. "People are getting involved in this who don't even have ties to Tony's business. They just don't like the idea of an untried, arrogant newcomer trucking into their territory and trying to set everybody aside who's been in the business for generations."

"I know several low-level bosses who hate Cotillo's guts and would love to move on him, There's even a rumor that one of the bigger New York families wants him out," Mikey said. "But Tony's the only one with the power to put him away. If Cotillo hadn't tried to frame him on that murder one charge, Cotillo would be running south as fast as his fat little legs would carry him."

"We've got the video you made," Paul told Mikey. "It's even got the time stamp."

"Sure," Mikey replied with a wry smile. "But the defense could swear that it was photoshopped, that I lied to save my friend."

"Not if you testify," McLeod replied. "You're the best insurance we've got that Cotillo can't bring his murderous operation into Jersey. Listen, nobody thinks you and Tony sing with the angels, okay?" he added. "But there are levels of criminals. Cotillo is a cutthroat with no conscience, who's only in it for the money. He'll kill anybody who gets in his way. Tony has more class than that. And you," he said to Mikey, "never hurt a person unless they hurt somebody you cared about."

Mikey flushed. "Cut it out," he muttered. "You'll ruin my image."

Paul chuckled. "He's right, though," he told his cousin. "Merrie said that after she'd painted you."

"Hell of a painting," Mikey replied. "And she didn't even know me."

"What painting?" McLeod asked.

"Wait a sec." Paul pulled out his cell phone and turned to the photo app. He thumbed through it and showed it to McLeod. It was the painting Merrie had done of Mikey, which Paul had photographed before he sent it to his cousin.

"Damn," McLeod said, looking from the portrait to Mikey. "And she didn't know what you did for a living?"

Mikey shook his head. "She painted that from some snapshots Paul had. Well, from a couple of digital images, from his cell phone, like that one. I was amazed. She did Tony, too. Some artist!"

"Some artist, indeed." McLeod agreed.

"Back to the problem at hand," Paul said when he put down the phone. "We need to double security. And you need to find another way to hang out with Bernie. A safer way than a drive-in theater in the country."

Mikey muttered under his breath. "What, like having tea in her bedroom in the boardinghouse? That'll help her rep."

"You can bring her here," Paul said. "We have the best security in town."

"You mean it?" Mikey asked.

"You bet," Paul told him. "You can watch movies together in the sunroom." He pursed his lips. "Where Cash Grier isn't likely to tap on the window."

"Which brings to mind a question," Mikey said. "Why was Grier looking for me at a movie theater out of town? Not his jurisdiction, is it?"

Chapter Six

"Cash was home and Sheriff Carson wasn't answering his phone," Paul said, "to make a long story short. Our police chief volunteered. His kids were protesting bedtime, so he pretty much walked off and left Tippy and Rory with it," he added, naming Cash's wife and young brother-in-law.

"In which case, he might want to spend the night at a friend's house," Mikey chuckled, "if what I've heard about his missus is true. Did she really use an iron skillet on that guy who came in her back door with a .45?"

"Absolutely she did," Paul confirmed. "She's still a celebrity for that, not to mention being a former model and movie star."

"And gorgeous," Agent Murdock said with a sigh. "Even two kids haven't changed that."

Paul chuckled. "Tell me about it. Not that I did bad

myself in the wife department. My Sari would give all the movie stars a run for their money."

"She's a doll," Mikey agreed. He sighed. "Well, what are you guys doing about Cotillo while he's plotting to have me and Tony killed?"

"We think he has somebody locally," Paul said, suddenly somber. "We don't know who. There are several people who just started working in Jacobsville recently, some of them with pronounced northern accents, like mine and yours."

Mikey grimaced. "I think I met one of them. She works with Isabel in the DA's office. A woman named Jessie." He shook his head. "Apparently she likes rich men and she's predatory. She actually got my cell phone number and called to ask me out."

"I'll bet that went over well," Paul replied tongue in cheek, because he knew his cousin inside out. Mikey didn't like aggressive women.

"It didn't go over at all," Mikey replied. "I told her the number was private and I wasn't interested. Then I hung up and blocked her number."

"I never attract women who want to date me." Murdock sighed. "I guess you have to be handsome."

"There's nothing wrong with you, Murdock, except the way you make coffee," Paul said. "And I did save you from that visiting attorney who mentioned how the ficus plant needed fertilizer."

"Yes, he was looking right at me when he said it," Murdock said and sighed. "Not my fault. Nobody else in the office will even try it."

"I would, but I'm never at my desk long enough."

"I live on the damned telephone," Murdock said heavily. "I get picked every time the boss needs information that he has to get from people out of town. I spend most of the day tracking down contacts."

"You should apply for the SWAT team," Paul suggested. "You'd do well."

"I'd get somebody killed is what I'd do," Murdock returned. "I don't think fast enough for a job like that. I guess, all in all, information gathering is important work and I'm pretty good at finding people."

"He used to be a skip tracer for a detective in Houston," Paul told Mikey. "He was good."

"I still am," Murdock said with a grin. "I tracked down an escaped murderer just a few days ago by calling his mother and telling her I was an old Army buddy. She told me exactly where he was. Sweet lady. I felt really guilty."

"People break the law, they do time," Paul said. "That's the rules."

"Rules are for lesser mortals," Mikey said with a hollow laugh. "I never followed any in my life."

"Until now," Paul said, with twinkling black eyes. "Rules are what's keeping you alive."

"Well, that and Bernie, I guess," Mikey said, and a faint ruddy color ran along his high cheekbones. "We went to the drive-in earlier. We were having a great time until Grier tapped on the window."

"What movie did you see?" Agent Murdock asked.

Mikey cleared his throat. "It was some sort of action movie, I think. The title escapes me."

"I'll bet it does," Paul said under his breath. "Isabel told me that Bernie poured coffee over ice when she went to get a cup, and then she toppled a bookcase, all in the same day. And she's not clumsy."

Mikey's eyes twinkled. "Well, well."

"She's a sweet woman," Paul said. "Sari's protective of her. That woman, Jessie, who works in the office, gives her a hard time."

"DA needs to take care of business and fire her," Mikey muttered.

"He's given her fair warning that she'll lose her job if she causes any more trouble," Paul replied. He put his hands in his pockets. "Back to the matter at hand, though. I phoned Marcus Carrera and asked him how things were going. He says Tony's getting restless. He doesn't like hiding from some cheap hood who wants to take over his territory. He's fuming that he didn't anticipate trouble from that quarter when the guy first moved in with his goons."

"If he comes back, he could die over here," Mikey said. "He knows that Cotillo will have people watching and waiting."

Paul nodded. "That's what I told Carrera. He said he'll talk some sense into Tony and make sure he stays put, no matter what it takes. He's got some old friends from his gangster days helping out. And he hired a group of mercs, one of whom used to live here—that Drake guy whose sister married the veterinarian, Bentley Rydel. Kell Drake, that was his name."

"That's some formidable backup," Mikey conceded. "I hope he won't have to stay there too long. But what about Cotillo?"

"We've got plans for him," Paul said. "I have friends in Jersey, too. They're doing some scouting for me. The agency turned one of our best field agents onto the case, and he's digging into Cotillo's background. With any luck, he'll find something we can use for leverage while we wait for Tony's trial to come up."

"Tony fled the country," Mikey said sadly. "That's going to go against him. Flight from prosecution."

"He didn't fly, he was flown—by us," Paul said with a grin. "So that's not a charge he'll be facing."

Mikey sighed. "His past isn't lily-white. Neither is mine. So far, Cotillo hasn't ever been charged with a crime, for all we know."

"That's right," Paul returned. "For all we know. That's why we're digging. There's a federal prosecutor also on the case, and using his own investigators to look at Cotillo and his associates. Eventually, somebody's going to talk."

"So long as they don't talk about me and Tony and what's in our pasts," Mikey said with a resigned breath. "I've been a bad man, Paulie. I hope it doesn't come back to bite me."

"Not that bad, and you don't have a single conviction," Paul told him.

"No," Mikey conceded with a sad smile. "But that doesn't mean I haven't deserved one."

Paul put a lean hand on Mikey's broad shoulder. "We go one day at a time and leave tomorrow to itself. Right?"

Mikey smiled. "Okay. Right. Well," he added, "I'd better take Bernie home. So much for the movies."

"We have movies on DVD and pay-per-view," Paul reminded him with a grin. "You can watch them together right here, where it's safe. And the door has a lock," he added with amused eyes when Mikey blushed.

Mikey told Bernie about it when he took her back to the boardinghouse, reluctantly. "I'm sorry we had to break it up tonight," he said gently. "But Paulie says we can watch pay-per-view at his place, whenever we want."

"I'd like that," she whispered as he drew her close.

"Me, too, baby." He kissed her hungrily and then put her gently away. "I'm going back over to the house for a while. But we'll make a new movie date later, okay?"

She beamed. "Okay!"

Later, over supper at the house, Mikey drank a second cup of black coffee. He was unusually quiet.

"What's biting you?" Paul asked.

He shrugged. "I was thinking about Cotillo and his stooges. You know, I never stopped having Santi drive me in the limo. I've been pretty visible here..."

"Disguises don't work with people like Cotillo," Paul replied. "Besides, this is one of the safest places in the world when somebody's hunting you. It saved Sari and Merrie."

"It did," Sari added to the conversation. "It will save you, too, and Tony, I hope. Merrie's very fond of him, you know."

Mikey smiled. "Baby Doll's fond of everybody. It's just the way she is."

"That's true."

"Why are you so morose?" Paul asked his cousin.

"I worry about taking Bernie out now that I know I'm being watched by Cotillo's hoods," he said, pushing his coffee cup around.

"We told you that you could bring her over here any time you like," Sari reminded him with a smile. "She's so sweet. I love working with her."

Mikey seemed to perk up a little. "You really meant that? You wouldn't mind?"

"Not at all," Sari replied. "There are plenty of places to walk within sight of the house. We have calves she can pet and cats in the barn, and there's also the sunroom." She cleared her throat and didn't dare look at Paul, because some momentous things had happened there before the two of them married.

Mikey chuckled. "Okay, then," he said. "Thanks."

"No problem," Paul told him, his dark eyes twinkling. "So. How about Saturday?"

"Saturday sounds fine," Mikey replied. "You guys are terrific."

"Thanks," Sari said.

"You're terrific, too, Mandy," Mikey added when the housekeeper came from the kitchen with a cake pan.

Mandy grinned. "Nice of you to say that, and I baked you a chocolate cake, too!"

Mikey hesitated, looked guilty. His face drew up. He didn't want to tell her.

"Mandy, he won't say, but he gets terrible migraine headaches," Paul told her gently. "Chocolate is one of his triggers."

"Oh, my goodness, I'm so sorry!" Mandy began.

"You're a sweetheart, and it's the thought that counts," Mikey told her with a smile. "I love chocolate. I just can't eat it."

"Well, I'll make you a nice vanilla pound cake tomorrow. How's that?" she teased.

"That, I'll eat, and thank you."

"It's no trouble at all. You helped keep my girls safe. I'll never forget you for it, not as long as I live."

Mikey flushed a little. "They're sweet girls, both of them." He glanced at Sari. "Sweet women," he amended.

Sari waved away the apology. "I don't get offended

at every single word people come up with. Besides," she added with twinkling blue eyes, "I got called a whole new word in court by a man I was prosecuting for assault. The judge turned him every which way but loose."

Mikey chuckled. "Good for the judge."

"She's a great judge," Paul agreed. "I had to get a search warrant from her several years ago. We had a long talk about Sari's mother. The judge was friends with her."

"My mother was sweet, kind of like Bernie," Sari said. "She loved to plant flowers and grow things."

"My grandmother did, too," Paul said.

"Yeah, she always had an herb garden, and she grew tomatoes out in the backyard," Mikey added. "It was hard, losing her. She was the only real family Paulie and I ever had. Our parents weren't around much."

"Which was just as well," Paul said grimly.

Mikey nodded.

"Well, I've got some research to do," Sari said, rising. She bent to kiss Paul. "Don't eat my part of that cake," she warned. "I'll be back for it later."

"Would I do that?" Paul said with mock defensiveness.

"Of course you would," she replied. She chuckled as she left the room.

"Damn, you got lucky," Mikey said after she'd gone.

"I did. Maybe you got lucky, too," Paul said. "Everybody who knows Bernie loves her." He grimaced. "Shame what happened to her," he added.

"Yeah, the arthritis is pretty bad," Mikey agreed.

Paul frowned and had started to speak when his phone went off. He looked at the number and groaned, but he answered it. "Fiore," he said.

He listened, glanced at Mikey, grimaced again. "I see. Yeah, I'll make sure he knows. We'll double up down here. No worries. I wouldn't want to risk Carrera getting mad at me, either, but these guys aren't playing with a full deck, if you know what I mean. Sure. Okay. Thanks."

"Trouble?" Mikey asked.

Paul nodded. "Somebody made an attempt on Tony, a new one. He's in custody and they're hoping he'll sing like a bird when they extradite him back here."

"A break, maybe."

"Maybe. If they don't suicide him, like they did the other one."

"Yeah." Mikey drew in a breath. "You know, my life was going along so well up until now. I've got the hotel. I've got all the money I'll ever need. I was really thinking about a home and a family. I guess I lost sight of what I've been, what I've done." He looked up at Paul. "Maybe the universe is set up so that you get back what you give out, every time, in double measure. I don't mind for me. I just don't want to put her in the crosshairs. She's the sweetest woman I've ever met."

Paul didn't need prompting to know that his cousin was talking about Bernadette. There was a look on Mikey's face that his cousin hadn't seen in many years. "We've got all our bases covered," he told Mikey. "You have to remember, outsiders stand out here. There's already gossip about that woman Jessie in Isabel's office, and even Barbara's new cook at the café. Outsiders draw attention."

"Did you check out Jessie and the cook?" Mikey asked.

Paul gave him a sardonic glance. "What do you think?"

"Sorry."

"No worries. But we dug pretty deep. I think we'd have found anything obvious, like an arrest record. Well, unless the guy's working for one of the letter agencies," he added, referring to the federal intelligence and justice community.

"True."

"You going to bring Bernie over Saturday?" Paul asked.

Mikey chuckled. "What do you think?" he said, throwing his cousin's own words back at him, and they both laughed.

Bernie couldn't sleep. It had been raining all day and the pain was pretty bad. She had pain relievers, massive doses of ibuprofen for when all else failed, but she didn't like it. The medicine messed her stomach up, even when she took it with food. Besides that, there was a limited amount of time that she could take it. It was so powerful that it could cause major problems with the liver and kidneys if people used it for a long period of time without a break. She was afraid of that.

But this was one time when she had to have some relief. She could barely hold back the tears.

She got out of bed painfully and pulled on her white chenille robe. She was going to have to go and get a bottle of water out of the fridge. Mrs. Brown, bless her heart, kept it for her tenants, who were always welcome to anything to drink or any bedtime snacks they could find in her spotless kitchen.

Bernie walked very slowly into the kitchen and almost collided with Mikey, in burgundy silk pajama bottoms with a matching robe. His broad, hair-roughened chest was bare, with the robe open. He looked handsome and sensuous. Bernie's heart jumped wildly at just the sight of him.

Mikey smiled. He could see all that in her face. She was totally without artifice, he thought. An honest woman, who never hid what she felt.

"You look pretty with your hair down, honey," he said gently.

She did. Her long platinum hair waved around her shoulders and down almost to her waist in back. With her cheeks faintly flushed and her pale green eyes twinkling despite the pain, she was a dish.

She laughed self-consciously. "I was just thinking how gorgeous *you* look," she confided with a bigger flush.

"What do you need?" he asked. He was holding a paper plate with crackers and sliced cheese on it, along with some slices of fresh pear.

"Just a bottle of water from the fridge and something to eat. I have to take one of the big pills. Pain's pretty bad," she said reluctantly.

"Here. Sit down. I'll get you some cheese and crackers."

"I can do that…"

"Don't fuss, honey," he said gently. He pulled out a chair and waited until she sat down. Then he fetched the water and sliced a little more cheese and put some more crackers on his paper plate. He sat down, too.

"The pears are nice," he said.

"I like fresh fruit," she said shyly.

They munched cheese in a pleasant silence. She

washed it all down with her bottle of water, wincing every time she shifted in the chair.

"I'm sorry you had to have a disease that makes you hurt all the time," he told her quietly.

"Life happens," she said. "I learned to live with it a long time ago."

He frowned. "You aren't that old."

"I'm twenty-four," she reminded him. "But I've had it since I was about nine."

"Nine years old!" he exclaimed.

"Some children are born with it," she replied. "Arthritis isn't just a disease of old people. There's a little boy, five, who goes to the same rheumatologist I do. He's got osteoarthritis and he has to take doses of ibuprofen just like I do."

Mikey winced. "What a hell of a life."

She nodded. "At least I've had it long enough to know how to cope with bad days and flares. It's much harder for a child."

"I can only imagine."

"Why are you up so late?" she wondered.

He moved crackers around on the plate, next to his opened soft drink. "You mentioned that I was worried about putting people in danger by living here," he said, recalling her uncanny perception.

She nodded. "You're in some kind of trouble, aren't you, and your cousin's trying to help."

"That's about the size of it." He leaned back with his soft drink in his hand. He looked gorgeous with his black, wavy hair tousled and his robe open.

He chuckled at her expression. "Your eyes tell me everything you're thinking, Bernie," he said softly. "You can't imagine how flattered I am by it."

"Really?" she asked, surprised.

He stared at her quietly. "I'm a bad man," he said after a minute, and he scowled. "Getting mixed up with me is unwise."

She just looked at him and sighed. "I never had much sense."

It took a minute for that to register. He burst out laughing. "Oh. Is that it?"

She grinned. "That's it."

"Then, what the hell. I've got all sorts of people looking out for me. That means they'll be looking out for you and everybody in the boardinghouse, too."

"Okay," she said, smiling.

He cocked his head. "Do you like chocolate cake?" he asked suddenly.

Her eyebrows arched. "Well, yes. It's my favorite."

"Mandy made me one and I couldn't eat it," he said with a grimace. "I get migraine headaches, real bad ones. Chocolate's a trigger."

"My dad used to get them," she replied. She frowned. "Isn't anything aged a trigger? I mean, like cheese?"

He looked at her and then at the plate of cheese and let out a breath. "Well, damn. I never thought about it. Every time I eat cheese I get a headache, and I never connected it!"

"Dad's neurologist said everybody's got more than one trigger, but sometimes they don't recognize them. He couldn't drink red wine or eat any dark fruit or cheese. And he loved cheese."

"How about chocolate?"

She laughed. "He never liked sweets, so it wasn't a problem."

"Do you get headaches?"

She shook her head. "I had one bad one when I was about thirteen. Never since."

"Lucky you," he told her.

"I guess so."

"Paulie says I can bring you over to the house to visit on Saturday, if you want."

Her heart skipped and ran away. "He did? Really?"

"So did Sari. There are kittens in the barn and horses to pet. I think there's a dog somewhere, too."

"Ooh, temptation," she cooed, and grinned at him.

He laughed. "I thought the kittens might do it."

She cocked her head and her eyes adored him. "The kittens would be a bonus. Spending time with you is the real draw."

He caught his breath. Amazing, the effect she had on him. He felt as if he could walk on air.

"It's like that with me, too, kid," he said softly. "I like being with you."

She felt exhilaration flow through her. "The cane doesn't put you off?"

He shrugged. "I'll get one, too. We'll look like a matched set."

Tears stung her eyes. She'd never dreamed that a man, especially a gorgeous, worldly man like this, would ever find her attractive and not be put off by her condition.

"Aw, now, don't do that," he said softly. He got up, lifted her into his arms and sat back down with her across his lap. "Don't cry. Everything's going to be all right. Honest."

She put her arms around his neck and snuggled close. "You think so?" she asked tearfully.

"Yes, I do." He rubbed her back, feeling protective.

The sound of a door opening broke the spell. But he wouldn't let Bernie up even when Mrs. Brown came into the kitchen.

"Oh, dear," she said, taking in Bernie's tears and Mikey comforting her. "Pain got you up, didn't it?"

"Yes. I came to get a bottle of water so I could take one of those horrible pills, but I have to eat something first. I hope you don't mind…"

"Bosh," Mrs. Brown said. "That's why I keep snacky foods and soft drinks in the fridge."

"The cheese is really good," Mikey said.

"It's hoop cheese," Mrs. Brown told him with a grin. "I get them to order me a wheel of it at the grocery store and I slice it and bag it up. I like it, too. I got peckish so I thought I'd get myself a snack. Is it bad, Bernie?" she added.

Bernie nodded. "I'm sorry if I woke you."

"I don't sleep much," Mrs. Brown said quietly. "You didn't bother me at all."

Bernie got off Mikey's lap reluctantly. "Thanks for the comfort," she said, wiping her eyes. "I don't feel sorry for myself, but the pain is pretty bad."

"Go to bed, honey. Don't forget your water," he told her. "Saturday, if you're better, we'll go see the kittens in Paulie's barn. Okay?"

Bernie's eyes lit up. "Okay."

"Want me to carry you down the hall?" he offered.

"Thanks," she said, a little self-conscious at Mrs. Brown's amused expression. "But I'm good. I hold on to the wall when I get wobbly. Good night," she added to both of them.

"Try to sleep, sweetheart," Mrs. Brown said. "If you need me, you call, okay?"

"I will. Thanks." She glanced at Mikey, flushed, smiled and went out the door.

"She's got grit," Mikey told the landlady.

"Yes, she really has," Mrs. Brown replied. "We all try to look out for her, as much as she'll let us. She's very independent."

"I noticed," he chuckled.

"You're eating cheese," she said worriedly. "Didn't you tell us that you got migraine headaches?"

"Well, yes…"

"Cheese is a trigger," she said. "Like red wine and chocolate."

He made a face. "I can't eat chocolate at all, but I never thought of cheese bringing on a headache." He laughed. "You know, I used to get headaches all the time and never knew why. It was always after I'd been out with a colleague of mine. He loved cheese, so he always had a platter of it with his dinner, wherever we ate. I nibbled on it and then almost died in the night when the pain came."

"Do you get the aura?" Mrs. Brown asked.

He grimaced. "Yeah. Flashy lights or blind in one eye until the pain hits."

"Do you have something to take for it?" she persisted.

"Just over-the-counter stuff."

"You should see a doctor and get something stronger," she told him. "They even have a drug that can prevent them, if you don't have drug allergies."

"They do?" he asked, and was really interested.

"They do." She laughed. "It's why I don't have them much anymore," she confessed. "Cheese is one of my biggest triggers. But I haven't had a migraine since back in the winter," she added.

"Maybe I should do that," he said. "They get worse as I get older."

"You're not old, Mr. Fiore," she teased.

He shrugged. "Thirty-seven," he confessed. "Really too old for Bernie…"

"Nonsense. I was fifteen years younger than my late husband, and we had a wonderful life together."

His eyebrows arched. "Did people talk about you?"

She nodded. She smiled. "We didn't care. It was nobody's business but ours." She sighed. "I'm so glad you and Bernie are friends. She's never had much in the way of companionship. She's so alone."

"Yeah, me, too," he confided. "After my grandmother died, all I had left was Paulie. He's a great guy."

"So I hear."

He got up. "Well, I'll go off to bed and hope the cheese doesn't do me in. But it was worth it," he added with a chuckle as he put his empty plate in the trash can. "Best cheese I've had in a long time."

"I'm glad you like it. And if you get the preventative, you can eat all you like of it," she laughed.

"I guess so. Sleep well."

"You, too."

But he didn't sleep well. He woke two hours later with a headache that almost brought him to tears. He walked into the bathroom, half-blind, and almost collided with Bernie, who was wetting a washcloth in the sink.

"My goodness, what's wrong?" she asked, because he was deathly pale.

"Migraine," he said roughly. "Any Excedrin in there?" he asked, indicating the medicine cabinet. "I can't find mine. I think I put it in here…"

She opened the cabinet and looked. "Yes, there is."

"Shake me out a tablet, will you, honey?"

"Oh, yes." She did and handed it to him. "You need this more than I do," she said, indicating the wet washcloth. "Come on. I'll help you back to bed."

"You should go," he said, swallowing hard.

"Why?"

"I get sick…" Before he could say anything else, he managed to make it to the commode and lost his supper, the cheese, the crackers, the soft drink and just about everything else.

When the nausea passed, he found Bernie on her knees beside him with the wet cloth, wiping his face. She flushed the toilet.

"Better now?" she asked.

He swallowed and drew in a breath. "Yeah. I think so. Honey, you shouldn't…" he began.

"You looked after me when I was having a flare," she reminded him. "Tit for tat."

He managed a smile. "Okay."

"Come on. I'll help you back to bed."

He let her lead him back into his bedroom and help him under the covers. She put the washcloth over his eyes.

"I'll go get you something to take the tablet with. Want water or a soft drink?"

"Ginger ale, if there's any in the fridge," he said weakly, loving the comfort of her touch, the compassion in her voice. All his life, women had wanted him for his wealth, his power. This woman only wanted him. It was a revelation.

"I'll be right back."

"You shouldn't be walking," he said.

"It's just to the kitchen, and I took the big pill. It's helping. I'll be right back."

Mrs. Brown was just getting ready for breakfast in the kitchen. She turned as Bernie came in.

"Do you want some coffee, sweetheart?" the landlady asked.

"I'd love some, but Mikey has a migraine. I found his migraine medicine, but he wants ginger ale to take it with."

"There's one bottle left that's cold," the older woman said. "I'll get some more and put them in there. Is he all right?"

"He lost his supper," Bernie said. "He's really sick. I'm going to sit with him for a few minutes."

"If you need me, just call. We can get one of the Coltrain doctors to come over here and give him a shot if he needs them to. Those headaches are horrible. I used to have them before I got on the preventative."

"He should see a doctor," she said as she got the ginger ale out of the fridge.

"You make him do that," Mrs. Brown said.

Bernie flushed and laugh. "As if I could."

"Bernie," Mrs. Brown said gently, "can't you see that the man is absolutely crazy about you?"

Chapter Seven

Bernie stared at Mrs. Brown as if she'd sprouted grass in her hair. "He what?"

"He absolutely adores you," the older woman replied, smiling. "Everybody noticed, not just me."

Bernie flushed. "Well," she said, stumped for a response.

"You just go take care of your fellow," Mrs. Brown said. "I'll get breakfast ready. If he can eat anything, I'll make him whatever he likes."

"I'll tell him," Bernie replied. "Thanks."

"You come and eat whenever you like. I'll make you up a plate that you can reheat, okay?"

"Okay!"

Bernie went back to Mikey's room and closed the door. She sat down on the edge of the bed. "Still got the tablet?" she asked, because she'd handed it to him earlier.

"I got it."

"Here. It's open." She'd already taken the top off the bottle before she handed it to him. He swallowed down the tablet and handed her back the bottle. "Thanks, honey."

"No problem." She put his drink on the side table. "Will it stay down?" she worried. "Mrs. Brown said we can call one of our local doctors and they'll come give you a shot if you need it."

He swallowed. "Maybe the pill will work."

"Does it usually?"

He smiled. "No. It helps just a little. Nothing stops it."

She smoothed back his cool, wavy black hair. "You just let me know what you need. I'll get it."

His eyes adored her. "There was never a woman in my whole life who'd have taken care of me the way you just did. Well, except for my grandmother."

"I'm sure there were plenty who wanted to," she teased.

"Maybe a couple. But I'm funny about women. Most of them are jaded and glitzy," he added, his eyes cold with memory.

"Maybe you've been looking in the wrong places for them," she said, tongue in cheek.

His black eyes twinkled at her. "Think so?"

"It's a possibility."

He lay back and closed his eyes, wincing. "Of all the things to get from cheese," he groaned. "It's my favorite food."

"You can find a new favorite one. Maybe squash," she teased. "Or okra."

"Stop! You're killing me!"

She laughed. Most of the men she worked around hated both vegetables with a passion.

"Frozen yogurt, then."

"That sounds nice."

They were quiet for a few minutes, but it was obvious that even when the tablet had time to work, it wasn't doing much.

"Pill helping at all?"

He put his hand over his eyes. "Not so much." He closed his eyes and winced. "It's just over-the-counter stuff."

"Let me call a doctor. Please."

He drew in a breath. "Okay," he said finally.

"Be right back."

She phoned Lou and Copper Coltrain's office. The nurse said she'd ask Lou to come right out. Lou was short for Louise, she was blond and sweet and she knew exactly what to do for Mikey.

"You should see a neurologist," she told him after she'd given him an injection for the pain. First, of course, she'd examined him, asked what he'd already taken for the headache and inquired about any drug allergies. He had none. "But in the meantime, I'll write you a prescription for the preventative and something for the headaches that works when you get one." She turned to Bernie. "I'll give these to you, Bernie. You get them filled today."

"I will," Bernie said, smiling at the physician. "Thanks for coming."

"You're most welcome. If you have any more issues, Mr. Fiore, you call the office, okay?"

"Yes, ma'am," he said complacently. He smiled up at her through dark-rimmed eyes. "Thanks, Doc."

"You're welcome."

"I didn't think doctors made house calls anymore," he said.

"Jacobsville's not like most small towns," she laughed. "We do what's needed." She glanced at Bernie. "I thought you might be dying, from Bernie's description. She was very upset."

He opened both eyes and stared at Bernie. "She was?" he asked softly, and smiled at her.

She flushed even more. He laughed. Lou hid a smile, said her goodbyes and left.

"Can I get you anything else?" Bernie asked.

"No, but you can give the prescriptions to Santi. I'll text him." He pulled out his cell phone and made a face. "Damn, I can't see it," he murmured.

"Just a sec." She took the phone from him, pulled up messaging and looked at Mikey. "What do you want to tell him?"

"Ask him to come over right away."

She typed it in. The response was immediate. "On my way," it read.

"He'll think I'm dying or that Cotillo got me," he chuckled.

She frowned. "Who's Cotillo?"

"A bad man. Even worse than me," he said in a husky tone. His eyes tried to focus on her face. "There's a lot you don't know about me, kid."

"Well, there's a lot you don't know about me, too," she said.

His big hand searched for hers and held it tight. "We'll learn about each other. It takes time. Right?"

She smiled. It sounded like a future. She felt herself glowing inside. "It takes time," she agreed.

He took a deep breath and closed his eyes. "I'm going to try to sleep. Santi has plenty of cash for the prescriptions."

"Okay." She got up. "If you need anything, you just call, okay?"

He smiled without opening his eyes. "Okay. Thanks, honey."

"You're very welcome."

She went out of the room, the soft words lingering, touching, making her feel valued.

There was a knock at the front door. She went to answer it. Santi was standing there.

"What's wrong with the boss?" he asked at once.

"Migraine," she said. "We had to call the doctor."

"It's a doctor you know, right?" he asked, and his broad face looked troubled.

"Oh, yes, Dr. Louise Coltrain. She came out and gave him these prescriptions. He asked you to get them filled for him at the drugstore."

He took them from her and nodded. "I'll get right on it." He grimaced. "I don't like being away from him at night, even with all those other guys watching out for him. Listen, you hear any strange noises or if anybody tries to get in the house, you text me. Got your cell phone with you?"

"Yes." She pulled it out and handed it to him.

He pulled up the contact screen and put information into it. He handed it back. "That's my cell phone number. The boss isn't twitchy, so he might pass over something that could be dangerous."

"I'll call you if anything happens here," she promised. "Thanks," she added softly.

He smiled. "You're a nice kid. I'm sorry we were rough on you when you fell in front of the car. It's just that women have tried that before in the boss's old neighborhood."

"Really?" she asked, and she was honestly surprised.

He nodded. "He's loaded, you know? Plenty of women would do anything for money."

She smiled. "I've known one or two of those myself. I like having enough to pay the bills and eat out once in a while. That's about all. Money doesn't make people happy. Very often, it does just the opposite."

"Yes, it does." He held up the prescriptions. "I'll get these filled and bring them back to you. The boss, you're sure he's okay?"

"Why don't you look in and see, before you go?" she asked, leading him down the hall. "He's had a rough night."

"I used to nurse him through these headaches," Santi said. "They're a nightmare."

"I can see that."

She knocked briefly and opened the door. Mikey turned his head, wincing at the pain. He managed a smile.

"Hey, Santi. Had to make sure I hadn't croaked, right?" he teased.

Santi chuckled. "Something like that. You okay?"

"Getting better by the minute."

"Okay. I'll go get your meds and be right back."

"Bernie," Mikey called, when she started to go out,

too. She went back in and paused by the bed. "You haven't even had breakfast, have you?" he asked.

"Well, not just yet…"

"Go eat something."

"Okay. Mrs. Brown said you can have anything you want to eat when you feel like food."

He smiled drowsily. "She's a doll. So are you. I'm not hungry yet. I think I'll just sleep for a while. Eat something."

"I will."

"Hey," he called softly when she was at the door.

She turned, her eyebrows arching.

"When I get better, suppose we take in another movie? Paulie says they've got all the latest movies on pay-per-view and DVD. And a door that locks," he added with a wicked smile.

She laughed, flushing as she remembered the last movie they'd gone to but not seen. The memory of his mouth on hers was poignant. "I'd like that," she said.

"Me, too."

"Get some rest. I'll check on you in a few minutes."

He sighed. "Sweet girl. Don't ever change."

"I'll do my best."

She went out and closed the door.

Paul came over to see about his cousin, alerted by Santi after the bodyguard had dropped off Mikey's prescriptions.

"You look rough," Paul said, sitting by his cousin's bedside. "I remember what a misery those headaches are."

"Misery is right. I lost everything I'd eaten. Bernie was right in the bathroom with me, mopping me up," he added. "What a hell of a woman. I never knew anybody like her."

"She's unique," Paul agreed. "Amazing how she keeps going. Her disability never seems to get her down."

"She has good days and bad ones."

"Don't they have shots for that condition now?"

"Yeah, they do," Mikey said. "I overheard her landlady saying what a shame it was that they were so expensive. Bernie can't afford them." His face tautened. "I can, but she'd never let me do it for her. She's proud."

"She is."

"Mikey, how well do you know Santi?" Paul asked.

Mikey's eyebrows rose. "As well as I know you," he said. "Honor's his big thing. He'd never sell me out because it would seem dishonorable to him. He takes his job seriously. Why do you ask?" he added.

"Just some gossip. They say Cotillo's got somebody close to you."

"It's got to be Mrs. Brown, then," Mikey said with twinkling dark eyes. "Right? I mean, she's the obvious choice. Friendly, sweet, just the sort to set you up for a hit."

Paul chuckled. "Okay. I see what you mean. Just the same, we're checking out everybody who lives here. Just in case."

"That's not a bad idea. You still got Billings somewhere with a sniper kit?"

Paul nodded. "I don't think he ever sleeps. He seems to get by on catnaps, but we have an alternate in place anyway."

Mikey drew in a breath and laughed huskily. "These damned headaches. I didn't know there was a way to prevent them. Doc prescribed something, along with a prescription to take when the pain gets bad." He grimaced. "I hate drugs, you know? But this is a sort of pain that makes you want to hit your head with a hammer just to make it stop throbbing."

"Grandmama used to get them," Paul recalled. "They were bad."

"So are mine. Imagine a woman who doesn't run for the hills when a man's losing the contents of his stomach," he said. "Bernie didn't leave me for a minute, not until after the doctor came."

"I hear you did pretty much the same for her the day you met, when she fell in front of the car."

"Yeah," Mikey's mouth pulled down. "I thought it was a trick. You know how women used to come on to me. One even pretended to fall down a flight of stairs. I didn't know Bernie from an apple. I assumed she liked the looks of the limo and wanted a ride. Bad call." He drew in a breath. "She asked us to look for her cane, and we didn't believe her. Santi found it. I felt like a dog."

"Your past isn't full of guileless women," Paul said with a grin. "Understandable mistake."

"I guess." He put a hand to his head. "At least the throbbing has stopped. That doctor's pretty good. Nice looking woman. She married to the redheaded doctor?"

"Copper Coltrain," Paul agreed. "There was a mismatch. She worked with him for almost a year, and he hated her guts for something her father did years ago. It wasn't until she started to leave the practice that he got his ducks in a row. It was a rocky romance."

Mikey just sighed. "Mine's not rocky at all," he said. "You know, I never thought about having a family before. Little girls are sweet."

"Yeah." Paul didn't say any more. He and his former wife had a little girl. His wife and the child were gunned down by one of Paul's enemies, in revenge for his arrest and conviction. It was a sad memory.

"Sorry," Mikey said, wincing. "I forgot."

"I try to," Paul said. "I mean, I'm happier than I ever dreamed I could be, with Sari. But there are times when I think of my little girl..." He broke off.

"We all have bad memories, Paulie," Mikey said. "Mine aren't as bad as yours. I'm sorry for what happened to you. But the guy paid for it," he added coldly.

Paul glanced at him. "Yeah, one of the marshals in Jersey said he thought you might have had something to do with that."

Mikey just pursed his lips. "Who, me? I go out of my way to be nice to people."

"Yeah, but you know people who don't."

Mikey chuckled. "Lots of them."

"Have you told her?" he asked, his head jerking toward the door.

Mikey knew who he meant. He leaned back against the pillows. "I don't know how. At first, I didn't think there was a reason I needed to tell her. Now, I'm scared of what she'll think of me."

"She's a sweet woman."

"Sweet, and innocent. She doesn't see wickedness. She always looks for the best in people. Even in me. I'm not what she thinks I am. But how do I tell her what my life has been like? How do I do that, and keep her?"

"You underestimate how she feels about you, Mikey," Paul said. "You don't love or hate people for their actions mostly. You care about them because of what they are, deep inside. Bernie knows you aren't as bad as you think you are."

"I hope you're right. It hasn't been a long time, but if I lose her, it will be like having an arm torn off, you know?"

"I do know. That's how I feel about Sari."

"She's a winner."

He smiled. "I agree. Hey, if you're not better Saturday, you can bring Bernie over for lunch Sunday, you'll be welcome. You can take her walking around the property, maybe even catch that movie you went to see at the drive-in. It wasn't a new one, because it's on pay-per-view now."

"That sounds nice," Mikey replied. "I hope this stupid headache goes away before then," he added. "They usually last two or three days."

"I remember. You take your meds. Maybe they'll cut this one short."

"I hope so. Thanks for the cousinly visit," he added. "Anything more from Carrera?"

Paul shook his head. "He's got Tony in a safe place, he says, and not to worry."

"I'm in a safer place," Mikey chuckled. "Little bitty town in the middle of nowhere, with half the retired mercs in the country. Lucky me."

Paul grinned. "I'll second that. Ask Bernie over Sunday."

"I will. Thanks."

"No problem. See you later."

"Yeah."

Bernie was delighted with the invitation. It did take Mikey a few days to get over the headache, but he was fine Sunday afternoon. "Are you sure they don't mind?" she asked.

"They wouldn't invite you if they minded, honey," he told her as they sped toward Paul and Sari's house. "You warm enough?"

"I'm fine," she said, huddling down in her warm berber coat. "It's chilly tonight."

"Imagine that, chilly in south Texas," he teased. "Now if you want to see chilly, you have to come to Jersey. We know about cold weather."

"I guess you get a lot of snow."

"We used to get more, when Paulie and I were kids. We had some great snowball battles in the neighborhood. These older boys would lie in wait for us and pelt us with frozen snowballs every chance they got. So Paulie and I got some ice cubes and put them inside our snowballs. Ouch! The bullies ran for their lives."

She laughed. "I'll bet they did."

"Our grandmother was so fierce that they were more afraid of her than even the big boss in the neighborhood," he recalled with a smile. "I told you about her hitting him with a salami. Chased him all the way out the front door with it, and his people didn't dare laugh. It taught him a whole new respect for women."

She laughed softly. "I wish I could have met your grandmother."

"Me, too, honey. She'd have loved you." His hand reached for hers and held it tight. "She had no time for modern women with modern ideas."

She sighed. "Me, neither. I'm a throwback to another generation, I guess. My dad pretty much raised me after we came back here." Her heart felt like lead in her chest. She hated remembering why they'd come to Jacobsville.

"What's wrong?" he asked, sensitive to her mood.

She grimaced. "Things I can't talk about. Bad things."

"Honey, I could write you a book on bad things," he commented. He drew in a breath. "One of these days we have to have a long talk about my past, and it isn't going to be nice."

"It won't matter," she said quietly. "The person you were isn't the man you are today."

"That's not as true as I wish it was," he replied.

"I can't believe you'd do anything terrible."

But he had. Really terrible things. They hadn't bothered him much until now. This sweet, kind woman beside him didn't have any idea about what sort of evil lived in his real world, the world she'd never seen.

"Listen, you read books?" he asked.

"Oh, yes. It's how I get through bad nights, when the pain overpowers the medicines I take for it."

"There's this book—I'll give you the title. It's about a man who paints houses."

"A painter?" she asked.

His fingers contracted. "It's a different sort of painting. If you read the book, you'll begin to get some idea of the sort of world I live in." His face tautened. "It's a hard life. Dog eat dog, and I mean that literally. The man I work for is hiding out from a man even worse than he is. What I know, what I've seen, can clear him. The feds just have to keep me alive long enough until the trial comes up." He turned and glanced at her. "It's a business. Like regular business, in a way. It's just that somebody wants what you have and thinks up ways to get it, most of them illegal and deadly."

She frowned. "I don't understand."

"How could you? Raised in a tiny little town, surrounded by law-abiding citizens, most of whom love you." His face hardened. "In my whole damned life, my grandmother was the only person who really loved me."

Her heart almost stopped. She loved him. And she'd only just realized it. She was faintly disconcerted by a revelation that should have occurred to her much sooner. "There's your cousin Paul," she said after a minute.

"Yeah, Paulie. We're fond of each other. He'd do anything he could to help me. In fact, he already is. But that's not the same way I felt about my grandmother."

"I don't remember mine very well," she said tightly.

He glanced at her. "Bad memories?"

She swallowed. "They don't get much worse."

His fingers linked into hers. "Can you tell me about it?"

She hesitated. He was insinuating that his life had been a little outside the law. Perhaps he might understand better than most men what it had been like for her, for her family.

"I want to," she said. "Can it wait until later?"

He laughed. "It can wait." He was flattered that she wanted to trust him with something that was obviously a secret, something she kept hidden. It was an indication of feelings she was beginning to have for him. He was beginning to have the same sort for her. If she had something traumatic in her past, it might help her relate to his own life.

Then he stopped and considered what he'd be letting her in for, after the trial, when he went back to

Jersey, back to the old life. He'd pledged his loyalty, his life, to the crime family he belonged to. Betraying that code, that omertà, would get him killed. Not that he had any plans to turn his people in to the feds. In fact, even Tony was working with the feds right now, to ward off the takeover by Cotillo. But that was a temporary truce. Nobody in Tony's employ was going to rat out anybody to the feds, least of all Mikey. That would get you killed quick.

On the other hand, if he wanted a life with the sweet woman at his side, and he was beginning to, how could he drag her into the shadows with him?

It would be her choice in the end. But she was sheltered and disabled. Not that his people would be bad to her, oh, no. Even the women would welcome her like a relative. His underlings would treat her like royalty. So it wouldn't be bad from that standpoint. But the rackets Tony and Mikey were mixed up in were illegal. They specialized in online gambling, in numbers running, in casinos in Vegas. One of Mikey's properties was a casino, in fact. He'd told Bernie that it was a hotel. It was a hotel, but it wasn't in Jersey. It was in Las Vegas, and big-name entertainers came regularly to appear there. He ran it like a legal business, but he did do things off the books that could land him in jail. Bernie was such a gentle, trusting soul. She liked the country, the outdoors, little animals. Mikey liked bright lights and casinos. It was going to be a difficult adjustment, if she was even willing to make it.

"You're brooding," she accused, watching the expressions cross his handsome face.

He laughed self-consciously. "I'm brooding." He turned his head for a minute and caught her eyes.

"Sorry. I have things on my mind." He made a face. "Paulie said they've got somebody close to me."

"They?"

"The guy who's after Tony and me," he explained. He chuckled. "I told him it was probably Mrs. Brown. You can tell she's just the kind of person who would set a man up," he added with a grin.

She burst out laughing. "Oh, that's wicked."

"I'm a wicked man, honey," he said, and he wasn't kidding.

She frowned. "He doesn't have any idea who it is?" she added.

"Not yet. He's checking people out."

"I'd check out that Jessie person in my office," she muttered. "She's one of the most horrible people I've ever known. She's always cutting at the other women in the office. Poor Glory has high blood pressure. It can be dangerous, you know, and she has a small child. Jessie makes all sorts of unpleasant remarks to her about the medicines she takes, even about the way she dresses."

"Your boss should get that woman out of the office," he commented.

"He'd like to, but he's the DA. He has to have a legitimate reason to let her go or she could take him to court. He'd like her to leave, too. She messes up appointments all the time, another reason Glory's so stressed."

His fingers stroked hers. "We all have our crosses, don't we, kid?"

She nodded. "Nobody gets through life without a few traumas." She sighed. "It's really sad, you know. She's so beautiful. How can a person who looks like that be such a pain to be around?"

"You never know what sort of background people

come from," he said simply. "A lot of times, kids turn out bad because of the way they were raised. You know, I only saw my dad a few times in my whole life. My mother died of a heart attack when she was just in her twenties, not too long after she had me. Her mother, my grandmother, took me in. Paulie's mom bit the dust about the same time, so he ended up with our grandmother, too." He grimaced. "Paulie's dad was even worse than mine. He took some licks when the old man was home. Fortunately, it wasn't often."

"Did your fathers work in some sort of away job, like construction?" she asked innocently.

"They worked for the big bosses. They went where they were told, and did what they were told." He smiled sadly. "That's the life, kid. You pledge to obey and you do it. There's a code of honor. We call it omertà. It means you pledge your loyalty to a don and you never forget it. You sell out your colleagues, you meet with a quick and sad end."

Her heart jumped. "But you're going to testify against a man who's a, what did you call him, a don?"

His fingers contracted comfortingly around hers. "That's a different thing," he said. "This guy Cotillo is trying to muscle in on territory that doesn't belong to him. The other families are as much against him as Tony's is."

She frowned. "Tony's your family? Is he a relation?"

He chuckled. "Tony's a character," he said. "No, we're not related, but we'd die for each other. So in that sense, yeah, I guess you could say he's family. The feds are protecting him. Me, too. What we know can put Cotillo away for a very long time. The families are working toward that end, even making a temporary truce with the feds to keep them from prying too closely into our business."

She blinked. "You talk about federal people as if they're the enemy," she said. "But your cousin works for a federal agency."

"It's just a figure of speech, honey," he said, back-tracking. "We're all grateful for their help. Nobody wants a guy like Cotillo in charge in Jersey. He's a weasel. First chance he got, he'd start lining up other families for elimination. They know that. So the feds are sort of the lesser of the two evils."

"I see."

"You don't, but you will," he promised. He sighed. "I just hope it isn't all going to be too much for you, Bernie. You've lived a sheltered life."

"Actually, I haven't. Not so much."

"Oh?"

"Well, I haven't lived in a commune or had lovers, or anything like that. But I'm anything but sheltered. I'll tell you," she added. "I promise."

He smiled. "I'll tell you, too."

"That's a deal."

Chapter Eight

They were heading down the long driveway to Graylings when his fingers contracted around hers. "No secrets from now on," he said. "I'll tell you about my life today and you can tell me about yours."

"It might matter..." she said worriedly.

"It won't." He sounded very positive. "Nothing you tell me will change anything." One side of his sensuous mouth pulled down. "On the other hand, what I have to tell you, well, that may change a lot of things," he added heavily, and he was regretting things in his past that might drive her out of his life. It was a terrible thought. She was already part of him.

"Whatever sort of trouble you're in, I'll stand by you," she said.

He wanted to pull her over into his lap and kiss the breath out of her for saying that, but he had to restrain himself. His fingers worked sensuously into hers, caressing them. "I never thought I'd get mixed up with a girl from a little town in Texas," he said, chuckling. "I feel just like Carrera must have."

"Carrera?" she asked. "Oh, yes, Delia's husband." She smiled. "Delia had a bad time of it. Her mother turned out to be a woman she'd always thought of as her sister, and her father turned out to be her mother's husband. She saved Mr. Carrera's life in the Bahamas, but she lost her baby. She came home and she was so miserable. It hurt me to see her when I had to go to the dry cleaner's." She sighed. "But then Mr. Carrera showed up with some sort of quilt he'd made for her, and the next thing we knew, they were getting married."

"Yeah, he quilts," he said with a soft laugh. "The guy looks like a wise guy. He's big and rough and he intimidates most people. The quilting habit gave him a lot of heat until he started throwing punches. Now nobody laughs at it. He wins international competitions with his designs, too."

She nodded. "They have one of his quilts in our library, on permanent display. It's a Bow Tie quilt. They say he has one just like it in a casino he owns. Gosh, imagine owning a casino! Those are the richest, flashiest places on earth!"

He hadn't told her that his hotel in Vegas was also a casino. "You ever been in one?" he asked.

"When I was small, my parents took me to the Bahamas on a cruise one year, on summer vacation. I wasn't allowed inside, but they drove me by one over on Paradise Island. It was fascinating to me, even as a child."

His fingers contracted. "Suppose I told you that the

hotel I own is actually a casino," he said slowly, "and it's in Las Vegas?"

Her eyes widened. "You own a casino in Las Vegas?" she exclaimed. "Wow!"

He laughed, surprised at her easy acceptance. "I run it legit, too," he added. "No fixes, no hidden switches, no cheating. Drives the feds nuts, because they can't find anything to pin on me there."

"The feds?" she asked.

He drew in a breath. "I told you, I'm a bad man." He felt guilty about it, dirty. His fingers caressed hers as they neared Graylings, the huge mansion where his cousin lived with the heir to the Grayling racehorse stables.

Her fingers curled trustingly around his. "And I told you that the past doesn't matter," she said stubbornly. Her heart was running wild. "Not at all. I don't care how bad you've been."

His own heart stopped and then ran away. His teeth clenched. "I don't even think you're real, Bernie," he whispered. "I think I dreamed you."

She flushed and smiled. "Thanks."

He glanced in the rearview mirror. "What I'd give for just five minutes alone with you right now," he said tautly. "Fat chance," he added as he noticed the sedan tailing casually behind them.

She felt all aglow inside. She wanted that, too. Maybe they could find a quiet place to be alone, even for just a few minutes. She wanted to kiss him until her mouth hurt.

He pulled into the long driveway and up to the house, which was all aglow with light. It was a huge two-story mansion with exquisite woodwork and a long, wide porch. The front door opened as Mikey helped her out of the car, retaining her hand in his as they approached the house.

"Paisano," Paul greeted him in Italian.

"Salve! Come stai?" Mikey replied, and let go of Bernie's hand long enough to hug his cousin.

"Sto bene, grazie, e tu?" Paul replied.

"Va bene," Mikey responded with a grin. *"Cosi, cosi. Non mi posso lamentare."*

"Benissimo!"

"English, English," Sari Fiore chided. "Bernie doesn't understand Italian," she laughed.

"Just greetings, honey," Mikey told her, and brought her hand to his lips. "I'll teach you some nice Italian words the minute we get some time together."

She grinned. "Okay."

"Come on in," Paul added as two feds got out of the sedan that had trailed Mikey's car. "McLeod, do you and Agent Murdock want coffee?"

"I'd love some," McLeod said, and glanced at Murdock. "As long as that guy doesn't offer to make it," he added firmly.

Murdock, a good-natured man, just chuckled. "I get stuck with making it at our office. People pour it in the ficus tree."

"Yeah, the poor damned thing shivers all the time," Paul commented on the way to the kitchen. "I think it's on the verge of a nervous breakdown. Hey, Mandy, can you make us a pot of coffee?" he called to the woman working to clean up the kitchen counters.

"Of course I can!" she exclaimed, and grinned. "Hey, Mikey! Hello, Bernie. Nice to see you both."

"Nice to see you, too, Mandy," Mikey replied, and

kissed her cheek. "I miss your cooking. Not that Mrs. Johnson isn't good."

"I know she is," Mandy replied. She gave Mikey and Bernie a secret smile when she saw them holding hands.

Mikey noticed, but he didn't let go, even when they sat down together at the long kitchen table with Paul and the two feds.

"Okay," Mikey said. "What's up? You guys tailed us the whole way here," he added to McLeod.

"Cotillo sent one of his boys down here after you," McLeod replied quietly, watching Mikey's face harden. "We caught him at the courthouse yesterday."

Mikey blinked. "How?"

"We have facial identification software," McLeod said simply. "I used it. He's got wants and warrants outstanding in Jersey. Our guys took him into custody and they're delivering him right back to the authorities there."

US Marshals, that was, Mikey knew without being told. He let out a breath. "I guess I'd better be more careful about taking Bernie out to public places."

Her fingers, unseen, contracted around his.

"Not at all," Agent Murdock said. "As long as they're pretty public. Drive-ins aren't a good idea. Too much opportunity for covert work."

Mikey sighed. "I guess so. Damn."

"It's okay," Bernie said. "We can sit in Mrs. Johnson's parlor anytime we like, and talk or watch television," she reminded him.

He smiled at her. "You're a rare girl, Bernie."

She flushed and laughed. "Not so much."

Mikey glanced at the government agents. "So why was he at the courthouse?" he asked.

"We think he was looking for a contact there. But he came after quitting time, so we didn't have the opportunity to find out. When we questioned him," McLeod added, "he said he was looking for San Antonio and got lost. He was just looking for directions."

"Oh, that sounds very sincere," Mikey said sardonically.

"Yeah, considering that he flew into the San Antonio airport," Paul added drily.

"Here's coffee," Mandy said. "And how about some nice pound cake? I made a chocolate one!"

Mikey made a face. "Gosh, I'd love that, but I'm just getting over a really bad migraine. Chocolate's one of my triggers," he reminded her.

"I'm sorry," Mandy said. She patted him on the shoulder. "But I've got a nice cherry pie?" she teased.

He chuckled. "I'll take that. Thanks. You know, she nursed me through the headache, sickness and all," he added, looking at Bernie with evident affection. "She never left me, and even called a doctor out to the boardinghouse to treat me. She's quite a girl."

Bernie's face flamed because everybody was looking at her.

"Yes, she is," Sari said, smiling. "At work, she's always the first one there and the last one to leave, and she never minds staying over if we need her." She made a face. "It's not the same with that new woman the boss hired. Jessie. She's constantly late and she makes clients uncomfortable. She made a real play for one of the wealthy married local ranchers, and the boss gave her warning." She sighed. "I wish she'd do something he could fire her for. Nobody likes her."

"She's an odd fit for a small town," Bernie said. "She's overly sophisticated."

"We have a few overly sophisticated people, like the police chief's wife, but she's nice," Mandy broke in, putting a platter of sliced pound cake, saucers and utensils on the table, along with a saucer containing a slice of cherry pie for Mikey.

"This looks delicious. Thanks, honey," he told the housekeeper and grinned at her.

"You're welcome. Go ahead, people, dig in. We don't stand on ceremony here."

"No, we don't," Sari said, smiling warmly at her husband.

"Oh, that's good coffee," Paul said with a long sigh. "I just hate trying to drink it at work," he added with a pointed glare at Murdock.

Murdock made a face. "Not my fault. My mother always drank tea. She never taught me how to make coffee and I never drink it."

"No wonder it tastes so bad," Paul teased.

Murdock sighed. "There have been threats, you know," he said complacently. "In fact, ASAC Jon Blackhawk's brother, McKuen Kilraven, was openly talking about men in ninja suits and a pickup truck and a big sack."

"You'd never fit in a sack, Murdock," Paul chuckled. "Besides, Kilraven's too occupied with their new daughter to do any such thing. That's two kids now. He and Winnie are over the moon."

"She still working 911 dispatch down here?" Murdock asked.

Paul shook his head. "She's got her hands full with two preschoolers. Kilraven's still with the company, but he's mostly administrative these days. No more hanging out of helicopters by one leg wrapped in camo netting while he fires at enemy agents."

"You're kidding!" Bernie gasped.

"Oh, no, I'm not," Paul chuckled. "The man was a maniac when he was after a perp. He's calmed down somewhat since he married, but he's still good at what he does."

"He was a patrolman here, working for Chief Grier as cover on a covert federal assignment, for a while," Bernie said as she nibbled cake and sipped coffee. She laughed. "There was gossip that Chief Grier wanted to put him in a barrel, drive him to the border and send him down the Rio Grande. They did butt heads a few times over procedure."

"The chief butts heads pretty good," Paul assured her. "He's lowered the crime rate with a vengeance since he's been in charge of our local police."

"Nobody thought he'd stay here when he first came," Bernie said. "He was really tough. Then they made a movie here with the Georgia Firefly, Tippy Moore, and before any of us realized it, he was married to her."

"She's a knockout," Paul said. He slid his hand over his wife's. "I'm partial to redheads, you know," he added, grinning as he studied Sari's red, red hair pinned up over big blue eyes.

She grinned back. "Thanks, sweetheart."

"So what do we do about Cotillo and the trial and Tony Garza?" Paul asked as he finished his pie and his coffee.

"First things first," Paul said. "We've got tails on Cotillo and his men, with interagency cooperation. Cotillo's killed a lot of people trying to forge new alliances and take over territory. He's made enemies."

"The killings are going to get him in trouble," Mikey said. "The big guys don't like that. It invites the feds in. They want problems solved with dialog, not automatic weapons."

"Well, they do kill people who rat them out," Paul replied solemnly.

Mikey nodded. "Omertà," he agreed. "Loyalty is life itself in the outfit. The number-one sin is selling out your people to the feds. Nobody likes a rat. They get put down and sometimes their whole families do as well, as a warning." He ground his teeth together when he saw his cousin's face. That had happened to Paul. His first family had been gunned down when Paul locked up one of the minor bosses and shut down a lucrative illegal operation. The man had gotten even in the worst possible way.

"I'm sorry," Mikey told his cousin. "Truly sorry. I should never have brought that up."

Paul's face relaxed. "It was a long time ago. Still stings," he said, and his eyes were filled with horrible memories.

"Just the same, I'm sorry."

Paul smiled. "We're family. Don't sweat it."

Mikey sighed. "You're the only family I've got. Well, except for Tony's family." He glanced at the feds. "I hope you guys understand that I'm only cooperating because Tony's being falsely accused. I'm not selling out my people. Not for anything."

"We know that, Mikey," Paul said quietly. "Nobody's asking you to rat out your colleagues."

Mikey sipped coffee, not looking at them. "I took

a blood oath," he said very quietly. "I made a solemn promise. I swore to it, like you'd make a vow in church. I won't break it. Not if they lock me up forever."

"We only lock up people when we can prove they've broken the law," Paul assured him. He leaned closer. "So make sure we can't prove anything on you," he chuckled.

Mikey laughed. "I don't do that stuff anymore. I have a legit casino and I run it like a legit business."

"I know that," Paul replied. "You're not as bad as you make out, Mikey. You saved Merrie's life," he added, referring to Sari's younger sister. Both women had been targeted by an enemy of their late father, victims of professional hit men. Mikey's input had helped save both of them. "In fact, you helped save Sari's, as well."

"I just made a few calls," Mikey replied.

"Well, those few calls helped us catch all the perps," Paul replied.

Mikey grinned. "I like Baby Doll," he said, referring to Merrie. "How's she doing?"

"She and Ren are expecting again," Sari said with a wide grin. "She's over the moon."

"She still painting?" Mikey asked.

"Oh, yes. She never gives that hobby up," Sari told him.

He glanced at Bernie with real hunger. "I'd love her to do a portrait of Bernie for me," he said.

"You know she'd be happy to!" Sari said. She glanced at Bernie, who was flushed and beaming. "Bernie, do you have a few photos of yourself that we could send her?"

Bernie grimaced. "Well, no, not a lot. I don't have anybody to take pictures of me…"

While she was speaking, Mikey took out his expensive cell phone and snapped photos of her from all angles. He showed them to her in his photo app.

"You're really good at this," she said, surprised as she looked at herself in the pictures. She looked happy, mysterious, almost pretty. She laughed. "These don't even really look like me!"

"They do. You don't laugh a lot," he replied. His face tightened. "I love it when you laugh, Bernie," he added. "You're beautiful when you're happy."

She felt her heart almost bursting. He thought she was beautiful. He wanted a painting of her. She could have floated up to the ceiling, she was so lighthearted.

"Thanks," she whispered.

He wrinkled his nose at her and grinned. "We'll have to wait until that movie we were watching comes out on pay-per-view and we can watch it together."

"I don't have pay-per-view," she said morosely.

"We do," Sari said, and grinned. "You can watch it in the library. In fact, we already have it. The drive-in is showing it, but it's not a first-run movie. Wouldn't you like to see the rest of it?"

Mikey pursed his lips. "Would I! It's a great movie."

"It is, but I'd need tissues," Bernie confessed. "One reviewer said it would twist your heart open."

"You can have tissues and more coffee," Sari said. "Mandy, can you do refills and find a box of tissues for Bernie?"

"You bet!" Mandy said, and went to get both.

The government agents left shortly after. Mikey took Bernie into the luxurious study with its plush couch and chairs and the expensive media center, with a fifty-five-inch television screen.

"Wow," Bernie said as Mikey closed the door behind them. "This is awesome."

"They've refurnished it since old man Grayling died," he told her as he went to turn on the television and set up the movie. "In fact, they've redone the whole house. It has some bad memories for Sari and her sister."

"I remember hearing about how badly their father treated them," Bernie said. "He must have been a horrible father."

"From what I hear, he was." He grimaced. "Mine was pretty bad, too."

"My dad was a sweet, kind man," Bernie said sadly. "He died much too young. He lived through a lot of trauma. I think it affects people, you know? Affects their health."

"Maybe so."

He turned on the movie and brought the controller back as he dropped down onto the plush couch beside Bernie. He put the controller on the coffee table and turned to Bernie.

"Gee, look, we're all alone," he said with a grin, "and there are no cars around us."

"Isn't that fascinating?" she laughed.

"Oh, you bet." He pulled her onto his lap, letting her head fall back on his shoulder. "And I have some really interesting ideas about what we could do while the movie runs."

Her arms looped around his neck and her eyes riveted to his wide, sensuous, chiseled mouth. "You do?" she whispered.

He drew her close and bent his head, smiling. "Oh, yes. Very, very interesting."

As he spoke, his mouth slowly covered hers. She sighed and sank against his big, muscular body, letting him take her weight while he kissed her.

"I could get used to this," he whispered.

She smiled under his lips. "Me, too."

He nibbled her upper lip and traced under it with just the tip of his tongue, loving the way she reacted to him. She wasn't coy or reticent. She met him halfway. If those long, soulful sighs were any indication, she loved what he was doing to her.

He shifted her and his fingers ran gently up and down her rib cage, setting fires, making her hungry. His mouth grew slowly insistent. She twisted against him, hungry and burning with new needs.

His big hand slid under the sweater she was wearing and teased around her breast while he kissed her slowly.

She moaned and twisted up toward that maddening hand whose touch was making her wild for more.

He smiled against her soft lips because he knew that. His thumb slowly trespassed under the lacy cotton cup and against her firm breast. She gasped under his mouth, but she didn't try to stop him. He loved that. His mouth opened on hers, deepening the kiss, diverting her while his hand went to the hooks that held the bra in place and snapped them open. His hand, warm and strong, moved slowly back around, teasing just under her breast. He could hear her breathing change, feel the need in her grow, as it grew in him.

"Oh, baby," he murmured as his mouth grew hard on hers and his big hand tenderly swallowed her breast up whole, his palm rubbing gently at the hard little nub he found.

She caught her breath and moaned.

"This is sweet," he ground out. "Oh, God, it's sweet like sugar candy…"

He moved, turning her so that she was lying under him, full length, on the plush couch. He was on his side, his elbow taking his weight as his hand moved the bra out of his way so that he could touch her more easily.

Her body arched, helpless, as she reacted to the intimate tracing of his hand. She couldn't even pretend not to want it. She was aching, throbbing with hungers she'd never felt in her life. A faint whimper escaped the mouth that his was devouring.

"Yes," he whispered huskily. "It's not enough, is it? Try not to cry out," he added as he slid the sweater and bra up under her chin. "They might hear us…"

What he was saying didn't make sense until his mouth lowered, and she felt it cover and consume her whole breast, taking it slowly into the moist, warm darkness, his tongue sliding over the nipple and making her throb from head to toe.

She had to stifle a cry. She sobbed under the expert touch of his mouth, shivering, arching as she pleaded for something more, something to ease the ache that was slowly consuming her.

He began to suckle her, hungrier than he could ever remember being with a woman. She sobbed as if he was hurting her, but he knew he wasn't. His long, powerful leg inserted itself between both of hers in the slacks she was wearing and began to move sensuously, making the hunger even worse.

He rolled over onto her completely, hesitating just

long enough to open the buttons of his shirt and pull it apart over the thick hair that covered his muscular chest. When he went down against her, it was bare skin against bare skin, something she'd never felt.

Her arms went under the shirt, around him, her hands digging into his bare back. Odd how it felt there, she thought dimly, because there was a definite depression, a coin-shaped one. But he was moving on her and she felt the power and heat of him, the sudden surge of his body that told her graphically how capable he was.

His mouth ground into hers. He groaned as he pushed between her long legs and right against the heart of her in that soft fork of her body. She lifted up, shivering, and he moved roughly on her, feeling the passion burn him alive.

But his mind froze the passion as he realized how innocent she was. This was wrong. He could live with it, he could love it, but it would shame her, make her feel soiled. He couldn't do that to her. He couldn't, even if it was agony to stop.

He rolled over, shivering, and pulled her hard against his side. "Don't move," he whispered unsteadily. "Just lie still. Please, honey. Help me. I hurt like hell!"

She managed that, just. She was on fire and he'd stopped. Why had he stopped? She wanted him so desperately, just as desperately as he wanted her.

But sanity slowly returned. Was this what she really wanted, to have sex with a man on a sofa in a room with an unlocked door, a man to whom she had no real ties except physical ones? She was religious. She didn't believe in sex before marriage. But she wanted Mikey. She wanted him so badly that she'd have given in right here, without a single protest. In fact, she'd done that.

But he'd stopped. She could feel how difficult it had been for him to do that. His body was shaking with unfulfilled needs. Now she felt guilty that she'd let it go so far. How would she have felt afterward? She didn't even know how to protect herself. What if she'd become pregnant? How would she live with that in a small town where everybody knew her, and knew that the only man she'd kept company with in recent years was the one lying so stiffly beside her right now? It would be no secret who the father was. Mikey had a casino in Las Vegas. He was a big-city man. It was highly unlikely that he'd throw all that up to live in a little town like Jacobsville with a woman who might end up an invalid in a very few years.

Besides that, he had a past, and bad men were after him because of a man he worked with, who was hiding from assassins. This was a terrible time to start an affair. In fact, she had to admit she wasn't the sort of woman who could even have an affair. It just wasn't like her, despite her aching hunger for Mikey and the violent attachment that she felt to him.

He was breathing easier now. He stretched and laughed softly when he felt her breasts against his bare rib cage.

"Well, that was a damned near thing," he whispered as he turned over, rolled her onto her back, and looked at her pretty firm pink breasts with their hard, dusky crowns. He touched them very gently. "I didn't want to stop."

"We're on a sofa," she began, flushing.

"Honey, all I had to do was push your pants down and go into you," he whispered blatantly, smiling at her expression. "It wouldn't have taken three minutes, as hot as I was. That's how easy it would have been. You didn't realize, did you?"

She caught her breath. "Not really," she confessed. "I haven't ever…"

"I noticed." He bent and brushed his mouth over her bare breasts. "God, woman, you're so beautiful," he whispered. "I'll dream of you every night of my life after this!"

"You will?" She thought how comfortable she was with him, how easily they'd slipped into intimacy. It felt so right. She wasn't even embarrassed.

He chuckled. "Yes, I will." He lifted his head and drew in a breath. "When all this is over, you and I are going to sit down and have a very serious talk." He brushed back her damp, disheveled hair. "Very serious."

She smiled slowly, her heart lifting. "Okay."

He laughed. "Everything's so easy with you, Bernie," he said, touching her cheek gently. "You never make waves, do you?"

"Not much, no."

"I love that about you," he said. "I feel at ease with you. Safe."

"I feel that way with you, too."

His big hand brushed tenderly over her breasts. "I guess we should put our clothes back on and watch the movie," he said with a sigh.

She nodded.

He pulled her up beside him, but before she could pull her sweater and bra back down, he turned her into his lap and pulled her inside his shirt, shivering as he felt her bare skin rub gently over his. His arms contracted hungrily and he held her, rocking her, in a blistering silence of passion.

"You'd do it with me, wouldn't you?" he whispered at her ear.

"Yes," she replied in a husky, shaky little voice.

"I don't even have anything to use," he confessed gruffly. He held her even closer. "You know what? I don't think I'd mind."

"You wouldn't?"

His hand went to the base of her spine, and he rubbed her against the hardness of him, holding her there firmly. "I like babies," he whispered.

She shivered. "Oh, Mikey," she sobbed, and her arms tightened.

He shivered, too. "Oh, God, I've got to get up and lock the door," he groaned. "On the sofa, on the damned carpet, against a wall—I have to have you, right now!"

"Yes," she whimpered, pushing closer. "Yes!"

He eased her away from him, his eyes blazing as he looked at her breasts. "I'll lock the door..." he said.

Just then, footsteps sounded down the wood floor of the hall and there was a sudden knock at the door.

"How's the movie going?" Sari called.

Mikey and Bernie looked at each other in a moment of shocked embarrassment while they waited for that doorknob to turn...

Chapter Nine

"Just a sec!" Mikey called in a strained, deep voice.

There was a muffled laugh from the door. "Mandy's got more coffee. Come on out when your movie finishes."

"We will. Thanks!" he called back.

The footsteps withdrew.

He let out the breath he'd been holding. Bernie sat beside him as if in a daze, her top still up around her neck, her breasts pressed hard into the thick hair on Mikey's broad chest. He looked down at her with wonder.

"I guess the jig would have been up if Sari had opened that door," he laughed.

She smiled dreamily up at him. "I guess."

He drew in a hard breath. "I suppose we'd better stop while we're ahead." He drew back and looked down at her bare breasts with fascination. "Over the years, I've seen a lot of women undressed," he murmured. "But none of them were half as beautiful as you are, honey." He stroked her soft, firm breast and leaned down, putting his lips reverently to it. "I'll live on this my whole life."

Her heart skipped. She just looked at him with everything she felt for him in her green eyes. His jaw clenched. He still wanted her, now more than ever. But he managed some control as he pulled down the bra and fastened it, then drew the sweater down over her waist.

She smiled and fastened the buttons of his shirt. He looked rumpled and his hair was mussed from her hands in it. She loved the way he looked. He was a little flushed, too, and his dark eyes danced as they met hers.

"You'd like Vegas," he said. "For visits, anyway, it's an exciting place. Plenty of music and neon lights. An oasis in the desert."

She put her hands on his chest, over the buttoned shirt. "I don't guess you'd like a little Texas town that draws the sidewalks in at dusk," she said without meeting his eyes.

"I'd like wherever you called home, Bernie," he said solemnly. "We come from different places. But that doesn't mean both of us can't adapt to something else, even if it's just for a little while." He bent and kissed her very softly. "I didn't want to stop. You go to my head like whiskey. It was like sailing on the clouds."

She laughed and pressed close. "For me, too."

His arms contracted, holding her close and rocking her. "We'd better finish watching the movie. There may be a quiz after."

She laughed with pure delight. "Okay."

He drew her gently down beside him and clasped her hand tight in his. They watched the screen until the credits came on. Mikey turned off the entertainment center and drew Bernie along with him out the door and into the kitchen.

Paul and Sari looked up as they came into the room. Both were grinning.

"Yeah, we got a little friendly," Mikey said defensively. "It was me, mostly."

"It was me, too," she said, and smiled up at him.

"You don't need to excuse anything to us," Paul chuckled. "We've only been married three years."

"He means, we're still on our honeymoon," Sari teased. "So how about that coffee?"

"Sounds lovely," Bernie said, and stars were in the eyes she turned toward Mikey, who looked like a cat who'd just eaten a canary.

That expression went along with Bernie to work the following Monday, where Jessie saw it and grew sarcastic and insulting.

"We all heard about you and Mikey going over to his cousin's place. Some mansion," Jessie drawled sarcastically, glancing at Sari as she paused by Bernie's desk. "Got your eyes on that nice rich fish, don't you? But do you think a little hick like you could land a man that sophisticated?"

Bernie's face flamed, but she didn't back down. "Backgrounds don't make much difference when people have feelings for one another," she said.

"As if he'd have feelings for you," Jessie said with a laugh. "I don't know him personally, but I know about him. He's had women who were movie stars, and debutantes and millionaires' daughters. He's not likely to take up with a woman who's looking at a wheelchair a few years down the road."

"That's enough," Sari said icily, standing up. "One more word and Mr. Kemp is going to get an earful."

Jessie knew when to quit. She shrugged. "Just stating facts, that's all."

"Ooh, somebody's so jealous she can't stand it," Olivia drawled with an amused look at Jessie. "What's the matter, sweetie, did he slap you down over at the courthouse and you're getting even?"

Jessie actually flushed. 'He did not," she spit. "I could have him if I wanted him."

"Do be my guest and try," Olivia taunted. "We heard that you made him sick."

Jessie was almost vibrating by now. She started to speak just as Mr. Kemp's door opened and he came out. She went quickly to her desk with a forced smile at the boss and pretended to work.

Kemp, no fool, looked from Bernie's flushed face to Sari's angry one and drew a conclusion. He didn't say a word, but the look he gave an oblivious Jessie wasn't one that would have encouraged her about her longevity in this office.

Glory Ramirez came in the door, a little fatigued. "Court is bound over until tomorrow," she told Mr. Kemp. Glory was an assistant DA, like Sari.

"Does it look like the jury will convict?" Sari asked.

Glory made a face. "Who knows what a jury will do?" she asked with a sigh. "I hope I'm good enough to put this guy away. He lured a fourteen-year-old girl in with promises of true love and she fell for it. He's thirty-five," she added coldly.

"What a mess," Sari said.

"It's worse than that. She's pregnant," Glory said.

"Oh, that's no problem," Jessie laughed. "She can just go to a clinic and have them take it out."

"She and her people are deeply religious," Glory replied. "Not everybody thinks of termination as birth control, Jessie."

There was a whip in her voice. The other women knew why. Glory had lost her first baby after a horrible fight with her husband when they were first married, before they really knew much about each other. It had taken her two years to get pregnant again. She and Rodrigo had one child, a boy, and Glory's precarious health made another unlikely. Her blood pressure was extremely high and she'd already had angioplasty for a blocked artery that had caused a mild heart attack.

"You people take everything so seriously," Jessie muttered.

"Babies are serious business," Mr. Kemp broke in. Everybody except Jessie knew that he'd been in love and engaged, and his fiancée had died after a local woman spiked her drink with a drug. The fiancée had been pregnant at the time, and the child died with her.

"Babies are a nuisance. They cry and keep everybody upset, and you never get your waistline back again. I'd never want one," Jessie said.

"I would," Bernie said on a long, happy sigh.

"Good luck with that, in your physical condition," Jessie said sarcastically.

"If I could have a child, with my blood pressure, there's no reason Bernie couldn't have one with her limitations."

Bernie smiled at her. "Thanks."

"Not a chance I'd take," Jessie muttered.

"Thank you for your input, Miss Tennison, and how about that call I asked you to make half an hour ago to the DA in Bexar County on the Ramsey matter?" Kemp asked shortly.

Jessie flustered. "Oh. Sorry. I forgot. I'll get him for you right now, Mr. Kemp!"

Kemp gave her an angry glance, smiled at the other women and went back into his office.

Bernie went to lunch at Barbara's Café and there was Mikey, holding down a table for them. He got up as she joined him, after she'd given her order and paid for it.

"I could have gotten the tab, honey," he said.

"I can pay for my own stuff," she teased. "But thanks for the thought."

His hand slid over hers and held it tight. "You don't look so good. Bad morning?"

"Sort of," she said. "But it's improving already," she added with a loving glance at his handsome face.

He grinned. "That's better. I like it when you're happy."

"I usually am." She didn't mention the confrontation with Jessie or the woman's harsh words. She pushed them to the back of her mind while she and Mikey had nice pieces of roast beef with perfect mashed potatoes and gravy and home-cooked green beans.

"This is so good," she sighed. "I love to cook, but it's hard for me to stand for long periods of time. Still, I used to do it when I lived at home with my parents."

"We were going to talk last night," he mused.

She flushed.

He laughed sensuously. "We didn't do a whole lot of talking, though, did we, baby," he whispered. "It's hard to think of things like that when I'm with you. I just go nuts when I touch you."

"I go nuts, too," she whispered back, and her face colored even more as she looked at his mouth and re-called the havoc it could create suckling at her breast. She caught her breath just with the memory of how it had felt.

"Oh, this won't do," Mikey said, and shifted uncomfortably. "We'd better not think too much about last night. Especially in a roomful of people."

She laughed softly.

He laughed, too.

"What sweet memories we're making, honey," he murmured as he forced himself to go back to his roast beef. "And we'll make plenty more, I promise you."

"You still have your shadow, I see," she replied under her breath, glancing out the front window at the black sedan parked there.

"They're being careful. After all, one guy almost got by them." He made a face. "It makes me wish I'd made fewer enemies along the way. This isn't the first time I've had somebody come after me over territory."

She was looking at him with open curiosity.

"What is it?" he asked.

"Nothing much. Just… Well, there's a coin-shaped depression in your back," she began. "I felt it last night."

"Noticed, did you?" He wasn't offended. He just smiled. "Yeah, I caught a bullet there when I was overseas in the Middle East. Punctured my lung and almost killed me, but I survived."

"I'm so glad you did," she said demurely, and she was unspeakably grateful that it had happened in a combat zone and not as a result of conflict with gangsters. He spoke of that world as if he knew it very well. Certainly he had to, if he was mixed up with a Mafia don whom he was protecting. It made her just a little uneasy. She didn't know much about organized crime. What she'd seen in movies and read in books was unlikely to be a mirror of the real thing. That word Mikey had used, *omertà*, she'd seen it in print somewhere. She couldn't recall where. She was going to do a search on Google when she got home that night, just to see if she could find the connection. No need to tell Mikey. She looked at him with hungry eyes that she couldn't help. He was becoming the most important thing in her life.

But what if Jessie was right? Mikey was rich and sophisticated. Yes, he liked going out with her and kissing her, but that wasn't a future. She knew some gangsters married, but most of them seemed to just live together. Or so she thought. And she couldn't do that.

It would break her heart if Mikey didn't feel the same way she did. If he was only playing with her, she was going to die.

"Hey, what's wrong?" he asked. "You look tragic."

She forced a smile. "It's been a long morning, that's all," she said brightly. "Lots of people breaking the law. Of course, that's not a bad thing for us."

"Not at all." He looked up and his dark eyes sparked.

Bernie followed his gaze and there was Jessie, just picking up a salad and coffee at the checkout. It was on a tray, which meant she wasn't leaving.

"The bubonic plague has arrived," Mikey muttered.

"Well, hi there, Bernie. I didn't know you were coming here for lunch. And Mikey, how's it going with you?" she added, almost purring.

He looked up at her with cold eyes and took a minute to answer. "We're having a private conversation, if you don't mind."

Jessie shrugged. "Well, excuse me, I'm sure," she drawled. She went to a table nearby, at the window, and put down her food.

Bernie was crestfallen. She'd hoped to have a nice quiet lunch with Mikey, but Jessie was already staring at them. Cooking up plots. Bernie was certain that the woman was searching for ways to split her from Mikey, because Mikey was rich and Jessie wanted him.

"Don't look like that," Mikey said, smiling at her. "She's trying to upset you. Don't let her."

"She really likes you," Bernie said, almost choking on the words.

"It isn't mutual."

The way he looked at her sent all her fears flying away. She smiled slowly. So did he. The rest of the world faded away until there were just the two of them.

They didn't look in Jessie's direction at all. She glared at both of them the whole time. She didn't stop even when they were walking out of the café.

"If looks could kill," Bernie said on a heavy sigh when they were back on the street.

"Why doesn't Kemp fire her?" he asked abruptly.

"I think he'd like to, but he has to have a reason that will hold up in court."

"Lawyers," he muttered.

She laughed. "You sound like one of the men we prosecuted for theft. He was sure that lawyers were all bound for a fiery end."

His hand caught hers. "I've gone my rounds with prosecutors," he mused as they walked toward her office.

"You have?" she asked, curious.

He looked down at her solemnly. "We really are going to have to have a talk," he told her. "There are things about me that you need to know."

She drew in a long breath. "There are things about me you need to know, too."

"Come over for lunch Sunday," he invited. "Paulie said Sari was going to ask you, anyway. We can walk down through the woods and talk without people watching us all the time."

"Would you be safe if we did that?" she worried. "I mean, snipers love deserted places, don't they?"

He chuckled. "The one who's watching me surely does," he pointed out.

"Oh! I forgot."

He grinned. "I'm glad. I don't want you upset. I can take care of myself, honey. I've been in worse jams than this. I'll tell you about it, Sunday." He paused and turned toward her. "You think you can live with my past. I'm not sure you can. But I'll leave the decision up to you."

"You undervalue yourself," she said, searching his dark eyes. "I said it wouldn't matter. I meant it."

He smiled and touched her cheek gently. "You think it wouldn't," he said sadly. "That may not be the case."

"You can tell me Sunday."

"And there you both are again," Jessie said from behind them.

"Yeah," Mikey said, glaring at her.

She made a face and went past them into the office, slamming the door behind her.

"Sore loser," he muttered after her.

Bernie smiled. It made her feel good that Mikey preferred her to the beautiful woman who'd just gone past them. She felt valued.

"Idiot," he whispered. "You're worth ten of a woman like that." His head jerked toward the office. "She's anybody's. She'll play up to a man for what he's got, nothing else. Women like that are after hard cash, not love."

"I don't care about money," Bernie said.

"I know that. It's one of your best traits, and you've got a lot of them."

"Me?" she laughed. "I'm just ordinary." She drew in

a breath. "You know, I have flares in the winter," she began. "I spend a lot of time in bed…"

He put his forefinger over her lips. "That won't matter, either. You nursed me through one of the worst headaches I've ever had. If you get down, I'll take care of you," he added huskily.

Tears stung her eyes. She lowered them to his broad chest.

"Don't cry," he whispered. "People will think I'm being mean to you."

She laughed. "Sorry. It's just that I've never really had anybody take care of me, not since my father died."

"I don't want to be your dad," he pointed out. He frowned. "You know, Bernie, I'm a lot older than you."

"Bosh," she mused, looking up into his face. "You'll never be old. Not to me."

His breath caught in his throat. He looked around. Cars everywhere. People on the sidewalks. Her boss, coming toward them.

"Oh, damn," he said under his breath.

Her eyebrows arched. "What?"

"Bernie, I want to kiss you so badly that it hurts and we're surrounded by people. Damned people!"

She grinned up at him. "There's Sunday," she teased.

He pursed his lips. His dark eyes twinkled. "Yeah. There's Sunday."

"Lunchtime's almost over, Bernie," Kemp teased as he came up beside them. "Back to boring routine."

"It's never boring, Mr. Kemp," she said, and meant it. "Tedious and maddening, but never boring!"

He grinned, nodded to Mikey, and went inside the building.

"I'd better go in. When?" she asked. "Sunday, I mean."

"About eleven suit you?"

She nodded. "That sounds great."

"I won't see you for a couple of days," he said. "I've got some people to see up in San Antonio. Santi and I have a room reserved for it. But I'll be here to pick you up Sunday, okay? And tell Mrs. Brown not to rent out my room while I'm gone!"

"I will, but she never would. She thinks you're terrific. So do the other boarders." She lowered her eyes to his chest. "So do I."

He bent and brushed a kiss over her forehead. "I think you're terrific, too, kid," he whispered. "Now go to work before I wrestle you down in the grass over there and do what I'm aching to do!"

Her breath caught. "It's in public view!"

"So would we be, and they'd be snapping pictures for the local paper, too," he assured her. "See you Sunday, honey. Be careful. Don't go out at night for any reason at all. You're being watched, but don't take chances. I couldn't live if anything happened to you." He touched her cheek and walked away before she could get the words out that she'd wanted to say.

No matter, she told herself. She could recite them on Sunday.

Jessie was wary of Sari and Glory, so she kept her hot words to herself. But just before quitting time, she stopped by Bernie when the other women were getting their coats and leaned close.

"You think he's hooked? You just wait," she threatened softly. "There's never been a man I couldn't get!"

And before Bernie could say a word, she was out the door and gone.

* * *

Bernie was agonizing over what she was going to have to tell Mikey on Sunday. She knew that he had a past, and she was sure she could live with whatever it was. But she wasn't so sure that he could live, not only with her disability issues, but with what had happened in her family. It was so horrible that she never spoke of it. Only a few people in Jacobsville knew. Her father was a good man, a kind man, who was wonderful to his daughter. But her grandfather had been a different story. He'd been notorious, in fact, and the story was so gruesome that it was fodder for the tabloids for the better part of a month.

None of that was Bernie's fault. She'd only been involved because he was part of her family, but it stung just the same. She felt dirty because of it. There had been survivors who were outraged. Her father had been targeted by one. Only the quick arrival of the sheriff's department had saved Bernie and her dad, because the man had been armed. She couldn't even blame him. The grief must have been horrible. But her father was no more responsible for it than Bernie was. It was just that the survivors couldn't get to the people responsible, so they went after the people who were left.

That had eventually blown over. Tempers cooled, people went back to church and remembered that part of their religious faith was the very difficult tenet of forgiveness for even the most horrible crimes. Bernie and her dad moved from Floresville back to Jacobsville, and distance helped. But that didn't mean that Bernie might not be a target in the future from some other relative who was frustrated by not having a means of vengeance.

She'd have to tell Mikey that. She'd also have to make him understand about her illness. There was no cure for rheumatoid arthritis. There were many treatments, most of which worked, but the most useful were beyond Bernie's pocket. Even with them, she would still have flares, days when she couldn't work at all. And because the drugs required worked at lowering her immune system to fight the RA, she was more disposed to illness than healthy people. She had bad lungs and often had respiratory infections. Mikey had to understand that just an occasional flare was the least of her health issues.

If he still wanted her after all that, well, it would make him a man in a million. Her family's notoriety was going to make things more complicated.

But it might work out, she told herself. They might actually be able to make it work, if they could keep Jessie at bay. She was an odd sort of person, very narcissistic and pretty horrible. She didn't feel compassion and she had an acid tongue. What in the world was she doing in a small town like Jacobsville when she was obviously more suited to big cities? It was a puzzle.

There was a cold rain on Friday afternoon just as Bernie was getting ready to go home. She hadn't worn a raincoat or brought an umbrella, and it was pouring outside. Even in south Texas, it could get pretty cold in autumn.

"Let me drop you off at your boardinghouse, Bernie," Sari offered. "You'll get soaked going home and you'll be sick."

"Yes, you have to stay well or Mikey won't be able to take you anyplace, will he, sweetie?" Jessie purred as she passed them outside, her umbrella raised.

"One day," Sari said with venom, and glared at the other woman.

Jessie made a harrumphing sound in her throat and

went on down the street to where her car was parked. Strangely, it was an expensive foreign one. How could she afford that on what she made as a stenographer and receptionist for the local DA, Sari wondered.

"You should have a car," Sari chided gently as the limousine driver started off down the street with his two passengers in back.

"They break down," Bernie said with a smile. "I can't afford to run one. And I can mostly walk to work, except when I'm having flares. Then I get a cab."

"You can always ride with me," Sari said. "Anytime you need to."

"Thanks," Bernie said. "But I do okay."

Sari laughed and shook her head. "Honestly, you're the hardest person to do anything for."

"I guess so. Sorry."

"It's not a bad trait. Jessie would do anything for someone with money," she added harshly. "That woman makes my blood boil."

"Mikey can't stand her," Bernie said with a wicked little smile.

Sari laughed. "So he said. I guess he's seen that sort so much in his life that he hasn't got any interest in them anymore."

"He said that he was a bad man," Bernie mentioned.

"Some bad, some good, like all of us."

Bernie looked at her warmly. "I told him it wouldn't matter, whatever he'd done."

"That's like you," Sari replied. She studied the other woman quietly. "He'll tell you the truth. I know about it from Paul. He and Mikey both had hard lives as children. They grew up with people who weren't good role models. Mikey went the wrong way. I think he's trying to leave that behind him now. But…" She hesitated, noticing how Bernie hung on every word. "But he'll have to tell you the rest. And you'll have to make a choice." She paused. She didn't want to say it. "That choice may be harder than you think right now."

Bernie drew in a long breath. "It's too late for choices," she said softly. "He's my whole world, Sari. He's…everything."

Sari smiled. "Paul is mine. I understand. It's just… Well, Mikey will explain it to you," she finished.

Bernie studied her hands, poised on her purse in her lap. "He's mixed up somehow with organized crime, I think," she said without noting Sari's sudden alertness. "I watched *The Godfather*, so I sort of know about that stuff."

She didn't know anything, not a thing, about the harshness and the blood and the savagery with which Mikey's associates did and could act. Sari didn't want to enlighten her, though. It was going to be up to Mikey. If Bernie truly loved him, they'd find a way to make it work.

"Paul says he's never seen Mikey so happy," Sari said, instead of voicing her thoughts.

Bernie beamed. "I've never been so happy, not in all my life." She looked at Sari. "You know all about my family, about what happened. Will Mikey be able to handle it? I mean, there are people who went after Daddy, when he was alive, because of what my grandfather did."

"Nobody's ever come after you, and nobody ever will. If they even try, we'll sic Mr. Kemp on them. He'll handle it. Okay?"

Bernie let out the breath she'd been holding. "Okay."

"And Mikey's the last person who'll blame you for something someone in your family did," she added.

"I was notorious for a while," Bernie said hesitantly.

"Only for a while, and never after you moved here with your dad," Sari added.

"I suppose so." She lowered her face. "I don't want Mikey to be ashamed of me."

"As if that would ever happen! Honestly, Bernie!" she laughed. "He's crazy about you. It won't matter."

Bernie smiled. "Okay."

"And the past doesn't matter. For either one of you."

"If I stay sick all the time, it may," Bernie voiced her other fear. "I've got a weak immune system already, and the medicines I have to take for RA make it even weaker. I get sick a lot, especially in cold weather."

"It won't matter," she said firmly. "Besides, Mikey could afford those outrageously expensive medicines that they think might help you," she added with a smile.

"As if I'd let him do that," Bernie began.

"Under certain circumstances, you would," Sari drawled, and laughed at the expression on her coworker's face. "Life is sweet. You're just finding that out."

"It's never been sweeter, in fact."

"So live one day at a time," Sari counseled, "and let tomorrow take care of itself."

"That sounds easy. It's not."

"Nothing is easy. But we get by. Right?"

"Right."

"And if Jessie makes one more snide remark about how unhealthy you are, I'm going to encourage Olivia to pour coffee on her head!"

"Oh, don't suggest that—Olivia would do it on a dare," Bernie laughed uproariously.

"I heard about the coffee incident after I got back from vacation this summer," Sari said mischievously. "Nobody had made coffee. Agent Murdock came to see the boss on a case, and he made coffee just for himself and turned off the pot. Olivia went to get herself a cup. It was barely lukewarm by then, but she thought she'd drink it anyway. She took a sip, spat it out, glared at Murdock, who was flushed by then, and she poured the whole carafe right over his head and his suit. Lucky it wasn't hot!"

"Mr. Kemp came out of his office to usher Agent Murdock in," Bernie recalled, laughing so hard she almost choked. "And when he saw Olivia with the empty pot and the full cup in Agent Murdock's hand, he put his hand over his mouth and went right back into his office and closed the door. I swear, he laughed for five minutes."

"What did Agent Murdock do?"

Bernie whistled. "He got up, in the ruins of his suit, stared at Olivia for a minute, and then poured the contents of his own coffee cup over her head."

"And?" Sari prompted.

"He walked out the door in a huff and she went home to change. We're still laughing about it. Except that when Agent Murdock comes through the door, they both pretend that the other one is invisible. It makes things interesting."

Sari just grinned.

Chapter Ten

Sunday morning, Mikey came by to pick up Bernie at Mrs. Brown's boardinghouse. He was preoccupied at first, frowning.

"What's wrong?" she asked gently. "Can I help?"

He turned toward her and smiled slowly, oblivious to Santi's quick and amused glance in the rearview mirror from the front seat. "There's that sweet compassion that I've hardly had in my whole life," he said. "You really are one in a million, kid."

She flushed. "So are you. But can I help?"

"You can listen, when we get to Paulie's house," he said. He glanced in the front seat. "And you can have the day off until I call you to take us home, Santi," he added with a grin. "You might go take in a movie."

"Not a bad idea, boss," Santi said with a big smile. "Thanks!"

He shrugged. "I'm not a bad guy."

Santi made a sarcastic noise, but Mikey ignored him. They got out at the front door of Paul's house, and Santi raised a hand and waved as he drove off.

Mikey held Bernie's hand tight in his and put his finger on the doorbell.

Before he could push it, the door opened. Sari and Paul welcomed them in.

"We have lunch," Sari announced. "Mandy made a macaroni and ginger and chicken salad, and sliced some fruit to go with it."

"That sounds wonderful," Bernie said.

"It does. Nobody cooks like Mandy," Mikey said.

"I heard that," Mandy called from the kitchen. "Come on in. I've almost got everything on the table."

She did. The place settings were immaculate, like the white linen napkins. Mikey pulled out a chair for Bernie and then one for himself.

Mandy came back in with a basket of blueberry muffins and put them on the table. "Who wants coffee?"

Every hand went up.

Mandy laughed. "That's what I figured," she mused. "Coming right up."

Bernie was a little self-conscious at first. She wasn't used to mansions and elaborate dining room place settings, and this was her first real meal with the Fiores. But the conversation and Mikey's attention thawed her out in no time at all.

"This is delicious," Bernie commented as she savored a bite of the chicken dish.

"We like it as a light meal," Sari said. "Neither of us likes anything heavy in the middle of the day. Or in the evening, for that matter."

"No wonder you're both so slender," Bernie teased.

"People in law enforcement have to be fast," Paul chuckled. "I had to run down a counterfeiter just last week," he added. "If I overeat, I lose my edge."

Mikey grinned at him. "Not likely," he commented. "You do okay, cousin."

"Sari says Jessie is giving you two a hard time," Paul noted.

Mikey's lip pulled down. "She's persistent, I'll give her that. But she has the appeal of a skunk on acid. Know what I mean?"

Paul laughed. "I do."

"Besides," Mikey said, his eyes on Bernie, "I have other interests."

Bernie beamed and almost spilled her coffee. Her heart was going so fast that it shook her blouse. Mikey noticed that and flashed her a wicked smile.

After lunch, Mikey took Bernie's hand and led her down the wooded path that eventually ended at the stables where the Grayling racehorses lived in luxury.

"I love it here," Bernie said, looking around at the leafless trees next to tall fir trees that were still green. "Fir trees are awesome."

"Yeah, they are," he agreed. "Out west, we've got Colorado blue spruce that go right up into the sky."

"Are they really blue, or is that just a description that stuck?"

"They're really blue," he replied. He stopped walking and turned to her. "Next time I go to Vegas, you can come with me. We'll go by way of Wyoming and have a look at Yellowstone and Old Faithful. It's a sight you'll never forget."

She hesitated.

He noticed that. "I have plans," he said softly. "First,

I have to take the heat off Tony and get him out of the mess he's in. He's family, you see?" he asked, scowling. "It's loyalty. You take a solemn vow. You fulfill it. If you don't, there are terrible penalties. Nobody ever sells out anybody in his family. If he does, the penalty is unspeakable." He didn't add that he'd participated in such retribution. He had to confess as much as he could to her, but there were things he had to keep to himself.

She looked up at him with her heart in her eyes. "It won't matter," she said stubbornly.

He touched her cheek with the tips of his fingers. "Bernie, I've been involved with the mob since I was old enough to carry a piece. I've done things…" He hesitated. It had never really bothered him before. Now it was hard to reconcile what he'd done with what he wanted to do now. He drew in a breath. "You've watched *The Godfather* movies, haven't you?"

"Oh, yes. They're great movies," she said.

"You remember about the horse's head being in bed with the producer who wouldn't give the outfit's singer a job?"

She nodded.

"And the way Michael's older brother was murdered, a hit organized by a rival family?"

She felt cold chills down her spine. "Yes," she said huskily. "I remember that, too."

"Well, that was glossed-over stuff," he said flatly. "Family hits are just plain gore. You don't know what happened to Paulie, do you?"

She just shook her head.

"He had a wife and a little girl, before he came down here to work for old man Grayling as a security expert," he said. "Paulie was the only person in our whole family who went straight. He worked with the FBI in Jersey, and he shut down one of the minor crime bosses. He felt great about it. But when he went home that night, his wife and his little girl had been done with a shotgun."

Bernie put a hand to her mouth. "Oh, the poor man!" she exclaimed, shocked.

"He took years getting over it," he said. "Eventually, he fell in love with Sari, but he got cold feet and made some excuse to quit. It was three years before he came back. In the meantime, Sari's father had beaten the girls to within an inch of their lives. Sari blamed Paul and had nothing to do with him when he worked out of the FBI office in San Antonio. But she was in a hurricane down in the Bahamas. Paul thought she was dead, but he and Mandy went to bring her home. She turned up alive and they were married the same week. Paulie never got over losing his family, though. He blamed himself for pushing the crime boss too hard and going after his whole organization."

"What happened to the man who killed his first family?" she asked.

His face grew hard. "I knew a guy who was inside," he said shortly. "I took care of it."

She felt the blood drain out of her face. "You…?"

"I took care of it," he repeated quietly. "Yes. I have that kind of power. I worked my way up through the organization for years, to get to where I am now. I own one of the biggest casinos in Vegas and I'm filthy rich. I was arrested once on a murder charge, but I had witnesses swear I was nowhere near the scene of the crime. They had no real evidence, so they dropped the case."

She moved to a big oak tree and leaned back against it. This was news she hadn't anticipated, and it was shocking. She looked up into cold dark eyes.

"I'm so sorry, honey. I didn't want to have to confess how bad a man I am. But you had to know," he said. Inside, he was churning like storm clouds. He hadn't wanted to tell her these things, but he couldn't offer her a future without making her aware of the past. "There's more," he told her. "A lot more. But this is enough for now."

Her lips parted on a long breath. She looked at him helplessly. She loved him. He was a criminal. He would probably never give up that life. He'd told her graphically what the family he belonged to would do if they were betrayed.

"Omertà," she whispered heavily.

He moved closer. "Yeah. Omertà," he replied. "It's the code we live by. Or die by, if we betray anybody in our family. They don't just kill you. They kill everybody you love. It's like erasing your whole life."

She leaned her head back against the hard bark of the tree and just looked at him. She didn't understand what he wanted from her, why he was telling her something so personal.

"So that's the secret I keep," he said. "It's bad. It's horrible. But it's a part of my life that you have to understand if we go forward together. So. What secrets are you keeping?" he added in a tender voice.

She took a deep breath. "My grandfather owned a little store over in Floresville. He and my grandmother ran it. We noticed that Granddaddy was forgetful, and sometimes he had rages, when he just went wild over something he saw on television, or something a politician said. We overlooked it because we thought it was just the product of normal aging."

He moved closer. "But it wasn't?"

"It wasn't. One day, he was listening to what a politician said about the economy and new regulations that were going to go into effect. Granddaddy started yelling that those people needed to be killed, slaughtered."

She hesitated, then plowed ahead without looking at him. "Maybe he would have calmed down, but the mayor was in his store buying some hardware, and he and Granddaddy got into an argument about politics. They were completely opposite in their views. The mayor tried to calm my grandfather down, and he thought he had. My grandmother chided him for being so violent over just stupid politics. She said he needed to lie down for a while. Granddaddy didn't argue with her. He went out from behind the counter without a word. My grandmother was relieved, she thought he was over his anger. Not five minutes later, he came back into the front of the store with an automatic pistol." She swallowed hard. "He killed my grandmother and the mayor, and then he turned the gun on three customers and killed them, too. The survivors screamed and ran out of the store. A local policeman heard the screams and went into the store with his pistol drawn. Granddaddy shot him dead the minute he walked into the store. The police called in the SWAT team from San Antonio. Granddaddy was holed up in the store, and he wouldn't come out and give up his gun." She sighed. "Long story short, the SWAT team went in and shot my grandfather. He died on the way to the hospital. My mother was so ashamed and sick at what her father had done, so grieved at the loss of her mother and the forthcoming fury of the townspeople, that she locked herself in the bathroom and slashed her own throat with a razor blade. We thought she was taking a bath." Her eyes closed. "By the time we realized something was wrong and Daddy got the door open, it was much too late. She died."

"Oh, God," he said. "You poor kid!"

She bit her lower lip. "Daddy sold the house and moved us here. It was horrible, the aftermath. We were hated by so many people who lost loved ones that day. I didn't blame them, you know, but Daddy and I had nothing to do with what happened. Nothing at all."

He moved forward and pulled her into his arms, folding her close, rocking her while she cried. "And I thought I'd had a hard life," he whispered at her ear. "Baby, I wish I'd known you then. Nobody would ever have hurt you!"

She pressed close, resting her wet cheek over his heart. "I thought you might not want anything else to do with me when you knew about what happened."

"Dopey girl," he murmured, and laughed softly. "I'm hooked. Haven't you noticed? Who do I hang around with all the time? Who do I take to movies and into rooms where we do naughty things together?"

She laughed through her tears. "Me, I guess."

"You." He drew in a long, slow breath. His arms tightened. "I pledged allegiance to Tony. I have to fulfill my vows. I can't let him die, whatever I have to do to save him."

"Family is more important than your own life, isn't it?"

"Yes." His breath was warm at her ear. "I'm mixed up in this in a bad way. I can't make commitments right now. But when it's over, when I clear Tony…"

She didn't move. Her eyes closed. "I told you," she whispered. "I meant it. It won't matter."

"God!" His mouth moved over hers and he kissed her with subdued passion, with pure hunger. He hadn't imagined that she could live with the things he'd done, that she could still want him after she knew them. She was an extraordinary woman. "Bernie," he said unsteadily, "you're the very breath in my body!"

She couldn't even find words to express what she felt, so she kissed him with her whole heart, her arms stealing up around his neck, her mouth answering his with the same hungry passion that he was showing her.

He groaned and his hands ran up and down her sides, his thumbs pressing under her breasts.

"Ahem."

Mikey lifted his head and stared at Bernie blankly. "What did you say?"

"I didn't say anything," she began.

"Ahem." It came again. Mikey frowned and felt around his lapel. There was a device that had been placed there in San Antonio. He glowered at it.

"Yes?" Mikey asked abruptly.

"I have a bead on you and quite frankly if you don't break that up, I'm going to have to leave you defenseless and go get several drinks of hard liquor."

Mikey's teeth ground together. "Damn it, Billings," he muttered.

"A lot of drinks," Billings continued. "Maybe a whole damned fifth. It's been a long dry spell and I have to watch you. Get it? Watch you."

Mikey drew a long breath and stared at Bernie with amused regret. "Okay. We'll go look at the horses."

"Good idea. Blakely's in there. You can drive him nuts!" There was a click and the device went silent.

Bernie was flushed and embarrassed.

"Hey," Mikey said, pushing back the unruly long, blond hair from her face. "Billings is right. This isn't the time or place."

"Did he hear all we said?" she worried.

"Not likely. He doesn't eavesdrop. I guess we were

getting pretty heated, huh?" He laughed. "Okay. Let's behave." He caught her fingers and entangled them with his. "Let's go look at the pretty horses."

She laughed. Life was sweet. He didn't mind her past. She didn't mind his. This was a relationship with a future. She'd never been so certain of anything.

They wandered through the stables. There was a man in charge of the thoroughbreds. He explained them to Bernie.

"They're descended from three stallions imported into England in the seventeenth and eighteenth centuries, the beginning of their line. We won the Kentucky Derby with this fellow," he said, smiling as he approached the big stall where the racehorse lived. "He has his own pasture and he's at stud. We get fabulous amounts of money from his colts. He's a grand old fellow."

Bernie looked at him with awe. He was grand, elegant and handsome, and he knew it, too. "He's gorgeous," she said.

The stable manager chuckled. "We think so, too. He has a colt that was born just two months ago. It's down here."

He led them down the paved aisle to another stall, where a handsome young thoroughbred was playing with a big ball.

"Horses play?" Bernie exclaimed.

The manager laughed. "Of course. They're like puppies or toddlers at this age. When they hit adolescence, or the horse equivalent, that's when the problems start. Right now, they're just children and it's a whole new world for them."

Bernie just watched the colt play, fascinated. "I've

never been around horses much," she confessed. "We had a small ranch in Floresville where my people had a few head of beef cattle. There were a few horses for the cowboys, but I never rode one. I was afraid of them."

"Never let a horse know that," the manager told her. "They'll take advantage."

"I'm not likely to be put on a horse anytime soon," she assured him.

"If you ever did want to ride, we have a fifteen-year-old gelding, very gentle, who would be perfect for you. If you ever did," he added.

Mikey chuckled and pressed her fingers with his. "There may come a day," he said with a gentle smile at Bernie, who returned it.

"There may," she said.

They went back to the house.

"You're back soon," Sari commented.

"Yeah," Mikey said with a rueful smile. "Billings is a wet blanket."

"Chet Billings? You saw him?" she asked.

"No. We heard him. He's got this device on me," he added, indicating the electronic thing on his lapel.

"Oh. He talked to you?"

"He threatened to get drunk is what he did." Mikey looked at Bernie and sighed. "I guess there's no real privacy left on earth."

"Yes, there is. The conservatory is very nice, very quiet and it has a door. However," she added mischievously, "not being stupid, I'll call you when supper is ready and I'll probably open the door to do it."

Mikey sighed. "Speak loudly, okay?" he teased.

Sari laughed. "Very loudly." She gave them a knowing look and went back into the kitchen, where she and

Mandy were sharing coffee. "Do you want coffee?" she called over her shoulder.

"Later," Mikey said. "When supper's ready. Thanks, Sari," he added.

"I wasn't always married," Sari replied, and grinned.

Mikey took off the lapel pen, put it on a table in the hall and drew Bernie into the room with him. He closed the door behind him and, as an afterthought, locked it.

"Just so you know," he said as he pulled her gently into his arms, "we're big on innocence. Some people might call us reactionary, but we respect our women and we don't dishonor them. You get what I mean?"

He was telling her that he wouldn't let it go too far. She smiled. "I guess you know all about me."

His mouth brushed hers. "I know that you're an innocent, Bernie," he whispered. "It excites me and maddens me, all at once."

"Maddens you?"

"Obstacles are frustrating," he mused. He kissed her with slow, hungry brushes of his mouth, feeling hers follow it helplessly. "But we'll muddle through. When things get too hot, and they might, all you have to do is remind me that I promised not to let things go too far."

She laughed. "Okay."

He smiled as he kissed her again. "You make me hungry for things I never wanted before," he murmured as he maneuvered her onto the cushy sofa and came down beside her. "A home, a family, roots," he whispered. He had her blouse off and her bra unsnapped in seconds. "Belonging," he murmured as his mouth opened over her taut nipple and suddenly suckled her, hard.

She came right off the sofa, a tiny, shocked cry pulsing out of her throat, a sound she'd never heard from it before.

"Shh," he whispered gruffly. "They'll hear."

She bit her lower lip and pulled his head closer, her fingers spearing through his thick, wavy black hair as his mouth made magic on her body.

"Glory!" she moaned. "Mikey, do it harder," she whispered frantically. "Harder!"

"I'll hurt you," he groaned.

"No. You won't. Please...!"

He took all of her firm breast into his mouth and his tongue worked on the nipple until she was writhing wildly under the sudden heavy press of his body.

One big hand was under her hip, grinding her against the growing hardness of him, letting her feel his need. It was desperate.

She felt guilty. She was inciting him, and they couldn't be intimate. She remembered suddenly what he'd told her about heavy petting, that he could have the clothes out of the way and be inside her in less time than it would take to react.

She thought about feeling him inside her, and she shivered with the sudden need.

Her nails bit into the back of his head as she held it closer, arching so that he could feed more easily on her breast. She shivered rhythmically as he suckled her, harder and harder. All at once she arched and sobbed and felt a shaft of pleasure pierce her that was beyond anything she'd ever dreamed. She convulsed, shuddered, flew up into the clouds and exploded.

Then she cried, embarrassed. He cuddled her close, denying his starved body the release it begged for. "It's all right," he whispered. "It's natural, baby. It's all right."

"It really is? Natural, I mean?" she whispered brokenly.

He laughed softly. "That only happens to one woman in a hundred," he said. "Maybe one in a thousand. I've never seen it happen to a woman I was with." His mouth brushed over hers. "God, what a thrill it was! You've never felt it, have you?"

"Not...until now," she managed.

He drew in a rough breath. "I'm better than I thought I was," he teased.

She laughed. "You're better than I thought you were, and that's saying something."

He lifted his head and looked down at her bare breasts. "You know that you belong to me, don't you?" he asked, and met her eyes with his. They were solemn. "You're mine, Bernie."

She melted into the sofa under the hard, sweet pressure of his body. "Yes. I know it."

He moved over her, his body pressing her down. He fought his shirt out of the way so that his muscular hair-roughened chest was rubbing against her bare breasts. He shivered.

She did, too. "If you want to," she said unsteadily, "I will."

"Right here?" he asked huskily.

"Right here."

"You don't know how much I want to," he bit off.

She moved her hips just a tiny bit. "Oh, yes, I do," she said, feeling him swell even more.

"Baby," he whispered. He moved between her legs and pushed up, so that he was intimately pressed against the heart of her.

She sobbed, because it was beyond anything she'd felt before. Her legs moved apart, inviting him.

"It would have to be quick," he said gruffly. "Very quick. And it will probably hurt."

"I don't...care," she said unsteadily.

He kissed her softly, and his hand went under the band of her slacks, under her briefs. She caught his wrist, embarrassed.

He lifted his head. "You have to let me do this," he whispered, his voice shaken. "I have to know how careful I need to be with you. Okay?"

She bit her lip. "I've never..."

"I know that. But you belong to me."

She let her body relax, let the hardness of him fit against her so that it was heaven to feel. "Yes," she said, her voice tender, her eyes wide and rapt on his taut face.

His hand smoothed over her belly and he thought of a baby who would look like her or like himself. He had something to use, but he didn't want to use it. And he didn't want to take her here in a rush, the way he'd taken women in his youth. She would need time, lots of time, and he couldn't give it to her if they went too far.

His fingers moved down. She hesitated and tightened as he suddenly began to probe where she was most a woman. She bit her lip hard enough to draw blood as he explored her intimately. Even loving him as she did, it was hard to give up control to another person.

He whispered, almost groaning as he drew his fingers back and smoothed them over her stomach, "It will hurt like hell, and I'm not sure I could even get through the barrier, you understand?"

"Oh!" She winced.

"Sorry." He rolled over onto his side and pulled her into his arms, grinding her breasts into his chest. "No, I'm sorry. I never meant to take it this far." His arms contracted. "God, Bernie, I want to get you pregnant so badly...!"

He kissed her shocked mouth and groaned again as he pushed her hips closer to his. "I want you. I want to go inside you, so deep, so hard, that you'll shoot up like a rocket!"

She flushed under the pressure of his hard mouth, moaning as she felt him move her rhythmically against his hips. "I'm so sorry..."

He managed a husky laugh. "Think of it as a chastity belt. It will keep me in line until we can make things legal."

She hid her face against his throat. Make it legal. Could he mean that he wanted to marry her? She was so entranced that she didn't even hear footsteps in the hall.

Neither did Mikey, who was kissing her as if he couldn't manage to stop.

The hard, insistent knock on the door and the rattling of the locked doorknob broke them apart.

"Supper!" Sari called.

Mikey laughed. "Okay! We'll be right there."

"I have a master key, you know. It fits all the locks," Sari threatened.

Bernie went beet-red. Mikey just chuckled. "We're behaving, starting right now!"

There was a laugh outside the door. "Fair warning. Five minutes and I unlock the door."

"Got it!" Mikey called.

Footsteps retreated.

Mikey took one long, last look at Bernie's half-nude body and groaned. "I hate dressing you," he muttered, as he refastened her bra and pulled her blouse down.

"I hate dressing you, too," she teased as she buttoned his shirt again. "I love the way you look undressed."

"Yeah. I feel exactly the same way about you."

"You're not upset by what I told you?" she asked, worried.

He cocked his head and stared at her. "I've done things almost as bad as your grandfather," he said flatly. "I can't sit in judgment on somebody else. Not my business. But now that you know what my business is," he added quietly, "you have to decide if you can live with it. There's no way I'll give it up. I can't. It's for life."

She was beginning to realize that even though he ran an honest gaming hotel in Las Vegas, he was firmly entrenched with a group that routinely broke the law. He could go to prison in certain circumstances. She'd have to be in the company of people who thought of crime as a way of life, an occupation. She'd be the outsider. Would the women in his organization hate her? And what about the women he'd had before her? Would they be around? Would they be like Jessie and make her life miserable?

"Deep thoughts, huh?" he asked quietly.

"Very deep." She drew in a breath. "Mikey, I'm not like you. I don't even jaywalk. My great-grandfather was a United States Marshal. I have a cousin who's a Texas Ranger. Law enforcement runs through my whole family."

"I see," he said heavily. "You don't think you could handle it."

"No!" She went close to him. "I'd be the outsider. The freak. They wouldn't accept me."

"Baloney," he mused. He smiled as he tangled his fingers in her hair. "You have no idea how much they'd accept you. They'd go places with you, protect you if you needed protection. They'd sit with you when you were sick, when you have flares. It's another whole world, baby. One you've never seen. It's violent, yes. But the people are just like anybody else. The women are a close-knit group, because there's always some danger involved that the men have to handle." He winced at her expression. "I don't know any other way of life, Bernie," he concluded. "I can't change what I am, what I do." He shrugged. "I don't want to. If that's selfish, I'm selfish."

She pressed herself close to him, sliding her arms around him. "I can try," she whispered.

His heart jumped. It lifted as if a dark cloud had dissipated in the sunlight. His arms tightened around her. "That's all I ask," he said. "That's all I want."

She smiled and closed her eyes.

There was a click and the door opened. Sari looked in with pursed lips when they turned toward her. She chuckled. "I warned you," she said, lifting the key to show them. "Supper."

Mikey grinned. "We're right behind you."

"Yes," Bernie agreed.

Mikey linked her fingers with his and the two of them looked, to Sari, like two halves of a whole. She had no doubt that there would be a wedding in the future.

Bernie clung to his hand and smiled. She looked up at Mikey with wonder, with adoration.

He saw that look and it made him feel a foot taller. His fingers contracted gently around hers. She tightened her own grip. She'd never known such wonder, such joy. It spilled out around her like sunshine. She smiled. So did Mikey. They both knew where this was leading, now more than ever.

Chapter Eleven

Supper was as uproarious as lunch had been. Paul had a dozen stories of things that had happened to him in the course of his duties. Foremost among those stories was the one he'd heard from Sari about agent Murdock. He recited it for Mikey and chuckled at his cousin's amusement.

"I like Olivia," Mikey said. "She seems very nice."

"She is," Bernie agreed. "Mr. Kemp hired her so that there would be another paralegal in the office on the days I can't work," she added, and felt uncomfortable talking about her limitations.

"You do very well, considering your obstacles," Sari told her. "We don't think of you as handicapped, you know," she added. "You have a disability. Lots of people have them. Look at poor Glory. She had dangerously high blood pressure and a light heart attack. But she overcame that to work here, where she and her husband and little boy live."

"I'd love a little boy," Mikey said, glancing at Bernie, who flushed. "Or a little girl. I'll bet little girls are sweet."

Bernie laughed. "I was never sweet," she teased. "I got into so much trouble when I was small. The worst time was when I climbed into the corncrib and couldn't get out, and a king snake decided to come in with me. He was huge. Over six feet long. I was terrified. But he didn't strike at me or even threaten me. He just stretched out on the corn and looked at me."

"Probably hunting rodents," Sari remarked. "They love corn."

"Probably," Bernie agreed. "All in all, he was a very polite snake. He didn't even seem bothered when Daddy came to find me and lifted me out of the corncrib."

"He might also have just eaten a few rats and was feeling lazy," Paul chuckled.

"Equally possible," Bernie laughed.

"Well, I've got briefs to read," Sari said.

"And I've got cases to work," Paul added as they both got to their feet. "You two can watch movies or just sit in the conservatory and watch the plants grow. You're both always welcome. Anytime."

"Thanks, Paul," Bernie said.

Mikey echoed the sentiment.

They were left with Mandy, who started to clear away the dishes. "You two want coffee?" she asked with a warm smile.

"Not for me," Mikey said. "I don't sleep good. It keeps me awake."

"Me, too," Bernie said.

Mikey stood up and helped Bernie out of her chair. "I think we'll go watch Sari's plants grow for a while, if you don't mind."

"Help yourselves," she said with a knowing grin.

Mikey led Bernie into the conservatory and locked the door.

"Nobody's likely to try it, but who knows?" Mikey teased. He took Bernie into his arms and kissed her hungrily. "Dessert," he whispered. "Sweeter than cake."

"Sweeter than honey," she agreed on a moan.

He picked her up and sat down with her in his lap, kissing her all the while.

She didn't protest his hands under her blouse. He was so familiar to her now, so dear, that she welcomed anything he did.

He knew that, and it kept him honest. He didn't want to take advantage of an attraction she couldn't help. She was very innocent. It made his head spin, that lack of sophistication. He loved it.

He eased her blouse and bra down to her waist and unbuttoned his shirt, pulling her hungrily inside it.

"Oh, glory," she choked when she felt thick, soft hair and warm muscles against her bare breasts. Her face sank into his throat while he caressed her.

"We're good together," he whispered. "Better than I dreamed. God, I want you!"

Her arms tightened around his neck. "I want you, too," she whispered back.

His hands smoothed over her hard-tipped breasts. "We've talked around it," he said after a minute. "But not any particulars." His hands moved her away and he looked at her breasts with possession and appreciation.

"You're beautiful like this, Bernie. It makes me hungry just to hold you. But this goes to my head like whiskey."

She arched backward, her body demanding, hungry, ignoring her mind's attempt to be sensible.

"This what you want, sweetheart?" he whispered, and his mouth swallowed up one small, taut breast almost whole.

She moaned and shivered.

"I thought so." His voice was rough, but his mouth was tender as he worked at the hard nipple slowly, tenderly, with a growing suction that very soon made her go stiff and then suddenly burst with pleasure that made her whole body convulse in his arms.

"God, I love this," he groaned against her breast. "I love that I can make you go off like a rocket when I suckle you!"

Her nails dug into him. It was a little embarrassing, but she was too exhausted with pleasure, with satisfaction, to protest. She shivered and clung to him in the aftermath. "I never felt anything like it in my whole life," she said brokenly. "It embarrasses me…"

His arms contracted. "Don't you dare be ashamed of something so beautiful," he whispered at her ear. "No two people ever belonged to each other more than we do right this minute, Bernie."

She swallowed, hard. "Do you feel that, too?"

He chuckled and turned her just a little, so that her hips were pressed to that part of him that was male and very hard. "Do you feel this?"

"Mikey!" she protested.

"A man can't fake that, honey," he said at her ear. "It's as honest as the way you react when I put my mouth on you." He drew back and looked down at her with pure possession. "There's nobody in the world like you."

She reached up and touched his cheek. "Or like you," she said solemnly.

He bent his dark head and smoothed his mouth over her breast tenderly. He drew in a breath. "We need to talk."

"We are."

"We need to talk when we're both dressed," he said with a droll smile.

"Oh."

He put her clothes back on and buttoned his shirt. When they were calmer, he drew her onto the love seat and sat holding her hand.

"Bernie, I'm not proud of what I'm about to tell you. But there's more about me that you need to know." He drew in a breath. "My family has belonged to what's known to outsiders as La Cosa Nostra for three generations. My father died working for them. I've been with Tony Garza since I was sixteen. I don't know any other way of life."

"You mean, you work outside the law," she said very calmly.

"That's exactly what I mean." He studied her face. She was a little pale, but she wasn't trying to get away from him. "We're like normal people. We pay our taxes, go to church, work for charitable causes, all that stuff. We just earn our living in ways that aren't conventional."

"I told you that I watched *The Godfather* movies," she said.

He brushed her disheveled hair back from her face. "That was a sanitized version of what really goes on," he said after a minute. "I won't, I can't, tell you how brutal it can be. You don't ever quit. And you don't rat out your associates. There are deadly penalties for that. Remember what I told you about Paulie's family?"

She just nodded. Her eyes were sketching his hard face as if she were painting it.

"I could go to jail one day," he persisted. "I could die."

"A meteor could land on the boardinghouse and take us all out," she said matter-of-factly. "Nobody is ever guaranteed even one more day."

He just looked at her.

"I'm not Italian," she said. "Would that make me an outsider?"

He smiled slowly. "The wives come from all sorts of backgrounds," he said, and noticed her flush at the word. "Some are American. Some are Italian and Spanish, even Polish. But they have one thing in common and that's family. We all belong to each other. If you shared that life with me," he said, "you'd be part of it. You'd never be an outsider. And if anything happened, anything at all, you'd be taken care of as long as you live. That's how it works."

She bit her lower lip. She drew in a breath. "Mikey, I won't get any better," she began. "There's no cure for what I have. They can control it with medicine, although I can't afford the kind that might make it easier. But they can't stop it. Eventually, I'll end up with twisted hands and feet, and even if I can walk with a cane at first, there's a good chance that one day I'll be in a wheelchair." She said it without a plea for pity. She just stated it as a fact.

He tilted her chin up. "I can live with your limitations. Can you live with my profession?"

She just nodded. She didn't say a word. She didn't have to.

He wrapped her up in his arms and just rocked her slowly, his face in her throat. They sat that way for a long time until there was a brief tap and the sound of a key in the lock.

Sari peered around the door and burst out laughing. "And I was afraid I'd have to run for my life when I opened this door…"

Mikey and Bernie both laughed.

Mikey got up and drew her up beside him. "We were talking about the future," he said, smiling. "It looks pretty sweet."

"Pretty sweet, indeed," Bernie said with a long sigh as she looked up at him.

"I'd better get her home," Mikey said. "She has to work tomorrow."

"I know. So do I," Sari wailed.

"There, there," Bernie comforted her. "But there's always next weekend!"

They all laughed.

Mikey took her back to the boardinghouse and left her at her door with a discreet kiss on her forehead because Mrs. Brown was lurking.

"It was a lovely day. Thank you," Bernie said.

"It was one of many to come," he replied. He smiled at her with his heart in his eyes. "See you in the morning, kid. Sweet dreams."

"Oh, they'll be sweet, all right," she whispered, and then flushed.

He wrinkled his nose at her and winked.

She watched him all the way down the hall before she went back into her room and closed the door.

Work was difficult. Bernie's happiness lit her up like a Christmas tree, and it showed. Olivia teased her. But Jessie watched and smoldered. She was furious that a plain little country girl like Bernie, one who was likely to end up living on disability, had attracted a man who could buy half a county with pocket change. Mikey was sophisticated, handsome and loaded. Jessie wanted him, and she couldn't get to first base. He avoided her like the plague when he was in town.

There had to be some way she could get him out of Bernie's life so that she had a chance with him. Being rude and unpleasant didn't do any good. But if she could play one of them against the other while pretending to turn over a new leaf... Well, that was a promising idea. She began to plot ways to accomplish it.

Her first step was to stop being abrasive to the other women in the office. She toned down her bad attitude and took on her share of the work instead of avoiding it. She offered to bring coffee to Olivia and Bernie when they were swamped with paperwork, and she even brought lunch back for them once.

Everyone was surprised, even Mr. Kemp, who actually praised Jessie for her changed attitude.

Nothing had changed at all except that Jessie was playing a new game. But she smiled and did her best to look humble. She even apologized for the way she'd behaved before. It was hard being a city girl in a small Texas town, she explained to the other women. She'd always had to fight to get ahead, where she'd come from, and it was difficult to stop. But she wanted to fit in. She was going to try harder. The other women in the office, suspecting nothing, warmed to her.

And Jessie just smiled to herself. So far so good, she thought. She even lost her fear of being fired, which she couldn't afford just now. She had a job to do. So she smiled and answered the phone and stopped flirting with rich men.

Bernie mentioned the changed attitude to Mikey on one of their dates, and he laughed. Bernie, he commented, was rubbing off on the other woman. He was happy to see it. So the next time he came across Jessie in the courthouse, where he'd gone with Paul to talk to a judge, he smiled and was pleasant to her.

Several days later, there was a complication. Bernie was walking back to the boardinghouse from work, after refusing a ride from Glory, and a car ran off the road, up onto the curb, and missed her by a few feet.

It sped away while she was getting back onto her feet. She was badly shaken. She picked up her pocketbook and her cane, and stood shivering while she tried to catch her breath. Had it been a car that just lost control, or was it deliberate? She worried the question all the way home.

She'd have told Mikey, but he was out of town on business. He'd mentioned at the boardinghouse that he had to meet with one of the deputy marshals in San Antonio, but he'd be back in time for a date they'd arranged for Saturday. He and Bernie had planned a sightseeing trip to San Antonio because they had plenty of chaperones. Bernie had always wanted to go through the Alamo, but there had never been time since she'd been an adult. Now she looked forward to seeing that part of Texas history with the love of her life.

Mikey picked her up in the limo, with Santi at the wheel, just after she got off work at one o'clock on Saturday. She was wearing a beige sweater and skirt with flats and a cane that matched her outfit.

"Color coordination, huh?" Mikey teased as he helped her into the back seat and climbed in beside her.

"I like things to match," she teased.

He indicated the beige suit he was wearing with a white shirt and a brown paisley tie. "And so we do," he laughed.

She grinned. "We do, indeed."

"I wanted to see the Alamo when I was here last time, when Merrie was in trouble. But I never had the time. You Texans are pretty proud of it, aren't you?"

She nodded. "We really are."

He sighed. "I don't know much about history, even in Jersey," he commented. "Well, maybe one sort of history, but it's not told in polite company," he chuckled.

"I won't ask," she returned, smiling up at him.

"You haven't carried the cane lately, until today," he pointed out. "Having a flare?"

"Well, not really. I had a fall the other day on my way home from work."

He scowled. "A fall?"

She nodded. She bit her lower lip. She hadn't wanted to mention it. "A driver lost control of his car and it came up on the curb where I was walking. It missed me by several feet," she added.

"What sort of car?" he asked with barely concealed anger.

She blinked. "That's the thing, I really didn't have time to notice. I fell and, while I was getting up, it sped away."

"Big car, small?"

She frowned. "Medium."

"What color?"

She tried to remember what it had looked like. "I think it was dark. Not black, but not a colored car, like blue or red or anything."

He looked troubled. He pulled out his cell phone and texted a message to someone. She couldn't tell who.

"I don't think it was deliberate, Mikey," she added softly. "I mean, it didn't come right at me."

"Warnings don't," he said curtly. He typed some more.

Her heart jumped. He was thinking it might be his enemy. But she was thinking it might be an enemy of her family, someone who'd tracked down the one surviving member and tried to avenge a loved one. It wouldn't be the first time it had happened. That worried her.

He put down the phone. "I wish you'd told me sooner," he said. His big hand reached out and touched her long hair lightly. "I couldn't bear it if anything happened to you, Bernie."

She beamed.

He caught her hand in his and held it tight. He leaned back against the seat, clearly concerned. "I sent a text to Paulie. Did you tell Sari about it?"

"No," she said. "She's been in court all week and then she had to go and depose a witness in an assault case she's prosecuting. And honestly, we've been pretty busy at work all week, too."

He was weighing it in his mind. He knew Cotillo was after him, that the man could also target Bernie. But it wasn't the way Cotillo did business. He'd already sent a cleaner after Mikey. That was how he handled threats. Aiming a car at a woman and missing her by several feet, that wasn't the way a man used to violence did business.

Bernie's hand in his tightened. "Maybe it was just an accident," she said. "People do lose control of their cars for all sorts of reasons."

"Yeah. They do. But it's suspicious."

She leaned her head on his shoulder and laughed. "That's you. Suspicious."

He kissed the top of her head. "I've spent my whole life being suspicious. It's why I'm still alive, kid," he teased.

"I suppose so." She looked up into his eyes. "It could be somebody from my own past, from my family's past, still hunting vengeance, you know. Daddy was almost killed once for it."

"How many years ago was that?" he asked.

"Well, quite a few," she recalled.

"It's more likely that it's somebody connected to me," he said. "But in any case, the feds will hash it out." He slid an arm around her shoulders. "Your coworker Jessie has changed," he commented. "Even Paulie said Sari's talking about it." He glanced down at her. "Is she pretending?"

She laughed. "You really are suspicious. She said that it was hard to come from the city and get used to a small town, that she was used to having to be on her guard with people."

"Did she say what city?"

She shook her head. "She came down here from San Antonio. But she's originally from somewhere up north, I think, like her friend Billie who works at the court-house. They room together."

He frowned. He hadn't considered that the two of them were both from up north. "Have they been here a long time?"

"Not really. Jessie's only been here a few weeks. I believe she and her friend moved from San Antonio together. Billie knew somebody at the courthouse who wanted a temporary secretary after his got sick. They know the cook at Barbara's, too—he's from New Jersey."

Mikey felt his heart stop and start again. He hadn't been asking the right questions. Neither had Paulie. What if the two women and the cook were part of Cotillo's bunch? If nothing else, the timing was right. He was going to suggest to Paulie that they get somebody to keep an eye on those three as well. It was too convenient to be a coincidence.

"You're worried," she said, breaking into his thoughts.

He smiled at her. "Nothing major," he said. "Just thinking. We're going to see the Alamo. No worries for today, at least. Okay?"

She grinned. "Okay!"

They walked around the old fort like tourists, holding hands and watching leaves drift down out of the trees.

"It's going to be Halloween next week," he pointed out.

She grinned at him. "Are we going trick-or-treating, then?"

He burst out laughing. "Oh, that would be one for the books, wouldn't it?"

"I used to go when I was a little girl," she recalled. "Mom and Dad would drive me up to some of the nice neighborhoods in San Antonio door-to-door so that I could get candy. We had only a couple of close neighbors, and they didn't celebrate it at all."

"Paulie and I went with a bunch of the guys from our neighborhood," Mikey recalled. "This one house, a little old lady always invited us in for hot chocolate. It was a hoot. She'd been a Hollywood agent in her younger days. She could tell some stories!"

"I'll bet!"

"I imagine kids in Jacobsville have a great time at Halloween. And the other holidays."

"They do. Christmas is the best time, though. They stretch garlands of holly and lights all over the streets and across them. There are Christmas trees everywhere, and the local toy store has trains running in the window." She sighed. "It's just magic."

He chuckled. His hand tightened on hers. "Grandma always made Christmas special for me and Paulie," he said. "Of course, we had to go with her to midnight mass every Christmas Eve and it went on for a couple of hours. You know how kids are. We squirmed and suffered, but we didn't dare complain. She was scary for a tiny little old lady," he added.

She smiled. "I know what you mean." Her eyes were sad. "My grandmother was so sweet. She was always baking for people who had family die and sitting with sick people. She was wonderful. My grandfather was violent and dangerous. Daddy said he'd been in trouble with the law a lot when he was a young man. But I never thought he'd do something so terrible."

"Listen, kid, lots of people do terrible things they never planned. Kids get on drugs and kill people. Old people get dementia and kill people. Alcoholics get behind the wheels of cars and kill people. I don't think most of them go out with the idea that they'll do harm. It just happens."

"I've never used drugs," she said.

He laughed softly. "Why am I not surprised?"

She leaned her head against his arm. "I'm predictable."

"Very. I love it," he whispered.

She drew in a long breath. "I've never been so happy in my whole life."

"Neither have I, baby," he said gently.

She looked up at him and he looked back, and the world vanished.

It took a car horn out in the street to snap them back to reality, and they both laughed.

They walked through the dark halls of the Alamo, paused at the door to the Long Barracks, looked at the graffiti on the walls where the last stand had been held. They were solemn as they filed into the gift shop for souvenirs.

"It's a sad history," she commented.

"Most history's sad," he returned. "Life is violent."

"I suppose it is."

"What would you like?" he teased, indicating the gifts in the glass display case. "Come on. Be daring. Pick out something outrageous."

She looked up at him, searching his dark eyes. She

looked down into the shelves and when the saleslady came over, she indicated a pretty inlaid turquoise ring."

Mikey's hand tightened on hers. "Yes," he said under his breath.

The saleslady handed it to her and she started to try it on her right hand, but Mikey stopped her and slid it onto her left ring finger, his eyes holding hers. It was a perfect fit.

"We'll take it," Mikey said.

The saleslady took the credit card he handed her while Bernie touched the pretty ring.

"You can think of it as an engagement ring until we can do the thing right," he whispered at her forehead.

She caught her breath and fought tears as she looked up into hungry dark eyes.

"An engagement ring?" she asked.

"I can't let you go," he said quietly. "I'd have no life left. Whatever happens."

She bit her lower lip. "Whatever happens, Mikey," she whispered huskily.

And just that simply, they were engaged.

Mrs. Brown cried when she saw the ring and heard the story. "It's a lovely ring!" she said.

"Not a diamond just yet," Mikey chuckled, "but it's standing in for one. I have to text Paulie and tell him." He bent and kissed Bernie's cheek. "I have to go up to San Antonio tomorrow, but we'll do this again next weekend, okay?"

"Okay," she said softly.

"I'll see you at breakfast in the morning, honey. You sleep well."

She reached up and kissed his own cheek. "You, too."

He laughed. "I doubt I'll sleep a wink." He grinned, smiled at Mrs. Brown, and went along to his room.

"Congratulations," Mrs. Brown said.

Bernie hugged her. "I'm so happy!" she exclaimed. And then the tears did, finally, fall.

Bernie showed her ring off at work. Olivia was overjoyed, so was Glory. And when Sari saw it, she just hugged Bernie.

"He's never been the sort of man who wanted to settle down and get serious about anyone," Sari told Bernie. "But I can see why he wants that with you."

"Me and my limitations," Bernie said with a sigh. "He could have any woman he wanted, you know. Somebody young and beautiful and, well, whole."

"Oh, you'll be fine," Jessie said, and she even smiled. "Men don't think about obstacles, you know. They just plow right ahead when they want something. Congrats," she added.

"Thanks," Bernie replied.

Jessie noticed that nobody thought she was the least bit insincere. Which worked to her advantage.

Later in the day, Billie alerted her to the fact that Mikey was at the courthouse with his cousin Paul, talking to a man in a black suit.

"I'm going to lunch early so I'll be here when all of you leave, is that all right?" Jessie asked them.

"Sure," Glory said.

"I won't be long," she added, and smiled again. They were so gullible, she thought smugly as she left. Nobody suspected a thing.

Mikey was by himself while Paul and the man in the suit went into an office nearby. Jessie walked up to him.

"Hi," she said breezily. "How's it going? We heard about the engagement. Congratulations!"

He grinned. "Thanks."

She sighed. "I know you'll be happy with her." She made a face. "It's just, she was talking about your past, you know? I couldn't help but overhear."

He felt his face go taut. "About my past?"

"She's such a straight arrow," she continued. "It's not surprising that she'd be upset when she knew your family had ties to organized crime. She said she gave her word and she'd keep it, but she didn't know how she was going to live with a man who was accused of murder, a man who lived with other men who killed people without guilt." She smiled sadly. "I'm really sorry. I guess I shouldn't have mentioned it…"

"No, it's okay," he said. "Really."

"She'd never tell you herself," Jessie added. "She's so sweet." She grimaced. "It will be hard for her to get used to another way of life. But, hey, she's young. She'll adjust, right?"

"Right," he said, but he didn't look convinced.

She glanced at her watch. "Oops, I'll be late getting back. I dropped by to see what Billie wanted for lunch. I'm bringing it to her." She smiled at him. "I've got two uncles who worked for a local crime boss in New York," she said. She shrugged. "I don't have a problem with it. But some people, you know, they don't quite understand the life. See you."

"Yeah. See you."

She walked toward Billie's office, feeling proud. She'd just put the first stick in the spokes of his relationship with Bernie. She had him off balance. Now it was just a matter of keeping him that way for some people she and Billie knew.

The next step was to talk to Bernie and make a similar confession to her about Mikey. Funny how easy it was to make them believe things about each other. But she knew people like Mikey. He'd never ask Bernie directly if she'd said such things because he wouldn't really want to know. He'd be afraid to hurt her feelings by accusing her of it, and of course she'd deny it—because it wasn't true. But he'd have doubts. Big doubts. Jessie was going to make them even bigger.

Chapter Twelve

Mikey went back to San Antonio with Paulie to talk to the feds, and he was morose. Could Bernie feel that way about his lifestyle and not be willing to tell him? She'd certainly been shocked when he'd told her about the man who'd killed Paulie's family. Well, he hadn't confessed that he'd ordered the hit—although he had. What he'd told her was enough to shock her, even without that. Had he been too truthful? Maybe he should have waited until they knew each other much better before he confessed just how full of violence and turmoil his life had been.

"Sari ever have a problem with your past?" he asked his cousin, who was driving them in a Bucar, the designation of a bureau vehicle used by the FBI.

Paul frowned. "Well, she wasn't overjoyed, if that's what you mean. She's an assistant district attorney, you know. A real straight arrow. I guess it bothered her some, but she loved me enough not to let it matter. Why? Is Bernie having second thoughts? She told Sari the two of you just got engaged."

"We did. But I told her a lot of it," Mikey said quietly. "She's got violence in her own past, something tragic. But hers was the result of an unbalanced relative. I'm not unbalanced. I've been a bad boy, Paulie. I'm not sure she can make a life with me, the way she is."

"You should talk to her."

"And say what? That I'll change? That I'll go straight and sell out my family? Fat chance, and you know why. You get in this racket for life. Nobody gets out except feet first."

"Marcus Carrera did," he was reminded.

"Yeah, Carrera. Well, he was a big fish and people were scared to death of him. Sure he got out. He always made his own rules. I'm not Carrera. I'm a small fry, compared to him."

"You own a casino in Vegas," Paul reminded him drily. "You drive a Rolls back home. You've got millions in overseas banks. And people are scared of you, too, kiddo."

"No kidding?"

"No kidding."

One corner of his mouth pulled down. "Well, that won't matter much if I turn my back on the outfit."

"Sadly, no, it won't. Hey, there's always the witness protection program," Paul teased.

"I noticed how well that worked out for the guy who squealed on the big bosses. He got hit right in protective custody, now, didn't he?" Mikey chuckled.

"He did."

"You don't get out. Hell, I don't want to get out," Mikey muttered. "It's the only life I've ever known, from the time we were kids. I like being part of a big family. I like the style and the cachet."

"Will Bernie like it? She's more of a butterflies and wildflowers girl than she is a showgirl."

"Yeah. I know that. But she's so sweet, Paulie," he replied heavily. "She's the sweetest human being I've ever known. And I don't think I can give her up, unless she wants me to. Even then, I don't know how I'd go on without her. It's only been a few weeks and I'm lonely when I'm not with her."

"It was that way with me when I was mooning over Sari and thinking how hopeless it all was. She was worth two hundred million, and I worked for wages."

"You're still working for wages," Mikey pointed out.

"I'm not a sit-at-home type of guy. I love my job." He glanced at Mikey. "So what are you going to do?"

"Rock along until I'm sure she can cope. Then I'm getting her to the nearest justice of the peace before she changes her mind," he chuckled.

Bernie, meanwhile, was still basking in the glory of her first proposal and looking forward to years of happiness with Mikey.

The others were getting ready to go to lunch. Bernie got to her feet a little unsteadily and picked up her cane.

"Rough day, huh?" Jessie asked in a gentle tone.

"Just a little," Bernie confessed. "I had a bad fall on my way home the other day. A car went out of control and almost hit me."

"Gosh, here in Jacobsville? People need to learn to drive!" Jessie muttered.

"Just what I was thinking."

"Bernie, we'll wait for you outside," Glory called as they went out the door.

"Be right there," she said, reaching for her purse.

"Mikey was in the courthouse when I went to take Billie her lunch," Jessie said. She made a face. "I really shouldn't tell you what I overheard him say to his cousin."

Bernie's heart dropped in her chest. "What?" she asked, and sounded a little breathless with worry.

Jessie sighed. "He told his cousin that he was worried about what you'd be like in a few years, because his grandmother had what you've got, and she was twisted like tree roots and almost helpless. He said that it was going to be hard to live with somebody who was sick so much. But that he'd made a promise and he was going to keep it. He said he was going to marry you because he gave his word. But that it was going to be like pulling teeth. He was used to women who could keep up with the pace. He went all over the world on trips for his family, vacationed in foreign countries. He didn't know how you'd manage the travel. It was hard for a healthy woman, but you'd never keep up. He said," she added with sad eyes, "that he'd rushed in because he was infatuated with you, and then it was too late to turn back after he'd thought about the difficulties."

"I see." Bernie's heart was beating like a drum. She felt sick inside.

"I knew I shouldn't have told you," Jessie groaned. "I'm sorry. But I thought you should know. I mean, he'd never tell you himself."

"Of course, he wouldn't."

"Please don't tell him I told you," Jessie pleaded. "I

don't want to make an enemy of him. He gets even with people. You don't know how dangerous he is," she added. "I come from up north. I've heard things about him. He scares people. Even bad people." She laughed hollowly. "I don't want to end up floating down a river..."

Bernie felt sick inside. Even Mikey had hinted at something of the sort, that he had power in his organization. She remembered what he'd said about taking care of the man who'd killed Paul's first wife and his child. It chilled her. "No, of course I won't tell."

"Thanks. I'm truly sorry. I know you're crazy about him."

Bernie managed a smile. She didn't answer. She went out onto the street with her coworkers and pretended that nothing at all had happened. But she was devastated.

Jessie smiled to herself. She was going to reap rich rewards for her little acts of "kindness." Throwing Mikey off balance had been the first step. Now she had Bernie doubting. The next thing was going to happen just as they'd planned it. And soon.

They spent all too much time in the Jacobs County courthouse, Mikey was thinking as he waited for Paulie to come out of an office where he was comparing notes with a contact in the probate judge's office.

He was staring at a plaque on the wall, denoting the building of the courthouse almost sixty years ago, and the names of the men on the county commission who'd authorized the construction. Farther down the wall were portraits of judges, many long gone. He was bored out of his mind.

"Fancy seeing you here again," Jessie said with a smile. She was carrying a box with food and a cup of coffee in it. "I came to bring lunch to poor Billie. She hurt her foot and she can't walk far."

"How're you doing?" he asked, and smiled, because she really did seem to have changed in the past week or so.

She shrugged. "Can't complain. It's just hard to get used to these Texans," she laughed. "They aren't like people up north."

"Nobody's like people up north. Where you from?"

She hesitated. "Upstate New York originally. You?"

"Jersey," he said. He grinned. "Doesn't the accent give it away?"

"It does, sort of." She cocked her head and studied him. "I've heard of your family. You were an underboss to Tony Garza, weren't you? Shame about him. He was a decent guy."

"He still is," Mikey said.

"I'm truly sorry that Bernie has such a hard time with your lifestyle…" She stopped and gritted her teeth. "Didn't mean to say that," she added quickly.

He scowled. "What did you mean?"

"Well, it's just," she hesitated. "Bernie doesn't understand the world you come from and she's afraid of it."

He felt his heart sinking. "She told you that?" he asked suspiciously.

"Of course not. She'd never talk to me about you," she said. "I told you about it before, remember? I heard her talking to Olivia, the other paralegal in our office. She said she was crazy about you, but that she wasn't sure she could cope with the way you made your living. She said she'd never fit in with a bunch of, well, criminals."

He could barely get words out. The pain went all the way through him. He'd wondered about the way Bernie accepted what he was, that she said it wouldn't matter. But she was a girl who'd never cheated in anything. She had a tragic past that predisposed her to loving the police. After all, they'd saved her and her father from a potential killer after the tragedy her grandfather had caused.

Apparently he hadn't been thinking straight at all. Rather, he'd been thinking with his heart instead of his brain. Bernie wasn't like him. They had different backgrounds, and she didn't understand the forces that honed his family into a criminal element over the years. The scandals of the Kennedy era, the unmasking of the five families, the scattering of bosses had been a wholesale offensive against organized crime. And it had largely succeeded. There were still bosses like Tony, who commanded power, but there was no more real commission that met and decided on who got hit, who had which territory, which politicians to support. Now the bosses were largely autonomous until they crossed the line. Nobody liked drawing attention to the outfit that was left, and people who did it got punished. Mostly, the days of wiping out a man's relatives to make a point were over. But there were still renegades who paid insults back with blood. Cotillo was one of those. That would never really end so long as there were power-mad people in the loop.

"I'm sorry," Jessie was saying. "I shouldn't have said anything."

"It isn't anything I wasn't already thinking," he confessed.

"You live in the fast lane. Fast cars, fast women, easy money," she said. "Bernie likes band concerts in the park and watching television in her room." Her mouth twisted. "Not a good mix."

"No." He wished he could forget what she'd told him about Bernie, the other day and now. But he knew it was true. He'd seen the way Bernie had reacted when he described his life to her. She'd said she could cope, that it wouldn't matter. It would matter.

"Please don't tell Bernie I said anything to you," she said softly. "I'd hate to have her mad at me now that we're getting along so well."

"I won't mention it to her," he said absently, and he was thinking that there was no way he could discuss it with Bernie without putting her on the defensive, making her ashamed of her feelings. He couldn't blame her. His lifestyle would be hard for any woman unless she came from a similar background. He'd been living in a dream. It was a sweet dream. But it wasn't real.

"I'd better get Billie's lunch to her. Nice seeing you." She walked away with a smile. It wouldn't do to lay it on with a trowel.

Paul came out of the probate judge's office with a worried look. He fell in beside Mikey and they walked outside. "Harvey," he said, referring to his contact inside, "told me that Billie and Jessie at Sari's office came down here at the same time. It's a little too cozy for coincidence."

"You think they're Cotillo's?" Mikey asked.

"They could be. We're going to do a thorough background search on all of them. What about that car that barely missed Bernie? Did she tell you anything about it?"

He shook his head and stuck his hands in his slacks pockets. "Only that it was a dark sedan. It happened too fast." He glanced at Paul. "Do you know about Bernie's grandfather and what he did?"

Paul nodded. "Tragic thing to happen to a child. There was a serious attempt on her father's life not long after it happened, by a member of a victim's family. He's doing time."

"She said it might have been somebody like that, trying to scare her." Mikey frowned. "It's not Cotillo's style, you know? He has people hit if he has a problem with them, like he tried to hit Tony and me. He doesn't make threats."

"Neither do you," Paul mused.

"Hey, I am what I am." He strolled along beside Paul. "I've been having second thoughts about this engagement," he confessed.

"What?" Paul stopped in the middle of the sidewalk. "But you're crazy about Bernie. She's crazy about you!"

Mikey took a breath and smiled cynically. "She likes small towns and band concerts, Paulie. She's never been in trouble with the law in her life. How's she going to like jetsetting, mixing with celebrities and crooks, wearing designer clothes, traveling around the world with me when I've got people to meet? How's she going to feel if I ever get arrested for something?"

Paul took a deep breath of his own. "I don't know. I don't live in that world. I never did."

"Well, I do. I have to." He grimaced. "And there's her health to consider. I remember our grandmother. She got twisted like a tree in a hurricane. She was in bed most of the time at the end. She got upset and she had flares, remember that? Bernie would be stressed-out all the time. It would affect her health."

"You've done a lot of thinking," Paul said. He wasn't saying anything, but his tone was full of curiosity and suspicion.

"Yeah. She's the sweetest woman I've ever known. I'd like her to stay that way. Involved with me for life? It would…kill something in her."

Paul didn't speak. He knew that Mikey's lifestyle involved stress. But he'd never seen Mikey involved with any woman to the extent he was involved with Bernie. He thought that love would resolve all those issues. Mikey clearly didn't.

"What are you going to do?" Paul asked.

"Ease off. Just a little at a time, so it doesn't look like I'm shooting her out of my life." He smiled sadly. "I want her to be happy. I can't give her the sort of life she deserves."

"You, being unselfish. Call the journalists," Paul drawled.

Mikey chuckled. "Out of character, isn't it?" he agreed.

Paul threw an arm around him. "Not anymore, it isn't, cuz," he said quietly. "But I'm sorry for both of you."

"Me, too," Mikey said. His eyes were solemn. "Me, too."

Mikey and Bernie were subdued at supper at Mrs. Brown's. Neither spoke much although they went through the motions of participating in the conversation.

But afterward, when Bernie started toward her room, Mikey stopped her.

"Listen," he began quietly, "I've been thinking—"

"Me, too," she interrupted.

She looked as uncomfortable as he did.

He shoved his hands into his pockets and felt his heart breaking inside him. He wanted to say something, but what could he say? His life wasn't butterflies and roses. And, realistically, she wasn't the sort of woman who could adjust to partying and casinos and jet travel and organized crime. It was impossible, but he hadn't realized it until Jessie told him what Bernie had said.

He looked down at her tenderly. She was so unworldly. It would be like her not to want to hurt his feelings or make him feel bad about what his world was like.

She was thinking the same thing about him, that he didn't want to hurt her feelings by admitting that he couldn't live with a woman who might be an invalid one day, a woman who could barely keep up with him on a slow walk in the woods. He needed somebody vibrant and healthy, who could thrive in his company, not a woman who would limit his activities.

"It might be an idea to cool it, just for a little while," Mikey said finally. "I've got people working on that car that almost hit you. We'll find out who it was."

"Probably somebody drunk who misjudged the curb," she replied with a faint smile. "It's a small town. Odd things happen here."

His dark eyes seemed even darker as they searched her light ones. "I've never enjoyed anything more than this time with you."

"Me, either," she confessed, and tried not to show that she was dying inside.

"But we need to give each other a little space. Just for now," he added quickly so it didn't sound like he was trying to dump her. He couldn't bear to hurt her feelings.

She nodded. "It's a good idea." She fingered the ring that stood in place of an engagement ring. She started to take it off.

His big hand went over both of hers. "No," he said, and sounded choked. "You keep that. You keep it forever. Think of me when you wear it."

She looked up, fighting tears. "I'll never forget you. No matter what."

"Yeah. It's like that with me, too." He hesitated. "Santi doesn't like having me apart from him at night, the way things are going."

Her eyes widened with worry. "They haven't sent somebody else after you…?" she asked almost frantically.

He almost bit his lip through. That soft concern made him hate himself. "No," he lied quickly. Some quick thinking by Paulie and the feds had saved him, already. "It's just that he thinks a bodyguard should stay with the boss, and he can't live in the room with me here. So…well, I'm moving over to the motel, and Santi and I can have adjoining rooms."

Her heart sank. She'd gotten used to seeing him at the table when they had meals, in the hallway, everywhere. "That's probably a good idea," she said softly. She looked up. "You take care of yourself, okay?"

His big hand touched her cheek. "You do that, too. Don't go out alone after dark. Be aware of your surroundings."

"I always do that. Well, almost always," she amended.

"But the car came out of nowhere. I didn't even hear it coming."

That wasn't surprising. Most newer model cars had quiet engines. It still bothered him that it didn't sound like an accident. Paul was checking. If there was anything sinister, he'd find it.

"So," Mikey said. "I'll see you around."

She forced a smile. "Yes. Well, goodbye."

She went into her room, resisting the urge to look behind her. She closed the door and let the tears fall silently. It was the biggest pain of her life, almost as bad as knowing what her grandfather had done, losing her sweet grandmother and the community where she'd grown up. It was like losing a loved one.

Outside the door, Mikey was feeling something similar. But he had to do it. If he stayed here, seeing her every day, he'd go nuts. He couldn't keep away from her, not unless he distanced himself from her. It was the hardest thing he'd ever done in his life. It was the only thing he could do. Bernie couldn't live with the man he was. He didn't blame her. It was just that she was the only woman he'd ever wanted to live with him.

He let out a weary breath and went into his room to pack.

"You moved out of the boardinghouse," Paul remarked a week later, when Mikey was having supper with him and Sari while Mandy bustled around in the kitchen making a cake.

"Yeah," Mikey said. He moved his cup around in the saucer. "Santi kept harping on it. He said he couldn't protect me if he was several blocks away. I finally listened."

Paul, remembering an earlier conversation, knew

what the truth was. Mikey was distancing himself from Bernie, removing temptation.

Sari glanced at Mikey's lowered head and started to speak, but a sharp jerk of the head from Paul silenced her. Instead, she started talking about a reality show she and Paul had been watching lately.

After Mikey went back to his motel, Sari questioned Paul about his odd behavior.

"He's doing it for her own good," Paul said on a sigh. "He thinks she couldn't cope with his lifestyle. You know, Isabel, it's not the same life as this one. Not at all. He's in constant company with people who break the law. He travels in high social circles just the same, rubs elbows with movie stars and politicians and gamblers. He couldn't settle down here if his life depended on it—well, except briefly, like he's having to do now. But Bernie would never fit into that sort of world."

Sari met his eyes and nodded sadly. "But she was so happy," she said softly. "Bright as the sun. She almost radiated with it. And now she's so quiet we hardly know she's around. She never jokes and smiles anymore."

"Neither does my cousin," Paul said. He pulled her close. "You and I came from different worlds, but we worked it out, because we loved one another. You can tell how Mikey and Bernie feel about each other just by looking at them. Why couldn't they work it out, too?"

"I don't know," she said with a sigh. She laid her head against his broad chest. "What about the sudden residents? Any new intel on them?"

"Not a lot," he confessed. "Jessie and her friend Billie are both from New York originally. They do have mob ties, but not to Cotillo or Tony Garza. Their connections aren't apparent, but we're trying to run them down.

There's still a family that operates in New York, even covertly, but it's fragmented and the boss is in prison."

"He can still run it from prison. It's not even hard."

"True. He has an underboss holding power for him. Jessie may have something to do with him. That wouldn't necessarily mean she or the boss favored Cotillo. He's an outsider and he does a bloody business. You know how well that goes over in mob circles. They don't like attention. Cotillo's getting them a lot of it."

"Wouldn't it be lovely if somebody in one of the old outfit families decided to take Cotillo out of the equation?" she asked on a sigh. "Shame on me. I work for the court system. I should be ashamed."

"Yes, you bad girl." He kissed her hungrily. "You need to be severely reprimanded. Come right over here and I'll do my best."

She laughed as he tugged her down onto the bed. "Oh, this is a reprimand I'm going to love," she teased.

He chuckled as he started to remove her gown. "You bet, you're going to love it!"

The driver of the car that almost hit Bernie was a local businessman who'd had three drinks too many out at Shea's Bar and misjudged the curb, just as Bernie had figured. He turned himself in to Cash Grier with many apologies and Cash got him into rehab.

Bernie listened to Cash's explanation in the office a couple of weeks after Mikey had moved out of the boardinghouse.

"I thought it was something like that," she said quietly. "I mean, if people in organized crime want to hurt you, they just kill you, don't they?"

"More or less." They were alone in the office. It was

just after lunch and the other women hadn't returned. "What about you and Mikey? I thought that was going to be permanent."

She flushed. "I'm not healthy," she said. "His grandmother had what I've got. She was an invalid, bedridden, when she was old. I'm likely to end up in that condition a lot sooner." She fought down panic at the thought that she might not even be able to work. She was far too proud to ask for government relief, even though she might one day be forced into it.

"There are new drugs," he pointed out.

She smiled sadly. "Chief Grier, the sort you're talking about costs over a thousand dollars a month. They do have programs to help people afford them, but it isn't that much of a reduction."

He grimaced.

"I get by. My rheumatologist has me on a regimen of medicines that mostly take care of the pain. I have flares, days when I can't get out of bed, and I have to use a cane from time to time. But there are lots of people worse off. Look at Glory in my office, and what she had to go through in her life. She still limps from time to time because her hip was broken long ago and it has arthritis in it, and her blood pressure is controlled but still subject to spikes. She lives with it. I live with my problems."

"But you don't think Mikey could?" he fished, his eyes piercing hers.

She toyed with a pen on her desk. "He was overheard telling his cousin that he wasn't sure that he could." She looked up. "Don't you dare repeat that, ever. It would hurt his feelings. He can't help what he thinks. He lives with glitzy people, rides in limousines, travels all over the world. I'm lucky if I can get from work to my boardinghouse without falling over my feet. How would I fit into that sort of lifestyle? I'd be a sparrow among peacocks, if you see what I mean."

He did see. But she was a sweet, kind woman. "If he loves you, it won't matter."

"That's the thing, though," she continued. "He said it would be better if we sort of let things cool off. And he's probably right. He has enough problems right now. They won't kill him, will they?" she asked, and looked agonized by the thought.

"He has powerful friends," he replied. "Marcus Carrera is one of them. Carrera runs a legitimate operation in the Bahamas, but he wasn't always a good guy, and his reputation still strikes fear in people who knew him back in the day." He chuckled. "He's got Tony Garza so surrounded by experienced mercs that only a suicidal maniac would try to get to him."

"Sari said that Mr. Garza gave her sister away at her wedding to that Wyoming rancher," Bernie said.

"He did. He's not what he seems." He cocked his head and studied her. "Neither is Mikey. His reputation is fearsome. But he's not as bad as people think he is."

"He was arrested once, though," she said.

He nodded. "And charged with attempted murder. But the charges were dropped," he reminded her. "Nobody's ever been able to bring him to trial on a major crime. For a man who operates outside the law, he's amazingly conventional."

She smiled sadly. "He's amazing, period," she said softly. "I'll never forget him." As she spoke, she twisted the turquoise-and-silver ring he'd given her. She wore it on her right hand, though, not her left. She didn't want it to get back to him that she considered herself engaged, not when he was backing away.

Cash muttered something about men being fools, smiled, and left her.

"What in the hell is wrong with you?" Cash asked Mikey when he saw him with Paul at Barbara's Café one day at lunch.

Mikey's eyebrows raised. "Excuse me?"

"You have almost as much money in foreign banks as I do," Cash said as he joined them for coffee and pie. "You could easily afford the newest treatments for rheumatoid arthritis, whatever they cost."

Mikey stared at him. "I don't have arthritis."

"Bernie does."

Mikey averted his eyes. "I know."

"She wouldn't let him, though," Paul said, and he was giving Cash expression cues that asked him to cool it. "She's too proud."

"Besides that, we're not... Well, we're not an item anymore," Mikey added. "She has her life, I have mine."

"Yes, but she..." Cash continued, ignoring Paul.

Before he could finish the sentence, Jessie came in the door, spotted Mikey and came right to the table, smiling.

"Don't forget, you're taking me to Don Alfonso's for supper, right?" she asked.

Mikey chuckled. "You bet, doll. Santi and I will pick you up about five."

"I thought maybe you could drive us both and leave Santi at home," she said with a husky laugh.

"Sorry. Santi drives, I don't."

"Well, okay. It doesn't matter. I'll be ready on time.

Hi, Chief Grier. Mr. Fiore," she added, a little unsettled when Paul just glared at her without speaking. "See you later."

She went to the counter to pick up her order. Paul glared at Mikey with much more venom than he'd shown the gorgeous, well-dressed woman waiting for her order.

"She doesn't mind riding around with a criminal," Mikey said sarcastically. "She loves casinos and fancy restaurants and she's classy enough to take to ritzy gatherings. So?"

"You're about to ruin your life," Paul said curtly. "What if Bernie finds out? Jessie works in the office with her, for God's sake!"

"I told you," Mikey said, averting his eyes. "Bernie and I are no longer an item. I can date any woman I like. Jessie's not so bad."

But Paul was thinking that Jessie was every bit as bad as she seemed. She was rubbing Bernie's nose in the fact that she had Mikey's attention. Not only that, she was pressuring Mikey to be alone with her, without Santi. That was suspicious. Very suspicious. He glanced at a taciturn Cash Grier and had the impression that the police chief was thinking the same thing.

"I need a night on the town, anyway," Mikey said as he finished his pie and washed it down with coffee. "I've been vegetating down here in cowboy town."

"You watch your step," Paul said shortly. "Don't forget that Cotillo may have people here that we don't even know about."

"Surely you don't think Jessie's one of them?" Mikey drawled. "You checked her out and found no connections to any of Cotillo's people."

"Yeah, I checked out our last limo driver, too, and

he almost got Merrie killed because the perp had connections I didn't ferret out," he was reminded.

"I can handle myself," Mikey reminded him curtly.

"You'd better have a concealed carry permit if you
walk around with a weapon in my town," Cash told him
humorously, but with a cold glint in his eyes.

"I got one the second day I was in town, for your information," Mikey said smugly. "I know you, Grier. No
way I'm stepping out of line around here!"

Cash just chuckled.

Paul cornered him after Grier left, while they were
waiting on the sidewalk for Santi to collect Mikey.

"This is going to ruin any chance you have of getting back together with Bernie," he told his cousin. "You
know that, right?"

Mikey's eyes were hollow with pain. "She can't live
with a crook, Paulie," he said shortly. "That's what she
said."

Paul's lower jaw fell. "She said that to you?"

"Of course, she didn't say it to me! She wouldn't hurt
my feelings for anything. But she was overheard saying it," he added, and flushed, remembering who'd told
him. "There's Santi. I gotta go. See you around, cuz."

"Watch your back!" Paul called after him.

Mikey waved and climbed into the limo.

Paul stood watching it pull away from the curb.
Something Mikey had said piqued his curiosity. He
was going to speak to Sari about it when he got home.

Chapter Thirteen

Sari was going over a brief when Paul walked into the study and closed the door.

"What's up?" she asked, because he looked worried.

"Did Bernie say anything to you about having an issue with Mikey's background?" he asked curiously.

"No," she replied. She grimaced. "But she doesn't really discuss Mikey with me," she added. "I guess she thinks I might tell him what she said." She put down the pencil she was using to edit the document she was working on. "Why?"

"He said she told somebody that she couldn't live with a man who made his living outside the law, with a criminal," he replied. "Would she tell somebody at work something so personal?" he persisted.

She frowned. "Well, I don't really think so. Bernie's a very private person. She's not the kind to blurt out intimate details of her life to people she works with. It's not the way she is. And there's not really anybody else she might tell, either. She has no close friends."

"That's what I thought. Mikey has the impression that she can't live with his past."

"I know that's not true," Sari said gently. "She loves him."

One side of his mouth pulled down. "I tried to tell him that. He wouldn't listen. He's destroying any chance that he could get back together with Bernie."

"How?"

"He's taking your coworker Jessie out on the town in San Antonio tonight," he said through his teeth.

"Oh, no!"

"I tried to warn him. It will ruin everything. But he wouldn't listen. He's convinced that he's so bad, only a bad woman would ever want him."

"What an idiot. Even if he is your cousin."

"Hey, no argument from me. I said the same thing, to his face."

"It will kill Bernie if she finds out."

He laughed coldly. "If? Jessie will tell the world tomorrow. I don't doubt she'll embroider it into something even more than it is."

"Jessie." Sari made a rough sound. "She was our worst nightmare for weeks. Then overnight she turned into a caring, worrying coworker who did everything she could to make things easier for us."

"And all an act," Paul said. "I can see right through her. I wish Mikey could."

"I didn't. Neither did Bernie or Glory or Olivia," Sari said.

"I've spent my life with people who bend the truth. I'm good at recognizing phonies."

"Poor Bernie."

"Poor Mikey, when he finally realizes he's been had," Paul said flatly. "I'm checking out an acquaintance of Jessie's in Upstate New York. I have a suspicion that she didn't just happen down here with her friend Billie."

"What about the cook from New Jersey who's working in Barbara's Café?"

He laughed. "I'll tell you about that," he said. "It's a hoot." And he did tell her.

"Now, this is my kind of place," Jessie said as they were seated in the five-star restaurant.

"Mine, too," Mikey said, but without any real enthusiasm. He studied the gorgeous woman across from him with only vague interest. She was wearing a couture cocktail dress with diamond earrings, necklace, bracelet and several rings. All diamonds. The best quality and set in 18 karat gold. He knew, because he'd spent a fortune on them for various women over the years. He was curious about how she afforded that kind of jewelry on a receptionist's salary.

Even as he had the thought, he felt cold chills inside. He was carrying. He had a snub .38 in a pancake holster behind his back, and a hidden gun in an ankle holster. He never went anywhere without being armed. Would he need to be? Santi was at the next table, apparently oblivious, but watching.

Odd, how he suddenly remembered that if the family ordered a hit on you, they sent your best friend to do it. He was warned that if he didn't, somebody else would, and he'd end up as dead as the intended victim. His blood ran cold as he stared at Santi.

But his bodyguard just grinned at him and went to

work on a huge plate of spaghetti. He was getting paranoid, Mikey considered, just like his old man.

He remembered his father with loathing. The man had been a dirty jobs soldier for the underboss in New Jersey, the one who'd preceded Tony Garza. Mikey's dad had killed men over and over again, never felt the least remorse, and spent his life at a local bar where the outfit hung out. Mikey rarely saw him, and if he ever did, his father treated him like a disease. He hated Mikey and made no secret of the fact that he thought the kid was some other man's son. Mikey's mother, long dead, had an affair, he'd told the boy one day, and Mikey was the result. It was to get even with him for something he'd done to her. So Mikey had no real family at all until his maternal grandmother, Paulie's grandmother, too, took both boys in and raised them. The old lady was Greek. She still spoke the old language. Mikey and Paulie had been schooled in Italian by the other kids and the families they associated with, but their grandmother taught them Greek, as well. Mikey could even read in it. Not a lot of people knew that. He kept his intelligence hidden; it gave him an advantage if his colleagues thought he was stupid.

"How was it you heard what Bernie said in the office?" he asked out of the blue.

Jessie's hand, which was holding her wineglass, jerked, but she recovered quickly. "Oh, she and Olivia didn't know I was there," she replied. "I'd just come out of Mr. Kemp's office and they were in the hallway."

"I see." He didn't know Bernie well, but it seemed unlike her to confide something so personal to an office worker, even one she was close to. She was, like him, a very private person.

"This place is nice," she said, changing the subject. She smiled at him alluringly. "You know, I have the use of a friend's apartment here in town," Her voice changed to a throaty purr. "We could be all alone there."

Mikey just stared at her. His dark eyes were cold, as cold as they'd ever been when he had another man at gunpoint. "Really?"

His glare disconcerted her. "You know, Bernie won't change her mind, and she'll never tell you what she really thinks of you," she said.

He cocked his head. "You're trying too hard."

"Excuse me?"

He just laughed, but it had a hollow sound. He was just beginning to believe he'd been had. And he was out with this jeweled barracuda, who would go back to the office Monday and tell Bernie all about this date, probably with some embroidering. He took a big sip of his Chianti and cursed himself silently through the rest of the meal.

"Oh, it was the most wonderful date!" Jessie enthused to the other women, including Bernie, the following Monday. "Mikey made me feel like a princess! And we went to this apartment a friend loans me…" She stopped when Bernie's face went white. "I'm so sorry, that was cruel," she added in a conciliatory tone. "But you know how he feels about you, honey."

"She knows what you told her," Olivia replied, her eyes narrow and suspicious.

"Odd, how you knew something so personal," Sari added her own comment to the discussion. "I mean, Mikey isn't the sort to discuss personal things with Paul, even in private, and Paul's the only person he's really close to."

Jessie looked uncomfortable. "It was just a comment he made—he didn't seem to think it was very personal."

Mr. Kemp's door flew open and he looked livid. "Miss Tennison!"

Jessie actually jumped. "Yes, sir?"

"Come into my office, please," he said icily.

Jessie collected herself quickly and forced a smile. "Yes, sir, at once." She jumped up and headed toward him without looking back.

"Don't you believe her," Sari told Bernie firmly. "Mikey never told Paul anything about you, not ever, in private. He would never blurt out something like that in a public place."

Bernie wasn't comforted. She forced a smile. "I could never keep up with him, don't you see?" she asked softly. "He lives in the fast lane. Some days, I can't even get out of bed. He'd get tired of it. I don't like bars and flashy places. I've never even owned an evening gown." She cocked her head and smiled at Sari. "The people in his circle would think he'd lost his mind if they ever got a look at me, and you know it."

Sari wasn't convinced. "Bernie, if somebody loves you, things like disabilities and things they've done in the past—none of it matters at all."

Bernie's green eyes were sad. "I believed that, once. But he took her out on the town," she added, indicating the door behind which Jessie was closeted with Mr. Kemp. "And he slept with her. It's over. I'm going to get on with my life. It's obvious that he's gotten on with his."

And she went back to work.

Jessie came out of Mr. Kemp's office with an absolute snarl on her face. "I'm fired," she said icily. "Just because I told that old man on the phone that Mr. Kemp didn't want to talk to him and not to go to court because I thought it was canceled that day!"

"What old man?" Olivia asked.

"Oh, some rancher named Regan."

Olivia's eyebrows arched. "Ted Regan?"

"Yes, I think that was it," Jessie muttered. She started pulling things out of desk drawers.

"Old man Regan," Sari told her, "is worth millions. He owns the second biggest ranch in Jacobs County, and properties all over the country. He's also a prime witness in a case we're prosecuting." She pursed her lips. "Or he was. I'm assuming Mr. Kemp lost the case, if you told Ted not to show up. Judge Drew was presiding and he didn't want to try the case to begin with."

Jessie just ground her teeth. "Well, it doesn't matter now, I'm fired," she muttered. She looked up and noted the pleased expressions on all the faces except Bernie's. Bernie wouldn't even look at her. "It's just as well," she commented. "I've done what I came to do. Aren't you the gullible bunch? I put on an act and all of you bought it. You pitiful little small-town people, you'll never know what life is all about."

"It's about family," Glory Ramirez said.

"It's all about family," Sari agreed. "Something you'll never understand."

"The only family I care about is the one I take orders from," Jessie muttered absently, and then looked up and flushed as she realized what she'd said. "My dad, I mean," she corrected, "and he's not from some little Texas town!"

But Sari picked up on what she'd said at once and hid her suspicions. She went back to work, ignoring Jessie.

"Well, so long," Jessie said as she carried the cardboard box with her things in it to the door. She turned and stared at Bernie. "I'll tell Mikey you said hello, Bernie," she purred. "After all, we're going to be seeing a lot of each other. I know his world and I love it. Unlike you, I don't mind being seen with him and his criminal friends," she drawled sarcastically.

Bernie felt shocked. "What do you mean?"

Jessie had slipped again. She shrugged. "Nothing at all. Goodbye."

She went out the door and closed it behind her.

Bernie didn't say a word. She brooded, though. Mikey was already involved with that vicious woman, but perhaps he liked that sort of person. Maybe he was frustrated because he'd wanted Bernie and she wasn't the sort to sleep around. But it still hurt to think of him in bed with Jessie. It hurt terribly.

"She was lying," Sari said gently.

Bernie looked up. Her eyes were sad and wise. "No, she wasn't," she said quietly. "And like I said, it doesn't matter. We were mismatched from the start. Opposites attract, don't they say, but the divorce rate for marriages like that is pretty dismal. I'd better get back to work."

Sari didn't say any more, but she was livid.

"Mikey did what?" Paul Fiore asked at supper, his fork poised in midair.

"He slept with Jessie," Sari said angrily.

He whistled, aware of Mandy's curious stare. "Well, damn, that's the end of it all."

"I know." Sari picked at her food. "Jessie was poison. I'm glad Mr. Kemp fired her. It was all an act, that sweetness and light attitude."

"No surprise, there."

"She let something slip when we were talking about families and how they mattered," Sari continued. "She said the only family she cared about was the one she took orders from."

Paul dropped the fork. "Families. Like Cotillo's."

"Maybe," Sari replied, watching him retrieve the utensil from the floor and carry it to the sink before he got another and returned to the table. "Don't you have somebody checking her out?"

"I do. I'll call him after we finish eating. Damn the luck! If she's involved with Cotillo, then her friend Billie may be, too. It's been right under our noses."

"What about that cook at Barbara's?" Mandy asked as she refilled coffee cups. She made a face at Sari. "And you should be drinking milk, not caffeine!"

Sari flushed. "Mandy..."

Mandy was grinning.

Paul, caught unaware, looked at Mandy's twinkling eyes and his own darted to his wife, looking flushed and guilty.

"Okay, spit it out," he told Sari. "What's going on that I don't know about?"

She cleared her throat and glared at Mandy. "I was going to tell you later."

"Tell me now," he persisted.

She drew in a breath. "I'm pregnant."

Paul sat very still for just a minute, then he rose, picked her up in his arms, and kissed her and kissed her, whooping in between at the top of his lungs.

Mandy pursed her lips. "Well," she said to nobody in particular, "I guess it's no secret that he's happy about it."

Bernie went home to a lonely apartment, her heart down in her shoes. Mikey was sleeping with that rat, Jessie. Mikey was a rat, too, she told herself. He'd taken her in, pretended to care about her, then backed off because she had an incurable disease.

If he'd been that concerned about her illness, why hadn't he stopped seeing her in the beginning? Why had he spent almost every day with her? Why had he bought her a ring and then asked her to marry him?

None of it made sense, unless he'd truly thought he could make it work and then decided he couldn't live with her limitations. She felt miserable. She couldn't help what was wrong with her. She couldn't cure it. Maybe she could have adjusted to travel, to his friends, to flashy places, if she'd been given the chance. But what did it matter now? She would never get over the fact that he'd promised to marry her and then cheated on her with another woman. She had too much pride.

"Are you out of your mind?" Paul demanded of Mikey the next day when they were having a quick lunch at the house.

Mikey blinked. "Excuse me?"

"Sleeping with Jessie. My God!"

Mikey's lips fell open. "Sleeping… Good Lord, do I look crazy to you? I wouldn't touch her with a pole!"

"You took her out on the town, didn't you?" he persisted.

Mikey grimaced. "I was feeling pretty low. I needed to feel like a man again."

"Great job."

"Bernie didn't want me!" he burst out. "She said she couldn't live with a man who'd been a criminal most of his life!"

"She told you this, huh?" Paul asked.

Mikey sighed. "No. She'd never want to hurt my feelings like that. She told somebody else and she was overheard."

"Let me guess—by Jessie."

Mikey scowled. "What?"

"Jessie told Bernie that you went with her to an apartment in San Antonio."

Mikey grimaced. He could only imagine how much that had hurt Bernie. He was hurting from her rejection, but it wounded him to think he'd caused her even more pain.

"She let something else slip. She has a 'family' that she takes orders from."

Mikey lost color. "Hell!"

"I've got a man digging hard into her past. He's hit a couple of dead ends, but he thinks he's onto something. I should have an answer today," Paul told him.

"You think she's on Cotillo's payroll."

"I think she might be," Paul replied. "Think about it. She and Billie are as out of place here as roaches in a ritzy hotel. So why are they here? Maybe to watch you and report on your movements to a third party."

"Like a cleaner," Mikey said, referring to a contract killer.

"Maybe. It depends on which family she has ties to. Cotillo's not the only man in the game. He has enemies. She's from New York. Cotillo's moving on Tony Garza in Jersey. Suppose another boss has Cotillo in his sights and wants to know if you're protected before he orders a hit."

Mikey toyed with his coffee cup. "That's a possibility."

"Cotillo's drawn a lot of attention to himself and to the outfit in general with this takeover thing. He's harking back to the mob wars in the past, which were bloody and public and ended in the congressional hearings that tore the Five Families apart. They can't really afford to make themselves too visible even today. Cotillo's a threat to them as well as to you and Tony. They might decide to act."

"If Jessie was lining up a hit, she had a perfect opportunity while we were at the restaurant," Mikey said. "Santi was at another table. Of course, I was watching the door. I know how hits go down."

"Which is why I don't think her boss is Cotillo."

Mikey drew in a long breath. "That might be." He looked into the coffee cup at the thick black liquid. "Bernie will never forgive me. I don't guess it matters. She didn't want me to begin with."

"Or so Jessie told you. She likes rich men. Kemp already called her down about it at least once. Of course, he fired her this morning."

"What?"

"She mouthed off to Ted Regan, of all people, and told him court had been canceled. Since she was calling from the DA's office, he believed her. He didn't show up and the case was thrown out of court. Kemp was livid."

"I guess so. She'll get another job, I guess."

"She and Billie left town late this afternoon," Paul

replied. "I got that from Mandy. She knows everything that goes on in this town. But I'm sure Jessie will keep in touch with you," he added sarcastically. "I mean, since you're dating her and all."

"You don't understand," he burst out. "I lost everything! Bernie couldn't live with what I am, and I don't know how I'm going to live without her! Jessie kept asking if we could get a meal somewhere and I said yes. I know I shouldn't have done it. I was so damned low I didn't care about how it would look."

"Jessie is poison," Paul said. "I'd bet real money that she told Bernie some tale about you, as well, to the tune of your not being able to live with a woman who might be an invalid later on."

Mikey was very still. He just stared at his cousin.

"Think about it. She told you that Bernie hated your past. Maybe she told Bernie that you hated her disease."

"Dear God," Mikey said huskily, and buried his face in his hands. "Oh, God, what am I going to do?"

"Talk to Bernie."

Mikey removed his hands from his face and drank the coffee. "Sure. I'm going to walk into the office, and she's going to throw me out headfirst, or the verbal equivalent. She thinks I slept with damned Jessie. She'll hate me."

"Sari hated me, too, when I first came back here." Paul grinned. "Remember what I did when she wouldn't speak to me?"

"Everybody in Jacobsville remembers," Mikey chuckled. "They even talked about it at the boarding-house and it was three years ago."

"Whatever works," he commented pointedly.

Mikey drew in a breath. "I'll think about it."

"Meanwhile, I have news."

"About Cotillo?"

Paul chuckled. "Not yet. About Sari."

Mikey's eyebrows arched.

"She's pregnant," Paul said, and smiled from ear to ear.

"Damn, that's great! Absolutely great!" Mikey burst out. "I'm happy for you."

"It's the nicest surprise," Paul confessed. "We've been trying for a long time, but, well, nothing happened and I thought maybe we couldn't have kids. It wouldn't have mattered. I love her so much. I'd rather have her and no kids than the biggest family in the country with any other woman."

"I know how that feels." Mikey put his cup down. "I wanted them with Bernie. Never with anybody else. Even with her limitations, she could carry a child. I asked a doctor." He flushed. "There are medicines she can't afford that I could have bought for her, and they would have helped. She could have private duty nurses, anything she needed. I'd have…taken care of her." He stopped, choking up.

"It isn't too late."

Mikey looked up, with the saddest expression Paul had ever seen. "Yes, it is, Paulie. It's too late. And I did it to myself, by not telling her what Jessie said and giving her a chance to tell me what she felt."

"We all make mistakes."

"Even you aren't in my class, cousin," Mikey said. He leaned back in the chair. "At least you're having that happy ending people dream about," he added with an affectionate smile. "You got lucky."

"I wish you had, too."

Mikey shrugged. "Let's just hope that Cotillo doesn't."

* * *

They were prophetic words. A day later, the story broke on all the major news networks. A New Jersey mob figure named Anthony Cotillo was found dead in his apartment of apparently natural causes. A friend said that the man had no apparent health problems and that it came as a shock to his associates.

"Can they detect an air embolism?" Mikey mused. "It doesn't matter—they'll have people in the coroner's office to make sure that doesn't go into the report."

Paul sighed. "Well, it's a novel way to take care of an interloper without getting the government all stirred up," he agreed. "No mess, no blood trail, no nothing. But I wonder who hit him?"

Mikey smiled. "Marcus Carrera has many friends from the old days," he pointed out. "Some of them owe him really big favors."

Paul's eyebrows arched.

"Really big," Mikey emphasized. And he smiled.

Tony Garza came home to New Jersey amid promises from an obscure New York outfit family that the loose association of bosses, the one that had existed since the Five Families were scattered by pressure from the feds, had no problem with him. They assured him that no more problems were expected, and that they had several people making sure of it. The message was clear—Carrera might not be a mob figure any longer, since he'd gone straight, but he was still a power to contend with in the States. A lot of people were afraid of him. Tony was going to be safe.

"So I guess I'll go home now," Mikey said sadly, when he was having supper with Paul and Sari. "I'll come back for the christening, though," he teased.

"Wrong church," Paul teased. "We're Methodist. Although, Reverend Blair does have a sort of christening ceremony, but not like the one you're thinking of."

"We can pretend. I'll come anyway." He toyed with his food. "So I guess Jessie and Billie worked for the New York boss."

"I guess so," Paul said.

"Carrera was a terror when he was younger," Mikey remarked with a smile. "You could just say his name ten years ago and people would start running for the door."

"It shocked everybody when he went legit," Paul said. "Even the feds. Now he's got a wife and two sons and he's the happiest man on earth."

"Families are nice," Mikey said absently.

"You should get married and have one," Sari said firmly.

"Chance would be a fine thing."

"You never know," she replied. "Strange things happen when you least expect them."

He smiled at her. "They do, don't they? What do you guys want, a boy or a girl?"

"Either," Paul said.

"Both," Sari said, and grinned.

"No twins on our side of the family, cousin," he told Paul.

"But there are loads on my side," Sari laughed. "Distant cousins, but at least three sets of twins among them."

"Son of a gun! You could have your whole family in one year."

Paul laughed. "Who knows?" he teased, and he looked at his wife with eyes that absolutely ate her. She looked back at him the same way.

Mikey felt more alone than he ever had in his whole life. Much more, although he was happy for his cousin. But he was leaving town. His heart would stay here, with that sad little woman who lived in Mrs. Brown's boardinghouse. She'd never forgive him for Jessie. He knew it without asking. It was the worst mistake of his life, and he couldn't fix it. Nobody could.

He packed his bags and Santi packed his. His heart was breaking. Bernie was the light of his life and he was leaving her behind. He hadn't felt so low since the death of his grandmother, and the murder of Paulie's wife and little girl. He felt the grief like a living thing.

"Where we going, boss," Santi asked. "Vegas or Jersey?"

"Vegas," Mikey said without missing a beat. "I need a diversion. A big, bright, flashy, glitzy diversion."

"Vegas is a nice place," Santi said. He grinned. "Lots of glitzy girls there."

"You're welcome to all you can find," his boss replied glumly. "You can have my share, too."

"That's nice," Santi replied.

They packed their things into the convertible. Mikey went to the office and took care of the bill. Santi was waiting just outside the door in the limousine as he came out.

Mikey put himself into the back seat and leaned against it wearily as Santi pulled out into traffic. It was early morning, so they'd probably hit the work traffic on the way to the airport. He didn't care. Santi had been a wheelman for Mikey in earlier times. He was still a great driver.

"Do me a favor," Mikey said suddenly.

"Sure, boss. What?"

"Drive through town. Past the courthouse."

Santi didn't say anything. He just smiled.

The women who worked in Kemp's office were just filing in. There was Glory Ramirez and Sari Fiore. Olivia was ahead of them all. And there, behind them, in an old tweed coat, walking slowly with a cane, was Bernie.

"Slow down, okay?" Mikey asked, sounding half out of breath as he watched Bernie's slow progress to the door. She was hurting. It was a cold, rainy day, and he imagined she was having one of her flares.

He remembered her sitting up with him when he'd had the migraine. He remembered carrying her into the boardinghouse the day they'd met, when she had fallen in front of the car and he thought she was playing him. It seemed so long ago.

She made her way into the building, not looking behind her. She'd screwed her beautiful blond hair up into a bun. She looked tired and in pain, worn-out. He grimaced as he watched her disappear into the office. The door closed behind her.

Mikey felt the loss of connection like a blow to his chest.

"We leaving now, boss?" he asked Mikey.

There was a hesitation, only a very brief one. "Yeah," Mikey said finally. He slumped a little. "Yeah, we're leaving. Let's get to the airport."

"Sure thing," Santi said, and sped up past the office building, leaving it and Bernie behind, perhaps forever.

Chapter Fourteen

Bernie, never a late sleeper, woke very early the next morning. She couldn't get what Sari had said out of her mind. Suppose Jessie had told lies to both her and Mikey? She had been too shy to speak to him about something so intimate, and he would probably have been reluctant to say anything to Bernie about her supposed distaste for his background.

Jessie had been putting on an act. Why? The woman was patently out of place in Jacobsville, which led to a worrying conclusion. What if she was a lookout for that man who was trying to have Mikey killed? It really bothered her.

She got up and dressed, aching and barely able to walk for the pain and stiffness. After a few minutes, she felt better, but she'd still need the cane, even on level ground. Rheumatoid arthritis flares were painful and fatiguing. She took her medicines regularly, but they'd begun to be less effective, as many drugs became over the years. She recalled the wonder shot that was used to control it, but even with a large discount, she'd never be able to afford the monthly expense. It might have made a difference in her quality of life. Days like this, cold and rainy, were agony to people who lived with arthritis.

She didn't tell the other women that she'd walked to work, because they'd have fussed. Any one of them would gladly have offered her a ride, but she wanted to be independent. It wasn't good to lean on people. Her father had always said that they had to take care of their own problems and not advertise them to the world. It was a burden that honorable people shared. She smiled, remembering the wonderful man who'd raised her. She missed him.

"You're just on time," Sari Fiore teased, smiling.

"I'm always on time," Bernie replied with a small laugh. "I wouldn't want Mr. Kemp to fire me."

"No danger of that, as long as you don't tell Ted Regan that court's been dismissed," Olivia said, tongue in cheek.

They all laughed as they filed into the office.

Bernie was the last one inside. She almost stumbled going in, but she regained her footing quickly, holding on to the doorknob. The back of her neck tingled. Odd, she thought, that feeling. But it was probably nothing. She ignored it and went on inside the building.

Sari was pregnant. It was happy news, and the whole office went wild when they knew. Even Mr. Kemp congratulated her, grinning from ear to ear.

"You'll find that babies are addictive," he teased. "Which is why we have another one on the way, too."

"That's wonderful," Sari said, smiling. "I know Violet's over the moon. Are the twins coping with your toddler?"

"The twins?" Bernie asked curiously.

"He has two Siamese cats," Sari explained. "He made them mad one day and they tag-teamed biting his ankles and ran under heavy furniture afterward."

Mr. Kemp chuckled. "They've calmed down. Well, a little. Violet learned early that they like salmon, so she keeps cans of it handy."

They all laughed. Bernie was thinking about children. She'd wanted one so badly with Mikey. Just as well, she realized, that she'd never been intimate with him, considering the way things had turned out.

In his world of glitzy women and casinos, he probably had a procession of beautiful women at his beck and call. Including Jessie.

But she remembered that Sari had told her Mikey was no longer in danger; nor was his boss, Tony Garza. Apparently a group of bosses had decided that Cotillo was calling too much attention to certain underworld figures, and he'd been taken out of the equation. It was called "natural causes," but Sari said it wasn't at all, that the mob knew how to cause sudden death that looked natural.

That was Mikey's world. Death. Violence. Glitter. Of course, she was well out of it. Her health wouldn't have allowed her to endure the stresses of his profession, much less the strenuous lifestyle he enjoyed.

But she missed him terribly. It had sent her into days of depression when she knew he was gone. He'd left without even bothering to say goodbye. But what, she reasoned, could he have said? That he couldn't live with a disabled woman, that he preferred her sexy coworker, that Jessie was great in bed? All those things? It would have tormented her forever. No. It was better the way it had happened—a quick ending, as painless as possible. It was over.

Now all she had to do was adjust to her new reality. Maybe one day she could look back and remember a handsome, dashing man who'd taken her places and kissed her as if he'd have died for her mouth, who'd seemed to love her. Maybe she could recall just the joy of being with him, without remembering how it had ended. It would be a pretty memory, tied up with ribbon and tucked away in a scrapbook.

Mikey watched people come and go in the casino with hardly any interest at all. Beside him, Tony Garza, who was breaking his California trip with a stop in Las Vegas to see Mikey, was sipping a whiskey highball.

"They ever find out who hit Cotillo?" Mikey asked.

"No. And they never will. The New York family arranged it all. Cotillo was about to point the finger at one of their underbosses. It would have devastated the family. So they sent Jack the Mackerel and Billy Tenspot down to visit Cotillo. They had a guy in the coroner's office swear it was a natural death."

"What about Cotillo's family?" Mikey persisted.

"Running scared. It wasn't that big, and most of them tried to talk Cotillo out of biting off more than he could chew. The New York boss even spoke to him personally and told him how it was. He didn't listen."

"Terminal error," Mikey commented.

"Very." He sighed. "At least we're off the hook. I

owe you, Mikey. Big-time. You ever need a favor, you know where to find me."

Mikey shrugged. "No sweat. You'd have done it for me, boss."

Tony chuckled. "Yeah. I would have." He paused. "What's this about some Texas girl you got involved with?"

Mikey's face closed up. "Closed chapter," he said tautly.

"I got a good look at Texas women when I gave Merrie Grayling away at her wedding," he reminded Mikey. "They're good people."

"She was. But she couldn't live with my profession."

"I heard you couldn't live with her maybe being an invalid one day."

Mikey turned. His eyes glittered. "I never said that," he replied. "Never! It wouldn't have mattered to me if she couldn't even walk. I'd have carried her—" He broke off, averting his eyes.

Tony laid a big hand on his shoulder. "Jessie Tennison belongs to the New York boss. She's his mistress," he continued. "She made trouble for you because it's what she does. Nobody likes her, and one day the wife is going to complain loudly enough that the boss will have to do something about her. Something unpleasant. She's making her own sad future and she doesn't even know it."

"I won't mourn her," Mikey said.

"Your cousin said she carried tales to both of you," he said. "She lied and you both believed her."

Mikey's face hardened. "Bernie told me herself that she was always on the right side of the law."

"And you told her that it didn't matter that she might become disabled one day, yes?"

Mikey's teeth clenched. "For all the good it did me."

"It's your life, *paisan*," he continued. "But you've been moping around here like a lost soul ever since I walked in the door, when we should both be celebrating. If I were you, I'd go back to Texas and talk to the woman. Really talk to her."

Mikey grimaced. "I took Jessie out on the town. I know, it was stupid. I was feeling low because of what I'd heard, what Jessie told me that Bernie said about my past. I wanted to feel better, so I took her up to San Antonio for supper. She told Bernie I slept with her. It's a lie, but Bernie had every reason to believe her. So even if I wanted to go back and talk it out, she'd never trust me again. She'd probably shut the door in my face."

"There are these things called roses," Tony mused. "Women go nuts over them. I know my late wife did. Chocolates. Greeting cards. I went through all those things while I was courting her." His eyes were wistful with memories. "She didn't even like me at first, but I wore her down. I was a bad man, too, Mikey, and her dad was a cop, but it didn't matter. She had leukemia," he added softly. "I took care of her when she had relapses, right up until the last one that took her out. I never minded. She knew it. We loved each other. None of the small stuff mattered. Love kept us together in spite of the difficulties we faced."

Mikey hadn't said anything. He just listened. "That's a lot like me and Bernie," he said after a minute.

"Yeah. How about that?"

Mikey took a deep breath. "I'll think about it." He glanced at the boss. "Roses, huh?"

"Might send yellow ones," Tony suggested. "Isn't there some song about yellow roses and Texas?"

Mikey actually laughed. It was the first time he had since he'd left Jacobsville.

It was the middle of the afternoon when the florist brought them in. Judy, who owned the flower shop, came herself, grinning from ear to ear as she carried them straight to a shocked Bernie at her desk and placed them on it.

"Oh!" Bernie's hand went to her throat. She couldn't believe what she was seeing. There must have been three dozen yellow roses in the arrangement, along with flowers of every single color, and greenery highlighting it all.

"I know, it's closer to Thanksgiving than spring," Judy laughed, "but the man said yellow roses, so that's what you get."

"The man?" Bernie was dumbfounded. Her coworkers were grinning from ear to ear.

"Read the card," Judy suggested, indicating it on a plastic stand inside the arrangement.

Bernie pulled it out with hands that held a faint trembling. She opened the envelope. The card only said, "Miss you terribly. Can you forgive?" And it was signed "Mikey."

Tears were rolling down her cheeks. She read the card again, just to be sure that she wasn't seeing things.

"Well?" Sari prompted. "What does it say? Who's it from? Or should we just guess?" she added with a grin.

"Mikey," Bernie said in a husky tone. "The flowers are from Mikey!"

"Doesn't he do things in a big way?" Olivia mused, studying the huge arrangement. "Amazing that your back didn't break under the weight, Judy," she teased the florist.

"I have liniment," Judy chuckled.

"They're so beautiful," Bernie said, caressing a petal on one of the roses, most of which were in bloom.

"I guess he thinks you are, too, sweetheart, because let me tell you, I could almost retire on what this arrangement cost," Judy laughed.

Bernie struggled to her feet and hugged the florist. "You always do the most beautiful arrangements, but this one is extraordinary."

"Thanks." Judy hugged her back.

Mr. Kemp came out of his office, stopped dead, and gaped at the arrangement that took up most of Bernie's desk. "Did somebody die?" he asked.

They all burst out laughing. Kemp grinned.

"Mikey, huh?" he asked Bernie, who flushed. "I figured he'd work it out sooner or later. Okay, people, back to work."

"Yes, sir," they chorused.

Bernie and Judy moved her beautiful floral arrangement to a side table so that the desk was clear, but all day Bernie's eyes went to it, and she felt as if she could walk on clouds.

Paul and Sari Fiore drove her home so that Paul could carry the arrangement inside for her. It was very heavy.

"Right there, if you don't mind," Bernie said, indicating the cleared-off part of her chest of drawers. "It's so beautiful!"

"Good thing that Judy makes arrangements that don't have a loud scent," Sari teased, "or you'd smother in here from the fumes."

"Oh, I wouldn't even mind." Bernie sighed. "Nobody ever sent me flowers in my whole life," she added softly.

Paul and Sari exchanged glances. It was obvious that Mikey's peace offering had struck pay dirt.

He phoned Paul that night.

"Well?" he asked. "Did she donate them to the hospital or her church?" he prompted, and sounded worried.

"No. She cried," Paul said. "Then Sari and I brought her home so I could carry them inside for her. God, Mikey, did you buy out a florist? I never knew there were that many yellow roses in the whole damned state," he added, chuckling.

"I wanted to make an impression," Mikey replied. There was a smile in his voice. "So she liked them, huh?"

"She loved them."

There was a sigh. "In that case, Santi and I might come down for a visit in a week or so. Just to get the lay of the land."

"I think that would be a very good idea," Paul replied.

Bernie was walking home late in the afternoon, wrapped in a coat against the chill, using her cane because it was rainy and her footing wasn't good.

A big, black limousine pulled up beside her and the window rolled down while her heart almost beat her to death.

"Now, don't fall under the wheels this time, okay?" said a man with a New Jersey accent.

Bernie laughed. "Hi," she said softly.

The door opened. Mikey got out, leaving Santi behind the wheel. He stuck his hands in his pockets and moved close to Bernie. His dark eyes searched her wan face in the late-afternoon dimness. They were intent, as if he was looking at something almost out of a fantasy.

"You look good," he said. "A little worn. You've lost weight, I think."

"Just a little," she confessed. Her eyes went over his lean face. "You look worn, too."

"I never slept with Jessie," he blurted out. "I like to stick to my own species."

She laughed in spite of herself.

"I did a dumb thing," he muttered. "I should have known that you wouldn't pour your heart out to somebody in a public place."

She grimaced. "I should have known the same thing about you."

He drew in a breath and smiled. "So. Suppose we start over? Hi. My name's Mikey. I sometimes break the law, but I'll try to restrict myself to jaywalking for the rest of my life if you'll take a chance on me."

Her heart leaped. "Hi. My name's Bernadette, but everybody calls me Bernie. I never break the law, but I'd take a chance on you no matter what you did for a living."

His lips parted on a husky breath. "Oh, baby," he said in a rough whisper. "God, I've missed you…!"

She would have told him the same thing, but he had her up in his arms and was kissing her as if there was no tomorrow. Her arms were around his neck, her cane was on the sidewalk somewhere getting wet. She was kissing him back.

Long minutes went by. The rain was coming down in buckets and they were both soaked. Finally Santi got out of the car and stopped beside them, coughing loudly.

Mikey drew back, shivering a little with the overwhelming hunger he felt for Bernie. He looked at Santi blankly. "What? You got a cold?"

"Boss, it's raining. Really raining. You know?"

Mikey blinked. Santi's hair was plastered to his head and face. He scowled and looked down at Bernie. Her hair was plastered to her head and face, too. He laughed out loud. "Damn. So it is! I guess we should find a dry place, huh?"

"I guess," Santi mused. He opened the car door.

"But I'm wet," Bernie wailed.

"The seats are leather, honey, they'll dry. Santi, find her cane, would you?"

"You bet!"

Santi closed the door.

"Now," Mikey murmured, drawing her close. "Where were we...?"

They were married in the courthouse, in the office of the justice of the peace. Bernie wore a winter-white coatdress and carried a bouquet of white roses. She had on a little saucy white hat that had a veil, and Mikey lifted it as he kissed her for the first time as Mrs. Michael Fiore.

Sari and Paul were their witnesses, and Tony Garza came down with his entourage for the wedding. In fact, Marcus Carrera and his Delia, and their little boys, also came to town for the event.

"I owe you a lot," Mikey told Marcus.

The big man waved away the thanks. "No sweat," he chuckled. "But if you come across a bolt of antique cloth, you know where to mail it, right?" he teased.

Mikey clapped him on the back. "You bet I do."

The honeymoon was in Jamaica, in Montego Bay, where they swam and acted like tourists. Well, at least, after the first night they were together.

"You don't need to worry about a thing," Mikey

whispered to her as he undressed her very slowly and eased her under the covers.

She shivered a little at the first contact with his nude body, but he kissed her and caressed her until she didn't care what he did as long as he didn't stop.

He carried her from one breathless plateau to another, from one side of the bed to the other, for what seemed hours before he finally moved over her with intent. She was so sensitized by then that she barely felt the little flash of pain that hallmarked his slow penetration of her welcoming body.

She was aching for him, so hungry that she knew nothing, saw nothing, except his face above her as the passion grew and grew and grew and finally exploded into pleasure beyond anything she'd ever dreamed.

"Oh, my goodness," she moaned as they finally moved apart. She shifted her hips and the exquisite sensations went on and on.

He chuckled, drawing her to his side. "It's addictive."

"Very!"

He pulled her onto him and looked up into her soft eyes. "I've never missed anyone the way I missed you. I was just ashamed to even call you, after what I did."

She bent and kissed him tenderly. "We both believed lies because we were insecure."

"But no more."

"Not ever," she agreed.

"There's still the matter of the little unlawful things," he said, grimacing. "But I've got a legitimate casino now, and two of the biggest mob bosses in history in my corner. So if I want to move out into the world, so long as I don't betray any secrets, I can leave the old life behind. Not that I'll give up my house in Jersey. You'll like it," he added softly. "It's old, but it's got character."

"I'll love anywhere you live," she said simply. "And I'll cope, however I have to." Her pale eyes met his dark ones. "I love you."

He hugged her close. "I love you, too, baby. And don't you dare think I mind about the cane and the days you have flares, or if you get sick. I can afford nurses, anything you need. But I'll take care of you myself," he added, lifting his head, and his eyes adored her. "Because you're the most important thing in the whole world."

"So are you to me," she whispered, and kissed him.

"Listen, I spoke to your doctor," he said. "Louise Coltrain said there are medicines you can inject, that will make your quality of life a hundred times better."

"Yes, but they're so expensive—"

"I could fund the treasury of a small country, honey," he interrupted. "It will be money well spent, especially when the kids come along. You won't need to try and keep up with me," he chuckled. "I'll carry you, if I need to. But you *will* need to keep up with our kids…"

She laughed with pure delight. "Are we having several?"

He grinned. "However many you want. And I'll learn to change diapers and give bottles, just so you know."

"We can do it together," she said softly.

"We'll do everything together," he replied quietly. "As long as we live. Yes?"

She bent and kissed him hungrily. "As long as we live."

And they did.

* * * * *

CIRCLE OF GOLD

Chapter One

Kasie Mayfield was excited. Her gray eyes were brimming with delight as she sat in the sprawling living room at the Double C Ranch in Medicine Ridge, Montana. There was a secretarial position available on the mammoth Double C, and she had the necessary qualifications. She was only twenty-two, but she had a certificate from secretarial school and plenty of initiative. Besides all that, the position was secretary to John Callister, the second son of the well-known family that headed not only a publishing empire in New York City, but a cattle empire out West.

There was a very interesting story about the ranch in a magazine that Kasie was reading while she waited her turn to be interviewed. The elder Callisters lived in New York, where they published, among others, a famous sports magazine. When they weren't in the city, they lived in Jamaica on an ancestral estate. The Callister who had founded the American branch of the family had been a British duke. He bought an obscure little magazine in New York City in 1897 and turned it into a publishing conglomerate. One of his sons had emigrated to Montana and founded the ranch. It eventually passed to Douglas Callister, who had raised the boys, Gilbert and John. Nobody talked about why the uncle had been given custody of both boys and left them the ranch when he died. Presumably it was some dark family secret. Apparently there wasn't a lot of contact between the boys and their parents.

Gilbert, the eldest at thirty-two, had been widowed three years ago. He had two young daughters, Bess, who was five, and Jenny, who was four. John had never married. He was a rodeo champion and did most of the traveling that accompanied showing the ranch's prize-winning pedigree black Angus bulls. Gil was the power in the empire. He was something of a marketing genius, and he dealt with the export business and sat on the boards of two multinational corporations. But mostly he ran the ranch, all thirty thousand acres of it.

There was a photograph of him in the magazine, but she didn't need it to know what he looked like. Kasie had gotten a glimpse of him on her way into the house to wait for her turn to be interviewed. One glimpse had been enough. It shocked her that a man who didn't even know her should glare at her so intently.

A more conceited woman might have taken it for masculine interest. But Kasie had no ego. No, that tall, lanky blond man hadn't liked her, and made no secret of it. His pale blue eyes under that heavy brow had pierced her skin. She wouldn't get the job. He'd make sure of it.

She glanced at the woman next to her, a glorious blonde with big brown eyes and beautiful legs crossed under a thigh-high skirt. Then she looked at her own ankle-length blue jumper with a simple gray blouse that matched her big eyes. Her chestnut hair was in a long braid down her back. She wore only a little lipstick on her full, soft mouth, and no rouge at all on her cheeks. She had a rather ordinary oval face and a small, rounded chin, and she wore contact lenses. She wasn't at all pretty. She had a nice figure, but she was shy and didn't make the most of it. It was just as well that she had good office skills, she supposed, because it was highly unlikely that anybody would ever want to actually marry her. She thought of her parents and her brother and had to fight down tears. It was so soon. Too soon, probably. But the job might keep her from thinking of what had happened....

"Miss Mayfield!"

She jumped as her name was called in a deep, authoritative tone. "Yes?"

"Come in, please."

She put a smile on her face as she clutched her small purse in her hands and walked into the paneled office, where plaques and photos of bulls lined the walls and burgundy leather furniture surrounded the big mahogany desk. A man was sitting there, with his pale eyes piercing and intent. A blond man with broad shoulders and a hard, lean face that seemed to be all rocky edges. It was not John Callister.

She stopped in front of the desk with her heart pounding and didn't bother to sit down. Gil Callister was obviously doing the interviews, and now she was sure she wouldn't get the job. She knew John Callis-

ter from the drugstore where she'd worked briefly as a
stock clerk putting herself through secretarial courses.
John had talked to her, teased her and even told her
about the secretarial job. He'd have given her a chance.
Gil would just shoot her out the door. It was obvious
that he didn't like anything about her.

He tossed a pen onto the desk and nodded toward
the chair facing it. "Sit down."

She felt vulnerable. The door was closed. Here she
was with a hungry tiger, and no way out. But she sat
anyway. Never let it be said that she lacked courage.
They could throw her into the arena and she would die
like a true Roman... She shook herself. She really had
to stop reading the Plinys and Tacitus. This was the new
millennium, not the first century A.D.

"Why do you want this job?" Gil asked bluntly.

Her thin eyebrows lifted. She hadn't expected the
question. "Because John is a dish?" she ventured dryly.

The answer seemed to surprise him. "Is he?"

"When I worked at the drugstore, he was always
kind to me," she said evasively. "He told me about the
job, because he knew I was just finishing my secretarial certificate at the vocational-technical school. I
got high grades, too."

Gil pursed his lips. He still didn't smile. He looked
down at the résumé she'd handed him and read it carefully, as if he was looking for a deficiency he could
use to deny her the job. His mouth made a thin line.
"Very high grades," he conceded with obvious reluc-
tance. "This is accurate? You really can type 110 words
a minute?"

She nodded. "I can type faster than I can take dictation, actually."

He pushed the résumé aside and leaned back. "Boy-friends?"

She was nonplussed. Her fingers tightened on her purse. "Sir?"

"I want to know if you have any entanglements that might cause you to give up the job in the near future," he persisted, and seemed oddly intent on the reply.

She shifted restlessly. "I've only ever had one real boyfriend, although he was more like a brother. He married my best friend two months ago. That was just before I moved to Billings," she added, mentioning the nearby city, "to live with my aunt. So, I don't date much."

She was so uncomfortable that she almost squirmed. He didn't know about her background, of course, or he wouldn't need to ask such questions. Modern women were a lot more worldly than Kasie. But she'd said that John was a dish. She flushed. Good grief, did he think she went around seducing men or something? Was that why he didn't want her in his house? Her expression was mortified.

He averted his eyes. "You have some odd character references," he said after a minute, frowning at them. "A Catholic priest, a nun, a Texas Ranger and a self-made millionaire with alleged mob ties."

She only smiled demurely. "I have unique friend-ships."

"You could put it that way," he said, diverted. "Is the millionaire your lover?"

She went scarlet and her jaw dropped.

"Oh, hell, never mind," he said, apparently disturbed that he'd asked the question and uncomfortable at the reaction it drew. "That's none of my business. All right, Kasie…" He hesitated. "Kasie. What's it short for?"

"I don't know," she blurted out. "It's my actual name."

One eye narrowed. "The millionaire's name is K.C.," he pointed out. "And he's at least forty."

"Thirty-seven. He saved my mother's life, while she was carrying me," she said finally. "He wasn't always a millionaire."

"Yes, I know, he was a professional soldier, a mercenary." His eyes narrowed even more. "Want to tell me about it?"

"Not really, no," she confided.

He shook his head. "Well, if nothing else, you'll be efficient. You're also less of a distraction than the rest of them. There's nothing I hate more than a woman who wears a skirt up to her briefs to work and then complains when men stare at her if she bends over. We have dress codes at our businesses and they're enforced—for both sexes."

"I don't have any skirts that come up to my…well, I don't wear short ones," she blurted out.

"So I noticed," he said with a deliberate glance at her long dress.

She fumbled with her purse while he went over the résumé one last time. "All right, Kasie, you can start Monday at eight-thirty. Did John tell you that the job requires you to live here?"

"No!"

His eyebrows arched. "Not in his room, of course," he added just to irritate her, and then looked satisfied when she blushed. "Miss Parsons, who has charge of my daughters, lives in. So does Mrs. Charters who does the cooking and housekeeping. We have other part-time help that comes infrequently. Board and meals are provided by us, in addition to your salary." He named a figure that made Kasie want to hold on to something. It was astronomical compared to what she'd made working at the drugstore part-time. "You'll be a private secretary," he added. "That means you may have to travel with us from time to time."

"Travel?" Her face softened.

"Do you like to travel?" he asked.

"Oh, yes. I loved it when I was little."

She wondered by the look he gave her if he assumed that her parents had been wealthy. He could not know, of course, that they were both deceased.

"Do you want the job?" he asked.

"Yes," she said.

"All right. I'll tell the others they can leave." He got to his feet, elegant and lithe, moving with a grace that was unequaled in Kasie's circle of acquaintances. He opened the office door, thanked the other young women for coming and told them that the position had been filled. There was a shuffle of feet, some murmuring, and the front door closed.

"Come on, Kasie," Gil said. "I'll introduce you to…"

"Daddy!" came a wail from the end of the hall. A little girl with disheveled long blond hair came running and threw herself at Gil, sobbing.

He picked her up, and his whole demeanor changed. "What is it, baby?" he asked in the most tender tone Kasie had ever heard. "What's wrong?"

"Me and Jenny was playing with our dollies on the deck and that bad dog came up on the porch and he tried to bite us!"

"Where's Jenny?" he demanded, immediately threatening.

A sobbing little voice answered him as the younger girl came toddling down the hall rubbing her eyes with dirty little fists. She reached up to Gil, and he picked her up, too, oblivious to her soiled dress and hands.

"Nothing's going to hurt my babies. Did the dog bite either of you?" Gil demanded.

"No, Daddy," Bess said.

"Bad doggie!" Jenny sobbed. "Make him go away!"

"Of course I will!" Gil said roughly, kissing little cheeks with a tenderness that made Kasie's heart ache.

A door opened and John Callister came down the hall, looking very unlike the friendly man Kasie knew from the drugstore. His pale eyes were glittering in his lean, dark face, and he looked murderous.

"Are they all right?" he asked Gil, pausing to touch the girls' hair. "It was that mangy cur that Fred Sims insisted on bringing with him when he hired on. I got between it and the girls and it tried to bite me, too. I called Sims up to the house and told him to get rid of it and he won't, so he's fired."

"Here." Gil handed his girls to his brother and started down the hall with quick, measured steps.

John stared after him. "Maybe Sims will make it to his truck before Gil gets him," he murmured. "But I wouldn't bet on it. Are my babies all right?" he asked, kissing their little damp cheeks as the girls clung to either shoulder.

"Bad old doggie," Bess sobbed. "Our Missie never bites people!"

"Missie's a toy collie," John explained to a silent Kasie with a smile. "She lives indoors. Nothing like that vicious dog Sims keeps. We've had trouble from it before, but Sims was so good with horses that we put up with it. Not anymore. We can't let it endanger the girls."

"If it would come right up on the porch and try to bite them, it doesn't need to be around children," Kasie agreed.

The girls looked at her curiously.

"Who are you?" Bess asked.

"I'm Kasie," she replied with a smile. "Who are you?"

"I'm Bess," the child replied. "That's Jenny. She's just four," she added, indicating the smaller child, whose hair was medium-length and more light brown than blond.

"I'm very glad to meet you both," Kasie said, smiling warmly. "I'm going to be Mr. Callister's secretary," she added with an apologetic glance at John. "Sorry."

"Why are you sorry?" John asked amusedly. "I only flog secretaries during full moons."

Her eyes crinkled with merriment and she grinned.

"Gil won't let me hire secretaries because I have such a bad track record," John confessed. "The last one turned out to be a jewel thief. You, uh, don't like jewels?" he added deliberately.

She chuckled. "Only costume jewelry. And unless you wear it, we shouldn't have a problem."

There was a commotion outside and John grimaced. "He'll come back in bleeding, as usual," he muttered. "I just glare at people. Gil hits." He gave Kasie a wicked grin. "Sometimes he hits me, too."

The girls giggled. "Oh, Uncle Johnny," Bess teased, "Daddy never hits you! He won't even hit us. He says little children shouldn't be hitted."

"Hit," Kasie corrected absently.

"Hit," Bess parroted, and grinned. "You're nice."

"You're nice, too, precious," Kasie said, reaching out to smooth back the disheveled hair. "You've got tangles."

"Can you make my hair like yours?" Bess asked, eyeing Kasie's braid. "And tie it with a pink ribbon?"

The opening of the back door stopped the conversation dead. Gil came back in with his shirt and jeans dusty and a cut at the corner of his mouth. As he came closer, wiping away the blood, his bruised and lacerated knuckles became visible.

"So much for that little problem," he said with cold satisfaction. His eyes were still glittery with temper until he looked at the little girls. The anger drained out of him and he smiled. "Dirty chicks," he chided. "Go get Miss Parsons to clean you up."

John put them down and Bess looked up at her father accusingly. "Miss Parsons don't like little kids."

"Go on. If she gives you any trouble, come tell me," Gil told the girls.

"Okay, Daddy!"

Bess took Jenny's hand and, with a shy grin at Kasie, she drew the other child with her up the winding staircase.

"They like Kasie already," John commented. "Bess said…"

"Miss Parsons takes care of the kids," Gil said shortly. "Show Kasie the way we keep records. She's a computer whiz in addition to her dictation skills. She should be able to get all those herd records onto diskettes for you. Then we can get rid of the paper clutter before we end up buried in it."

"Okay," John said. He hesitated. "Sims get off okay?"

"Sure," Gil said easily. "No problem." He wiped the

blood away from his mouth with a wicked look at his brother before he turned and went up the staircase after the children.

John just shook his head. "Never mind. Come on, Kasie. Let's get you started."

Kasie moved into the house that weekend. Most of her parents' things, and her own, were at Mama Luke's, about ten miles away in Billings, Montana, to whom she'd come for refuge after losing her family. She had only the bare necessities of clothing and personal items; it barely filled one small suitcase. When she walked into the ranch house with it, Gil was on the porch with one of his men. He gave her a curious appraisal, dismissing the man.

"Where's the rest of your stuff?" he asked, glancing past her at the small, white used car she drove, which she'd parked beside the big garage. "In the trunk?"

"This is all the stuff I have," she said.

He looked stunned. "Surely you have furniture…?"

"My other things are at my aunt's house. But I don't have much stuff of my own."

He stepped aside to let her go inside, his face curious and his eyes intent on her. He didn't say a word, but he watched her even more closely from then on.

The first week on the job, she lost a file that Gil needed for a meeting he was flying to in the family Piper plane. It was an elegant aircraft, twin-engine and comfortable. Gil and John could both fly it and did, frequently, trucking the livestock they were showing from one state to the next with employees. Kasie wished she could go with the livestock, right now. Gil was eloquent about the missing file, his deep voice soft and filled with impatience.

"If you'll just be quiet for a minute, Mr. Callister, I'll find it!" she exclaimed finally, driven to insubordination.

He gave her a glare, but he shut up. She rustled through the folders on her desk with cold, nervous hands. But she did find the file. She extended it, sheepishly, grimacing at the look in his eyes.

"Sorry," she added hopefully.

It didn't do any good. His expression was somber and half-angry. His eyes glittered down at her. She thought absently that he looked very nice in a gray vested suit. It suited his fair hair and light eyes and his nice tan. It also emphasized the excellent fitness of his tall, muscular body. Kasie thought idly that he must have women practically stalking him when he went to dinner meetings. He was striking just to look at, in addition to that very masculine aura that clung to him like his expensive cologne.

"Where's John?" he asked.

"He had a date," she said. "I'm trying to cope with the new tax format."

His eyes narrowed. "Surely they taught tax compilation at your school?"

She grimaced. "Well, actually, they didn't. It's a rather specialized skill."

"Buy what you need from the bookstore or the computer store and have them send me the bill," he said shortly. "If you can't cope, tell me that, too."

She didn't dare. She wouldn't have a job, and she had to support herself. She couldn't expect Mama Luke to do it. "I can cope, sir," she assured him.

His eyes narrowed as he stared down at her. "One

thing more," he added curtly. "My girls are Miss Parsons's responsibility, not yours."

"I only read them a story," she began, blushing guiltily.

His eyebrows arched. "I was referring to the way you braided Bess's hair," he said. "I thought it was an isolated incident."

She swallowed. Hardly isolated. The girls were always somewhere close by when Kasie stopped for lunch or her breaks. She shared her desserts with the children and frequently read to them or took them on walks to point out the various sorts of flowers and trees around the ranch house. Gil didn't know that and she'd hoped the girls hadn't said anything. Miss Parsons was curt and bullying with the children, whom she obviously disliked. It was inevitable that they'd turn to Kasie, who adored them.

"Only one story," she lied.

He seethed. "In case you didn't get the message the first time, Kasie, I am not in the market for a wife or a mother for my daughters."

The insult made her furious. She glared up at him, forgetting all her early teachings about turning cheeks and humility. "I came to work here because I need a job," she said icily. "I'm only twenty-two, Mr. Callister," she added. "And I don't have any interest in a man almost old enough to be my father, with a ready-made family to boot!"

His reaction was unexpected. He didn't fire back. He grew very quiet. He turned and went out of the room without another word. A minute later, she heard the front door close and, soon, an engine fire up.

"So there," she added to herself.

* * *

Gil came home from his trip even quieter than when he'd left. There was tension between him and Kasie, because she hadn't forgotten the insulting remark he'd made to her before he left. As if she'd come to work here just so she could chase him. Really! But there was another complication now, as well. Kasie was a nervous wreck trying to keep him from seeing how much time she actually spent with his little girls. She didn't need to worry when he was off on his frequent business trips, but they suddenly stopped. He started sending Brad Dalton, his manager, to seminars and conferences. He stayed home on the pretext of overseeing massive improvements on the property.

It was just after roundup, when the cattle business was taking up a little less of his time. But there were new bunkhouses being built, as well as new wells being dug in the pastures and new equipment brought in for tagging and vaccinations of new calves. The trucks were being overhauled, along with the other farm machinery such as tractors and combines that harvested the grain crops. The barns were repaired, a new silo erected. It was a busy time.

Kasie found herself involved unexpectedly with Gil when John went out of state to show two new bulls at a pedigree competition and Gil's secretary, Pauline Raines, conveniently sprained her thumb and couldn't type.

"I need these yesterday," he said without preamble, laying a thick sheaf of papers beside Kasie's neat little hand on the desk. "Pauline can't do them. She missed the tennis ball and hit her thumb with the tennis racket."

She managed not to make a disparaging comment—

barely. She didn't like Pauline any more than Gil's daughters did. The woman was lazy and seductive, and always hanging on Gil like a tie. What little work she actually did was of poor quality and she was pitifully slow as well. She worked at the ranch office near the front of the house three days a week, and Kasie had already inherited a good deal of her work. Pauline spent her time by the pool when Gil wasn't watching. Now, Kasie thought miserably, she was going to end up doing not only John's paperwork, including the unbelievably complex taxes that she was still struggling to understand, but Gil's as well.

"I don't guess she could type with her toes?" she murmured absently.

There was an odd sound, but when she looked up, Gil's hard face was impassive. "How long will it take?" he persisted.

She looked at the pages. They weren't data, as she'd first thought, but letters to various stock producers. They all had different headings, but the same basic body. "Is this all?" she asked with cool politeness.

He glowered at her. "There are fifty of them. They'll have to be done individually…"

"No, they won't," she said gently. "All you have to do—" she opened a new file, selected the option she needed and began typing "—is type the body of the letter once and then just type the various addresses and combine them. An hour's work."

He looked as if he'd been slapped. "Excuse me?"

"This word processor does all that for you," she explained. "It's very simple, really."

He looked angry. "I thought you had to type all fifty individually."

"Only if you're using a prehistoric typewriter and carbon system," she pointed out.

He was really angry now. "An hour?" he repeated.

She nodded. "Maybe less. I'll get right on it," she added quickly, hoping to appease him. Heaven only knew what had set him off, but she recognized that glitter in his eyes.

He left her and went to make some phone calls. When he came back, Kasie was printing the letters out, having just finished the mailing labels. There was a folding machine that made short work of folding the letters. Then all she had to do was stuff, lick, stamp and mail the envelopes.

Gil put on the stamps for her. He watched her curiously. Once, when she looked up into his eyes, it was like an electric shock. Surprised, she dropped her gaze and blushed. Really, she thought, he had a strange effect on her.

"How do you like your job so far?" he asked.

"Very much," she said. "Except for the taxes."

"You'll get used to doing them," he assured her.

"I suppose so."

"Can you manage John's load and mine as well, or do you want me to get a temporary to help you?"

"There isn't a lot," she pointed out. "If I get overwhelmed, I'll say so."

He finished stamping the envelopes and stacked them neatly to one side. "You're very honest. It's unusual in most people." He touched a stamp with a floral motif. "My wife was like that." He smiled. "She said that lies were a waste of time, since they got found out anyway." His eyes were far away. "We were in grammar school together. We always knew that we'd marry one day."

The smile faded into misery. "She was a wonderful rider. She rode in the rodeo when she was younger. But a gentle horse ran away with her and a low-lying limb ended her life. Jenny was only a year old when Darlene died. Bess was two. I thought my life was over, too."

Kasie didn't know what to say. It shocked her that a man like Gil would even discuss something so personal with a stranger. Of course, a lot of people discussed even more personal things with Kasie. Maybe she had that sort of face that attracted confidences.

"Do the girls look like her?" she asked daringly.

"Bess does. She was blond and blue-eyed. She wasn't beautiful, but her smile was." His eyes narrowed in painful memory. "They had to sedate me to make me let go of her. I wouldn't believe them, even when they swore to me that no means on earth could save her..." His fingers clenched on top of the envelope and he moved his hand away at once and stood up. "Thanks, Kasie," he said curtly, turning away, as if it embarrassed him to have spoken of his wife at all.

"Mr. Callister," she said softly, waiting until he turned to continue. "I lost...some people three months ago. I understand grief."

He hesitated. "How did they die?"

Her face closed up. "It was...an accident. They were only in their twenties. I thought they had years left."

"Life is unpredictable," he told her. "Sometimes unbearable. But everything passes. Even bad times."

"Yes, that's what everyone says," she agreed.

They shared a long, quiet, puzzling exchange of sorrow before he shrugged and turned away, leaving her to her work.

Chapter Two

Kasie was almost tearing her hair out by the next afternoon. John's mail was straightforward, mostly about show dates and cancellations, transportation for the animals and personal correspondence. Gil's was something else.

Gil not only ran the ranch, but he dealt with the majority of the support companies that were its satellites. He knew all the managers by first names, he often spoke with state and federal officials, including well-known senators, on legislation affecting beef production. Besides that, he was involved in the scientific study of new grasses and earth-friendly pesticides and fertilizers. He worked with resource and conservation groups, even an animal rights group; since he didn't run slaughter cattle and was rabidly proconservation, at least one group was happy to have his name on its board of directors. He was a powerhouse of energy, working from dawn until well after dark. The problem was, every single task he undertook was accompanied by a ton of paperwork. And his part-time secretary, Pauline Raines, was the most disorganized human being Kasie had ever encountered.

John came home late on Friday evening, and was surprised to find Kasie still at work in the study.

He scowled as he tossed his Stetson onto a rack. "What are you doing in here? It's almost ten o'clock! Does Gil know you're working this much overtime?"

She glanced up from the second page of ten that she was trying to type into the computer. None of Pauline's paperwork had ever been keyed in.

She held up the sheaf of paperwork in six files with a sigh. "I think of it as job security," she offered.

He moved around beside the desk and looked over what she was doing. "Good God, he's not sane!" he muttered. "No one secretary could handle this load in a week! Is he trying to kill you?"

"Pauline hurt her thumb," she said miserably. "I get to do her work, too, except that she never put any of the records into the computer. It's got to be done. I don't see how your brother ever found anything in here!"

"He didn't," John said dryly, his pale eyes twinkling. "Pauline made sure of it. She's indispensable, I hear."

Kasie's eyes narrowed. "She won't be for long, when I get this stuff keyed in," she assured him.

"Don't tell her that unless you pay up your life insurance first. Pauline is a girl who carries grudges, and she's stuck on Gil."

"I noticed."

"Not that he cares," John added slowly. "He never

got over losing his wife. I'm not sure that he'll ever re-marry."

"He told me."

He glanced down at her. "Excuse me?"

"He told me specifically that he didn't want a mother for the girls or a new wife, and not to get my hopes up." She chuckled. "Good Lord, he must be all of thirty-two. I'm barely twenty-two. I don't want a man I'll have to push around in a wheelchair one day!"

"And I don't rob cradles," came a harsh, angry voice from the doorway.

They both jumped as they looked up to see Gil just coming in from the barn. He was still in work clothes, chaps and boots and a sweaty shirt, with a disreputable old black Stetson cocked over one eye.

"Are you trying to make Kasie quit, by any chance?" John challenged. "Good God, man, it'll take her a week just to get a fraction of the information in these spread-sheets into the computer!"

Gil frowned. He pulled off his hat and ran a hand through his sweaty blond hair. "I didn't actually look at it," he confessed. "I've been too busy with the new bulls."

"Well, you'd better look," John said curtly.

Gil moved to the desk, aware of Kasie's hostile glare. He peered over her shoulder and cursed sharply. "Where did all this come from?" he asked.

"Pauline brought it to me and said you wanted it con-verted to disk," she replied flatly.

His eyes began to glitter. "I never told her to land you with all this!"

"It needs doing," she confessed. "There's no way you can do an accurate spreadsheet without the com-parisons you could use in a computer program. I've re-worked this spreadsheet program," she said, indicating the screen, "and made an application that will work for cattle weight gain ratios and daily weighing, as well as diet and health and so forth."

"I'm impressed," Gil said honestly.

"It's what I'm used to doing. Taxes aren't," she added sheepishly.

"Don't look at me," John said. "I hate taxes. I'm not learning them, either," he added belligerently. "Half this ranch is mine, and on my half, we don't do tax work." He nodded curtly and walked out.

"Come back here, you coward!" Gil muttered. "How the hell am I supposed to cope with taxes and all the other routine headaches that you don't have, because you're off somewhere showing cattle!"

John just waved his hand and kept walking.

"Miss Parsons knows taxes inside out," Kasie ven-tured. "She told me she used to be an accountant."

He glared at her. "Miss Parsons was hired to take care of my daughters." He kept looking at Kasie, and not in any friendly way. It was almost as if he knew...

She flushed. "They couldn't get the little paper ship to float on the fish pond," she murmured uneasily, not looking at him. "I only helped."

"And fell in the pond."

She grimaced. "I tripped. Anybody can trip!" she added in a challenging tone, her gray eyes flashing at him.

"Over their own feet?" he mused.

Actually it had been over Bess's stuffed gorilla. The thing was almost her size and Kasie hadn't realized it was there. The girls had laughed and then wailed, thinking she'd be angry at them. Miss Parsons had fussed for hours when Bess got dirt on her pretty yellow dress. But Kasie didn't scold. She laughed, and the girls were so relieved, she could have cried. They really didn't like Miss Parsons.

He put both hands on his lean hips and studied her with reluctant interest. "The girls tell me everything, Kasie," he said finally. He didn't add that the girls worshiped this quiet, studious young woman who didn't even flirt with John, much less the cowboys who worked for the family. "I thought I'd made it perfectly clear that I didn't want you around them."

She took her hands off the keyboard and looked up at him with wounded eyes. "Why?"

The question surprised him. He scowled, trying to think up a fair answer. Nothing came to mind, which made him even madder.

"I don't have any ulterior motives," she said simply. "I like the girls very much, and they like me. I don't understand why you don't want me to associate with them. I don't have a bad character. I've never been in trouble in my life."

"I didn't think you had," he said angrily.

"Then why can't I play with them?" she persisted. "Miss Parsons is turning them into little robots. She won't let them play because they get dirty, and she won't play with them because it isn't dignified. They're miserable."

"Discipline is a necessary part of childhood," he said curtly. "You spoil them."

"For heaven's sake, somebody needs to! You're never here," she added shortly.

"Stop right there, while you still have a job," he interrupted, and his eyes made threats. "Nobody tells me how to raise my kids. Especially not some frumpy little backwoods secretary!"

Frumpy? Backwoods? Her eyes widened. She stood up. She was probably already fired, so he could just get it from the hip. "I may be frumpy," she admitted, "and I may be from the backwoods, but I know a lot about little kids! You don't stick them in a closet until they're legal age. They need to be challenged, made curious about the world around them. They need nurturing. Miss Parsons isn't going to nurture them, and Mrs. Charters doesn't have time to. And you aren't ever here at bedtime, even if you're not away on business," she repeated bluntly. "Whole weeks go by when you barely have time to tell them good-night. They need to be read to, so they will learn to love books. They need constructive supervision. What they've got is barbed wire and silence."

His fists clenched by his sides, and his expression darkened. She lifted her chin, daring him to do anything.

"You're an expert on children, I guess?" he chided.

"I took care of one," she said, her eyes darkening. "For several months."

"Why did you quit?"

He was assuming that she'd meant a job. She didn't. The answer to his question was a nightmare. She couldn't bear to remember it. "I wasn't suited to the task," she said primly. "But I won't corrupt your little girls by speaking to them."

He was still glowering. He didn't want Kasie to grow close to the girls. He didn't want her any closer to him than a desk and a computer was. His eyes went involuntarily to the desk piled high with Pauline's undone work. The files were supposed to have been converted to computer months earlier, when he'd hired the woman. He'd assumed that it had been done, because she was always ready with the information he needed. He felt suddenly uneasy.

"Check out Black Ribbon's growth information for me," he said suddenly.

She hesitated, but apparently she was still working for him. She sat down and pulled the information up on the computer. He went to his desk and pulled a spreadsheet from a drawer. He brought it to Kasie and had her compare it with the figures she'd just put into the computer. There was a huge difference, to his favor.

He said a word that caused Kasie's face to grow bright red. That disturbed him, but he didn't allude to it. "I've made modifications to improve what seemed like a deficiency in diet. Now it looks as if it wasn't even necessary. How long will it take you to get the breeding herd information transcribed?"

"Well, I've done about a third of it," she said. "But John has letters and information to be compiled for this new show..."

"You're mine until we get this information on the computer. I'll make it all right with John."

"What about Pauline?" she asked worriedly.

"Pauline is my concern, not yours," he told her.

"Okay, boss. Whatever you say."

He made an odd gesture with one shoulder and gave her a long scrutiny. "I told you to let me know if there was too much work. Why didn't you?"

"I thought I could keep up," she said simply. "I

wouldn't have complained as long as I could do it within a couple of weeks, and I can."

"Working fourteen-hour shifts," he chided.

"Well, work is work," she said. "I don't mind. It's not as if I have an active social life or an earthshaking novel to write or anything. And I get paid a duke's ransom as it is."

He frowned. "Why don't you have a social life?"

"Because cowboys stink," she shot right back.

He started to speak, burst out laughing and walked to the door. "Stop that and go to bed. I'll have you some help by morning. Good night, Kasie."

"Good night, Mr. Callister."

He hesitated, turned, studied her, but he didn't speak. He left her tidying up and went upstairs to change out of his work clothes and have a shower.

The next morning, when she went into the office, Pauline was there and so was Gil. They stopped talking when Kasie walked in, so she assumed that they'd been talking about her. Apparently it hadn't been in a friendly way. Pauline's delicate features were drawn in anger and Gil's eyes were narrow and glittery.

"It's about time you got down here!" Pauline said icily.

"It's eight twenty-five," Kasie said, taken aback. "I'm not supposed to be in here until eight-thirty."

"Well, let's get started, then," Pauline said, flopping down at the computer.

"Doing what, exactly?" Kasie asked, disconcerted.

"Teach her how to put information on the computer," Gil said in a voice that didn't invite argument. "And while she's doing that, you can tackle John's work."

Kasie grimaced. Her pupil didn't look eager or willing. It was going to be a long morning.

It was, too. Pauline made the job twice as tedious, questioning every keystroke twice and grumbling—when Gil was out of the office—about having to work with Kasie.

"Look, this wasn't my idea," Kasie assured her. "I could do it myself if Mr. Callister would just let me."

Pauline didn't soften an inch. "You're trying to get his attention, playing up to those kids," she accused. "You want him."

Kasie just looked at her. "I love children," she said quietly. "But I don't want to get married."

"Who said anything about marriage?" Pauline chided.

Kasie averted her eyes. "I needed a job and John needed a secretary," she murmured as she turned a spreadsheet page.

"Funny. You call him John, but Gil is 'Mr. Callister.' Why?"

The younger woman blinked. "John is just a few years older than I am," she replied.

Pauline frowned. "How old are you?"

"Twenty-two."

There was a long pause. "Well!" she said finally. She pursed her lips and entered a number into the computer. "You think Gil is old, do you?"

"Yes." She didn't, really, but it seemed safer to say so. She did, after all, have to work with this perfumed barracuda for the immediate future.

Pauline actually smiled. But only for a minute.

"What do I do now?" she asked when she finished entering the last number.

Kasie showed her, faintly disturbed by that smile. Oh, well, she'd figure it out later, maybe.

Pauline went home at five o'clock. By now, she had a good idea of how to use the computer. Practice would hone her skills. Kasie wondered why Gil, who had the lion's share of the work, only had a part-time secretary.

When he came back in, late Saturday night, dressed in evening clothes with a black tie and white ruffled shirt, Kasie was still in the office finalizing the spreadsheets. She looked up, surprised at how handsome he was dressed like that. Even if he wasn't really good-looking, he had a natural authority and grace of carriage that made him stand out. Not to mention a physique that many a Hollywood actor would have coveted.

"I thought I told you to give up this night work," he said curtly.

She spared him a glance while she saved the information onto a diskette. "You won't let me play with the girls. I don't have anything else to do."

"Watch television. We have all the latest movies on pay-per-view. You can watch any you like. Read a book. Take up knitting. Learn Dutch. But," he added with unnatural resentment, "stay out of the office after supper."

"Is that an order?" she asked.

"It damned well is!"

He was absolutely bristling, she thought, frowning as she searched his pale blue eyes. She closed the files and shut down the program, uneasy because he was glowering at her.

She got up, neat and businesslike in her beige pantsuit, with her chestnut hair nicely braided and hanging down her back.

But when she went around the desk to go to the door, he blocked her path. She wasn't used to men this close and she backed up a step, which only made things worse. He was so tall that she wished she were wearing high heels. The top of her head barely came up to his nose.

His pale eyes glittered even more. "Old age isn't contagious," he said with pure venom in his deep voice.

"Sir?"

"And don't call me sir!"

She swallowed. He was spoiling for a fight. She couldn't bear the thought of one. Her early life had been in the middle of a violent battleground, and loud noises and voices still upset her. "Okay," she agreed immediately.

He slammed his hands into his pockets and glared more. "I'm thirty-two. Ten years isn't a generation and I'm not a candidate for Social Security."

"Okay," she repeated uneasily.

"For God's sake, stop agreeing with me!" he snapped.

She started to say "Okay" again, and bit her tongue. She was as rigid as a ruler, waiting for more explosions with her breath trapped in her throat.

He took his hands out of his pockets and they clenched at his sides as he looked down at her with more conflicting emotions than he'd ever felt. She wasn't beautiful, but there was a tenderness in her that he craved. He hadn't had tenderness in his life since Darlene's untimely death. This young woman made him hungry for things he couldn't grasp. He didn't understand it, and it angered him.

Kasie was wavering between a dash for the door or backing up again. "Do you want me to quit?" she blurted out.

His teeth ground together. "Yes."

She swallowed. "All right. I'll leave in the morning." She moved around him to the door, trying not to take it personally. Sometimes people just didn't like other people.

"No!"

His voice stopped her with her hand on the doorknob.

There was a long pause. Kasie turned, surprised by his indecision. From what she already knew of Gil Callister, he wasn't a man who had trouble making decisions. But he seemed divided about Kasie.

She went toward him, noticing the odd expression on his face when she stopped within arm's length and folded her hands at her waist.

"I know you don't like me," she said gently. "It's all right. I'll really try hard to stay away from the girls. Once Pauline learns how to input the computer files, you won't even have to see me."

He seemed troubled now. Genuinely troubled. He sighed as if he were carrying the weight of the world on his shoulders. At that moment, he looked as if he needed comforting.

"Bess would love it if you took her and Jenny to one of those cartoon movies," she said out of the blue. "There's a Sunday matinee at the Twin Oaks Cinema."

He still didn't speak.

She searched his cold eyes. "I'm sorry that I've gone behind your back to spend time with them. It's not what you think. I mean, I'm not trying to worm my way into your family, even if Pauline does think so. The girls...

remind me...of my own little niece." Her voice almost broke but she controlled it quickly.

"Does she live far away?" he asked abruptly.

Her eyes darkened. "Very...far away...now," she managed. She forced a smile. "I miss her."

She had to turn away then, or lose control of her wild emotions.

"You can stay for the time being," he said finally, reluctantly. "It will work out."

"That's what my aunt always says," she murmured as she opened the door.

"I didn't know you had family. Your parents are dead, aren't they?"

"They died years ago, when I was little. My aunt was in charge of us until we started school."

"Us?"

She couldn't say it, she couldn't, she couldn't. "I ha... have a twin brother," she corrected quickly.

She lifted her head, praying for strength. "Good night, Mr. Callister."

She heard the silence of his disapproval, but she was too upset to care. She went up the staircase with no hesitation at all, straight to her room. She locked the door and lay down on the covers, crying silently so that no one would hear.

There was a violent storm that night. The lightning lit up the whole sky. Kasie heard engines starting up and men's voices yelling. The animals must be unsettled. She'd read that cattle didn't like lightning.

She got up to look out the window, and then she heard the urgent knocking at her door.

She went to it, still in her neat thick white cotton

gown that concealed the soft lines of her body. Her hair was loose down her back, disheveled, and she was barely awake.

She opened the door, and looked down. There were Bess and Jenny with tears streaming down their faces. Bess was clutching a small teddy bear, and Jenny had her blanket.

"Oh, my babies, what's wrong?" she asked softly, going down on her knees to pull them close and cuddle them.

"The sky's making an awful noise, Kasie, and we're scared," Bess said.

She threw caution to the winds. She was already in so much trouble, surely a little more wouldn't matter.

"Do you want to climb in with me?" she asked softly.

"Can we?" Bess asked.

"Of course. Come on."

They climbed into bed with her and under the covers, Jenny on one side and Bess on the other.

"Want a story," Jenny murmured.

"Me, too," Bess seconded.

"Okay. How about the three bears?"

"No, Kasie, that's scary," Bess said. "How about the mouse and the lion?"

"Aren't you scared of lions?" she asked the girls.

"We like lions," Bess told her contentedly, cuddling closer. "Daddy took us to the zoo and we saw lions and tigers and polar bears!"

"The lion it is, then."

And she proceeded to tell them drowsily about the mouse who took out the thorn in the lion's paw and made a friend for life. By the time she finished, they were both asleep. She kissed their pretty little sleeping faces and folded them close to her as the lightning flashed and the thunder rolled. She wondered just before she fell asleep how much trouble she'd be in if their father came home and found them with her, after she'd just promised not to play with them. If only, she thought, Gilbert Callister would get a thorn in his paw and she could pull it out and make friends with him....

It was almost two in the morning when Gil and John got back from the holding pens. There had been a stampede, and two hundred head of cattle broke through their fences and spilled out into the pasture that fronted on a highway. The brothers and every hand on the place were occupied for three hours working in the violent storm to round them up and get them back into the right pasture and fix the fence. It helped that the lightning finally stopped, and in its wake came a nice steady rain. But everyone was soaked by the time they finished, and eager for a warm, dry bed.

Gil stripped off his wet clothes and took a shower, wrapping a long burgundy silk robe around his tall body before he went to check on the girls. He opened the door to the big room they shared and his heart skipped a beat when he realized they were missing.

Where in hell was Miss Parsons and where were his children? He went along to her room and almost knocked at the door, when he realized suddenly where the girls were most likely to be.

With his lips making a thin line, he went along the corridor barefoot to Kasie's room. Without knocking, he opened the door and walked in. Sure enough, curled up as close as they could get to her, were Bess and Jenny.

He started to wake them up and insist that they go back to bed, when he saw the way they looked.

It had been a long time since he'd seen their little faces so content. Without a mother—despite the housekeeper and Miss Parsons—they were sad so much of the time. But when they were around Kasie, they changed. They smiled. They laughed. They played. He couldn't remember the last time he'd seen them so happy. Was it fair to deny them Kasie's company just because he didn't like her? On the other hand, was it wise to let them get so attached to her when she might quit or he might fire her?

The question worried him. As he pondered the situation, Kasie moved and the cover fell away from her sleeping form. He moved closer to the bed in the dim light from the security lights outside, and abruptly he realized that she was wearing the sort of gown a dowager might. It was strictly for utility, plain and white, with no ruffles or lace or even a fancy border. He scowled. Kasie was twenty-two. Was it normal for a woman her age to be so repressed that she covered herself from head to toe even in sleep?

She moved again, restlessly, and a single word broke from her lips as the nightmare came again.

"Kantor," she whispered. "Kantor!"

Chapter Three

Without thinking, Gil reached down and shook Kasie's shoulder. "Wake up, Kasie!" he said firmly.

Her eyes opened on a rush of breath. There was horror in them for a few seconds until she came awake and realized that her boss was standing over her. She blinked away the sleepiness and pulled herself up on an elbow. Her beautiful thick chestnut hair swirled around her shoulders below the high neck of the gown as she stared at him.

"You were having a nightmare," he said curtly. "Who's Kantor?"

She hesitated for a few seconds. "My brother," she said finally. "My twin." She noticed that he was wearing a long robe and apparently nothing under it. Thick dark blond hair was visible in the deep vee of the neckline. She averted her eyes almost in panic. It embarrassed her to have him see her in her nightgown; almost as much as to see him in a robe.

"Why do you have nightmares about him?" he asked gently.

"We had an argument," she said. She pushed back her hair. "I don't want to talk about it."

His eyes narrowed. Apparently it was a painful subject. He let it drop. His eyes went to the girls and not without misgiving. "Why are they in here with you?"

"The storm woke them up. They got scared and came to me," she said defensively. "I didn't go get them."

He was studying them quietly. His expression was hard, grave, wounded.

"I'm sure they went to look for you first," she began defensively.

His eyes glittered down into hers. "We've had this conversation before. Miss Parsons is supposed to be their governness," he emphasized.

"Miss Parsons is probably snoring her head off," she said curtly. "She sleeps like the dead. Bess had a fever week before last, and she didn't even get up when I woke her and told her about it. She said that a fever never hurt anybody!"

"That was when she had strep and I took her to the doctor," he recalled. "Miss Parsons said she was sick. I assumed that she'd been up in the night with her."

"Dream on."

He glared at her. "I'll excuse it this time," he said, ignoring the reference he didn't like to Miss Parsons and her treatment of Bess. He'd have something to say to the woman about that. "Next time, come and find me if you can't wake Miss Parsons."

She just stared back, silent.

"Did you hear me, Kasie?" he demanded softly.

"All right." She glanced from one side of her to the other. "Do you want to wake them up and carry them back to their own beds?"

He looked furious. "If I do, we'll all be awake the rest of the night. We had cattle get out, and we got soaked trying to get them back in. I'm worn-out. I want to go to sleep."

"Nobody here is stopping you," she murmured.

His pale eyes narrowed. "I should have let you go when you offered to resign," he said caustically.

"There's still time," she pointed out, growing more angry by the minute.

He cursed under his breath, glared at her again and walked out.

The next morning, Kasie woke to soft pummeling little hands and laughing voices.

"Get up, Kasie, get up! Daddy's taking us to the movies today!"

She yawned and curled up. "Not me," she murmured sleepily. "Go get breakfast, babies. Mrs. Charters will feed you."

"You got to come, too!" Bess said.

"I want to sleep," she murmured.

"Daddy, she won't get up!" Bess wailed.

"Oh, yes, she will."

Kasie barely had time to register the deep voice before the covers were torn away and she was lifted bodily out of the bed in a pair of very strong arms.

Shocked, she stared straight into pale blue eyes and felt as if she'd been electrified.

"I'll wake her up," Gil told the girls. "Go down and eat your breakfast."

"Okay, Daddy!"

The girls left gleefully, laughing as they went to the staircase.

"You look like a nun in that gown," Gil remarked as he studied his light burden, aware of her sudden stillness. Her face was very close. He searched it quietly. "And you've got freckles, Kasie, just across the bridge of your nose."

"Put...put me down," she said, unnerved by the proximity. She didn't like the sensations it caused to feel his chest right against her bare breasts.

"Why?" he asked. He gazed into her eyes. "You hardly weigh anything." His eyes narrowed as he studied her face thoroughly. "You have big eyes," he murmured. "With little flecks of blue in them. Your face looks more round than oval, especially with your hair down. Your mouth is—" he searched for a word, more touched than he wanted to be by its vulnerability "—full and soft. Half-asleep you don't come across as a fighter. But you are, aren't you?"

Her hands were resting lightly around his neck and she stared at him disconcertedly while she wondered what John or Miss Parsons would say if they walked in unexpectedly to find them in this position.

"You should put me down," she said huskily.

"Don't you like being carried?" he murmured absently.

She shivered as she remembered the last time she'd been carried, by an orderly in the hospital...

She pushed at him. "Please."

He set her back down, scowling curiously at the

odd pastiness of her complexion. "You're mysterious, Kasie."

"Not really. I'm just sleepy." She folded her arms over her breasts and flushed. "Could you leave, please, and let me get dressed?"

He watched her curiously. "Why don't you date? And don't hand me any bull about stinking cowboys."

She was reluctant to tell him anything about herself. She was a private person. Her aunt, Mama Luke, always said that people shouldn't worry others with their personal problems. She didn't.

"I don't want to get married, ever."

He really scowled then. "Why?"

She thought of her parents and then of Kantor, and her eyes closed on the pain. "Love hurts too much."

He didn't speak. For an instant, he felt the pain that seemed to rack her delicate features, and he understood it, all too well.

"You loved someone who died," he recalled.

She nodded and her eyes met his. "And so did you."

For an instant, his hard face was completely unguarded. He was vulnerable, mortal, wounded. "Yes."

"It doesn't pass away, like they say, does it?" she asked softly.

"Not for a long time."

He moved a step closer, and this time she didn't back up. Her eyes lifted to his. He slid his big, lean hand into the thick waves of her chestnut hair and enjoyed its silkiness. "Why don't you wear your hair down, like this?"

"It's sinful," she whispered.

"What?"

"When you dress and wear your hair in a way that's

meant to tempt men, to try to seduce them, it's sinful," she repeated.

His lips fell open. He didn't know how to answer that. He'd never had a woman, especially a modern woman, say such a thing to him.

"Do you think sex is a sin?" he asked.

"Outside of marriage, it is," she replied simply.

"You don't move with the times, do you?" he asked on an expulsion of breath.

"No," she replied.

He started smiling and couldn't stop. "Oh, boy."

"The girls will be waiting. Are you really taking them to a movie?" she asked.

"Yes." One eye narrowed. "I need to take you to one, too. Something X-rated."

She flushed. "Get out of here and stop trying to corrupt me."

"You're overdue."

"Stop or I'll have Mama Luke come over and lecture you."

He frowned. "Mama Luke?"

"My aunt."

"What an odd name."

She shrugged. "Our whole family runs to odd names."

"I noticed."

She made a face. "I work for you. My private life is my own business."

"You don't have a private life," he said, and smiled tenderly.

"I'm a great reader. I love Plutarch and Tacitus and Arrian."

"Good God!"

"There's nothing wrong with ancient history. Things were just as bad then as they are now. All the ancient writers said that the younger generation was headed straight to purgatory and the world was corrupt."

"Arrian didn't."

"Arrian wrote about Alexander the Great," she reminded him. "Alexander's world was in fairly good shape, apparently."

"Arrian wrote about Alexander in the distant past, not his own present." His eyes became soft with affection as he looked at her. "Why don't I like you? There isn't a person in my circle of acquaintances who would even know who Arrian was, much less what he wrote about."

"I don't like you much, either," she shot right back. "But I guess I can stand it if you can."

"I'll have to," he mused. "If I let you walk out, the girls will push me down the staircase and call you back to support them at my funeral."

She shivered abruptly and wrapped her arms around herself. Funeral. Funeral...

"Kasie!"

Her somber eyes came up. She was barely breathing. "Don't...joke about things like that."

"Kasie, I didn't mean it that way," he began.

She forced a smile. "Of course not. I have to get dressed."

He lifted an eyebrow. "You might as well come as you are. I haven't seen a gown like that since I stayed with my grandmother as a child." He shook his head. "You'd set a lingerie shop back decades if that style caught on."

"It's a perfectly functional gown."

"Functional. Yes. It's definitely functional. And about as seductive as chain mail," he added.

"Good!"

He burst out laughing. "All right, I'm leaving."

He went out, sparing her a last, amused glance before he closed the door.

Kasie dressed in jeans and a dark T-shirt. She put her long hair in a braid and pulled on sneakers. She felt a twinge of guilt because she'd missed so many Sunday sermons in past months. But she couldn't reconcile her pain. It needed more time.

The whole family was at the table when she joined them for breakfast. John gave her a warm smile.

"I hear you had visitors last night," he told Kasie with a mischievous glance at the two little girls, who were wolfing down cereal.

"Yes, I did," Kasie replied with a worried glance that encompassed both Gil and Miss Parsons.

"You should have called me, Miss Mayfield," Miss Penny Parsons said curtly and glanced at Kasie with cold dark eyes. "I take care of the children."

Kasie could have argued that point, but she didn't dare. "Yes, Miss Parsons," she said demurely.

Gil finished his scrambled eggs and lifted his coffee cup to his firm lips. He was wearing slacks and a neat yellow sports shirt that emphasized his muscular arms. He looked elegant even in casual wear, Kasie thought, and remembered suddenly the feel of those strong arms around her. She flushed.

He noticed her sudden color and caught her gaze. She couldn't seem to look away, and he didn't even try to. For a space of seconds, they were fused in some sort of bond, prisoners of a sensual connection that made Kasie's full lips part abruptly. His gaze fell to them and lingered with unexpected hunger.

Kasie dropped her fork onto her plate and jumped at the noise. "Sorry!" she said huskily as she fumbled with the fork.

"Didn't get much sleep last night, did you?" John asked with a smile. "Neither did any of us. About midnight, I thought seriously about giving up cattle ranching and becoming a door-to-door vacuum cleaner salesman."

"I felt the same way," Gil confessed. "We're going to have to put a small line cabin out at the holding pens and keep a man there on stormy nights."

"As long as I'm not on your list of candidates," John told his brother.

"I'll keep that in mind. Bess, don't play with your food, please," he added to the little girl, who was finished with her cereal and was now smearing eggs around the rim of her plate.

"I don't like eggs, Daddy," she muttered. "Do I gotta eat 'em?"

"Of course you do, young lady!" Miss Parsons said curtly. "Every last morsel."

Bess looked tortured.

"Miss Parsons, could you ask Mrs. Charters to see me before she plans the supper menu, please?" Gil asked.

Miss Parsons got up. "I will. Eat those eggs, Bess."

She left. Gil gave his oldest daughter a sign by placing his forefinger across his mouth. He lifted Bess's plate, scraped the eggs onto his, and finished them off before Miss Parsons returned.

"Very good," she said, nodding approvingly at Bess's plate. "I told you that you'd grow accustomed to a balanced breakfast. We must keep our bodies healthy. Come on, now, girls. We'll have a nice nap until your father's ready to go to the movies."

Bess grimaced, but she didn't protest. She got up with Jenny and was shepherded out by the governess.

"Marshmallow," John chided the older man, poking the air with his fork. "You should have made her eat them herself."

"When you start eating liver and onions voluntarily, I'll make Bess eat eggs," Gil promised. "Want to come with us to the movies?" He named the picture they were going to see.

"Not me," John said pleasantly. "I'm going to Billings to see a man about some more acreage." He glanced at Kasie speculatively. "Want to tag along, Kasie?"

The question surprised her. While she was trying to think of a polite way to say she didn't, Gil answered for her.

"Kasie's going with us to the movies," he replied, and his pale eyes dared her to argue. "The girls will have conniptions if we leave her behind. Besides, she likes cartoons. Don't you, Kasie?"

"I'm just crazy about them, Mr. Callister," she agreed with a tight smile, angry because he'd more or less forced her into agreeing to go.

"Mr. Callister was our father," Gil said firmly. "Don't use it with us."

She grimaced. "I work for you. It doesn't seem right."

John was gaping at her. "You're kidding."

"No, she isn't," Gil assured him. "When you have a

free minute, get her to tell you why she braids her hair. It's a hoot."

She glared at Gil. "You cut that out."

He wiped his mouth with a white linen napkin and got to his feet. "I've got some phone calls to make before we go. We'll leave at one, Kasie."

"Phone calls on Sunday?" she asked John when his brother had left them alone.

"It's yesterday in some parts of the world, and tomorrow in some other parts," he reminded her. "You know how he is about business."

"Yes," she agreed.

"What amazes me," he mused, watching her, "is how much he grumbles about you. He loves women, as a rule. He's always doing little things to make the job easier for Mrs. Charters. He lets Pauline get away with only working three days of the week, when he needs a full-time secretary worse than I do. But he's hard on you."

"He doesn't like me," she said quietly. "He can't help it."

"You don't like him, either."

She smiled sheepishly. "I can't help it, either." She picked up on something he'd said earlier. "How can Pauline make ends meet with only a part-time job?" she asked curiously.

"She's independently wealthy," John told her. "She doesn't need a job at all, but she caught Gil at a weak moment. He doesn't have many of them, believe me. I think she attracted him at first. Now things have cooled and he's stuck with her. She's tenacious."

"Why would she need to work?" she wondered aloud.

"Because Gil needed a secretary, of course. She

hasn't had any business training, and I don't doubt that the files are in a hellacious mess."

"Couldn't he get somebody else?"

"He tried to. Pauline cried all over him and he gave up."

"He doesn't look like a man who'd even notice tears," she said absently.

"Appearances are deceptive. You saw how he was when the dog threatened the girls," he reminded her. "He's not immune to tears."

"I'd need convincing," she said and grinned wickedly.

He leaned back in his chair with his coffee cup in his hand and studied her. "You're good with the kids," he said. "You must have spent a lot of time around children."

She lowered her eyes to her empty plate. "I did. I'm not formally taught or anything, but I do know a few things."

"It shows. I've never seen Bess respond to any of her various governesses. She liked you on sight."

"How many governesses has she had?" she asked curiously.

"Four. This year," he amended.

Her eyebrows arched. "Why so many?"

"Are you afraid of spiders, garter snakes, or frogs?" he asked.

She shook her head. "Why?"

"Well, the others were. They got downright twitchy about opening drawers or pulling down bedcovers," he recalled with a chuckle. "Bess likes garter snakes. She shared them with the governesses."

"Oh, dear," Kasie said.

"You see the point. That's why Miss Parsons was hired. She's the next best thing to a Marine DI, as you may have noticed."

Her face lightened. "So that's why he hired her. I did wonder."

John sighed. "I wish he'd hired her to do the tax work on the payroll instead. She's a natural, and since she's a retired accountant that experience would make her an asset. We have a firm of C.P.A.'s to do yearly stuff, but our bookkeeper who did payroll got married and moved to L.A. just before we hired you."

"And Miss Parsons got hired to look after the girls. She really dislikes children," she added.

"I know. But Gil refuses to believe it. He's been lax about work at the ranch for a while. He stayed on the road more and more, avoiding the memories after Darlene died. I felt bad for him, but things were going to pot here. I have to travel to show the bulls," he added, "because the more competitions we win, the higher the prices we can charge for stud fees or young bulls. The ranch can't run without anybody overseeing it." He pursed his lips as he studied her. "I gather that you said something to him about neglecting the girls. I thought so," he mused when she shifted uncomfortably. "I've told him, too, but he didn't listen to me. Apparently he listens to you."

"He's already tried to fire me once," she pointed out.

"You're still here," he replied.

"Yes. But I can't help but wonder for how much longer," she murmured, voicing her one real fear. "I could go back and live with my aunt, but it isn't fair to her. I have to work and support myself. This was the only full-time job that I was qualified for. Jobs are thin on the ground, regardless of the reports coming out about how great the economy is."

"How did you end up in Medicine Ridge in the first place?" he wondered.

"I was living with my aunt in Billings when I saw the ad for this job in the local paper. I'd already been all over Billings hoping for a full-time job and couldn't find one. This one seemed tailor-made for me."

"I'm glad you applied for it," he said. "There were a lot of candidates, but we ruled out most of them in less than five minutes each. You were the only woman out there who could even type."

"You're kidding."

"No. They thought I wanted beauty instead of brains. I didn't." He smiled. "Not that you're bad on the eyes, Kasie. But I wasn't running a pageant."

"I was surprised that your brother hired me," she confessed. "He seemed to dislike me on sight. But when he found out how fast I could type, he was a lot less antagonistic."

He wasn't going to mention what Gil had said to him after he hired Kasie. It had been against Gil's better judgment, and he'd picked her appearance and her pert manner to pieces. It was interesting that Gil was antagonistic toward her. Very interesting.

"You're a whiz at the computer," John said. "A real asset. I didn't realize what you could do with a spreadsheet program until you modified ours. You're gifted."

"I love computers," she said with a smile. "Pauline is going to enjoy them, too, when she learns just a little more. Once she discovers the Internet, she'll be even more efficient. There are all sorts of Web sites dedicated to the cattle industry. It would be great for com-parisons—even for buying and selling bulls. You could have your own Web site."

John let out a low whistle. "Funny, I hadn't even considered that. Kasie, it might revolutionize the way we do business, not to mention cutting down on the amount of travel we have to do every year."

"That's what I thought, too," she said, smiling at him.

"Mention it to Gil when you go to the movies," he coaxed. "Let's see what he thinks."

"He might like the idea better if it came from you," she said.

"I think he'll like it, period. I already do. Can you make a Web site?"

She grimaced. "No, I can't. But I know a woman who can," she added. "She works out of Billings. I met her when we were going to secretarial school. She's really good, and she doesn't charge an arm and a leg. I can get in touch with her, if you like."

"Go ahead. We do a lot of communication by e-mail, but neither of us even thought about putting cattle on our own site. It's a terrific idea!"

"You sound like Bess," Gil said from the doorway. "What's terrific?"

"We're going on the Internet," John said.

His big brother frowned. "The Internet?"

"Kasie can tell you what she's proposed. It could open new doors for us in marketing. It's international."

Gil was quick. He caught on almost at once. "You mean, get a Web site and use it to buy and sell cattle," he said.

"It will save you as much time as sending e-mail back and forth between potential buyers and sellers already does," she added.

"Good idea." Gil studied her with a curious smile. "Full of surprises aren't you, Miss Mayfield?"

"She's gifted," John said, grinning at his brother. "I told you so. Now maybe you can stop talking about firing her, hmm?"

Gil pressed his lips together and refused to rise to the bait. "It's almost one o'clock. If we're going to the movies, let's go. Kasie, fetch the girls."

She almost saluted, but he looked vaguely irritated. It looked as though nothing she suggested was ever going to please him. She wondered why she didn't just walk out and leave him to it. The thought was painful. She went up to get the little girls, more confused than ever.

Chapter Four

The girls chattered like birds all the way to town in Gil's black Jaguar. Kasie sat in front and listened patiently, smiling, while they told her all about the movie they were going to see. They'd seen the previews on television when they watched their Saturday morning cartoons.

It was a warm, pretty day, and trees and shrubs were blooming profusely. It should have been perfect, but Kasie was uneasy. Maybe she shouldn't have mentioned anything about Web sites, but it seemed an efficient way for Gil and John to move into Web-based commerce.

"You're brooding," Gil remarked. "Why?"

"I was wondering if I should have suggested anything about Internet business," she said.

"Why not? It's a good idea," he said, surprising her. "John told me about the Web site designer. Tomorrow,

I want you to get in touch with her and get the process started."

"She'll need you to tell her what you want on the site."

"Okay."

She glanced in the back seat where the girls were sharing a book and enthusing over the pop-up sections.

"I brought it home for them yesterday," he commented, "and forgot to give it to them. They love books."

"That's the first step to getting them to love reading," she said, smiling at the little heads bowed over the books. "Reading to them at night keeps it going."

"Did your mother read to you?" he asked curiously.

"She probably did," she mused, smiling sadly. "But Kantor and I were very young when she and our father... died. Mama Luke read to us, when we were older."

"I suppose you liked science fiction," he murmured.

"How did you know?" she asked.

"You love computers," he said with a hint of a smile.

"I guess they do fit in with science fiction," she had to admit. She eyed him curiously. "What sort of books did you like to read?"

"Pirate stories, cowboy stories. Stuff like that. Now, it's genetics textbooks and management theory," he added wryly. "I hardly ever have time to read just for fun."

"Do your parents help you with the ranch?"

He seemed to turn to ice. "We don't talk about our parents," he said stiffly.

That sounded odd. But she was already in his bad books, so she didn't pursue it. "It's nice of you to take the girls to the movies."

He slowed for a turn, his expression taut. "I don't spend enough time with them," he said. "You were right about that. It isn't a lack of love. It's a lack of delegation.

You'd be amazed how hard it is to find good managers who want to live on a cattle ranch."

"Maybe you don't advertise in a wide enough range," she suggested gently.

"What?"

She plunged ahead. "There are all sorts of trade magazines that carry ads with blind mailboxes," she said. "You can have replies sent to the newspaper and nobody has to know who you are."

"How do you know about the trade magazines?" he asked.

She grinned sheepishly. "I read them. Well, I ought to know something about cattle, since I work for a ranch, shouldn't I?"

He shook his head. "You really are full of surprises, Kasie."

"Kasie, what's this big word?" Bess asked, thrusting the book at her. Kasie took it and sounded the word out phonetically, coaching the little girl in its pronunciation. She took the book back and began to teach the word to Jenny.

"You're patient," Gil remarked. "I notice that Miss Parsons doesn't like taking time to teach them words."

"Miss Parsons likes numbers."

"Yes. She does." He pulled into the theater parking lot, which was full of parents and children. He got everyone out and locked the door, grimacing as they walked past several minivans.

"They're handy for little kids," Kasie said wickedly. "Mothers love them, I'm told."

"I love my kids, but I'm not driving a damned minivan," he muttered.

She grinned at his expression. The little girls ran to get in line, and struck up a conversation with a child they knew, whose bored mother perked up when she saw Gil approaching.

"Hi, Gil!" she called cheerily. "We're going to see the dinosaur movie! Is that why you're here?"

"That's the one," he replied, pulling bills out of his wallet. He gave one to each of the little girls, and they bought their own tickets. Gil bought his and Kasie's as they came to the window. "Hi, Amie," he called to the little girl with Bess and Jenny, and he smiled. She smiled back. She was as dark as his children were fair, with black eyes and hair like her mother's.

"We're going to sit with Amie, Daddy!" Bess said excitedly, waving her ticket and Jenny's.

"I guess that leaves me with you and…?" the other woman paused deliberately.

"This is Kasie," Gil said, and took her unexpectedly by the arm, with a bland smile at Amie's mom. "You're welcome to join us, of course, Connie."

The other woman sighed. "No, I guess I'll sit with the girls. Nice to have seen you," she added, and moved ahead with the girls, looking bored all over again.

Gil slid his hand down into Kasie's. She reacted nervously to the unexpected touch, but his fingers clung, warm and strong against her own. He drew her along to the line already forming alongside the velvet ropes as the ticket takers prepared to let people through to the various theaters.

"Humor me," he said, and it looked as though he were whispering sweet nothings into her ear. "I'm the entrée, in case you haven't noticed."

Kasie glanced around and saw a number of women with little children and no man along, and two of them gave him deliberate, wistful glances and smiled.

"Single moms?" she whispered back, having to go on tiptoe.

He caught her around the waist and held her against his hip. "No. Get the picture?"

Her breath caught. "Oh, dear," she said heavily.

He looked down into her wide eyes. "You're such a child sometimes," he said softly. "You don't see ugliness, do you? You go through life looking for rainbows instead of rain."

"Habit," she murmured, fascinated by the pale blue lights in his eyes.

"It's a rather nice habit," he replied. The look lasted just a few seconds too long to be polite, and Kasie felt her heart begin to race. But then, the line shifted and diverted him. He moved closer to the ticket-taker, keeping the girls ahead carefully in sight while his arm drew Kasie along with him.

She liked the protectiveness of that muscular arm. He didn't look like a body-builder, all his movements were lithe and graceful. But he worked at physical labor from dawn until dusk most days. She'd seen him throw calves that had to be doctored. She'd seen him throw bulls, too. He was strong. Involuntarily she relaxed against him. It was delicious, the feeling of security it gave her to be close to him, to the warm strength of him.

The soft movement caught him off guard and sent a jolt of sensation through him that he hadn't felt in a long time. He looked down at her with curious, turbulent eyes that she didn't see. She was smiling and waving at the girls, who were darting off down into the theater with the little girl and her mother.

"They like you," he said.

"I like them."

He handed their tickets to the uniformed girl, who smiled as she handed back the stubs and pointed the way to the theater that was showing the cartoon movie.

Gil caught Kasie's hand in his and drew her lazily along with him through the crowd of children and parents until they reached the theater. But instead of going down to the front, he drew Kasie to an isolated double-seat in the very back row and sat down beside her. His arm went over the back of the chair as the theater darkened and the previews began showing.

Kasie was electrified by the shift in their relationship. She felt his lean fingers on her shoulder, bringing her closer, and his cheek rested against her temple. She hadn't ever been to a movie with a man. There had been a blind double date once, and the boy sat on his own side of the seat and looked nervous until they got home again. This was worlds away from that experience.

"Comfortable?" he asked at her ear, and his voice was like velvet.

"Yes," she said unsteadily.

His chest rose and fell and he found himself paying a lot more attention to the feel of Kasie's soft hair against his skin than the movie. She smelled of spring roses. Her hair was soft, and had a faint herbal scent of its own. Twenty-two. She was twenty-two. He was thirty-two, and she'd already said that he was too old for her.

He scowled as he thought about that difference. She needed someone as young as she was, with that same vulnerable, kind, generous spirit. He had two little girls and a high-pressure business that gave him little free time. He was still grieving, in a way, for Darlene, whom he'd loved since grammar school. But there was something about Kasie that made him hungry. It wasn't desire, although he was aware of heady sensations when she was close to him. No, it was the sort of hunger a man got when he was standing outside in the snow with a wet coat and soaked jeans, looking through the window at a warm, glowing fireplace. He couldn't really explain the feelings. They made him uneasy.

He noticed that she was still a little stiff. He touched a curl at her ear. "Hey," he whispered.

She turned her head and looked up at him in the semidarkness.

"I'm not hitting on you," he whispered into her ear. "Okay?"

She relaxed. "Okay."

The obvious relief in her voice made him feel guilty and offended. He moved his arm back to the chair and forced himself to watch the movie. He had to remember that Kasie worked for him. It wasn't fair to use her to ward off other women. But...was it really that?

The dinosaur movie was really well-done, Kasie thought as she became involved in the storyline and the wonder of creatures that looked really alive up there on the screen. It was a bittersweet sort of cartoon, though, and she was sorry for the little girls. Because when it was over, Bess and Jenny came to them crying about the dinosaurs that had died in the film.

"Oh, sweetheart, it was only a movie," Kasie said at once, and bent to pick up Bess, hugging her close. "Just a movie. Okay?"

"But it was so sad, Kasie," cried the little girl. "Why do things have to die?"

"I don't know, baby," she said softly, and her eyes

closed for an instant on a wave of remembered pain. She'd lost so many people she loved.

Gil had Jenny up in his arms, and they walked out of the theater carrying the children. Behind them, other mothers were trying to explain about extinction.

"There, there, baby," he cooed at Jenny and kissed her wet eyes. "It was only make-believe. Dinosaurs don't really talk, you know, and they had brains the size of peas." He shifted her and smiled. "Hey, remember what I told you about chickens, about how they'll walk right up to a rattlesnake and let it strike them? Well, dinosaurs didn't even have brains that big."

"They didn't?" Bess asked from her secure hold on Kasie.

"They didn't," Gil said. "If a meteor had struck them, they'd be standing right in its path waiting for it. And they wouldn't be discussing it, either."

Kasie laughed as she looked at Gil, delighted at the way he handled the sticky situation. He was, she thought, a marvelous parent.

"Can we get some ice cream on the way home?" Bess asked then, wiping her tears.

"You bet. We'll stop by the yogurt place."

"Thanks, Daddy!" Bess cried.

"You're the nicest daddy," Jenny murmured against his throat.

"You really are, you know," Kasie agreed as they strapped the little girls into the back seat.

His eyes met hers across the children. "I'm a veteran daddy," he told her dryly.

"Is that what it is?" Kasie chuckled.

"You get better with practice, or so they tell me. Do

you like frozen yogurt? I get them that instead of ice cream. It's healthy stuff."

"I like it, too," Kasie said as she got into the front seat beside him.

"We'll get some to take home for Mrs. Charters and Miss Parsons," he added, "so that we don't get blamed for ruining their appetites for supper."

"Now that's superior thinking," Kasie had to admit.

He started the engine and eased them out of the crowded parking lot.

The yogurt shop was a few miles from home. They stopped and got the treat in carryout cups, because Gil was expecting a phone call from a buyer out of state.

"I don't like to work on Sundays," he remarked as they drove home. "But sometimes it's unavoidable."

"Do you ever take the girls to church?"

He hesitated. "Well…no."

She was watching him with those big, soft gray eyes, in which there wasn't condemnation or censure. It was almost as if she knew that his faith had suffered since the death of his wife. No, for longer than that. It had suffered since childhood, when his parents had…

"I haven't gone for several months, myself," Kasie remarked quietly. She twisted her purse slowly in her hands. "If I…start back, I could take them with me, if you didn't mind."

"I don't mind," he replied.

Her eyes softened and she smiled at him.

He tore his gaze away from that warm affection and forced it back to the road. His hands tightened on the steering wheel. She really was getting to him. He wished he knew some way to head off trouble. He found her far too attractive, and she continued to make her lack of receptiveness known. He didn't want to do something stupid and send her looking for another job.

"I enjoyed today," he said after a minute. "But you remember that Miss Parsons is supposed to be responsible for the girls," he added with a stern glance. "You have enough to do keeping John's paperwork current. Understand?"

"Yes, I do. I'll try very hard to stop interfering," she promised.

"Good. Pauline is out of town for the next week, but she'll be home in time for the pool party we're giving next Saturday. She'll be in the office the following Monday morning. You can give her another computer lesson."

She grimaced. "She doesn't like me."

"I know. Don't let it worry you. She's efficient."

She wasn't, but apparently she'd managed to conceal it from Gil. Kasie wondered how he'd managed not to notice the work Pauline didn't do.

"Did John have a secretary before me?" she asked suddenly.

"He did, and she was a terrific one, too. But she quit with only a week's notice."

"Did she say why?" she fished with apparent unconcern.

"Something about being worked to death. John didn't buy it. She didn't have that much to do."

She did, if she was doing John's work and having Gil's palmed off on her as well. Kasie's eyes narrowed. Well, she wasn't going to get away with it now. If Pauline started expecting Kasie to do her job for her, she was in for a surprise.

"Funny," Gil murmured as he turned onto the black

shale ranch road that led to the Double C. "Pauline said she couldn't use the computer, but she always had my herd records printed out. Even if they weren't updated properly."

Kasie didn't say a word. Surely he'd work it out by himself one day. She glanced back at the girls, who were still contentedly eating frozen yogurt out of little cups. They were so pretty and sweet. Her heart ached just looking at them. Sandy had been just Bess's age...

She bit down hard on her lip. She mustn't cry. Tears were no help at all. She had to look ahead, not backward.

Gil pulled up in front of the house and helped Kasie get the girls out.

"Thanks for the movie," Kasie told him, feeling shy now.

"My pleasure," he said carelessly. "Come on, girls, let's get you settled with Miss Parsons. Daddy's got to play rancher for a while."

"Can't we play, too?" Bess asked, clinging to his hand.

"Sure," he said. "Just as soon as you can compare birth weight ratios and compute projected weaning weight."

Bess made a face. "Oh, Daddy!"

"I'll make a rancher out of you one day, young lady," he said with a grin.

"Billy's dad said he was sure glad he had a son instead of girls. Daddy, do you ever wish me and Jenny was boys?" she asked.

He stopped, dropped to one knee and hugged the child close. "Daddy loves little girls," he said softly. "And he wouldn't trade you and Jenny for all the boys in the world. You tell Billy I said that."

Bess chuckled. "I will!" She kissed his cheek with a big smack. "I love you, Daddy!"

"I love you, too, little chick."

Jenny, jealous, had to have a hug, too, and they ended up each clinging to a strong, lean hand as they went into the house.

Kasie watched them, feeling more lost and alone than she had in months. She ached to be part of a family again. Watching Gil with the girls only emphasized what she'd lost.

She went up onto the porch and up the staircase slowly, her hand smoothing over the silky wood of the banister as she tried once again to come to grips with her loss.

She was curled up in her easy chair watching an old movie on television when there was a soft knock at the door just before it opened. Bess and Jenny sneaked in wearing their gowns and bathrobes and slippers, peering cautiously down the hall before they closed the door.

"Hello," Kasie said with a smile, opening her arms as they clambered up into the big chair with her and cuddled close. "You smell nice."

"We had baths," Bess said. "Miss Parsons said we was covered with chocolate sauce." She giggled. "We splashed her."

"You bad babies," she chided softly and kissed little cheeks.

"Could you tell us a story?" they asked.

"Sure. What would you like to hear?"

"The one with the bears."

"Okay." She started the story, speaking in all the different parts, while they snuggled close and listened with attention.

Just to see if they were really listening, she added, "And then the wolf huffed and puffed..."

"No, Kasie!" Bess interrupted. "That's the pig story!"

"Is it?" she exclaimed. "All right, then. Well, the bears came home..."

"Huffing and puffing?" came a deep, amused query from the doorway. The little girls glanced at him, looking guilty and worried. "Miss Parsons is looking for you two fugitives," he drawled. "If I were you, I'd get into my beds real fast. She's glowering."

"Goodness! We got to go, Kasie!" Bess said, and she and Jenny scrambled to their feet and ran past their father down the hall, calling good-nights as they went.

Gil studied Kasie from the doorway. She was wearing her own white gown, with a matching cotton robe this time, and her long hair waved around her shoulders. She looked very young.

"You weren't reading from a book. What did you do, memorize the story?" he asked curiously.

"I guess so," she confided, smiling. "I've told it so many times, I suppose I do have it down pretty well."

"Who did you tell it to?" he asked reasonably.

The smile never faded, but she withdrew behind it. "A little girl who stayed with us sometimes," she replied.

"I see."

"They came in and asked for a story," she explained. "I hated telling them to go away..."

"I haven't said a word."

"You did," she reminded him worriedly. "I know that Miss Parsons looks after them. I'm not trying to interfere."

"I know that. But it's making things hard for her when they come to you instead," he said firmly.

She grimaced. "I can't hurt their feelings."

"I'll speak to them." He held up a hand when she started to protest. "I'll speak to them nicely," he added. "I won't make an issue of it."

She hesitated. "Okay."

"You have your own duties," he continued. "It isn't fair to let you take on two jobs, no matter how you feel about it. I don't pay Miss Parsons to sit and read tax manuals."

Her eyes widened. "You're kidding," she said, sitting up straight. "She reads tax manuals? What for? Did you ask her?"

"I did. She says she reads them for pleasure," he said. "Apparently she didn't really want to retire from the accounting business, but she was faced with a clerical position or retirement," he added with a droll smile.

"Oh, dear."

He pushed away from the door facing. "Don't stay up too late. John needs to get an early start. He'll be away for a week showing Ebony King on the road."

"He's the new young bull," Kasie recalled. "He eats corn out of my hand," she added with a smile. "I never thought of bulls as being gentle."

"They're a real liability if they're not," he pointed out. "A bull that size could trample a man with very little difficulty."

"I guess he could." She stood up, with her hands in the pockets of the cotton robe. "I'm sorry about the girls coming in here."

"Oh, hell, I don't mind," he said on a rough breath. "But it isn't wise to let them get too attached to you, Kasie. You know it, and you know why."

"They think you're going to marry Pauline," she blurted out, and then flushed at having been so personal with him.

"I haven't thought a lot about remarrying," he replied quietly. His eyes went over her with a suddenly intent appraisal. "But maybe I should. They're getting to the age where they're going to need a woman's hand in their lives. I love them, but I can't see things from a female point of view."

"You've done marvelously with them so far," she told him. "They're polite and generous and loving."

"So was their mother," he remarked and for a few seconds, his face was lined with grief before he got it under control. "She loved them."

"You said Bess was like her," she reminded him.

"Yes," he said at once. "She had long, wavy blond hair, just that same color. Jenny looks more like me. But Bess is more like me."

She smiled. "I've noticed. She has a very hard head when she doesn't want to do something."

He shrugged. "Being stubborn isn't always a bad thing. Persistence is the key to most successes in life."

"Yes." She searched his hard face, seeing the years of work and worry. It was a good, strong face, but it wasn't handsome.

He was looking at her, too, and something stirred inside him, a need that he had to work to put down. He moved out the door. "Sleep well, Kasie," he said curtly.

"You, too."

He closed the door behind him, without looking at her again. She went back to her movie, but with much less enthusiasm.

Chapter Five

The week went by slowly, and the girls, to Kasie's dismay, became her shadows. She worried herself sick trying to keep Gil from noticing, especially after the harsh comments he'd made about her job responsibilities. It didn't help that she kept remembering the feel of his arm around her at the movie theater, and the warm clasp of his big lean hand in her own. She was afraid to even look at him, because she was afraid her attraction to him might show.

Saturday came and the house was full of strangers. Kasie found it hard to mix with high-society people, so she stuck to Miss Parsons and the girls. Miss Parsons took the opportunity to sneak back inside the house while Kasie watched the girls. Everything went well at first, because Gil was too busy with guests to notice that Miss Parsons was missing. But not for long. Kasie had given the girls a beach ball to play with, which was her one big mistake of the morning.

It wouldn't have been so bad if she'd just let the children's beach ball fly into the swimming pool in the first place. The problem was that, if she didn't stop it, Pauline was going to get it in the mouth, which wouldn't improve the already-bad situation between her and Kasie. Bess and Jenny didn't like Gil Callister's secretary. Neither did Kasie, but she loved the little girls and didn't want them to get into trouble. So she gave in to an impulse, and tried valiantly to divert the ball from its unexpecting target.

Predictably, she overreached, lost her footing and made an enormous splash as she landed, fully clothed, in the deep end. And, of course, she couldn't swim...

Gil looked up from the prospectus he'd been reading when he heard the splash. He connected Kasie's fall, the beach ball, and his two little blond giggling daughters at once. He shook his head and grimaced. He put aside the prospectus and dived in to save Kasie, Bermuda shorts, Hawaiian shirt and all.

Her late parents had lived long enough to see the irony of the second name they'd given her. Her middle name was Grace, but she wasn't graceful. She was all long legs and arms. She wasn't pretty, but she had a lovely body, and the thin white dress she was wearing became transparent in the water. It was easily noticed that she was wearing only the flimsiest of briefs and a bra that barely covered her pert breasts. Just the thing, she thought miserably, to wear in front of the Callisters' business partners who were here for a pool party on the big ranch. Feline blond Pauline Raines was laughing her head off at Kasie's desperate treading of water. Just you wait, lady, she fumed. Next time I'll give Bess a soccer ball to bean you with and I won't step in the way...!

Her head went under as her arms gave out. She took a huge breath as powerful arms encircled and lifted her clear of the deep water. It would have to be Gil who rescued her, she thought miserably. John wasn't even looking their way. He'd have dived in after her in a minute, she knew, if he'd seen her fall. But while he was nice, and kind, he wasn't Gil, who was beginning to have a frightening effect on Kasie's heart. She glanced at Pauline as she spluttered. Kasie wished that she was beautiful like Pauline. She looked the very image of an efficient secretary. Kasie had great typing speed, dictation skills and organizational expertise, but she was only ordinary-looking. Besides, she was a social disaster, and she'd just proved it to Gil and all the guests.

Gil had been unexpectedly kind to her at the theater when he'd taken her with the girls to see the movie. She still tingled, remembering his hand holding hers. This, however, was much worse. Her breasts were almost bare in the thin blouse, and she felt the hard muscular wall of his chest with wonder and pleasure and a little fear, because she'd never felt such heady sensations in her body before. She wondered if he'd fire her for making a scene at his pool party, to which a lot of very wealthy and prominent cattlemen and their wives had been invited.

To give him credit, she hadn't exactly inspired confidence on the job in the past few weeks. Two weeks earlier, she tripped on the front steps and landed in a rosebush at the very feet of a visiting cattleman from Texas who'd almost turned purple trying not to laugh. Then there had been the ice-cream incident last week, which still embarrassed her. Bess had threatened Kasie with a big glop of chocolate ice cream. While Kasie was backing away, laughing helplessly, Gil had come into the house in dirty chaps and boots and shirt with his hat jerked low over one blue eye and his mouth a thin line, with blood streaming from a cut on his forehead. Bess had thrown the ice cream at Kasie, who ducked, just in time for it to hit Gil right in the forehead. While he was wiping it off, Kasie grabbed the spoon from Bess and waited for the explosion as her boss wiped the ice cream away and looked at her. Those blue eyes could cut like diamonds. They actually glittered. But he hadn't said a word. He'd just looked at her, before he turned and continued down the hall to the staircase that led up to his room.

Now, here she was half-drowned from a swimming pool accident, having made a spectacle of herself yet again.

"I wonder if I could get work in Hollywood?" she sputtered as she hung on for dear life. "There must be a market for terminal clumsiness somewhere!"

Gil raised an eyebrow and gave her a slow, speaking glance before he pulled her close against his chest and turned toward the concrete steps at the far end. He walked up out of the pool, streaming water, and started toward the house. "Don't struggle, Kasie," he said at her temple, and his voice sounded odd.

"Sorry," she coughed. "You can put me down, now. I'm okay. I can walk."

"If I put you down, you're going to become the entertainment," he said enigmatically at her ear. He looked over his shoulder. "John, look after the girls until I get back!" he called.

"Oh, I'll watch them, Gil!" Pauline interrupted lazily. "Come over here, girls!" she called, without even looking in their direction.

"John will watch them," Gil said emphatically and didn't move until his lean, lanky brother jumped up and went toward his nieces, grinning.

Gil went up the staircase with Kasie held close to his chest. "Why can't you swim?" he asked.

His deep, slow voice made her feel funny. So did the close, almost intimate contact with him. She nibbled on her lower lip, feeling soggy and disheveled and embarrassed. "I'm afraid of the water."

"Why?" he persisted.

She wouldn't answer him. It would do no good, and she didn't want to remember. Probably he'd never seen anyone drown. "Sorry I messed up the pool party," she murmured.

He shook her gently as they passed the landing and paused at her bedroom door. "Stop apologizing every second word," he said curtly as he put her down. He held her there with two big, lean hands on her upper arms and studied her intently in the dim light of the wall sconces.

The feel of all that warm strength against her made her giddy. She'd never been so close to him before. He was ten years older than Kasie, and he had an authority and maturity that must have been apparent even when he'd been her age. She had tried to think of him as Bess and Jenny's daddy, but after their closeness at the movie theater, it was almost impossible to think of him as anything but a mature, sexy man.

"I can't seem to make you understand that the girls are Miss Parsons's responsibility, not yours!" He saw her faint flush and scowled down at her. "Speaking of Miss Parsons, where in hell is she?"

She cleared her throat and pushed back a soggy strand of dark hair. "She's in the office."

"Doing what?"

She shifted, but he didn't let go of her arms. That unblinking, ferocious blue stare robbed her of a smart retort. "All right," she said heavily. "She's doing the withholding on John's tax readout." He didn't speak. She looked up and grimaced. "Well, I'm not up on tax law, and she is."

"So you traded duties without permission, is that it?"

She hesitated. "Yes. I'm sorry. But it's just for today! You already know that she doesn't...well, she doesn't like children very much, really, and I hate taxes..."

"I know."

"I shouldn't have given them the beach ball. I thought they were going into the shallow part of the pool with it. And then Bess threw it..."

"Right at Pauline's expensive new coiffure," Gil finished for her. He pursed his sensuous lips and searched her face. "You won't tell on them, of course. You took the blame for the ice cream, too. And when one of Jenny's toys tripped you on the front steps and you went into the rosebush, you blamed that on clumsiness."

"You knew?" she asked, surprised.

"I've been a father for five years," he mused. "I know all sorts of things." His pale blue eyes slid very slowly down Kasie's wet dress and narrowed on what was showing. She had the most delicious body. Every line and curve of it was on view where the thin dress was plastered to her body. Her breasts were perfectly shaped and the nipples were dusky. The feel of her against his chest, even through her wet blouse and his cotton shirt, had almost knocked the breath out of him. It upset him that he was noticing these things about her. He was beginning to react to them, too. He had to get out of here. She was so young…

He cursed under his breath. "You'd better change," he said curtly. He turned on his heel and went toward the staircase.

"About Miss Parsons…!" she called after him, in one last attempt to ward off retribution.

"You might as well consider the girls your job from now on," he said angrily. "I can see that it's a losing battle to keep you away from them. I'll give Miss Parsons to John. He won't enjoy the view as much, but keeping out of prison because we can't figure out tax forms might sweeten the deal," he said, without breaking stride. "When you have some spare time, you can continue giving Pauline computer lessons. That includes Monday morning. Mrs. Charters can watch the girls while you work with Pauline."

"But I'm not a trained governess. I'm a secretary!" she insisted.

"Great. You can let Bess dictate letters to you for her dolls."

"But…!"

It was too late. He never argued. He just kept walking. She threw up her hands and went back into her room. She started toward the bathroom to change out of her wet things when she got a look at herself in the mirror. The whole outfit was transparent. She remembered Gil's intent stare and blushed all the way to her toes. No wonder he'd been looking at her. Everything she had was on view! She wondered how she'd ever be able to look him in the eye again.

She changed and went back to the pool party, dejected and miserable. It was hard to believe that she'd not even had a mild crush on John when she first went to work for the Callisters. He was handsome, and very sexy, but she just didn't feel that way about him. Fortunately he'd never felt that way about her, either. John had some secret woman in his past, and now he didn't get serious about anyone. Kasie had heard that from Mrs. Charters, who was a veritable storehouse of information about it. John didn't look to Kasie like a man with a broken heart. But maybe he played the field to camouflage it.

Kasie had never really been in love. She'd had crushes on TV celebrities and movie stars, and on boys at school—and one summer she'd had a real case on a boy who lived near Mama Luke, her aunt, in Billings. But those had all been very innocent, limited to kisses and light caresses and not much desire.

All that had changed when Gil Callister held her hand at the movies. And when Gil had carried her up the staircase this morning, she was on fire with pleasure. She was still shivery with new sensations, which she didn't understand at all. Gil was her boss and he disliked her. She'd been spending more time with the girls than the grown-ups because John didn't like to do paperwork and he was always dodging dictation. He could usually be found out with the men on the ranch, helping with whatever routine task was going on at the time. Gil did that, too, of course, but not because he didn't like paperwork. Gil rarely ever sat still.

Mrs. Charters said it was because he'd loved his wife and had never gotten over her unexpected death from a freak horseback-riding accident. She was only twenty-six years old.

That had been only three years ago. Since then, Gil had hired a succession of nurses, at first, and then motherly governesses to watch over the girls. Old Mrs. Harris had retired and then Gil had hired Miss Parsons in desperation, over a virtual flood of young marriageable women who had their eye on either Gil or John. Kasie remembered Gil saying that he had no interest in marriage ever again. At that time, she couldn't have imagined feeling attracted to a widowed man with two children who had the personality of a spitting cobra.

For her first few weeks on the job, he'd watched Kasie. He hadn't wanted his children around Kasie, and made it plain. Amazing, how much that had hurt.

They were such darling little girls.

At least, she thought, now she could spend time with them and not have to sneak around doing it. Gil might not like her, but he couldn't deny that his daughters did. Probably he felt that he didn't have a choice.

Kasie was going to miss the secretarial work, and she wondered how Gil would manage with Pauline, who absolutely hated clerical duties. The woman only did it to be near Gil, but he didn't seem to realize it. Or if he did, he didn't care.

She tried to picture Gil married to Pauline and it wounded her. Pauline was shallow and selfish. She didn't really like the girls, and she'd probably find some way to get them out of her hair when she and Gil married, if they did. Kasie hated the very idea of such a marriage, but she was a little nobody in the world and Gil Callister was a millionaire. She couldn't even tease him or flirt with him, because he might think she was after him for his wealth. It made her self-conscious, so she became uneasy around him and tongue-tied to boot.

That made him even more irritable. Sunday afternoon there was another storm and he and the men had to go out and work the cattle. He came in just after dark, drenched, unfastening his shirt on the way into the office. His hair was plastered to his scalp and his spurs jingled as he walked, his leather bat-wing chaps making flapping noises with every stride of his long, powerful jean-clad legs. His boots were soaked, too, and caked with mud.

"Mrs. Charters will be after you," Kasie remarked as she lifted her eyes from the badly scribbled notes John had left, which Miss Parsons had asked her to help decipher. Miss Parsons had already gone up to bed, anticipating a very early start on work the next morning.

"It's my damned house," he shot at her irritably, running a hand through his drenched hair to get it off his forehead. "I can drip wherever I please!"

"Suit yourself," Kasie replied. "But red mud won't come out of Persian wool carpets."

He gave her a hard glare, but he sat down in a chair and pulled off the mud-caked boots, tossing them onto the wide brick hearth of the fireplace, where they wouldn't soil anything delicate. His white socks were soaked as well, but he didn't take them off. He sat down behind his desk, picked up the telephone and made a call.

"Where are the girls?" he asked while he waited for the call to be answered.

"Watching the new *Pokémon* movie up in their room," Kasie said. "Miss Parsons can't read John's handwriting, so I'm deciphering this for her so she can start early tomorrow morning on the payroll and the quarterly estimated taxes that are due in June. If that's all right," she added politely.

He just glared at her. "Hello, Lonnie?" he said suddenly into the telephone receiver he was holding. "Can you give me the name of that mechanic who worked on Harris's truck last month? Yes, the one who doesn't need a damned computer to tell him what's wrong with the engine. Got his number? Just a minute." He fished in the drawer for a pen, grabbed an envelope and wrote a number on it. "Sure thing. Thanks." He hung up and dialed again.

While he spoke to the mechanic, Kasie finished transcribing John's terrible handwriting neatly for Miss Parsons.

Gil hung up and got to his feet, retrieving his boots. "If you've got a few minutes free, I need you to take some dictation for me," he told Kasie.

"I'll be glad to."

He gave her a narrow appraisal. "I've got a man coming over to look at my cattle truck," he added. "If he gets here while I'm in the shower, show him into the living room and don't let him leave. He can listen to an engine and tell you what's wrong with it."

"But it's Sunday," she began.

"I need the truck to haul cattle tomorrow. I'm sure he went to church this morning, so it's all right," he assured her dryly. "Besides…"

The ringing of the phone interrupted him. He jerked up the receiver. "Callister," he said.

There was a pause, during which his face became harder than Kasie had ever seen it. "Yes," he replied to a question. "I'll talk to John when he gets back in, but I can tell you what the answer will be." He smiled coldly. "I'm sure that if you use your imagination, you can figure that out without too much difficulty. No, I don't. I don't give a damn. Do what you please with them." There was a longer pause and Kasie thought she'd never seen such coldness in a man's eyes. "I don't need a thing, thanks. Yes. You do that."

He hung up. "My parents," he said harshly. "With an invitation to come and bring the girls to their estate on Long Island next week."

"Are you going?"

He looked briefly sardonic. "They're hosting a party for some people who are interested in seeing what a real cattleman looks like," he said surprisingly. "They're trying to sell them on an advertising contract for their sports magazine and they think John and I might be useful." He sounded bitter and angry. "They try this occasionally, but John and I don't go. They can make money on their own. I'll be upstairs if the mechanic comes. Tell him the truck's in the barn with one of my men. He can go right on out."

"Okay."

He walked out and Kasie stared after him. The conversation with his parents hadn't been pleasant for him. He seemed to dislike them intensely. She knew that they were never mentioned around the girls, and John never spoke of them, either. She wondered what they'd done to make their sons so hostile. Then she remembered what Gil had said, about their being used by their parents only to make money, and it all began to make sense. Perhaps they didn't really want children at all. What a pity, that their sons were nothing more than sales incentives to them.

The mechanic did come while Gil was upstairs. Kasie went with him onto the long porch and showed him where the barn was, so that he could drive on down there and park his truck. The rain had stopped, though, so he didn't have to worry about getting wet. There was a pleasant dripping sound off the eaves of the house, and the delicious smell of wet flowers in the darkness.

Kasie sat down in the porch swing and rocked it into motion. It was a perfect night, now that the storm had abated. She could hear crickets, or maybe frogs, chirping all around the flowering shrubs that surrounded the front porch. It reminded her, for some reason, of Africa. She vaguely remembered sitting in a porch swing with her mother and Kantor when their father was away working. There were the delicious smells of cooking from the house, and the spicy smells drifting from the harbor nearby, as well as the familiar sound of African workers singing and humming as they worked around the settlement. It was a long time ago, when she still had a family. Now, except for Mama Luke, she was completely alone. It was a cold, empty feeling.

The screen door suddenly opened and Gil came out onto the porch. His blond hair was still damp, faintly unruly at the edges and tending to curl. He was wearing a blue checked Western shirt with clean jeans and nice boots. He looked just the way a working cowboy should when he was cleaned up, she thought, trying to imagine him a century earlier.

"Is the mechanic here?" he asked abruptly when he spotted Kasie in the swing.

"Yes, I sent him on down to the barn."

He went down the steps gracefully and stalked to the barn. He was gone about five minutes and when he came out of the barn, so did the mechanic. They shook hands and the mechanic drove off.

"A fuse," he murmured, shaking his head as he came up the steps and dropped into the swing at Kasie's side.

"A damned fuse, and the whole panel went down. Imagine that."

"Sometimes it's the little things that give the most trouble," she murmured, shy with him.

He put an arm behind her and rocked the swing into motion. "I like the way you smell, Kasie," he said lazily. "You always remind me of roses."

"I'm allergic to perfume," she confided. "The florals are the only ones I can wear without sneezing my head off."

"Where are my babies?" he asked.

"Mrs. Charters is baking cookies with them in the kitchen," she said, smiling. "They love to cook. So do I. We've all learned a lot from Mrs. Charters."

He looked down at her in the darkness. One lean hand went to the braid at the back of her head, and he tugged on it gently. "You're mysterious," he murmured. "I don't really know anything about you."

"There's not much to tell," she told him. "I'm just ordinary."

He shifted, and she felt his powerful thigh against her leg. Her body came alive with fleeting little stabs of pleasure. She could feel her breath catching in her throat as she breathed. He was too close.

She started to move, but it was too late. His arm curled her into his body, and the warm, hard pressure of his mouth pushed her head back against the swing while he fed hungrily on her lips.

Part of her wanted to resist, but a stronger part was completely powerless. She reached up and put her arms around his neck and opened her lips for him. She felt him stiffen, hesitate, catch his breath. Then his mouth became rough and demanding, and he dragged her across his legs, folding her close while he kissed her until her mouth was swollen and tender.

He nibbled her upper lip, fighting to breathe normally. "Don't let me do this," he warned.

"You're bigger than I am," she murmured breathlessly.

"That's no excuse at all."

Her fingers trailed over his hard mouth and down to his chest where they rested. She stared at the wide curve of his mouth with a kind of wonder that a man like this, good-looking and charming and wealthy, would look twice at a chestnut mouse like Kasie. Perhaps he needed glasses.

He touched her oval face, tracing its soft lines in a warm, damp darkness that was suddenly like an exotic, faraway place. Kasie felt as if she'd come home. Impulsively, she let her head slide down his arm until it rested in the crook of his elbow. She watched his expression harden, heard his breathing change. His lean fingers moved down her chin and throat until they were at the top button of her shirtwaist dress. They hesitated there.

She lay looking up at him patiently, curiously, ablaze with unfamiliar longings and delight.

"Kasie," he whispered, and his long fingers began to sensually move the top button out of its buttonhole. As it came free, he heard her soft gasp, felt the jerk of her body, and knew that this was new territory for her.

His hand started to slide gently into the opening he'd made. He watched Kasie, lying so sweetly in his embrace, giving him free license with her innocence, and he shivered with desire.

But even as he felt the soft warmth of the skin at her collarbone, laughing young voices came drifting out onto the porch as the front door opened.

Gil moved Kasie back into her own seat abruptly and stood up.

"Daddy's home!" Bess cried, and she and Jenny ran to him, to be scooped up and kissed heartily.

"I'll, uh, just go and get my pad so that you can dictate that letter you mentioned," Kasie said as she got up, too.

"You will not," Gil said, his voice still a little husky. "Go to bed, Kasie. It can wait. In the morning, you can tutor Pauline on the computer, so that she can take over inputting the cattle records. John won't be in until late tonight, and he leaves early tomorrow for the cattle show in San Antonio. There's nothing in the office that can't wait."

She was both disappointed and relieved. It was getting harder to deny Gil anything he wanted. She couldn't have imagined that she was such a wanton person only a few weeks ago. She didn't know what to do.

"Okay, I'll call it a night," she said, trying to disguise her nervousness. "Good night, babies," she told Bess and Jenny with a smile. "Sleep tight."

"Will you tell us a story, Kasie?" Bess began.

"I'll tell you a story tonight. Kasie needs her rest. All right?" he asked the girls.

"All right, Daddy," Jenny murmured, laying her sleepy head on his shoulder.

They all went upstairs together. Kasie didn't quite meet his eyes as she went down the hall to her own room. She didn't sleep very much, either.

Chapter Six

Pauline Raines was half an hour late Monday morning. Gil had already gone out to check on some cattle that was being shipped off. John had left before daylight to fly to San Antonio, where the cattle trailer was taking his champion bull, Ebony King, for the cattle show. While the girls took their nap, Kasie helped Miss Parsons with John's correspondence and fielded the telephone. Now that it was just past roundup, things weren't quite as hectic, but sales reports were coming in on the culled cattle being shipped, and they weren't even all on the computer yet. Neither were most of the new calf crop.

Miss Parsons had gone to the post office when Pauline arrived wearing a neat black suit with a fetching blue scarf. She glared at Kasie as she threw her purse down on the chair.

"Here I am," she said irritably. "I don't usually come in before ten, but Gil said I had to be early, to work on this stupid computer. I don't see why I need to learn it."

"Because you'll have to put in all the information we're getting about the new calves and replacement heifers," Kasie explained patiently. "It's backing up."

"You can do that," Pauline said haughtily. "You're John's secretary."

"Not anymore," she replied calmly. "I'm going to take care of the girls while Miss Parsons takes my place in John's office. She's going to handle all the tax work."

That piece of information didn't please Pauline. "You're a secretary," she pointed out.

"That's what I told Mr. Callister, but it didn't change his mind," Kasie replied tersely.

"So now I'll have to do all your work while Miss Parsons does taxes? I won't! Surely you'll have enough free time to put these records on the computer! Two little girls don't require much watching. Just put them in front of the television!"

Kasie almost bit her tongue right through keeping back a hot reply. "It isn't going to be hard to use the computer. It will save you hours of paperwork."

Pauline gave her a glare. "Debbie always put these things on the computer."

"Debbie quit because she couldn't do two jobs at once," Kasie said, and was vindicated for the jibe when she saw Pauline's discomfort. "You really will enjoy the time the computer saves you, once you understand how it works."

"I don't need this job, didn't anyone tell you?" the older woman asked. "I'm wealthy. I only do it to be near Gil. It gives us more time together, while we're seeing how compatible we are. Which reminds me, don't think you're on to a cushy job looking after those children," she added haughtily. "Gil and I are going to be looking for a boarding school very soon."

"Boarding school?" Kasie exclaimed, horrified.

"I've already checked out several," Pauline said. "It isn't good for little girls to become too attached to their fathers. It interferes with Gil's social life."

"I hadn't noticed."

Pauline frowned. "What do you mean, you hadn't noticed?"

"Well, Mr. Callister is almost a generation older than I am," she said deliberately.

"Oh." Pauline smiled secretively. "I see."

"He's a very kind man," Kasie emphasized, "but I don't think of him in that way," she added, lying through her teeth.

Pauline for once seemed speechless.

"Here, let's get started," Kasie said as she turned on the computer, trying to head off trouble. She hoped that comment would keep her out of trouble with Pauline, who obviously considered Gil Callister her personal property. Kasie had enough problems without adding a jealous secretary to them. Even if she did privately think Gil was the sexiest man she'd ever known.

Pauline seemed determined to make every second of work as hard as humanly possible for Kasie. She insisted on three coffee breaks before noon, and the pressing nature of the information coming in by fax kept Kasie working long after Pauline called it a day at three in the afternoon and went home. If Mrs. Charters hadn't helped out by letting Bess and Jenny make cookies, Kasie wouldn't have been able to do as much as she did.

She'd only just finished the new computer entries when Gil came in, dusty and sweaty and half out of humor. He didn't say a word. He went to the liquor cabinet and poured himself a scotch and water, and he drank half of it before he even looked at Kasie.

It took her a minute to realize that he was openly glaring at her.

"Is something wrong?" she asked uneasily.

"Pauline called me on the cell phone a few minutes ago. She said you're making it impossible for her to do her job," he replied finally.

Her heart skipped. So that was how the other woman was going to make points—telling lies.

"I've been showing her how to key in this data, and that's all I've done," Kasie told him quietly. "She hates the computer."

"Odd that she's done so well with it up until now," he said suspiciously.

"Debbie did well with it," Kasie replied bluntly, flushing a little at his angry tenseness. "She was apparently having to put her own work as well as Pauline's into the computer."

He took another sip of the drink. He didn't look convinced. "That isn't what Pauline says," he told her. "And I want to know why you suddenly want my girls in a boarding school, after you've spent weeks behind my back and against instructions winning them over, so they're attached to you." He added angrily, "I meant it when I said I have no plans to marry. So if that changes your mind about wanting to take care of them, say so and I'll give you a reference and two weeks severance pay!"

He really did look ferocious. Kasie's head was spinning from the accusations. "Excuse me?"

He finished the drink and put the glass down firmly on the counter below the liquor cabinet. His pale eyes were glittery. "John and I spent six of the worst years of our lives at boarding school," he added unexpectedly. "I'm not putting my babies in any boarding school."

Kasie felt as if she were being attacked by invisible hands. She stood up, her mind reeling from the charges. Pauline had been busy!

"I haven't said anything about boarding school," she defended herself. "Pauline said…"

He held up a hand. "I know Pauline," he told her. "I've known her most of my life. She doesn't tell lies."

Boy, was he in for a shock a little further on down the road, she thought, but she didn't say anything else. She was already in too much trouble, and none of it of her own making.

She didn't say a word. She just looked at him with big, gray, wounded eyes.

He moved closer, his mind reeling from Pauline's comments about Kasie. He didn't want to believe that Kasie was so two-faced that she'd play up to the girls to get in Gil's good graces and then want to see them sent off to boarding school. But what did he really know about her, after all? She had no family except an aunt in Billings, or so she said, and except for the information on her application that mentioned secretarial school, nothing about her early education was apparent. She was mysterious. He didn't like mysteries.

He stopped just in front of her, his face hard and threatening as he glared down at her.

"Where were you born?" he asked abruptly.

The question surprised her. She became flustered. "I, well, I was born in…in Africa."

He hadn't expected that answer, and it showed. *"Africa?"*

"Yes. In Sierra Leone," she added.

He frowned. "What were your parents doing in Africa?"

"They worked there."

"I see." He didn't, but she looked as if she hated talking about it. The mystery only deepened.

"Maybe you're right," she said, unnerved by his unexpected anger and the attack by Pauline, which made her look like a gold digger. "Maybe I'm not the best person to look after the girls. If you like, I'll hand in my notice…!"

He had her by both shoulders with a firm grip and the expression on his face made her want to back away.

"And just for the record, ten years isn't a generation!" he said through his teeth as he glared down at her. His gaze dropped to her soft, generous mouth and it was like lightning striking. He couldn't help himself. The memory of her body in his arms on the porch swing took away the last wisp of his willpower. He bent quickly and took that beautiful softness under his hard lips in a fever of hunger, probing insistently at her tight mouth with his tongue.

Kasie, who'd never been kissed in any intimate way, even by Gil, froze like ice at the skillful, invasive intimacy of his mouth. She couldn't believe what was happening. Her hands against his chest clenched and she closed her eyes tightly as she strained against his hold.

Slowly it seemed to get through to him that she was shocked at the insistence. He lifted his demanding mouth and looked at her. This was familiar territory for him. But, it wasn't for her, and it was apparent. After the way she'd responded to him the night before, he was surprised that she balked at a deep kiss. But, then, he remembered her chaste gowns and her strange attitude about wearing her beautiful hair loose. She wasn't fighting him. She looked…strange.

His lean hands loosened, became caressing on her upper arms under the short sleeve of her dress. "I'm sorry. It's all right," he breathed as he bent again. "I won't be rough with you. It's all right, Kasie…"

His lips barely brushed hers, tender now instead of demanding. A few seconds of tenderness brought a sigh from her lips. He smiled against her soft mouth as he coaxed it to part. He nibbled the full upper lip, tasting its velvety underside with his tongue, enjoying her reactions to him. He felt her young body begin to relax into his. She worked for him. She was an employee. He'd just been giving her hell about trying to trap him into marriage. So why was he doing this…? She made a soft sound under her breath and her hands tightened on the hard muscles of his upper arms. His brows began to knit as sensation pulsed through him at her shy response. What did it matter *why* he was doing it, he asked himself, and threw caution to the winds.

His arms went around her, gently smoothing her against the muscular length of him, while his mouth dragged a response under its tender pressure. He felt her gasp, felt her shiver, then felt her arms sliding around his waist as she gave in to the explosion of warm sensation that his hungry kiss provoked in her.

It was like flying, he thought dizzily. He lifted her against him, feeding on the softness of her mouth, the clinging wonder of her arms around him. It had been years since a kiss had been this sweet, this fulfilling. Not since Darlene had he been so hungry for a woman's mouth. Darlene. Darlene. Kasie was so much like her...

Only the need to breathe forced him to put her down and lift his head. His turbulent eyes met her dazed ones and he had to fight to catch his breath.

"Why did you do that?" she asked unsteadily.

He was scowling. He touched her mouth with a lean forefinger. "I don't know," he said honestly. "Do you want me to apologize?" he added quietly.

"Are you sorry?" she returned.

"I am not," he said, every word deliberate as he stared into her eyes.

That husky statement made her tingle all over with delicious sensations, but he still looked formidable. His lean fingers caught her shoulders and gently moved her away. She looked as devastated as he felt.

Her eyes searched his quietly. She was shaking inside from the delicious crush of his mouth, so unexpected. "What did you mean, about ten years not being a generation?" she asked suddenly.

"You harp on my age," he murmured coolly, but he was still looking at her soft, swollen mouth. "You shouldn't tell Pauline things you don't want me to hear. She can't keep a secret."

"I wouldn't tell her my middle name," she muttered. "She hates me, haven't you noticed?"

"No, I hadn't."

"It would never have been my idea to send the girls to boarding school," she insisted. "I love them."

His eyebrows lifted. Kasie didn't appear to be lying. But Pauline had been so convincing. And Kasie was mysterious. He wanted to know why she was so secretive about her past. He wanted to know everything about her. Her mouth was sweet and soft and innocent, and he had to fight not to bend and take it again. She was nervous with him now, as she hadn't been before. That meant that the attraction was mutual. It made him feel a foot taller.

"Pauline wants to go down to Nassau for a few days with the girls. I want you to come with us," he said abruptly.

She gaped at him. "She won't want me along," she said with conviction.

"She will when she has to start looking out for Bess and Jenny. Her idea of watching them is to let them do what they please. That could be disastrous even around a swimming pool."

She grimaced. It would be a horrible trip. "We'd have to fly," she said, hating the very thought of getting on an airplane. She'd lost everyone she'd ever loved in the air, and he didn't know.

"The girls like you," he persisted gently.

"I'd really rather not," she said worriedly.

"Then I'll make it an order," he said shortly. "You're coming. Have you got a current passport?"

"Yes," she said without thinking.

He was surprised. "I was going to say that if you didn't have one, a birth certificate or even a voter's registration slip would be adequate." He was suspicious. "Why do you keep a passport?"

"In case I get kidnapped by terrorists," she said, tongue in cheek, trying to put aside the fear of the upcoming trip.

He rolled his eyes, let her go and walked to the door.

"We'll go Friday," he said. "Don't take much with you," he added. "We'll fly commercial and I don't like baggage claim."

"Okay."

"And stop letting me kiss you," he added with faint arrogance. "I've already made it clear that there's no future in it. I won't marry again, not even to provide the girls with a grown-up playmate."

"I do know that," she said, wounded by the words. "But I'm not the one doing the grabbing," she pointed out.

He gave her an odd look before he left.

She could have told him that she didn't have much to take anywhere, and she almost blurted out why she was afraid of airplanes. But he was already out the door. She touched her mouth. She tasted scotch whiskey on her lips and she was amazed that she hadn't noticed while he was kissing her. Why had he kissed her again? she wondered dazedly. The other question was why had she kissed him back? Her head was reeling with the sudden shift in their relationship since the night before. Kissing seemed to be addictive. Perhaps she should cut her losses and quit right away. But that thought was very unpleasant indeed. She decided that meeting trouble head-on was so much better than running from it. She had to conquer her fear and try to put the past behind her once and for all. Yes, she would go to Nassau with him and the girls—and Pauline. It might very well put things into perspective if she saw Pauline and Gil as a family, while there was still time to stop her rebellious heart from falling in love.

Kasie's seat was separated from Gil's, Pauline's and the girls' by ten rows. Gil didn't appear pleased and he tried to change seat assignments, but it wasn't possible. Kasie was rather relieved. She was uncomfortable with Gil since he'd kissed her so passionately.

Pauline was furious that Kasie had been included in the trip. She was doing everything in her power to get Kasie out of Gil's life, but nothing was going the way she planned. She'd envisioned just the four of them in the exquisite islands, where she could convince Gil that they should get married. He agreed to her suggestion about the trip more easily than she'd hoped, and then he said Kasie would have to come along to take care of the girls. He didn't even mention boarding school, as if he didn't believe Kasie had suggested it. Pauline was losing ground with him by the day. She could cheerfully have pushed Kasie out of the terminal window. Well, she was going to get rid of Miss Prim over there, whatever it took. One way or another, she was going to get Kasie out of Gil's house!

They boarded the plane, and Kasie smiled with false bravado as she passed the girls with a wave and found her window seat. There was only one seat next to hers. She was watching the people file in while she fought her own fear. Seconds later, a tall blond man wearing khakis swung into the seat beside hers and gave her an appreciative smile.

"And I thought this was going to be a boring flight," he chuckled as he stuffed his one carry-on bag under the seat in front of him and fastened his seat belt. "I'm Zeke Mulligan," he introduced himself with a smile. "I write freelance travel articles for magazines."

"I'm Kasie Mayfield," she replied, offering her small hand with a wan smile. "I'm a governess to two sweet little girls."

"Where are the sweet little girls?" he asked with a grin.

"Ten rows that way," she pointed. "With their dad and his venomous secretary."

"Ouch, the jealousy monster strikes, hmm?" he asked. "Does she see you as competition?"

"That would be one for the books," she chuckled. "She's blond and beautiful."

"What are you, chestnut-haired and repulsive?" he chided. "Looks aren't everything, fellow adventurer."

"Adventuress," she corrected. She glanced out the window and noticed the movement of the motorized carts away from the plane. It was going to take off soon. Sure enough, she heard the rev of the engines and saw the flight attendants take up their positions to demonstrate the life vests even as the plane started to taxi out of its concourse space. "Oh, gosh," she groaned, tightening her hands on the arms of her seat.

"Afraid of flying?" he asked gently.

"I lost my family in a plane crash," she said in a rough whisper. "This is the first time I've flown, since I lost them. I don't know if I can...!"

She'd started to pull at her seat belt. He caught her hand and stilled it. "Listen to me," he said gently, "air travel is the safest kind. I've been knocking around on airplanes for ten years, I've been around the world three times. It's all right," he stressed, his voice low and deep and comforting. His fingers contracted around hers. "You just hold on to me. I'll get you through takeoff and landing. Once you've conquered the fear, you'll be fine."

"Are you sure?" she asked on a choked laugh.

"I walked away from a crash once," he told her quietly. "A week later I had to get on a plane for Paris. Yes," he added. "I'm sure. If I could do it, I know you can."

Her lips parted as she let out the breath she'd been holding. He was nice. He was very nice. He made her feel utterly safe. She clung to his hand as the airplane taxied to the runway and the pilot announced that they were next in line to take off.

"Here we go," her seat companion said in her ear. "Think of *Star Trek* when the ship goes into light speed," he added on a chuckle. "Think of it as being flung up into the stars. It's exciting. It's great!"

She held on tighter as the plane taxied onto the runway, revved up its engines and began to pick up speed.

"We can even sing the Air Force song as we go," he said. "I spent four years in it, so I can coach you if you can't remember the words. Come on, Kasie. Sing!"

Kasie started to hum the words of the well-known song.

The passengers around them noticed Kasie's terror and her companion's protective attitude, and suddenly they all started singing the Air Force song. It diverted Kasie with uproarious laughter as the big airplane shot up into the blue sky, leaving her stomach and her fears far behind.

"I'm very grateful," she told him when they were comfortably leveled off and the flight attendants were getting the refreshment cart ready to take down the aisle. "You can't imagine how terrified I was to get on this plane."

"Yes, I can. I'm glad I was here. Where are you staying in Nassau?" he added.

She laughed. "I'm sorry. I don't know! I didn't realize that until just now. My boss will have all the details in hand, and a driver to meet us when we land. I didn't ask."

"New Providence is a small island," he told her.

"We'll see each other again. I'm at the Crystal Palace on Cable Beach. You can phone me if you get a few free minutes and we'll have lunch."

"Do you go overseas to do stories?" she asked.

He nodded. "All over the world. It's a great job, and I actually get paid to do it." He leaned close to her ear. "And once, I worked for the CIA."

"You didn't!" she exclaimed, impressed.

"Just for a year, while I was in South America," he assured her. "I might have kept it up, but I was married then and she didn't want me taking chances, especially while she was carrying our son."

"She doesn't travel with you?" she asked curiously.

"She died, of a particularly virulent tropical fever," he said with a sad smile. "My son is six, and I leave him with my parents when I have to go away during his school year. During the summer, he goes places with me. He loves it, too."

He pulled out his wallet and showed her several photographs of a child who was his mirror image. "His name's Daniel, but I call him Dano."

"He really is cute."

"Thanks."

The flight attendant was two rows away, with snack meals and drinks. Kasie settled down to lunch with no more reservations. She'd landed on her feet. She wondered what Gil would think if he saw her with this nice young man. Nothing, probably, she thought bitterly, not when he was so wrapped up in Pauline. Well, she wasn't going to let that spoil her trip.

Nassau was unexpected. Kasie fell in love with it on first sight. She'd seen postcards of the Bahamas, and she'd always assumed that the vivid turquoise and sapphire color of the waters was exaggerated. But it wasn't. Those vivid, surreal colors were exactly what the water looked like, and the beaches were as white as sugar. She stared out the window of the hired car with her breath catching in her chest. She'd gone overseas with her parents as a child, but to distant and primitive places. She remembered the terror of those places far better than she remembered the scenery, even at so young an age. Even now, it was hard to think about how she'd lost the parents who'd loved her and Kantor so much. It was harder to think of Kantor...

"Do stop pressing your nose against the glass, Kasie. You look about Jenny's age!" Pauline chided from her seat beside Gil.

"That's funny," Bess said with a giggle, not understanding the words were meant to hurt.

"I've never seen anything so beautiful," Kasie murmured a little shyly. "It really does look like paradise."

Pauline yawned. Gil ignored her and watched Kasie a little irritably as she and the girls enthused over the beach.

"When can we go swimming in the ocean, Daddy?" Bess asked excitedly.

"We have to check into the hotel first, baby," Gil told her. "And even then, the beach is dangerous. Kasie doesn't swim."

"Oh, we can take them with us," Pauline said lazily. "I'll watch them."

It occurred to Gil that he never trusted Pauline with his children. She wasn't malicious, she just didn't pay attention to what they were doing. She'd be involved in putting on sunscreen and lying in the sun, not watching children who could become reckless. Bess was especially good at getting into trouble.

"That's Kasie's job," Gil said, and put a long arm around Pauline just to see the reaction it got from Kasie. It was a constant source of anger that he couldn't keep his hands off Kasie when he was within five feet of her, and he still didn't trust her.

Kasie averted her eyes. Odd, how much it hurt to see Pauline snuggle close to Gil as if she were part of him. Remembering the hungry, masterful way he'd kissed her in the study, Kasie flushed. She knew things about Gil Callister that she shouldn't know. He made her hungry. But he was showing her that he didn't feel the same way. It was painfully obvious what his relationship was with Pauline. Even though she'd guessed, it hurt to have it pointed out to her like this.

She knew then that she was going to have to resign her job when they got back to the States. If he married Pauline, there was no way she could live under the same roof with them.

Gil saw the reaction that Kasie was too young to hide, and it touched him. She felt something. She was jealous. He could have cheered out loud. It didn't occur to him then why he was so happy that Kasie was attracted to him.

"Who was the man you were talking to on the concourse, Kasie?" Gil asked unexpectedly.

"His name was Zeke," she replied with a smile. "He had the seat next to mine."

"I noticed him. He's good-looking," Pauline said. "What does he do?"

"He's a freelance writer for several travel magazines," Kasie told her. "He's down here doing a story on a new hotel complex."

Gil didn't look pleased. "Apparently you made friends quickly."

"Well, yes," she confessed. "I was a little nervous about flying. He talked to me while we got airborne." She grinned. "Didn't you hear us all singing the Air Force song?"

"So that's what it was," Pauline scoffed. "Good Lord, I thought the plane was full of drunks."

"Why were you afraid of flying?" Gil persisted.

Kasie averted her eyes to the girls. "My family died in an airplane crash," she said, without mentioning under what circumstances.

He shifted uncomfortably and looked at his daughters, who were watching for exciting little glimpses of people playing in the surf on the white beaches as they passed them.

"I'm all right now," she said. "The flight wasn't so bad."

"Not with a handsome man to hold your hand," Pauline teased deliberately.

"He *was* handsome," Kasie agreed, but without enthusiasm, and without noticing that Gil's eyes were beginning to glint with anger. He leaned back, glaring at Kasie.

She wondered what she'd done to provoke that anger. It made her uneasy. Pauline obviously didn't like it, either, and the woman was giving Kasie looks that promised retribution in the near future. Kasie had a feeling that Miss Raines would make a very bad enemy, and deep in her stomach, she felt icy cold.

Chapter Seven

It took an hour to get checked into the luxury hotel. The girls played quietly in the marble-floored lobby with a puzzle book Kasie had brought along for them, while Pauline complained loudly and nonstop about the inconvenience of having to wait for a room to be made ready. By the time the clerk motioned them to the desk, Gil was completely out of humor. He hadn't smiled since they got off the plane, in fact. When they were given keys to a two-bedroom suite and a single adjoining room, Pauline's expression lightened.

"Oh, that's nice of you, darling, letting Miss Mayfield have a room of her own."

Gil gave her a look that combined exasperation with impatience. "The girls can't be alone at night in a strange hotel," he said curtly. "Kasie's staying in the room with them, and the other bedroom in the suite is mine. You get the single."

"Why can't I just share with you, darling?" Pauline purred, enjoying Kasie's sudden flush.

Gil looked furious. He glared down at her from his superior height. "Maybe you've forgotten that I don't move with the times," he said quietly.

Pauline laughed a little nervously. "You're kidding. What's so bad about two…friends sharing a room?"

"I'm not kidding," Gil said flatly. He handed Pauline her key and motioned for Kasie and the girls to follow him.

Pauline stomped into the elevator, fuming. She gave Kasie a ferocious glare before she folded her arms over her chest and leaned back against the wall. The bellboy signaled that he'd wait for the next elevator to bring their luggage up, because six other people had jumped into the elevator right behind Pauline.

Gil and Pauline led the way down the hall, with Kasie and the girls following suit.

"At least, you can take me out tonight," Pauline told Gil, "since Kasie's along to baby-sit. Come on, darling, please? They have the most beautiful casino over on Paradise Island, and floor shows, too."

"All right," he said. "Let me get the girls and Kasie settled first, and find out about room service. You will want to have supper up here, won't you?" he asked Kasie stiffly.

"Of course," she said, not wanting to make things worse than they were—if that was possible.

"Good. Kasie can take the girls out to the beach while I check with the concierge about reservations," he added, watching Pauline's face beam. "I'll pick you up at your room at five-thirty."

"But that only gives me an hour to dress," she moaned.

"You'd look beautiful in a pillowcase, and you know it," he chided. "Go on."

"Okay." Pauline walked off to her own room without a word to the girls or Kasie.

Gil opened the door, noting that the bellboy was coming down the hall toward them with the luggage on a rolling carrier. He motioned Kasie and the girls inside.

"The bedrooms both have two double beds," he told Kasie stiffly. "And there's a balcony off the sitting room, if you want to sit outside and watch the surf after the girls get to sleep," he added, indicating the French doors that led onto a small balcony with two padded chairs.

"We'll be fine," she told him.

"Don't let them stay up past eight, no matter what they say," he told her. "And don't you stay up too late, either."

"I won't."

He hesitated at the door to his own room and looked at Kasie for a long moment, until her heart began to race. "You didn't tell me that you lost your family in an air crash. Why?"

"The subject didn't come up," she said gruffly.

"If it had," he replied curtly, "you wouldn't have been sitting alone, despite Pauline's little machinations with the seat assignments."

She was taken aback by the anger in his tone. "Oh."

"You make me feel like a gold-plated heel from time to time, Kasie," he said irritably. "I don't like it."

"I was all right," she assured him nervously. "Zeke took care of me."

That set him off again. "You're getting paid to take care of my children, not to holiday with some refugee from a press room," he pointed out, his voice arctic.

She stiffened. "I hadn't forgotten that, *Mr.* Callister," she added deliberately, aware that the girls had stopped playing and were staring up at the adults with growing disquiet. She turned away. "Come on, babies," she said with a forced smile. "Let's go change into our bathing suits, then we can go play on the beach!"

"All of you stay out of the water," Gil said shortly. "And I want you back up here before I leave with Pauline."

"Yes, sir," Kasie said, just because she knew it made him angry.

He said something under his breath and slammed the door to his own room behind him. Kasie had a premonition that it wasn't going to be much of a holiday.

She and the girls played in the sand near the ocean. On the way outside, Kasie had bought them small plastic buckets and shovels from one of the stores in the arcade. They were happily dumping sand on each other while, around them, other sun-worshipers lay on towel-covered beach chaise lounges or splashed in the water. The hotel was near the harbor, as well, and they watched a huge white ocean liner dock. It was an exciting place to visit.

Kasie, who'd only ever seen the worst part of foreign countries, was like a child herself as she gazed with fascination at rows of other luxury hotels on the beach, as well as sailboats and cruise ships in port. Nassau was the brightest, most beautiful place she'd ever been. The sand was like sugar under her feet, although hot enough to scorch them, and the color of the water was almost too vivid to believe. Smiling, she drank in the warmth of the sun with her eyes closed.

But it was already time to go back up to the room. She hated telling the girls, who begged to stay on the beach.

"We can't, babies," she said gently. "Your dad said we have to be in the room when he leaves. There's a television," she added. "They might have cartoons."

They still looked disappointed. "You could read us stories," Bess said.

Kasie smiled and hugged her. "Yes, I could. And I will. Come on, now, clean out your pails and shovels, and let's go."

"Oh, all right, Kasie, but it's very sad we have to leave," Bess replied.

"Don't want to go." Jenny pouted.

Kasie picked her up and kissed her sandy cheek. "We'll come out early in the morning, and look for shells on the beach!"

Jenny's eyes lit up. She loved seashells. "Truly, Kasie?"

"Honest and truly."

"Whoopee!" Bess yelled. "I'll get Jenny's pail, too. Can we have fish for supper?"

"Anything you like," Kasie told her as she put Jenny down and refastened her swimsuit strap that had come loose.

Above them, at the window of his room, Gil watched the byplay, unseen. He sighed with irritation as he watched the girls respond so wholeheartedly to Kasie.

They loved her. How were they going to react if she decided to quit? She was very young; too young to think of making a lifelong baby-sitter. Pauline said she'd been very adamant about sending the girls away to school, but that was hard to believe, watching her with them. She was tender with them, as Darlene had been.

He rammed his hands hard into the pockets of his dress slacks. It hurt remembering how happy the two of them had been, especially after the birth of their second little girl. In the Callister family, girls were special, because there hadn't been a girl in the lineage for over a hundred years. Gil loved having daughters. A son would have been nice, he supposed, but he wouldn't have traded either of his little jewels down there for anything else.

It wounded him to remember how cold he'd been to Kasie before and after the plane trip. He hadn't known about her family dying in a plane crash. He could only imagine how difficult it had been for her to get aboard with those memories. And he'd been sitting with Pauline, talking about Broadway shows. Pauline had said that Kasie wanted to sit by herself, so he hadn't protested.

Then, of course, there was this handsome stranger who'd comforted her on the flight to keep her from being afraid. He could have done that. He could have held her hand tight in his and kissed her eyes shut while he whispered to her...

He groaned out loud and turned away from the window. She was worming her way not only into his life and his girls' lives, but into his heart as well. He hadn't been able to even think about Pauline in any romantic way since Kasie had walked into his living room for the job interview. Up until then, he'd found the gorgeous blonde wonderful company. Now, she was almost an afterthought. He couldn't imagine why. Kasie wasn't really pretty. Although, she had a nice figure and a very kissable mouth and those exquisitely tender eyes...

He jerked up the phone and dialed Pauline's extension. "Are you ready to go?" he asked.

"Darling, I haven't finished my makeup. You did say five-thirty," she reminded him.

"It is five-thirty," he muttered.

"Give me ten more minutes," she said. "I'm going to make you notice me tonight, lover," she teased. "I'm wearing something very risqué!"

"Fine," he replied, unimpressed. "I'll see you in ten minutes."

He hung up on her faint gasp of irritation. He didn't care if she wore postage stamps, it wasn't going to cure him of the hunger for Kasie that was tormenting him.

He heard the suite door open and the sound of his children laughing. Strange how often they laughed these days, when they'd been so somber and quiet before. She brought out the best in people. Well, not in himself, he had to admit. She brought out the worst in him, God knew why.

He went out into the big sitting room, still brooding.

"Daddy, you look nice!" Bess said, running to him to be picked up and kissed heartily. "Doesn't he look nice, Kasie?" she asked.

"Yes," Kasie said, glancing at him. He was dishy in a tuxedo, she thought miserably, and Pauline probably looked like uptown New York City in whatever she was wearing. Pauline was like a French pastry, while Kasie was more like a stale doughnut. The thought amused her and she smiled.

"Bess, get the menu off the desk and take it into your room. You and Jenny decide what you want to eat," Gil told them.

"Yes, Daddy," Bess said at once, scooping up the menu and her sister's hand as they left the room.

"Don't let them fill up on sweets," he cautioned Kasie. His pale eyes narrowed on her body in the discreet, one-piece blue bathing suit she was wearing with sandals and a sheer cover-up in shades of blue. Her hair was down around her shoulders. She looked good enough to eat.

"I won't," she promised, moving awkwardly toward the bathroom with the towel she'd been sunbathing on.

"Next time, get a towel from the caretaker down on the beach," he said after she'd put the towel in the bathroom. "They keep them there for beach use."

She flushed. "Sorry. I didn't know."

He moved toward her. In flats, she was even shorter than usual. He looked down at her with narrow, stormy eyes. The curves of her pretty breasts were revealed in the suit and he thought for one insane instant of bending and putting his mouth right down on that soft pink skin.

"Mr. Callister," she began, the name almost choking her as his nearness began to have the usual effect on her shaking knees.

His lean hand moved to her throat and touched it lightly, stroking down to her bare shoulder and then back to her collarbone. "You've got sand on your skin," he observed.

"We had a little trouble making a sand castle, so

the girls covered me up instead," she said with an unsteady laugh.

His hand flattened on the warm flesh and he looked into her huge, soft eyes, waiting for a reaction. Her pulse became visible in her throat. His blood began to surge, hot and turbulent, in his veins. His fingers spread out deliberately, so that the touch became intimate.

She wasn't protesting. She hadn't moved an inch. She didn't even seem to be breathing as she looked up into his pale, glittery eyes and waited, spellbound, for whatever came next.

Without saying a word, his fingers slid under the strap that held up her bodice. They inched into the suit and traced exquisite patterns on the soft, bare flesh that had never been exposed to the sun, or to a man's eyes. He watched her lips part, her eyes dilate with fascination and curiosity.

His hand stilled as he realized what he was doing. The girls were right in the next room, for God's sake. Was he losing his mind?

He jerked his hand back as if he'd scalded it and his expression became icy. "You'd better change," he said through his teeth.

She didn't move. Her eyes were wide, curious, apprehensive. She didn't understand his actions or his obvious anger.

But he was suspicious of her. He didn't trust her, and he didn't like his unchecked response to her. She could be anybody, with any motive in mind. She dressed like a repressed woman, but she never resisted anything physical that he did to her. He began to wonder if she was playing up to him with marriage in mind—or at least some financially beneficial liaison. He knew that she wasn't wealthy. He was. It put him at a disadvantage when he tried to puzzle out her motives. He knew how treacherous some women could be, and he'd been fooled once in recent months by a woman out for what she could get from him. She'd been kind to the girls, too, and she'd played the innocent with Gil, leading him on until they ended up in her bedroom. Of course, she'd said then, they'd have to get married once they'd been intimate...

He'd left her before the relationship was consummated, and he hadn't called her again. Not that she'd given up easily. She'd stalked him until he produced an attorney and a warrant, at which point she'd given up the chase.

Now, he was remembering that bad experience and superimposing her image over Kasie's innocent-looking face. He knew nothing about her. He couldn't take the risk of believing what he thought he saw in her personality. She could be playing him for a sucker, very easily.

"You don't hold anything back, do you?" he asked conversationally, and it didn't show that he'd been affected by her. "Are you like that all the way into the bedroom?" he added softly, so that the girls wouldn't hear.

Kasie drew in a long breath. "I wouldn't know," she said huskily, painfully aware that she'd just made an utter fool of herself. "I'll get dressed."

"You might as well, where I'm concerned," he said pleasantly. "You're easy on the eyes, Kasie, but in the dark, looks don't matter much."

She stared at him with confusion, as if she couldn't believe she was hearing such a blatant remark from him.

He slid his hands into his pockets and studied her arrogantly from head to toe. "You'd need to be prettier," he continued, "and with larger...assets," he said with a deliberate study of her pert breasts. "I'm particular about my lovers these days. It takes a special woman."

"Which, thank God, I'm not," she choked, flushing. "I don't sleep around."

"Of course not," he agreed.

She turned away from him with a sick feeling in her stomach. She'd loved his touch. It had been her first experience of passion, and it had been exquisite because it was Gil touching her. But he thought she was offering herself, and he didn't want her. She should be glad. She wasn't a loose woman. But it was a deliberate insult, and she wondered what she'd done to make him want to hurt her.

Her reaction made him even angrier, but he didn't let it show. "Giving up so easily?" he taunted.

She kept her back to him so that he wouldn't see her face. "We've had this conversation once," she pointed out. "I know that you don't want to remarry, and I've told you that I don't sleep around. Okay?"

"If I catch you in bed with that hack writer, I'll fire you on the spot," he added, viciously.

She turned then and glared at him from wet eyes. "What's the matter with you?" she asked.

"A sudden awakening of reason," he said enigmatically. "You look after the girls. That's your job."

"I never thought it involved anything else," she said.

"And it doesn't," he agreed. "The fringe benefits don't include the boss."

"Some fringe benefit," she scoffed, regaining her composure. "A conceited, overbearing, arrogant rancher who thinks he's on every woman's Christmas list!"

He lifted an eyebrow over eyes with cynical sophistication gleaming in them. "Don't look for me under your Christmas tree," he chided.

"Don't worry, I won't." She turned and kept walking before he could say anything worse. Of all the conceited men on earth!

He watched her go with mixed emotions, the strongest of which was desire. She made him ache all over. He checked his watch. Pauline's ten minutes were up, and he wanted out of this apartment. He called a goodnight to the girls and went out without another word to Kasie.

When he got back in, at two in the morning, he paused long enough to open Kasie's door and look in.

She was wearing another of those concealing cotton gowns, with the covers thrown off. Jenny was curled up against one shoulder and Bess was curled into the other. They were all three asleep.

Gil ground his teeth together just looking at the picture they made together. His girls and Kasie. They looked more like mother and daughters. The thought hurt him. He closed the door with a little jerk and went back into his own room. Despite Pauline's alluring gown and her spirited conversation, he had been morose all evening.

Pauline had noticed, and knew the reason. She was, she told herself, going to get rid of the competition. It only needed the right set of circumstances.

Fate provided them only two days later. Kasie and Gil were barely speaking now. She avoided him, and he did the same to her. If the girls noticed, they kept their thoughts to themselves. Impulsively Kasie phoned

Zeke at his hotel and asked if he'd like to come over and have lunch with her at the hotel, since she couldn't leave the girls.

He agreed with flattering immediacy, and showed up just as Kasie was drying off the girls.

"Surely you aren't going to take them to lunch with you?" Pauline asked, laughing up at Zeke, who attracted her at once. "I'll watch them while you eat."

"Please can't we stay and play in the pool?" Bess asked Kasie. "Miss Raines will watch us, she said so."

"Please," Jenny added with a forlorn look.

"You'll be right inside, won't you?" Pauline asked cunningly. "Go ahead and enjoy your lunch. I'm not going anywhere."

For an instant, Kasie recalled that Gil didn't trust Pauline with the girls. But it was only for a few minutes and, as Pauline had said, they were going to be just inside the nearby restaurant that overlooked the pool.

"Well, all right then, if you really don't mind," she told Pauline. "Thank you."

"It's my pleasure. Have fun now," Pauline told her. "And don't worry. Gil's not going to be back for at least a half hour. He's at the bank."

Kasie brooded over it even while she and Zeke ate a delicious seafood salad. They were seated at a window overlooking the swimming pool, but a row of hedges and hibiscus obscured the view so that only the deep end of the pool could be seen from their table.

"Stop worrying," Zeke told her with a grin. "Honestly, you act as if they were your own kids. You're just the governess."

"They're my responsibility," she pointed out. "If anything happened to them…"

"Your friend is going to watch them. Now stop arguing and let me tell you about this new hotel and casino they're opening over on Paradise Island."

"Okay," she relented, smiling. "I'll stop brooding."

Outside by the pool, Pauline had noticed that Kasie and her companion couldn't see beyond the hedges. She smiled coldly as she looked at the little girls. Jenny was sitting on the steps of the wading pool, playing with one of her dolls in the water.

Closer to Pauline, Bess was staring down at the swimming pool where the water was about six feet deep—far too deep for her to swim in.

"I wish I could dive," she told Pauline.

"But it's easy," Pauline told her, making instant plans. "Just put your arms out in front of you like this," she demonstrated, "and jump in. Really, it's simple."

"Are you sure?" Bess asked, thrilled that an adult might actually teach her how to dive!

"Of course! I'm right here. How dangerous can it be? Go ahead. You can do it."

Of course she could, Bess thought, laughing with delight. She put her arms in the position Pauline had demonstrated and shifted her position to dive in. There wasn't anybody else around the pool to notice if she did it wrong. She'd show her daddy when he came back. Wouldn't he be surprised?

She moved again, just as Pauline suddenly turned around. Her leg accidentally caught one of Bess's. Pauline fell and so did Bess, but Bess's head hit the pavement as she went down. The momentum kept her going, and she rolled into the pool, unconscious.

"Oh, damn!" Pauline groaned. She got to her feet and looked into the pool, aware that Jenny was screaming. "Do shut up!" she told the child. "I'll have to get someone…"

But even as she spoke, Gil came around the corner of the hotel, oblivious to what had just happened.

"Daddy!" Jenny screamed. "Bess falled in the swimmy pool!"

Gil didn't even break stride. He broke into a run and dived in the second he was close enough. He went to the bottom, scooped up his little girl and swam back up with all the speed he could muster. Out of breath, he coughed as he lifted Bess onto the tiles by the pool and climbed out himself. He turned the child over and rubbed her back, aware that she was still breathing by some miracle. She coughed and water began to dribble out of her mouth, and then to gush out of it as she regained consciousness.

"Call an ambulance," he shot at Pauline.

"Oh, dear, oh, dear," she murmured, biting her nails.

"Call a damned ambulance!" he raged.

One of the pool boys saw what was going on and told Gil he'd phone from inside the hotel.

"Where's Kasie?" Gil asked Pauline with hateful eyes as Jenny threw herself against him to be comforted. Bess was still coughing up water.

There it was. The opportunity. Pauline drew in a quick breath. "That man came by to take her to lunch. You know, the man she met on the plane. She begged me to watch the girls so they'd have time to talk."

Gil didn't say anything, but his eyes were very expressive. "Where is she?"

"I really don't know," Pauline lied, wide-eyed. "She didn't say where they were going. She was clinging to him like ivy and obviously very anxious to be alone with him," she added. "I can't say I blame her, he's very handsome."

"Bess could have died."

"But I was right here. I never left them," she assured him. "The girls mean everything to me. Here, let me have Jenny. I'll take care of her while you get Bess seen to."

"Want Kasie," Jenny whimpered.

"There, there, darling," Pauline said sweetly, kissing the plump little cheek. "Pauline's here."

"Damn Kasie!" Gil bit off, horrified at what might have happened. Kasie knew he didn't trust Pauline to watch the girls. Why had Kasie been so irresponsible? Was it to get back at him for what he'd said the night they arrived in Nassau?

When the ambulance arrived, Kasie and Zeke left their dessert half-eaten and rushed out the door. Zeke had to stop to pay the check, but Kasie, apprehensive and uneasy without knowing exactly why, rounded the corner of the building just in time to see little Bess being loaded onto the ambulance.

"Bess! What happened?!" Kasie asked, sobbing.

"She hit her head on the pool, apparently, and almost drowned, while you were away having a good time with your boyfriend," Gil said furiously. The expression on his face could have backed down a mob. "You've got a ticket home. Use it today. Go back to the ranch and start packing. I want you out of my house when I get back. I'll send your severance pay along, and you can thank your lucky stars that I'm not pressing charges!"

"But, but, Pauline was watching them—" Kasie began, horrified at Bess's white face and big, tragic eyes staring at her from the ambulance.

"It was your job to watch them," Gil shot at her. "That's what you were paid to do. She could have died, damn you!"

Kasie went stark white. "I'm sorry," she choked, horrified.

"Too late," he returned, heading to the ambulance. "You heard me, Kasie," he added coldly. "Get out. Pauline, take care of Jenny until I get back."

"Of course, darling," she cooed.

"And get her away from the swimming pool!"

"I'll take her up to my room and read to her. I hope you'll be fine, Bess, darling," she added.

Kasie stood like a little statue, sick and alone and frightened as the ambulance closed up and rushed away, its lights flashing ominously.

Pauline turned and gave Kasie a superior appraisal. "It seems you're out of a job, Miss Mayfield."

Kasie was too sick at heart to react. She didn't have it in her for a fight. Seeing Bess lying there, so white and fragile was acutely painful. Even Jenny seemed not to like her anymore. She buried her face against Pauline and clung.

Pauline turned and carried the child back to her chaise lounge to get her room key. Not bad, she thought, for a morning's work. One serious rival accounted for and out of the way.

Zeke caught up with Kasie at the pool. "What happened?" he asked, brushing a stray tear from Kasie's cheek.

"Bess almost drowned," she said huskily. "Pauline promised to watch her. How did she hit her head?"

"I wouldn't put much past that woman," he told Kasie somberly. "Some people won't tolerate rivals."

"I'm no rival," she replied. "I never was."

Having noted the expression on her boss's face at the airport when he'd said goodbye to Kasie, he could have disputed that. He knew jealousy when he saw it. The man had been looking at him as if he'd like to put a stake through his heart.

"He fired me," Kasie continued dazedly. "He fired me, without even letting me explain."

"Trust me, after whatever she told him, it wouldn't have done any good. Go home and let things cool down," he added. "Most men regain their reason when the initial upset passes."

"You know a lot about people," Kasie remarked as they started up to her room.

"I'm a reporter. It goes with the territory. I'll go with you to the airport and help you change the ticket," he added grimly. "Not that I want to. I was looking forward to getting to know you. Now we'll be ships that passed in the night."

"So we will. Do you believe in fate?" she asked numbly.

"I do. Most things happen for a reason. Just go with the flow." He grinned. "And don't forget to give me your home address! I won't be out of the country forever."

Chapter Eight

It didn't take long for Kasie to pack. She wouldn't let herself think of what was ahead, because she'd cry, and she didn't have time for tears. She changed into a neat gray pantsuit to travel in, and picked up her suitcase and purse to put them by the door. But she stopped long enough to find the phone number of the hospital and check on Bess. The head nurse on the floor, once Kasie's relationship to the girls was made clear, told her that the child was sitting up in bed asking for ice cream. Kasie thanked her and hung up. She wondered if the news would have been quite as forthcoming if she'd mentioned that she'd just been fired.

She moved out into the sitting room with her heart like a heavy weight in her chest. She looked around to make sure she hadn't forgotten anything and went into the hall with her small piece of carry-on luggage on wheels and her pocketbook. It was the most painful moment of her recent life. She thought of never seeing the girls and Gil again, of having Gil hate her. Tears stung her eyes, and she dashed at them impatiently with a tissue.

As she passed Pauline's room, she hesitated. She wanted to say goodbye to little Jenny. But on second thought, she went ahead to the elevator, deciding that it would only make matters worse. Besides, Pauline was probably still at the hospital with Gil. She wished she knew what had really happened by the pool. She should never have left the girls with Pauline, despite the other woman's assurances that she'd look after them. Gil had said often enough that she was responsible for them, not Pauline. She should have listened.

Downstairs, Zeke was waiting for her. He put her small bag into the little car he'd rented at the airport and drove her to the airport to catch her flight.

At the hospital, Bess was demanding ice cream. Gil hugged her close, more frightened than he wanted to admit about how easily he could have lost her forever.

"I'm okay, Daddy," she assured him with a grin.

"Does your head hurt?" he asked, touching the bandage the doctor had placed over the cut, which had been stitched.

"Only a little. But ice cream would make it feel better," she added hopefully.

"I'll see what I can do," he promised with a strained smile.

The nurse came in, motioning Pauline and Jenny in behind her. "I thought it might help to let her sister see her," she told Gil confidentially.

"Hi, Bess," Jenny said, sidling up to the bed. "Are you okay?"

"I'm fine," Bess assured her. "But it was real scary." She glared at Pauline. "It was your fault. You tripped me."

"Bess!" Gil warned his daughter while wondering at Pauline's odd expression.

"I did not trip you!" Pauline shot back.

"You did so," Bess argued. "I wouldn't dive in, and you tripped me so I'd fall in."

"She's obviously delirious," Pauline said tautly.

"You told Kasie you'd stay right with us," she continued angrily. "And she told us not to go swimming, but you showed me how to dive and you told me to dive into the pool. And when I didn't, you tripped me!"

Pauline was flushed. Gil was looking vaguely murderous. "She did hit her head, you know," she stammered. "I was telling her how to dive, I didn't tell her to actually do it!"

"You tripped me and I hurt myself!" Bess kept on.

Pauline backed away from Gil. "What do I know about kids?" she asked impatiently. "She said she wanted to learn how to swim. I showed her a diving position. Then I slipped on the wet tiles and fell against her. It was an accident. I never meant to hurt her. You must know that I wouldn't deliberately hurt a child!" she added fiercely.

He was still silent, as the fear for Bess began to fade and his reason came back to him.

Pauline grabbed up her purse. "I was just trying to do Kasie a favor," she muttered. "That reporter wanted to take her to lunch and I told her to go ahead, that I'd watch the kids. Besides, she was just in the restaurant next to the pool!"

Gil felt his stomach do a nosedive. So Kasie hadn't deserted the kids. Pauline had told her to go, and she'd been right inside. He'd fired Kasie, thinking she was at fault!

"I imagine that reporter went home with her," Pauline continued deliberately. "They were all over each other when he came to pick her up. Besides, governesses are thick on the ground. It won't be hard to replace her."

"Or you," he said coldly.

She looked shocked. "You can't mean you're firing me?"

"I'm firing you, Pauline," he said, feeling like a prize idiot. Kasie was gone, and it was as much Pauline's fault as it was his own. He knew she didn't like Kasie. "I need a full-time secretary. We've discussed this before."

She started to argue, but it was obvious that there was no use in it. She might still be able to salvage something of their relationship, just the same, if she didn't make a scene. "All right," she said heavily. "But we might as well enjoy the vacation, since we're here."

His face became hard. He thought of Kasie going back to Montana, packing, leaving. For an instant he panicked, thinking that she might go so far away that he'd never find her.

Then he remembered her aunt in Billings. Surely she wouldn't be that hard to locate. He'd give it a few days, let Kasie get over the anger she must be feeling right now. Maybe she'd miss the girls and he could persuade her to come back. God knew, she wouldn't miss him, he thought bitterly. He'd probably done more damage than he could ever make up to her. But when they got back, he was going to try. Misjudging Kasie seemed to be his favorite hobby these days, he thought miserably.

"Yes," he told Pauline slowly. "I suppose we might as well stay."

Pauline had hardly dared hope for so much time with him. She was going to try, really try, to take care of the girls and make them like her.

"Bess, shall I go and ask if they have chocolate ice cream?" she asked, trying to make friends. "I'm really sorry about accidentally knocking you into the pool."

"I want Kasie," Bess muttered.

"Kasie's gone home," Gil said abruptly, not adding that he'd fired her.

"Gone home?" Bess's face crumpled. "But why?"

"Because I told her to," he said shortly. "And that's enough about Kasie. We're going to have a good time... Oh, for God's sake, don't start bawling!"

Now it wasn't just Bess crying, it was Jenny, too. Pauline sighed heavily. "Well, we're going to have a very good time, aren't we?" she said to nobody in particular.

Mama Luke never pried or asked awkward questions. She held Kasie while she cried, sent her to unpack and made hot chocolate and chicken soup. That had always been Kasie's favorite meal when she was upset.

Kasie sat down across from her at the small kitchen table that had a gaily patterned tablecloth decorated with pink roses and sipped her soup with a spoon.

"You don't have to say a word," Mama Luke told her gently, and smiled. She had eyes like her sister, Kasie's mother, dark brown and soft. She had dark hair, too, which she kept short. Her hands, around the mug, were thin and wrinkled now, and twisted with arthritis, but they were loving, helping hands. Kasie had always envied her aunt her ability to give love unconditionally.

"I've been a real idiot," Kasie remarked as she worked through her soup. "I should never have let Pauline look after the girls. She isn't really malicious, but she's hopelessly irresponsible."

"You haven't had a man friend in my recent memory," Mama Luke remarked. "I'm sure you were flattered to have a handsome young man want to take you out to lunch."

"I was. But that doesn't mean that I should have let Pauline talk me into leaving the girls with her. Bess could very easily have drowned, and it would have been my fault," she added miserably.

"Give it time," the older woman said gently. "First, let's get you settled in. Then you can help me with the garden," she added with a grin.

Despite her misery, Kasie laughed. "I see. You're happy to have me back because I'm free labor."

Mama Luke laughed, too. It was a standing joke, the way she press-ganged even casual visitors into taking a turn at weeding the garden. She prescribed it as the best cure for depression, misery and anxiety. She was right. It did a lot to restore a good mood.

In the days that followed, Kasie worked in the garden a lot. She thought about Gil, and the hungry way he'd kissed her. She thought about the girls and missed them terribly. She'd really expected Gil to phone her. He knew she had an aunt in Billings, and it wouldn't have taken much effort for him to track her down. In fact, she'd put Mama Luke's telephone number down on her job application in case of emergency.

The thought depressed her even more. He knew where she'd be, but apparently he was still angry at her. God knew what Pauline had said at the hospital about how the accident happened. She'd probably blamed the whole thing on Kasie. Maybe the girls blamed her, too, for leaving them with Pauline, whom they disliked. She'd never felt quite so alone. She thought of Kantor and grew even sadder.

Mama Luke came out into the garden and caught her brooding. "Stop that," she chided softly. "This is God's heart," she pointed out. "It's creation itself, planting seed and watching little things grow. It should cheer you up."

"I miss Bess and Jenny," she said quietly, leaning on her hoe. She was dirty from head to toe, having gotten down in the soil to pull out stubborn weeds. There was a streak of it across her chin, which Mama Luke wiped off with one of the tissues she always carried in her pocket.

"I'm sure they miss you, too," the older woman assured her. "Don't worry so. It will all come right. Sometimes we just have to think of ourselves as leaves going down a river. It's easy to forget that God's driving."

"Maybe He doesn't mind back seat drivers," Kasie said with a grin.

Mama Luke chuckled. "You're incorrigible. Almost through? I made hot chocolate and chicken with rice soup."

"Comfort food." Kasie smiled.

"Absolutely. Stop and eat something."

Kasie looked at the weeding that still had to be done with a long sigh. "Oh, well, maybe the mailman has some frustrations to work off. He's bigger than I am. I'll bet he hoes well."

"I'll try to find out," she was assured. "Come on in and wash up."

It was good soup and Kasie had worked up an appetite. She felt better. But she still hated the way she'd left the Callister ranch. Probably everybody blamed her for Bess's accident. Especially the one person from whom she dreaded it. "I guess Gil hates me."

The pain in those words made Mama Luke reach out a gentle hand to cover her niece's on the table. "I'm sure he doesn't," she contradicted. "He was upset and frightened for Bess. We all say things we shouldn't when our emotions are out of control. He'll apologize. I imagine he'll offer you your job back as well."

Kasie shifted in the chair. "It's been a week," she said. "If he were going to hire me back, he'd have been in touch. I suppose he still believes Pauline and thinks he's done the best thing by firing me."

"Do you really?" Her aunt pursed her lips as her keen ears caught the sound of a car pulling up in the driveway. "Finish your hot cocoa, dear. I'll go and see who that is driving up out front."

For just a few seconds, Kasie hoped it would be Gil, come to give her back her job. But that would take a miracle. Her life had changed all over again. She was just going to have to accept it and get a new job. Something would turn up somewhere, surely.

She heard voices in the living room. One of them was deep and slow, and she shivered with emotion as she realized that she wasn't dreaming. She got up and went into the living room. And there he was.

Gil stopped talking midsentence and just looked at

Kasie. She was wearing old jeans and a faded T-shirt, with her hair around her shoulders. He'd missed her more than he thought he could miss anyone. His heart filled with just the sight of her.

"I believe you, uh, know each other," Mama Luke said mischievously.

"Yes, we do," Kasie said. She recalled the fury in his pale eyes as he accused her of causing Bess's accident, the fury as he fired her. It was too painful to go through again, and he didn't look as if he'd come to make any apologies. She turned away miserably. "If you'll excuse me, I have to clean up," she called over her shoulder.

"Kasie…!" Gil called angrily.

She kept walking down the hall to her room, and she closed and locked the door. The pain was just too much. She couldn't bear the condemnation in his eyes.

Gil muttered under his breath. "Well, so much for wishful thinking," he said almost to himself.

"Come along and have some hot cocoa, Mr. Callister," Mama Luke said with a gentle smile. "I think you and I have a lot to talk about."

He followed her into the small, bright kitchen with its white and yellow accents. She motioned him into a chair at the table while she poured the still-hot cocoa into a mug and offered it to him.

"I'm Sister Luke," she introduced herself, noting his sudden start. "Yes, that's right, I'm a nun. My order doesn't wear the habit. I work with a health outreach program in this community."

He sipped cocoa, feeling as if more revelations were in store, and that he wasn't going to like them.

She sipped her own cocoa. He was obviously waiting for her to speak again. He studied her quietly, his blue eyes troubled and faintly disappointed at Kasie's reception.

"She's still grieving," she told Gil. "She didn't give it enough time before she started back to work. I tried to tell her, but young people are so determined these days."

He latched on to the word. "Grieving?"

"Yes." Her dark eyes were quiet and soft as they met his. "Her twin, Kantor, and his wife and little girl died three months ago."

His breath caught. "In an airplane crash," he said, recalling what Kasie had said.

"Airplane crash?" Her eyes widened. "Well, I suppose you could call it that, in a manner of speaking. Their light aircraft was shot down—"

"What?" he exploded.

She frowned. "Don't you know anything about Kasie?"

"No. I don't. Not one thing!"

She let out a whistle. "I suppose that explains some of the problem. Perhaps if you knew about her background…" She leaned back in her chair. "Her parents were lay missionaries to Africa. While they were working there, a rebel uprising occurred and they were killed." She nodded at his look of horror. "I had already taken my vows by then, and I was the only family that Kasie and Kantor had left. I arranged to have them come to me, and I enrolled them in the school where I was teaching, and living, at the time. In Arizona," she added. "Kantor wanted nothing more than to fly airplanes. He studied flying while he was in school and later went into partnership with a friend from college. They started a small charter service. There was an opportunity in Africa for a courier service, so he decided to go there and set up a second headquarters for the company. While he was there, he married and had a little girl, Sandy. She and Lise, Kantor's wife, came and stayed with Kasie and me while Kasie was going through secretarial school. Kantor didn't want them with him just then, because there was some political trouble. It calmed down and he came and rejoined his family. He wanted to bring everyone home to Africa."

She grimaced. "Kasie didn't want him to go back. She said it was too risky, especially for Lise and Sandy. She adored Sandy…" She hesitated, and took a steadying breath, because the memory was painful. "Kantor told her to mind her own business, and they all left. That same week, a band of guerrillas attacked the town where he had his business. He got Lise and Sandy in the plane and was flying them to a nearby town when someone fired a rocket at them. They all died instantly."

"My God," he said huskily.

"Kasie took it even harder because they'd argued. It took weeks for her to be able to discuss it without breaking down. She'd graduated from secretarial college and I insisted that she go to work, not because of money, but because it was killing her to sit and brood about Kantor."

He wrapped both hands around the cocoa mug and stared into the frothy liquid. "I knew there was something," he said quietly. "But she never talked about anything personal."

"She rarely does, except with me." She studied him. "She said that your wife died in a riding accident and that you have two beautiful little girls."

"They hate me," he said matter-of-factly. "I fired

Kasie." He shrugged and smiled faintly. "John, my brother, isn't even speaking to me."

"They'll get over it."

"They may. I won't." He wouldn't meet her eyes. "I thought I might persuade her to come back. I suppose that's a hopeless cause?"

"She's hurt that you misjudged her," she explained. "Kasie loves children. It would never occur to her to leave them in any danger."

"I know that. I knew it then, too, but I was out of my mind with fear. I suppose I lashed out. I don't know much about families," he added, feeling safe with this stranger. He looked up at her. "My brother and I were never part of one. Our parents had a governess for us until we were old enough to be sent off to school. I can remember months going by when we wouldn't see them or hear from them. Even now," he added stiffly, "they only contact us when they think of some new way we can help them make money."

She slid a wrinkled hand over his. "I'm sorry," she said gently. She removed her hand and pushed a plate of cookies toward him. "Comfort food," she said with a gleeful smile. "Indulge yourself."

"Thanks." He bit into a delicious lemon cookie.

"Kasie says you love your girls very much, and that you never leave them with people you don't trust. She's hating herself because she did leave them against her better judgment. She blames herself for the accident."

He sighed. "It wasn't her fault. Not really." His eyes glittered. "She wanted to have lunch with a man she met on the plane. A good-looking, young man," he added bitterly. "Pauline admitted causing the accident, but I was hot because Kasie was upset about flying and I didn't know it until it was too late. She was sitting all by herself." His face hardened. "If I'd known what you just told me, we'd have gone by boat. I'd never have subjected her to an airplane ride. But Kasie keeps secrets. She doesn't talk about herself."

"Neither do you, I think," she replied.

He shrugged and picked up another cookie. "She looks worn," he remarked.

"I've had her working in my garden," she explained. "It's good therapy."

He smiled. "I work cattle for therapy. My brother and I have a big ranch here in Montana. We wouldn't trade it for anything."

"I like animals." She sipped cocoa.

So did he. He looked at her over the mug. "Kasie mentioned she was named for the mercenary K.C. Kanton."

She raised an eyebrow amusedly. "That's right. I'm not sure how much she told you, but when Jackie, her mother, was carrying her, there was a guerrilla attack on the mission. Bob, my brother-in-law, was away with a band of workers building a barn for a neighboring family. They'd helped a wounded mercenary soldier hide from the same guerrillas, part of an insurgent group that wanted to overthrow the government. He was well enough to get around by then, and he got Jackie out of the mission and through the jungle to where Bob was. Kasie and Kantor were born only a day later. And that's why she was named for K.C. Kantor."

"They both were named for him," he realized. "Amazing. What I've heard about Kantor over the years doesn't include a generous spirit or unselfishness."

"That may be true. But he pays his debts. He'd

still like to take care of Kasie," she added with a soft chuckle. "She won't let him. She's as independent as my sister used to be."

It disturbed him somehow that Kasie was cherished by another man who could give her anything she wanted. "He must be a great deal older than she is," he murmured absently.

"He doesn't have those kind of feelings for her," she said quietly, and there was pain in her soft eyes. "He missed on family life and children. I think he's sorry about that now. He tried to get her to come and stay with him in Mexico until she got over losing her twin, but she wouldn't go."

"One of her other character references was a Catholic priest."

She nodded. "Father Vincent, in Tucson, Arizona. He was the priest for our small parish." She sighed. "Kasie hasn't been to mass since her brother died. I've been so worried about her."

"She mentioned taking the girls with her to church," Gil said after a minute. "If I can get her to come back to work for me, it might be the catalyst to help her heal."

"It might at that," she agreed.

Gil took another cookie and nibbled it. "These are good."

"My one kitchen talent," she said. "I can make cookies. Otherwise, I live on TV dinners and the kindness of friends who can cook."

He sipped cocoa and thought. "How can I get her to go back with me?" he asked after a minute.

"Tell her the girls are crying themselves to sleep at night," she suggested gently. "She misses Sandy even more than her twin. She and the little girl were very close."

"She's close to my girls," he remarked with a reminiscent smile. "If there's a storm or they get frightened in the night, I can always find them curled up in Kasie's arms." His voice seemed to catch on the words. He averted his eyes toward the hallway. "The light went out of the house when she left it."

She wondered if he even realized what he was saying. Probably not. Men seemed to miss things that women noticed at once.

"I'll go and get her," she said, pushing back her chair. "You can sit by my fishpond and talk with the goldfish."

"My uncle used to have one," he recalled, standing. "I haven't had one built because of the girls. When they're older, I'd like to put in another one."

"I had to dig it myself, and I'm not the woman I used to be. It's only a little over a foot deep. One of my neighbors gave me his used pond heater when he bought a new one. It keeps my four goldfish alive all winter long." She moved to the door. "It's just outside the back door, near the birdbath. I'll send Kasie out to you."

He went out, his hands in his pockets, thinking how little he'd known about Kasie. It might be impossible for them to regain the ground they'd lost, but he wanted to try. His life was utterly empty without her in it.

Mama Luke knocked gently at Kasie's door and waited until it opened. Kasie looked at her guiltily.

"I was rude. I'm sorry," she told the older woman.

"I didn't come to fuss," Mama Luke said. She touched Kasie's disheveled hair gently. "I want you to go out and talk to Mr. Callister. He feels bad about the things he said to you. He wants you to go back to work for him."

Kasie gave her aunt a belligerent look. "In his dreams," she muttered.

"The little girls miss you very much," she said.

Kasie grimaced. "I miss them, too."

"Go on out there and face your problem squarely," Mama Luke coaxed. "He's a reasonable man, and he's had a few shocks today. Give him a chance to make it up to you. He's nice," she added. "I like him."

"You like everybody, Mama Luke," Kasie said softly.

"He's out by the goldfish pond. And don't push him in," she added with a wicked little smile.

Kasie chuckled. "Okay."

She took a deep breath and went down the hall. But her hands trembled when she opened the back door and walked outside. She hadn't realized how much she was going to miss Gil Callister until she was out of his life. Now she had to decide whether or not to risk going back. It wasn't going to be an easy decision.

Chapter Nine

Gil was sitting on the small wooden bench overlooking the rock-bordered oval fishpond, his elbows resting on his knees as he peered down thoughtfully into the clear water where water lilies bloomed in pink and yellow profusion. He looked tired, Kasie thought, watching him covertly. Maybe he'd been away on business and not on holiday with Pauline after all.

He looked up when he heard her footsteps. He got to his feet. He looked elegant even in that yellow polo shirt and beige slacks, she thought. He wasn't at all handsome, but his face was masculine and he had a mouth that she loved kissing. She averted her eyes until she was able to control the sudden impulse to run to him. Wouldn't that shock him, she thought sadly.

He looked wary, and he wasn't smiling. He studied

her for a long time, as if he'd forgotten what she looked like and wanted to absorb every detail of her.

"How are the girls?" she asked quietly. "Is Bess going to be all right?"

"Bess is fine," he replied. "She told me everything." He grimaced. "Even Pauline admitted that she'd told you to go and have lunch with what's-his-name, and she'd watch the girls. She said she slipped and tripped Bess. I imagine it's the truth. She's never been much of a liar, regardless of her faults," he returned, his voice flat, without expression. "They told me you phoned the hospital to make sure Bess was all right."

"I was worried," she said, uneasy.

He toyed with the change in his pocket, making it jingle. "Bess wanted you, in the hospital. When I told her you'd gone home, she and Jenny both started crying." The memory tautened his face. "For what it's worth, I'm sorry that I blamed you."

She'd never wanted to believe anything as much as that apology. But it was still disturbing that he'd accused her without proof, that he'd assumed Bess's accident was her fault. She wanted to go back in the house. But that wouldn't solve the problem. She had to try and forget. He was here and he'd apologized. They had to go from there. "It's all right," she said after a minute, her eyes on the fish instead of him. "I understand. You can't help it that you don't like me."

"Don't…like you?" he asked. The statement surprised him.

She toyed with the hem of her shirt. "You never wanted to hire me in the first place, really," she continued. "You looked at me as if you hated me the minute you saw me."

His eyes were thoughtful. "Did I?" He didn't want to pursue that line of conversation. It was too new, too disturbing, after having realized how he felt about her. "Why do you call your aunt Mama Luke?" he asked to divert her.

"Because when I was five, I couldn't manage Sister Mary Luke Bernadette," she replied. "She was Mama Luke from then on."

He winced. "That's a young age to lose both parents."

"That's why I know how Bess and Jenny feel," she told him.

His expelled breath was audible. "I've made a hell of a mess of it, haven't I, Kasie?" he asked somberly. "I jumped to the worst sort of conclusions."

She moved awkwardly to the other side of the fish-pond and wrapped her arms around her body. "I wasn't thinking straight. I knew you didn't trust Pauline to take care of the girls, but I let myself be talked into leaving them with her. You were right. Bess could have drowned and it would have been my fault."

"Stick the knife right in, don't be shy," he said through his teeth. His blue eyes glittered. "God knows, I deserve it."

Her eyes met his, wide with curiosity. "I don't understand."

She probably didn't. "Never mind." He stuck his hands into his pockets. "I fired Pauline."

"But…!"

"It wasn't completely because of what happened in Nassau. I need someone full-time," he interrupted. "She only wanted the job in the first place so that she could be near me."

The breeze blew her hair across her mouth. She

pushed it back behind her ear. "That must have been flattering."

"It was, at first," he agreed. "I've known Pauline for a long time, and her attention was flattering. However, regardless of how Bess fell into the water, Pauline didn't make a move to rescue her. I can't get over that."

Kasie understood. She'd have been in the pool seconds after Bess fell in, despite the fact that she couldn't swim.

His piercing blue eyes caught hers. "Yes, I know. You'd have been right in after her," he said softly, as if he'd read the thought in her mind. "Even if you'd had to be rescued as well," he added gently.

"People react differently to desperate situations," she said.

"Indeed they do." His eyes narrowed. "I want you to come back. So do the girls. I'll do whatever it takes. An apology, a raise in salary, a paid vacation to Tahiti…"

She shrugged. "I wouldn't mind coming back," she said. "I do miss the girls, terribly. But…"

"But, what?"

She met his level gaze. "You don't trust me," she said simply, and her eyes were sad. "At first you thought I was trying to get to you through the girls, and then you thought I wanted them out of the way. In Nassau, you thought I left them alone for selfish reasons, so that I could go on a lunch date." She smiled sadly. "You have a bad opinion of me as a governess. What if I mess up again? Maybe it would be better if we just left things the way they are."

The remark went through him like hot lead. He hadn't trusted Kasie because she was so mysterious about her past. Now that he knew the truth about her, knew of the tragedies she'd suffered in her young life, lack of trust was no longer going to be a problem. But how did he tell her that? And, worse, how did he make up for the accusations he'd made? Perhaps he could tell her the truth.

"The girls' last governess was almost too good to be true," he began. "She charmed the girls, and me, until we'd have believed anything she told us. It was all an act. She had marriage in mind, and she actually threatened me with my own children. She said they were so attached to her that if I didn't marry her, she'd leave and they'd hate me."

She blinked. "That sounds as if she was a little unbalanced."

He nodded, his eyes cold with remembered bitterness. "Yes, she was. She left in the middle of the night, and the next morning the girls were delighted to find her gone."

He shook his head. "She was unstable, and I'd left the kids in her hands. It was such a blot on my judgment that I didn't trust it anymore. Especially when you came along, with your mysterious past and your secrets. I thought you were playing up to me because I was rich."

It hurt that he'd thought so little of her. "I see."

"Do you? I hope so," he replied heavily, and with a smile. "Because if I go back to Medicine Ridge without you, I wouldn't give two cents for my neck. John's furious with me. He's got company. Miss Parsons glares at me constantly. Mrs. Charters won't serve me anything that isn't burned. The girls are the worst, though," he mused. "They ignore me completely. I feel like the ogre in that story you read them at bedtime."

"Poor ogre," she said quietly.

He began to smile. He loved the softness of her voice

when she spoke. For the first time since his arrival, he was beginning to think he had a chance. "Feeling sorry for me?" he asked gently. "Good. If I wear on your conscience, maybe you'll feel sorry enough to come home with me."

She frowned. "What did Mama Luke tell you?" she asked suddenly.

"Things you should have told me," he replied, his tone faintly acidic. "She told me everything, in fact, except why you don't like the water."

She stared down into the fishpond, idly watching the small goldfish swim in and out of the vegetation. "When I was five, just before my parents were…killed," she said, sickened by the memory, "one of my friends at the mission in Africa got swept into the river. I saw her drown."

"You've had a lot of tragedy in your young life," he said softly. He moved a step closer to her, and another, stopping when he was close enough to lift a lean hand and smooth his fingers down her soft cheek. "I've had my own share of it. Suppose we forget the past few weeks, and start over. Can you?"

Her eyes were troubled. "I don't know if it's wise," she said after a minute. "Letting the girls get attached to me again, I mean."

His fingers traced her wide, soft mouth. "It's too late to stop that from happening. They miss you terribly. So do I," he added surprisingly. He tilted her chin up and bent, brushing his lips tenderly over her mouth. His heavy eyebrows drew together at the delight that shafted through him from the contact. "When I think of you, I think of butterflies and rainbows," he whispered against her mouth. "I hated the world until you came to work for John. You brought the light in with you. You made me laugh. You made me believe in miracles. Don't leave me, Kasie."

He was saying something, more than words. She drew back and searched his narrow, glittery eyes. "Leave...you?" she questioned the wording.

"You don't have an ego at all, do you?" he asked somberly. "Is it inconceivable that I want you back as much as my girls do?"

Her heart jumped. She'd missed him beyond bearing. But if she went back, could she ever be just an employee again? She remembered the hard warmth of his mouth in passion, the feel of his arms holding her like a warm treasure. She hesitated.

"I don't seduce virgins," he whispered wickedly. "If that wins me points."

She flushed. "I wasn't thinking about that!"

He smiled. "Yes, you were and that's the main reason I won't seduce you."

"Thanks a lot."

He cocked an eyebrow. "You might sound a little more grateful," he told her. "Keeping my hands off you lately has been a world-class study in restraint."

Her eyes widened. "Really?"

She was unworldly. He loved that about her. He loved the way she blushed when he teased her, the way she made his heart swell when she smiled. He'd been lonely without her.

"But I'll promise to keep my distance," he added gently. "If you'll just come back."

She bit her lower lip worriedly. She did need the job. She loved the girls. She was crazy about Gil. But there were so many complications...

"Stop weighing the risks," he murmured. "Say yes."

"I still think..."

"Don't think," he whispered, placing a long forefinger over her lips. "Don't argue. Don't look ahead. We're going to go home and you're going to read the girls to sleep every night. They miss their stories."

"Don't you read to them?" she asked, made curious by a certain note in his voice.

"Sure, but they're getting tired of *Green Eggs and Ham*."

"They have loads of other books besides Dr. Seuss," she began.

He glowered at her. "They hid all the other books, including *Green Eggs and Ham*, but at least I remember most of that story. So they get told it every night. Two weeks of that and I can't even look at ham in the grocery story anymore without gagging..."

She was laughing uproariously.

"This is not funny," he pointed out.

"Oh, yes, it is," she said, and laughed some more.

He loved the sound. It reminded him of wind chimes. His heart ached for her. "Come home before I get sick of eggs, too."

"All right," she said. "I guess I might as well. I can't live here with Mama Luke forever."

"She's a character," he remarked with a smile. "A blunt and honest lady with a big heart. I like her."

"She must like you, too, or she wouldn't have threatened to have you break down my bedroom door."

He pursed his lips. "Nice to have an ally with divine connections."

"She does, never doubt it," she told him, laughing. "I'll just go throw a few things into my suitcase."

He watched her go with joy shooting through his

veins like fireworks. She was coming back. He'd convinced her.

Now all he had to do was make her see him as something more than an intolerant, judgmental boss. That was not going to be the easiest job he'd ever tackled.

Kasie kissed Mama Luke goodbye and waited while she hugged Gil impulsively.

"Take care of Kasie," her aunt told him.

He nodded slowly. "This time, I'll do better at that."

Mama Luke smiled.

They got into his black Jaguar and drove away, with Kasie leaning out the window and waving until her aunt was out of sight.

Gil watched her eyes close as she leaned back against the leather headrest. "Sleepy?"

"Yes," she murmured. "I haven't slept well since I came back from Nassau."

"Neither have I, Kasie," he said.

Her head turned and she looked at him quietly. It made her tingle all over. He was really a striking man, all lean strength and authority. She'd never felt as safe with anyone as she did with him.

He felt her eyes on him; warm, soft gray eyes that gave him pleasure when he met them. Kasie was unlike anyone he'd ever known.

"Did Pauline finish keying in the herd records to the computer before she left?" she asked, suddenly remembering the chore that had been left when they went to Nassau.

"She hasn't been around since we came home," he said evasively. "I think she's visiting an aunt in Vermont."

She traced a line down the seat belt that stretched across her torso. "I thought you were going to marry her."

He had a good idea where she'd heard that unfounded lie. "Never in this lifetime," he murmured. "Pauline isn't domestic."

"She's crazy about you."

"The girls don't like her."

She pursed her lips. "I see."

He chuckled, glancing at her while they stopped for a red light. "Besides, after they found out that I'd fired you, they made Pauline's life hell. Their latest escapade was to leave her a nice present in her pocketbook."

"Oh, dear."

"It was a nonpoisonous snake," he said reassuringly. "But she decided that she'd be better off not visiting when the girls were around. And since they were always around..."

She shook her head. "Little terrors," she said, but in a tone soft with affection.

"Look who's talking," he said with a pointed glare.

"I've never put snakes in anybody's purse," she pointed out. "Well, not yet, anyway."

He gave her an amused glance. "Don't let the girls corrupt you."

She smiled, remembering how much fun she'd had with the little girls. It made her happy that they wanted her back. Except for her aunt, she was alone in the world. She missed being part of a whole family, especially on holidays like Christmas.

The light changed and he pulled back out into traffic. Conversation was scanty the rest of the way home, because Kasie fell asleep. The lack of rest had finally caught up with her.

She was jolted awake by a firm hand on her shoulder.

"Wake up. We're home," Gil said with a smile.

She searched his blue eyes absently for a moment before the words registered. "Oh." She unfastened her seat belt and got out as he did.

The girls were sitting on the bottom step of the staircase when the door opened and Kasie walked in with Gil.

"Kasie!" Bess cried, and got up to run and throw herself into Kasie's outstretched arms.

"Bess!" Kasie hugged her close, feeling tears sting her eyes. She was so much like Sandy.

Jenny followed suit, and Kasie ended up with two arms full of crying little girls. She carried them to the staircase and sat down, cuddling them both close. Her face was wet, but she didn't care. She loved these babies, far more than she'd realized. She held them and rocked them and kissed wet little cheeks until the sobs eased.

"You mustn't *ever* leave us again, Kasie," Bess hiccuped. "Me and Jenny was ever so sad."

"Yes, we was," Jenny murmured.

"Oh, I missed you!" Kasie said fervently as she dug into her pocket for a tissue and wiped wet eyes all around.

"We missed you, too," Bess said, burying her face in Kasie's shoulder while Jenny clung to her neck.

Gil watched them with his heart in his throat. They looked as if they belonged together. They looked like a family. He wanted to scoop all three of them up in his arms and hold them so tight they'd never get away.

While he was debating that, John came down the hall and spotted Kasie. He grinned from ear to ear. "You're back! Great! Now maybe Mrs. Charters will cook something we can eat again!"

"That's not a nice way to say hello," Kasie chided with a smile.

"Sure it is! What good is a man without his stomach?" John asked. He moved closer to Kasie and the girls and bent to kiss Kasie's wet cheek. "Welcome back! It's been like a ballpark in January. Nobody smiled."

"I'm happy to be back," Kasie said. "But what about all those herd records that need putting into the computer?" she asked, realizing that Gil never had answered her when she'd questioned him about them.

"Oh, those. It turns out that Miss Parsons is a computer whiz herself," he said to Kasie's amusement. "She's got everything listed, including the foundation bloodlines. And remember that Internet site you suggested? It's up and running. We're already getting three hundred hits a day, along with plenty of queries from cattlemen around the country!"

"I'm so glad," Kasie said sincerely.

"So are we. Business is booming. But the babies have been sad." He glanced at his older brother meaningfully. "We missed you."

"It's nice to be back," Kasie said.

"Are we ever going to have lunch?" John asked then. "I'm fairly starved. Burned eggs and bacon this morning didn't do a lot for my taste buds."

"Mine, either," Gil agreed. "Go tell Mrs. Charters Kasie's back and is having lunch with us," he suggested. "That might get us something edible, even if it's only cold cuts."

"Good thinking," John said, smiling as he went out to the kitchen.

"Our eggs wasn't burned," Bess pointed out.

"Mrs. Charters wasn't mad at you, sweetheart," Gil

told her. "You two need to run upstairs and wash your hands and faces before we eat."

"Okay, if Kasie comes, too," Bess agreed.

Kasie chuckled as both girls grabbed a hand and coaxed her to her feet. "I gather that I'm to be carefully observed from now on, so I don't make a run for the border," she murmured to Gil.

"That's right. Good girls," Gil said, grinning. "Keep her with you so she doesn't have a chance to escape."

"We won't let her go, Daddy," Bess promised.

They tugged her up the staircase, and she went without an argument, waiting in their rooms while they washed their hands and faces.

"Daddy was real mad when we came home," Bess told Kasie. "So was Uncle Johnny. He said Daddy should go and get you and bring you home, but Daddy said you might not want to, because he'd been bad to you. Did he take away your toys, Kasie, and put you into time-out?"

"Heavens, no," she said at once.

"Then why did you go away?" the child insisted. "Was it on account of Pauline said you left us alone? We told Daddy the truth, and Pauline went away. We don't like her. She's bad to us when Daddy isn't looking. He won't marry Pauline, will he, Kasie?"

"I don't think so," she said carefully.

"Me and Jenny wish he'd marry you," Bess said wistfully. "You're so much fun to play with, Kasie."

Kasie didn't dare say anything about marriage. "You can't decide things like that, sweetheart," she told Bess. "People don't usually marry unless they fall in love."

"Oh."

The child looked heartbroken. Kasie went down on her knees and caught Bess gently by the waist. "What do you want to do after we have lunch?" she asked, changing the subject.

"Could we swim in the pool?"

She'd forgotten that the family had a swimming pool. "I suppose so," she said, frowning. "But it's pretty soon after your accident, Bess. Are you sure you want to?"

"Daddy and me went swimming the day after we came home," Bess said matter-of-factly. "Daddy said I mustn't be afraid of the water, after I fell in, so he's giving me swimming lessons. I love to swim, now!"

So some good had come out of the accident. That was reassuring. "Let's go down and eat something. Then we have to wait a little while."

"I know. We can pick flowers while we wait, can't we? There's some pretty yellow roses in a hedge behind the swimming pool," Bess told her.

"I love roses," Kasie said, smiling. "But perhaps we'd better not pick any until someone tells us it's all right."

"Okay, Kasie."

They went downstairs and Kasie helped Mrs. Charters set the table. She was welcoming and cheerful about having Kasie back again. John talked easily to Kasie and the children. Gil didn't. He picked at his food and brooded. He watched Kasie, but covertly. She wondered what was going on in his mind to make him so unhappy.

He looked up and met Kasie's searching eyes, and she felt her stomach fall as if she was on a roller coaster. Her hands trembled. She put them in her lap to hide them, but her heartbeat pounded wildly and her nervousness was noticeable. Especially to the man with the arrogant smile, who suddenly seemed to develop an appetite.

Chapter Ten

For the next few days, Gil seemed to watch every move Kasie made. He was cordial with her, but there was a noticeable difference in the way he treated her since her return. He was remote and quiet, even when the family came together at mealtimes, and he seemed uncomfortable around Kasie. She noticed his reticence and understood it to mean that he was sorry for the way he'd treated her before. He didn't touch her at all these days, nor did he seem inclined to include her when he took the girls to movies and the playground, even though he asked her along. But she always refused, to the dismay of the children. She excused it as giving them some time alone with their father. Gil knew that wasn't the truth. It made matters worse.

John left Thursday for a conference that Gil had been slated to attend, and Gil stayed home. Kasie noticed that he seemed unusually watchful and he was always around the ranch even when he wasn't around the house. He didn't explain why. Kasie would have loved thinking that it was because he was interested in her, but she knew that wasn't the reason. There was more distance between them now than there had ever been before.

Mrs. Charters mentioned that there was some uneasiness among the cowboys because of a threat that had been made. Kasie tried to ask Gil about it. He simply ignored the question and walked away.

He was missing at breakfast early one Monday morning. The girls were sleeping late, so Kasie walked into the dining room and found only John at the table.

"Pull up a chair and have breakfast," he invited with a grin. "I have to move bulls today, so I'm having seconds and thirds. I have to keep up my strength."

"If you keep eating like that, you could carry the bulls and save gas," she said wickedly. "I thought you had to go to Phoenix to show a bull this week?"

He averted his eyes. "I thought I'd put it off for another couple of weeks." He sipped coffee and studied Kasie quietly. "There's a new movie showing at the theater downtown. How would you like to pack up the girls and go with me to see it?"

Her eyes lit up. "I'd love to," she said at once.

He grinned. "Okay. We'll go tomorrow night. I, uh, noticed that you don't like going to movies with my brother, even if the girls go along."

"I just thought he'd like some time alone with them," she hedged. "After all, I'm just the governess."

He poured himself more coffee before he replied. "That's a bunch of hogwash, Kasie."

She drew in a long breath. "He makes me uncomfortable," she said. "I always feel like he's biding his time, waiting for me to make another mistake or do something stupid."

He chuckled. "He doesn't lie in wait to ambush you," he said softly. "He meant it when he apologized, you know. He was sorry he misjudged you. Believe me, it's a rare thing for him to make a mistake like that. But he's had some hard blows from women in recent years."

"I felt really bad about what happened," she said with a wistful sadness in her eyes. "I should have remembered that he never trusted Pauline to look after the girls. I'd met this man on the plane, and he invited me to lunch. I liked him. He kept me from being afraid on the way to Nassau."

John's face sobered, and she realized that Gil must have told him about her past. "I'm sorry about your brother and his family," he said, confirming her suspicions. "Gil and I haven't really been part of a family since our uncle died."

"Don't you ever go to see your parents?" she asked curiously.

"There was a time when they offered an olive branch, but you know Gil," he said soberly. "He's slow to get over things, and he refused to talk to them. Maybe they did neglect us, but I never thought it was malicious. They had kids before they were ready to have them. Lots of people are irresponsible parents. But you can't hold grudges forever." He frowned. "On second thought, maybe Gil can."

She smiled and reached across the table to lay her hand over his. "Maybe one day you can try again. It would be nice for the girls to have grandparents."

"The only ones they have left are our parents. Darlene's died years ago." He caught her hand in his and held it tight. "You make the hardest things sound simple. I like myself when you're around, Kasie."

She laughed gently. "I like you, too," she said.

"I never believed you had anything to do with Bess getting hurt," he said somberly. "Anyone could see how much you care about the girls."

"Thanks. It's nice to know that at least one grown-up person in your family believed I was innocent," she said, oblivious to the white-faced, angry man standing in the hall with an armload of pale pink roses. "It hurt terribly that Gil thought I'd ever put the girls at risk in any way, least of all by neglecting them. But it wasn't the first time he's accused me of ulterior motives. I should be used to it by now. I think he's sorry he rehired me, you know," she added sadly, clinging to his hand. "He looks through me when he isn't glaring at me."

"Gil's had some hard knocks with women," John repeated, letting go of her hand. "Just give him time to adjust to being wrong. He rarely is." He picked up a forkful of eggs. "If it's any consolation, he roared around here for two weeks like every man's nightmare before he went after you. He wanted you to have enough time to get over the anger and let him explain his behavior. He would have gone sooner, he said, but he wasn't sure he could get in the front door."

She remembered her lacerated feelings when she'd arrived at her aunt's house. "It would have been tricky, at that," she agreed. "He was the last person on earth I wanted to see when I first came back from Nassau."

Footsteps echoed out in the hall and a door slammed. Kasie frowned.

"Sounds like Gil's going to bypass breakfast again

this morning," John remarked as he finished his eggs. "He doesn't have much of an appetite these days."

"I'll just check and make sure it isn't the girls," Kasie said.

"Suit yourself, but I know those footsteps. He only walks that way when he's upset. God help whatever cowboy he runs into on his way."

Kasie didn't reply. She walked into the hall and there, on the hall table, was an armload of pink roses with the dew still clinging to the silky, fragrant petals. It took a few seconds for her to realize that Gil must have heard every word she'd said. She groaned inwardly as she gathered up the roses. Well, that was probably the end of any truce, she thought. He'd think she couldn't forgive him, and that would make him even angrier. Unless she missed her guess, he was going to be hell to live with from now on.

She took the roses to the kitchen and found a vase for them, which she filled with water before she arranged the flowers in it. With a sigh, she took them upstairs to her room and placed them on the dresser. They were beautiful. She couldn't imagine what had possessed Gil Callister to go out and cut her a bouquet. But the gesture touched her poignantly.

Sure enough, when Gil came in early for supper, he was dusty and out of humor. He needed a shave. He glared at everybody, especially Kasie.

"Aren't you going to clean up first?" John asked, aghast, when he sat down to the table in his chaps.

"What for?" he muttered. "I've got to go right back out again." He reached for his coffee cup, which Mrs. Charters had just filled, and put cream in it.

"Is something wrong?" John asked then, con-cerned.

"We've got a fence down." His eyes met his brother's. "It wasn't broken through. It was cut."

John stared at the older man. "Another one? That makes two in less than ten days."

"I know. I can't prove it, but I know it was Fred Sims."

John nodded slowly. "That makes sense. One of the cowboys who was friendly with him said Sims hasn't been able to find another job since we fired him."

Gil's pale blue eyes glittered. "That damned dog could have bitten my babies," he said. "No way was he going to keep it here after it chased them onto the porch."

"Bad doggie," Jenny agreed.

Bess nodded. "We was scared, Daddy."

"Sims is going to be scared, if I catch him within a mile of my property," Gil added.

"Don't become a vigilante," John cautioned his older brother. "Call the sheriff. Let him handle it. That's what he gets paid to do."

"He can't be everywhere," Gil replied, eyes narrowed. "I want all the cowboys armed, at least with rifles. I'm not taking any chances. If he's brazen enough to cut fences and shoot livestock, he's capable of worse."

Kasie felt her heart stop. So that was why he'd been around the ranch so much lately. The man, Sims, had threatened vengeance. Apparently he was killing cattle as well as cutting fences to let them escape. She pictured Gil at the end of a gun and she felt sick all over.

"I'll make sure everyone's been alerted and prepared for danger," John agreed. "But you stay out of it. You're the one person around here that Sims would enjoy shooting."

"He'd be lucky to get off a shot," Gil replied imperturbably. He finished his meal and wiped his mouth. "I've got to get back out there. We haven't finished stringing wire, and it's not long until dark."

"Okay. I'll phone the vet about those carcasses we found. I want him to look for bullet wounds."

"Good idea."

Gil finished the last sip of his coffee in a grim silence that seemed to spread to the rest of the family. The girls, sensing hidden anger in the adults around them, excused themselves and went upstairs to play in their room while Mrs. Charters cleaned away the dishes. John went to make a phone call.

Gil got to his feet without looking at Kasie and started toward the front door. Kasie caught up with him on the porch. It was almost dark. The sky was fiery red and pink and yellow where the sun was setting.

"Thank you," she blurted out.

He stopped and turned. "For what?"

His hat was pulled low over his eyes, and she couldn't see the expression in them, but she was pretty sure that he was scowling.

She went closer to him, stopping half an arm's length away. "For the roses," she said hesitantly. "They're beautiful."

He didn't move. He just stood there, somber, quiet. "How do you know they were meant for you?" he drawled. "And how do you know I brought them?"

She flushed scarlet. She didn't know for sure, but she'd assumed.

He averted his eyes, muttering under his breath. "You're welcome," he said tersely.

"That man, Sims," she continued, worried. "The day

you fired him, John said that he had a mean temper and that he carried a loaded rifle everywhere with him. You…you be careful, okay?"

She heard the soft expulsion of breath. He moved a step closer, his lean hands lifting her oval face to his. She could see the soft glitter of his blue eyes in the faint light from the windows.

"What do you care if I get myself shot?" he asked huskily. "I'm the one who sent you packing without even giving you the chance to explain what happened in Nassau."

"Pauline didn't like me," she said. "And you trusted her. I was just a stranger."

"Not anymore, Kasie," he said gruffly.

"I mean, you didn't know anything about me," she persisted. She searched his eyes, feeling jolts of electricity flow into her at the exquisite contact. "I was upset and I behaved badly when you came to Mama Luke's. But deep inside, I didn't blame you for not trusting me."

His lean hands tightened on her face. "I've done nothing but torment you since the first day you came here," he bit off. "I didn't want you in my life, Kasie," he whispered as he bent toward her. "I still don't. But a man can only stand so much…!"

His mouth caught hers hungrily. His arms swallowed her up against him, so that not an inch of space separated them. For long, achingly sweet seconds, they clung to each other in the soft darkness.

He drew away from her finally and stood just looking at her in a tense, hot silence. His hands were firm around her arms, and she swayed toward him helplessly.

She felt her knees go shaky, as if they had jelly in

them instead of bone and cartilage. "Look, I'm very old-fashioned," she began in a choked tone.

"I almost never make love to women on the floor of the front porch."

She stared at him dimly, only slowly becoming aware that he was smiling and the words were both affectionate and teasing.

A tiny laugh burst from her swollen lips, although the kiss had rattled her.

"That's better," he said. His eyes narrowed. "How do you feel about my brother?"

Her mind refused to function. "How do I what?"

"Feel about John," he persisted coolly. "When I asked you why you wanted this job, you said it was because John was a dish. I know you had a crush on him. How do you feel now?"

She was at a loss to know what to say. "I like…him," she blurted out. "He's been kind to me."

"Kinder than I have, for damned sure," he agreed at once. "And he believed you were innocent when I didn't."

She frowned. "You explained why."

His hands tightened on her arms and his lips flattened. "He's younger than I am, single and rich and easygoing," he said harshly. "Maybe he'd be the best thing that ever happened to you."

Her eyes widened. "Thank you. I've always wanted a big, strong man to plan my future for me."

He let her go abruptly, angry. "You said it yourself. I'm a generation older than you with a ready-made family."

She couldn't make head or tail of what he was saying. Her mind was spinning as she looked up at him.

"Maybe you're what he needs, too," he added coldly. "Someone young and optimistic and intelligent."

"Are you going to buy the ring, too?"

He turned away. "That wasn't funny."

"I don't want to marry your brother. Thanks, anyway."

He kept walking.

She ran after him. "That man Sims has got a gun," she called. "Don't you dare go out there and get shot!"

He paused on the top step and looked back at her as if he had doubts about her sanity. "John's going out with me as soon as he finishes his phone calls."

"Great!" she exclaimed angrily. "I can worry about both of you all night!"

"Worry about my daughters," he told her bluntly. "That's your only responsibility here. You work for me, remember?"

"I remember," she replied irritably. "Do you?"

"Stay in the house with the girls until I tell you otherwise. I don't want any of you on the porch or in the yard until we settle this, one way or another."

He did think there was danger. She heard it in every word. "I won't let anything happen to Bess and Jenny. I promise."

He glared at her. "Can you shoot?"

She shook her head. "But I know how to dial 911."

"Okay. Keep one of the wireless phones handy, just in case."

She moved toward him another step, wrapping her arms tight around her body. "Have you got a cell phone?"

He indicated the case on his belt. That was when she noticed an old Colt .45 strapped to his other hip, under the denim shirt he was wearing open over his black T-shirt.

Her breath caught. Until that minute, when she saw the gun, it was a possibility. But guns were violent, chaotic, frightening. She bit her lower lip worriedly.

"I'll be late. Make sure you lock the doors before you go upstairs. John and I have keys."

"I will," she promised. "You be careful."

He ignored the quiet command. He took one long, last look at her and went on down the steps to his pickup truck, which was parked nearby.

She stood at the top of the steps until he drove away, staring after him worriedly. She wanted to call him back, to beg him to stay inside where he'd be safe from any retribution by that man Sims. But she couldn't. He wasn't the sort of man to run from trouble. It wouldn't do any good to nag him. He was going to do what he needed to do, whether or not it pleased her.

She got the girls ready for bed and tucked them in. She read them a Dr. Seuss book they hadn't heard yet. When they grew drowsy, she pulled the covers over them and tiptoed to the door, pausing to flick off the light switch as she went out into the hall.

She left the door cracked and went on down the hall to her own room. She got ready for bed and curled up on her pillows with a worn copy of Tacitus's *The Histories*. "I wonder if you ever imagined that people in the future would still be reading words you wrote almost two thousand years ago," she murmured as she thumbed through the well-read work. "And nothing really changes, does it, except the clothes and the everyday things. People are the same."

Her heart wasn't in the book. She laid it aside and turned off the lights, thinking how it would have been two thousand years ago to watch her husband put on his armor and march off to a war in some foreign country behind one of the Roman generals. That made her think of Gil and she gnawed her lip as she lay in the darkness, waiting for some sound that would tell her he was still all right.

It was two o'clock in the morning before she heard a pickup truck pull up at the bottom of the steps out front. She threw off the covers and ran to the window, peering out through the lacy curtain just in time to see Gil and John climb wearily out of the truck. John had a rifle with the breech open under one arm. He led the way into the house, with Gil following behind.

At least, thank God, they were both still alive, she thought. She went back to bed and pulled the covers up to her chin. Relieved, she slept.

She'd forgotten John's invitation to the movies, but he hadn't. And he looked odd, as if he was pondering something wicked, when he waited for her to come down the stairs with the girls.

Kasie was wearing a pretty dark green silk pantsuit with strappy sandals and her hair around her shoulders. She smiled at the little girls in their skirt sets. They looked like a family, and John was touched. He went forward to greet them, pausing to kiss Kasie's cheek warmly.

Gil, who was working in the office, came into the hall just in time to see his brother kissing Kasie. His eyes splintered with unexpected helpless rage. His fists clenched at his sides. She wouldn't leave the house with him, but here she was dressed to the nines and all eager to jump into a car with his brother.

John glanced at him warily and hid a smile. "We're off to the movies! Want to come?"

"No," Gil said abruptly. He avoided looking at Kasie. "I've got two more hours of work to finish in the den."

"Let Miss Parsons do it and come with us," John persisted.

"I gave Miss Parsons the day off. She's visiting a friend."

"Let it wait until tomorrow, then."

"No chance. Go ahead and enjoy yourselves, but don't get too comfortable. Watch your back," he said tersely, and returned into the study. He closed the door firmly behind him.

John, for some ungodly reason, was rubbing his hands together with absolute glee. Kasie gave him a speaking glance, which he ignored as he herded them out into the night.

The movie was one for general audiences, about a famous singer. John didn't really enjoy it, but Kasie and the girls did. They ate popcorn and giggled at the funny scenes, and moaned when the heroine was misjudged by the hero and thrown out on her ear.

"That looks familiar, doesn't it?" John murmured outrageously.

"She should hit him with a brickbat," Kasie muttered.

"With a head that hard, I don't know if it would do any good," he said, and Kasie thought for a minute that it didn't sound as if he were referring to the movie. "But I have a much better idea, anyway. Wait and see."

She pondered that enigmatic remark all through the movie. They went home, had dinner and watched TV, but it wasn't until the girls went up to bed and the study door opened that Kasie began to realize what John was up to. Because he waited until his brother had an unobstructed view of the two of them at the foot of the staircase. And then he bent and kissed Kasie. Passionately.

Kasie was shocked. Gil was infuriated. John winked at Kasie before he turned to face his brother. "Oh, there you are," he told Gil with a grin. "The movie was great. I'll tell you all about it tomorrow. Sleep well, Kasie," he added, ruffling the hair at her temple.

"You, too," she choked. She could barely manage words. John had never touched her before, and she knew that it hadn't been out of misplaced passion or raging desire that he'd kissed her. He'd obviously done it to irritate his big brother. And it was working! Gil looked as if he wanted to bite somebody.

He moved close to Kasie when John was out of sight up the steps, whipping out a snow-white handkerchief. He caught her by the nape and wiped off her smeared lipstick.

"You aren't marrying my brother," he said through his teeth.

"Excuse me?"

"I said, you aren't marrying John," he repeated harshly. "You're an employee here, and that's all. I am not going to let my brother become your meal ticket!"

She actually gasped. "Of all the unfounded, unreasonable, outrageous things in the world to say to a woman, that really takes the cake!" she raged.

"I haven't started yet," he bit off. He threw the handkerchief down on the hall table and pulled her roughly into his arms. "I've never wanted to hit a man so badly in all my life," he ground out as his mouth went down over hers.

She couldn't breathe. He didn't seem to notice, or care. His mouth was warm, hard, insistent. She clung to his shirtfront and let the sensations wash over her like fire. He was insulting her. She shouldn't let him. She should make him stop. It was just that his mouth was so sweet, so masterful, so ardent. She moaned as the sensations piled up on themselves and left her knees wobbling out from under her.

He caught her closer and lifted her against him, devouring her mouth with his own. She felt her whole body begin to shiver with the strength of the desire he was teaching her to feel. Never in her life had she known such pleasure, but even the hungry force of the kiss still wasn't enough to ease the ache in her.

Her arms went up and around his neck and she held on as if she might die by letting go. He groaned huskily as his body began to harden. He wanted her. He wanted to lay her down on the Persian carpet, make passionate love to her. He wanted...

He dragged his mouth from hers and looked down at her with accusation and raging anger.

"I'm mad," he growled off. "You aren't supposed to enjoy it."

"Okay," she murmured, trying to coax his mouth back down onto hers. She had no will, no pride, no reason left. She only wanted the pleasure to continue. "Come back here. I'll pretend to hate it."

"Kasie..."

She found his mouth and groaned hoarsely as he gave in to his own hunger and crushed her against the length of his tall, fit body. It was the most glorious kiss of her entire life. If only it would never end…

But it did, all too soon, and he shot away from her as if he'd tasted poison. His eyes glittered. "If you ever let him kiss you again, I'll throw both of you out a window!"

She opened her mouth to speak, but before she could manage words, the front doorbell rang.

It was one of the cowboys. Two more head of cattle had been shot, and the gunman was still out near the line cabin. One of the cowboys had him pinned down with rifle fire and needed reinforcements. It took Gil precisely five minutes to call John, load his Winchester and get out the door. He barely took time to caution Kasie about venturing outside until the situation was under control. She didn't even get a chance to beg him to be careful. She went upstairs, so that she'd be near the girls, but she knew that this was one night she wouldn't sleep a wink.

Chapter Eleven

Kasie lay awake for the rest of the night. When dawn broke, she still hadn't heard Gil come into the house. And once she'd thought she heard a shot being fired. Remembering how dangerous the man Sims was supposed to be made her even more uneasy. What if Gil had been shot? How would she live? She couldn't bear the thought of a world without Gil in it.

She got up and dressed just as Mrs. Charters went into the kitchen to start breakfast. John and Gil were nowhere in sight.

"Have they come in at all?" she asked Mrs. Charters.

"Not yet," the older woman said, and looked worried. "There were police cars and sheriff's cars all over the place about two hours ago," she added. "I saw them from my house."

"I thought I heard a shot, but I didn't see anything," Kasie said, and then she really worried.

"You couldn't have seen them, it was three miles and more down the road. But I'm sure we'd have heard if anything had happened to Gil or John."

"Oh, I hope so," Kasie said fervently.

"I'll make coffee," she said. "You can have some in a minute."

"Thanks, Mrs. Charters. I'm going to go sit on the front porch."

"You do that, dear."

The ranch was most beautiful early in the morning, Kasie thought, when dawn broke on the horizon and the cattle and horses started moving around in the pastures. She loved this part of the day, but now it was torment to sit and wonder and not be able to do anything. Had they found Sims? Was he in custody or still at large? And, most frightening of all, was the memory of that single gunshot. Had Gil been hurt?

She nibbled at her fingernails in her nervousness, a habit left over from childhood. There didn't seem to be a vehicle in the world. The highway was close enough that the sound of moving vehicles could be heard very faintly, but at this hour there was very little traffic. In fact, there was none.

She got up from the porch swing and paced restlessly. What if Gil had been shot? Surely someone would have phoned. John would, she was certain. But what if the wound was serious, so serious that he couldn't leave his brother's side even long enough to make a phone call? What if…!

The sound of a truck coming down the long ranch road caught her attention. She ran to the top of the steps and stood there with her heart pounding like mad. It was one of the ranch's pickup trucks. She recognized it. Two men were in the cab. They were in a flaming rush. Was it John and one of the hands, come to tell her that Gil was hurt, wounded, dying?

Dust flew as the driver pulled up sharply at the front steps. Both doors flew open. Kasie thought she might faint. John got out of the passenger side, whole and undamaged and grinning. Gil got out on the other side, dusty and worn, with a cut bleeding beside his mouth. But he was all in one piece, not injured, not shot, not...

"Gil!" She screamed his name, blind and deaf and dumb to the rest of the world as she came out of her frozen trance and dashed down the steps, missing the bottom one entirely, to rush right into his arms.

"Kasie..." He couldn't talk at all, because she was kissing him, blindly, fervently, as if he'd just come back from the dead.

He stopped trying to talk. He kissed her back, his arms enfolding her so closely that her feet dangled while he answered the aching hunger of her mouth.

She was shaking when he lifted his head. His eyes were glittery with feeling as he searched her eyes and saw every single emotion in her. She loved him. She couldn't have told him any plainer if she'd shouted it.

John just chuckled. "I'll go drink coffee while you two...talk," he murmured dryly, bypassing them without a backward glance.

Neither of them heard him or saw him go. They stared at each other with aching tenderness, touching faces, lips, fingertips.

"I'm all right," he whispered, kissing her again. "Sims took a shot at us, but he missed. It took two sheriff's deputies, the bloodhounds and a few ranch hands, but we tracked him down. He's in jail, nursing his bruises."

She traced the dried blood on his cheek. "He hit you."

He shrugged. "I hit him, too." He smiled outrageously. "So much for pretending that you only work for me, Kasie," he said with deliberate mischief in his tone.

She touched his dusty hair. "I love you," she said huskily. Her eyes searched his. "Is it all right?"

"That depends," he mused, bending to kiss her gently. "We discussed being old-fashioned, remember?"

She flushed. "I wasn't suggesting..."

He took her soft upper lip in both of his and nibbled it. "This is the last place in the world that you and I could carry on a torrid affair," he pointed out. "The girls can take off doorknobs if they have the right tools, and Mrs. Charters probably has microphones and hidden cameras in every room. She always knows whatever's going on around here." He lifted his head and searched her eyes. "I'm glad you love children, Kasie. I really don't plan to stop at Bess and Jenny."

She flushed softly. "Really?"

"We should have one or two of our own," he added quietly. "Boys run in my family, even if Darlene and I were never able to have one. If we had a son or two, it would give Bess and Jenny a chance to be part of a big family."

Her eyes grew dreamy. "We could teach all of them how to use the computer and love cattle."

He smiled tenderly. "But first, I think we might get married," he whispered at her lips. "So that your aunt doesn't have to be embarrassed when she tells people what you're doing."

"We wouldn't want to embarrass Mama Luke," she agreed, bubbling over with joy.

"God forbid," he murmured. He kissed her again, with muted passion. "She can come to the wedding." He hesitated and his eyes darkened. "I'm not sure about my brother. I could have decked him for kissing you!"

"I still don't know why he did," she began.

He chuckled. "He told me. He wanted to see if I was jealous of you. I gave him hell all night until Sims showed up. He laughed all the way back to the ranch. So much for lighting fires under people," he added with a faint grin. "I'll let him be best man, I guess, but he's going to be the only man in church who doesn't get to kiss the bride!"

She laughed. "What a wicked family I'm marrying into," she said as she reached up to kiss him. "And speaking of wicked, we have to invite K.C.," she added shyly.

He froze, lifting his head. "I don't know about that, Kasie…"

"You'll like him. Really you will," she promised, smiling widely.

He grimaced. "I suppose we each have to have at least one handicap," he muttered. "I have a lunatic brother and you're best friends with a hit man."

"He's not. You'll like him," she repeated, and drew his head down to hers again. She kissed him with enthusiasm, enjoying the warm, wise tutoring of his hard mouth. "We should go and tell the babies," she whispered against his mouth.

"No need," he murmured.

"Uncle John, look! Daddy's kissing Kasie!"

"See?" he added with a grin as he lifted his head

and indicated the front door. Standing there, grinning also, were John, Bess, Jenny, Mrs. Charters, and Miss Parsons.

The wedding was the social event of Medicine Ridge for the summer. Kasie wore a beautiful white gown with lace and a keyhole neckline, with a Juliet cap and a long veil. She looked, Gil whispered as she joined him at the altar, like an angel.

Her excited eyes approved his neat gray vested suit, which made his hair look even more blond. At either side of them were Bess and Jenny in matching blue dresses, carrying baskets of white roses. Next to them was John, his brother's best man, fumbling in his pocket for the wedding rings he was responsible for.

As the ceremony progressed, a tall, blond man in the front pew watched with narrowed, wistful eyes as his godchild married the eldest of the Callister heirs. Not bad, K.C. Kantor thought, for a girl who'd barely survived a military uprising even before she was born. He glanced at the woman seated next to him, his eyes sad and quiet, as he contemplated what might have been if he'd met Kasie's aunt before her heart led her to a life of service in a religious order. They were the best of friends and they corresponded. She would always be family to him. She was the only family he had, or would ever have, except for that sweet young woman at the altar.

"Isn't she beautiful?" Mama Luke whispered to him.

"A real vision," he agreed.

She smiled at him with warm affection and turned her attention back to the ceremony.

As the priest pronounced them man and wife, Gil lifted the veil and bent to kiss Kasie. There were sighs all around, until a small hand tugged hard at Kasie's skirt and a little voice was heard asking plaintively, "Is it over yet, Daddy? I have to go to the bathroom!"

Later, laughing about the small interruption as they gathered in the fellowship hall of the church, Kasie and Gil each cuddled a little girl and fed them cake.

"It was nice of Pauline to apologize for what she did in the Bahamas," Kasie murmured, recalling the telephone call that had both surprised and pleased her the day before the ceremony.

"She's really not that bad," Gil mused. "Just irresponsible and possessive. But I still didn't want her at the wedding," he added with a grin. "Just in case."

"I still wish you'd invited your parents," Kasie told Gil gently.

"I did," he replied. "They were on their way to the Bahamas and couldn't spare the time." He smiled at her. "Don't worry the subject, Kasie. Some things can't be changed. We're a family, you and me and the girls and John."

"Yes, we are," she agreed, and she reached up to kiss him. She glanced around them curiously. Mama Luke intercepted the glance and joined them.

"He left as we were coming in here," she told Kasie. "K.C. never was one for socializing. I expect he's headed for the airport by now."

"It was nice of him to come."

"It was," she agreed. She handed a small box to Kasie. "He asked me to give this to you."

She frowned, pausing to open the box. She drew out a gold necklace with a tiny crystal ball dangling from it. Inside the ball was a tiny seed.

"It's a mustard seed," Mama Luke explained. "It's from a Biblical quote—if you have even that amount of faith, as a mustard seed, nothing is impossible. It's to remind you that miracles happen."

Kasie cradled it in her hand and looked up at Gil with her heart in her eyes. "Indeed they do," she whispered, and all the love she had for her new husband was in her face.

The next night, Kasie and Gil lay tangled in a king-size bed at a rented villa in Nassau, exhausted and deliciously relaxed from their first intimacy.

Kasie moved shyly against him, her face flushed in the aftermath of more physical sensation than she'd ever experienced.

"Stop that," he murmured drowsily. "I'm useless now. Go to sleep."

She laughed with pure delight and curled closer. "All right. But don't forget where we left off."

He drew her closer. "As if I could!" He bent and kissed her eyes shut. "Kasie, I never dreamed that I could be this happy again." His eyes opened and looked into hers with fervent possession. "I loved Darlene. A part of me will always love her. But I would die for you," he added roughly, his eyes blazing with emotion.

Overwhelmed, she buried her face in his throat and shivered. "I would die for you," she choked. She clung harder. "I love you!"

His mouth found hers, hungry for contact, for the sharing of fierce, exquisite need. He drew her over his relaxed body and held her until the trembling stopped. His breath sighed out heavily at her ear. "Forever, Kasie," he whispered unsteadily.

She smiled. "Forever."

* * *

They slept, eventually, and as dawn filtered in through the venetian blinds and the sound of the surf grew louder, there was a knock on the door.

Gil opened his eyes, still drowsy. He looked down at Kasie, fast asleep on her stomach, smiling even so. He smiled, too, and tossed the sheet over her before he stepped into his Bermuda shorts and went to answer the door.

The shock when he opened it was blatant. On the doorstep were a silver-haired man in casual slacks and designer shirt, and a silver-haired woman in a neat but casual sundress and overblouse. They were carrying the biggest bouquet of orchids Gil had ever seen in his life.

The man pushed the bouquet toward Gil hesitantly and with a smile that seemed both hesitant and uncertain. "Congratulations," he said.

"From both of us," the woman added.

They both stood there, waiting.

As Gil searched for words, there was movement behind him and Kasie came to the door in the flowered cotton muu-muu she'd bought for the trip, her long chestnut hair disheveled, smiling broadly.

"Hello!" she exclaimed, going past Gil to hug the woman and then the man, who both flushed. "I'm so glad you could come!"

Gil stared at her. "What?"

"I phoned them," she told him, clasping his big hand in hers. "They said they'd like to come over and have lunch with us, and I told them to come today. But I overslept," she added, and flushed.

"It's your honeymoon, you should oversleep," Gil's mother, Magdalene, said gently. She looked at her son nervously. "We wanted to come to the wedding," she said. "But we didn't want to, well, ruin the day for you."

"That's right," Jack Callister agreed gruffly. "We haven't been good parents. At first we were too irresponsible, and then we were too ashamed. Especially when Douglas took you in and we lost touch." He shrugged. "It's too late to start over, of course, but we'd sort of like to, well, to get to know you and John. And the girls, of course. That is, if you, uh, if you…" He shrugged.

Kasie squeezed Gil's hand, hard.

"I'd like that," he said obligingly.

Their faces changed. They beamed. For several seconds, they looked like silver-haired children on Christmas morning. And Gil realized with stark shock that they were just that—grown-up children without the first idea of how to be parents. Douglas Callister had kept the boys, and he hadn't approved of his brother Jack, so he hadn't encouraged contact. Since the elder Callisters didn't know how to approach their children directly, they lost touch and then couldn't find a way to reach them at all.

He looked down at Kasie, and it all made sense. She'd tied the loose ends up. She'd gathered a family back together.

She squeezed Gil's hand again, looking up at him with radiant delight. "We could get dressed and meet them in the restaurant. After we put these in water," she added, hugging the bouquet to her heart and sniffing them. "I've never had orchids in my life," she said with a smile. "Thank you!"

Magdalena laughed nervously. "No, Kasie. Thank *you*."

"We'll get dressed and meet you in about fifteen minutes, in the restaurant," Gil managed to say.

"Great!" Jack said. He took his wife's hand, and they both smiled, looking ten years younger. "We'll see you there!"

The door closed and Gil looked down at Kasie with wonder.

"I thought they might like to visit us at the ranch next month, too," Kasie said, "so they can get to know the babies."

"You're amazing," he said. "Absolutely amazing!"

She fingered the necklace K.C. had given her at the wedding. "I like miracles, don't you?"

He burst out laughing. He picked her up and swung her around in an arc while she squealed and held on to her bouquet tightly. He put her down gently and kissed her roughly.

"I love you," he said huskily.

She grinned. "Yes, and see what it gets you when you love people? You get all sorts of nice surprises. In fact," she added with a mischievous grin, "I have all sorts of surprises in store for you."

He took a deep breath and looked at her with warm affection. "I can hardly wait."

She kissed him gently and went to dress. She gave a thought to Gil's Darlene, and to her own parents, and her lost twin and his family, and hoped that they all knew, somehow, that she and Gil were happy and that they had a bright future with the two little girls and the children they would have together. As she went to the closet to get her dress, her eyes were full of dreams. And so were Gil's.

* * * * *

"Sweet dreams, little one," he said and stepped out of
the room.

She took off Hannah's shoes and jeans, then tucked
her in for the night. With a bolstering breath, she braced
herself for being alone with her fantasy man.

He stood in the center of the living room, looking
around like he'd never seen his own house. She
followed Anson's gaze to the built-in shelves she'd
filled with precious and painful memories. Things she
wasn't ready to share with him. Before he could ask any
questions, she opened the front door.

HSEEXP1020

"Even though we were coerced, thank you for carrying her home. And for the house tour." Their "moment" in his bedroom flashed before her. *Damn, why'd I bring that up?*

"Anytime." Anson's blue-eyed gaze danced with amusement before he ducked his head and stepped outside. "Sleep well, Tess."

Fat chance of that.

She closed the door to prevent herself from watching him walk away. Tonight, Anson hadn't treated her indifferently like before and, in fact, seemed to be fighting his own temptations. Sometimes shutters would fall over his eyes as he distanced himself, then she'd blink and he'd wear his devil's grin, drawing her in with flirtation. Maybe he wasn't as immune to their attraction as she'd thought.

"I can't figure you out, Chief Anson Curry. But why am I even bothering?"

Don't miss
A Sheriff's Star *by Makenna Lee,*
available November 2020 wherever
Harlequin Special Edition books and ebooks are sold.

Harlequin.com

HSEEXP1020

HARLEQUIN
SPECIAL EDITION

**Believe in love. Overcome obstacles.
Find happiness.**

Save **$1.00**

on the purchase of ANY
Harlequin Special Edition book.

Available wherever books are sold,
including most bookstores, supermarkets,
drugstores and discount stores.

Save $1.00

on the purchase of ANY Harlequin Special Edition book.

Coupon valid until December 31, 2020.
Redeemable at participating outlets in the US and Canada only.
Not redeemable at Barnes & Noble stores. Limit one coupon per customer.

52616831

5 65373 00076 2   (8100)0 12468

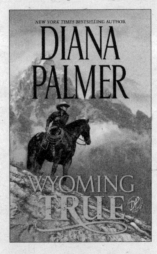